Frost could feel the
It was a slowly build
at the core of her :
each beat of her hear

She reached beyond
storm and made a clawing motion with her
hand.

A violet shaft lanced downward, shattered the
overhanging stones and blasted a gaping hole in
the parapet. An awful odor swirled up in thick,
vaporous clouds. Bits of wood and stone exploded outward.

Again Frost reached out and pulled lightning
from the sky. For an instant the darkness was
transformed to painful white. The tower lurched
fearsomely under the force of the blast. A black
crater yawned where the gates had been and the
surrounding earth burned.

Her witch powers were back. Frost stared
into the storm with an awful trepidation. Then,
just to prove she could do it, she sent another
bolt hurtling earthward.

BLOODSONGS

Look for these Tor books by Robin W. Bailey

BLOODSONGS
SKULL GATE

ROBIN W. BAILEY
BLOODSONGS

A TOM DOHERTY ASSOCIATES BOOK

BLOODSONGS

Copyright © 1986 by Robin W. Bailey

First printing: April 1986

A TOR Book

Published by Tom Doherty Associates
49 West 24 Street
New York, N.Y. 10010

Cover art by Kevin Johnson

ISBN: 0-812-53141-8
CAN. ED.: 0-812-53142-6

Printed in the United States

0 9 8 7 6 5 4 3 2 1

Chapter One

Mother, I need you
Take me back and cradle me
In boughs and branches
Clothe me in green leaves
Suckle me on fresh flower petals
Soothe me with wind songs
I am lost, alone,
For you will not come near me
Where I wander now.

The music wove a wild, insistent fury in her brain; its tempestuous rhythms drove her, inspired her movements. The strings of the *saz* and the *oud* rang out in frenzied quarter-tone harmonies. The *dumbeki* drum shivered and pulsed and quivered. The *zils* on her fingers made brass thunder in the air.

All through the inn men and women hawked and cried encouragement, ignoring food and drink and companions while they watched her dance. Samidar's dance.

Her hips shimmied, stilled suddenly, then described small, tantalizing circles and half circles. Above the low band of her several skirts her belly fluttered, rolled sensuously. The navel seemed to drift around her body of its own free motion. She began to spin ever more rapidly on the smooth tabletop. Skirts flew about, exposing legs and the bells she wore on her left ankle. Dark hair formed a cloud about her face. The jeweled halter that contained her breasts glittered in the lamplight that illuminated the inn; the gems flashed with mesmeric fire in response to every subtle movement.

She clanged the *zils,* and the deep voice of the *dumbeki* throbbed in answer. The *saz* and the *oud* dared, and her hips courted brazenly. Perspiration made thick rivulets along her face, throat, torso, creating slick puddles that menaced her intricate footwork.

She danced, danced until the faces were blurred and the voices were indistinct rumbles of no significance, until nothing touched her or seemed real but the drum and the music and the dance.

From the shadowy darkness coins struck her breasts and belly, then clattered on the table around her feet. It was impossible to recognize the value or the mint. She glanced at the man who threw them, then regarded him through seductively lowered lids, a gaze that promised everything and nothing, by design. Generosity deserved some reward after all. She shook her hips for him, turned, bent slowly backward until her hair brushed the top of the table. Her shoulders and breasts began a provocative quiver as she arched even lower.

It was part of the dance, that look, that beguiling, teasing gaze. It drew the customers in, made them part of the dance, too. It invited them to share in her joy and excitement.

The *dumbeki* called her back with an urgent, low fluttering, and she gave herself to its rhythm like a lover, riding every throbbing beat, feeling the drum's power coursing through her.

Then the drum stopped, and it was like the huge hand of some cruel god had suddenly crushed her heart. She collapsed, both legs bent back beneath her, breasts heaving, one hand flung back dramatically, eyes closed, skirts pooled between her damp, open thighs.

For a long instant the inn was silent. Then, the crowd erupted. She shielded her eyes from the shower of coins that shimmered in the air and fell on or around her. Kirigi, the drummer, rose from his seat before the *dumbeki* to help her gather them. He grinned at her as she sat up. Some of the coins had stuck to her sweat-sheened flesh. She picked them off and dropped them in Kirigi's cupped hands. Plenty of coins, she discovered. A good night.

Hands reached up to help her down from the table.

They were a good lot, these men and women. Their mirth
threatened to burst the walls of her poor place. They called
zaghareets and shouted to her, and she answered with bawdy
joviality.

"I hope you've a father or an older brother, Conn," she
gibed. "I doubt you're man enough, yourself!" That brought
laughter from all but the boasting, red-faced young townsman.

· "Make 'er no offers, lad," cried old Tamen. Once, he'd
been a warrior in the northern lands. Now, he was Dashrani's
blacksmith. "She'll no' accept 'em from the likes o' ye."

Samidar reached out and tweaked the old man's iron-gray
beard, wondering briefly if anyone noticed such streaks in her
own black tresses. "With a man like you around"—she
grinned, teasing—"hot young studs like Conn haven't a
chance."

"Ah, his sword's too rusty to cut piss," shouted a stranger,
one of the caravan merchants who frequented Dashrani's bars
and brothels. "Let alone carve on good hams like yours!"

That brought another outburst from the crowd.

Old Tamen jumped to his feet, parted his trousers, and
exposed himself. "Who said that? Speak, ye son o' a bitch,
an' up against the wall wi' ye! We'll talk o' swords!"

A flurry of taunts, insults, challenges, and bets filled the
inn as a dozen others exposed themselves. Samidar cried out
over the din, "Put those things away before the straw thrash-
ers come for an early harvest! You'll find no one here to test
the mettle of those dirks."

The laughter was interrupted this time as someone called
from the far corner, "How about those three monkeys by the
door? I'll wager they've sat on a few dirks in their days."

She turned to see whom the caller meant. The customers
seemed to part for her.

Three soldiers, dressed in the livery of the king, hunched
around a small table separate from the rest. Two of them
clutched half-empty mugs of ale. The third leaned back on
his bench, resting against the wall, drinking nothing. She'd
noticed them earlier. They'd sat quietly most of the evening,
watching and muttering among themselves.

She stopped before their table and folded her arms. "Well,
what say you men of King Riothamus? Will you cross swords
with my fine gibbons?" She waved at the men who, moments
ago, had exposed themselves.

The soldier who leaned on the wall folded his arms over his chest, perhaps to mock her, and regarded her with a cool, sober gaze. "We never cross swords with peaceful citizens."

Did she imagine it, or was there a hint of displeasure in his tone, a note of warning? It annoyed her. This was her place; she ruled it.

A little pout formed on her lips, and she drew her hair over one shoulder so it covered a breast. Her hand drifted down along one hip in an exaggeratedly seductive motion. "But you do sheathe your blades now and then"—she made a small thrust with her pelvis and grinned—"in a few of those peaceful citizens?"

Someone shouted from the crowd, "I sheathe it in me wife ever' night, an' she's real peaceful!" That sparked another uproarious outburst.

But an odd tension settled over the inn.

Only two days before, a farmer and his family had been slaughtered on the far side of Dashrani. The youngest son had lived just long enough to accuse a band of soldiers. A hasty search by a group of outraged townsmen found no soldiers in the area. However, it was general conversation among the caravan merchants that King Riothamus was taking little time to verify allegiances in his hunt for an elusive group of bandit-rebels.

Now, here were three soldiers. Could they have had anything to do with the farm attack?

The soldier unfolded his arms, leaned forward on one elbow. He fixed her with a stare. "We sheathe our blades where our king orders." He glanced at his two companions. They continued to sip their ale, but they watched the crowd carefully. "Where *your* king orders," he added pointedly.

"To the insensate joy of wives and daughters everywhere, I'm sure." Samidar spread her skirts and made a mocking curtsey, hiding a smile. "Kirigi, my fine son!" she called, straightening. "More brew for these duteous soldiers." She leaned on the table, then, until she could smell the beer on their breath. "Enjoy my hospitality, sirs, but pray keep all your weapons sheathed. I run neither a brothel nor a charnel house."

She turned and glowered at old Tamen, who stood close behind her. "And if you let that mouse out of its hole again, I'll take a broom to it."

Again the inn shook with laughter, and Tamen was made the butt of many jests. He took them all in good humor, though, secure in the knowledge that, if any cared to look, it was no mere mouse that filled his trousers.

She pushed her way through the throng and passed through a door into the kitchen. The smells of roasted meats were nearly overwhelming in the small room, despite the two unshuttered windows. She snatched up a long tunic from a peg on the wall and pulled it over her head. The hem fell past her knees; to protect her skirts it was much better than an apron.

Half a side of beef and several fowl sizzled on spits in the huge firepit. She dipped a ladle into a jar of grease and herb-seasoned drippings that sat on the hearth. She poured it carefully over the meats, and blue spurts of flame leaped up as the juices drooled down on the crackling coals.

Kirigi came in, bearing a wooden tray and four mugs. His linen shirt was opened to the waist, revealing his smooth, sweaty chest. He paused long enough to wipe his brow and smile at her.

"You danced like a wind-devil tonight, Mother," he said as he dipped each mug into a large cask of frothy beer.

"You drummed like the thunder-goddess herself," she called after his departing back.

Alone again, she bent over a blackened pot of stew that simmered on the edge of the coals and stirred the contents with a heavy spoon. As an afterthought, she added water to thin it. When that was done, she moved to the other side of the kitchen, where loaves of hard-crusted bread and blocks of cheeses occupied a row of shelves. Only two cheeses were left. Tomorrow she would have to go into Dashrani to the shop of Khasta the merchant. His cheeses were the finest; she dealt only with him.

Filling a mug with beer for herself, she rejoined her customers.

They were hers, these men and women of Dashrani, neighbors who walked or rode out from town to relax from the day's labors or to escape their wives for a little while. Some came to forget their troubles, some came to enjoy the company of good fellows. There were other inns inside the city's walls, but they had no dancers, or they watered the wine, or the owners were surly. Not that her place was a playpen for children; she served the occasional cutpurse and murderer, she was sure. But she minded her own business. And at her place, she reflected with a sly grin, if one was robbed or murdered, it happened in good humor.

Yes, they were hers. For twenty years she had lived among them, served them, and entertained them. She knew their troubles, and they knew hers. And though she was not native to Dashrani or even to the kingdom of Keled-Zaram, they accepted her. They were as close to her as kin, these men and women, these friends.

A movement near the front door caught her eye. Riothamus's soldiers slid out quietly into the night. She crooked a finger at Kirigi, who served a table on the other side of the inn. With a subtle nod, he set down his tray and followed them out. Moments later, he returned and took up his duties again.

"Away from town," he reported, mouthing the words so she could read his soundless lips.

Samidar put the soldiers out of her mind. There was business to see after, and it was almost time to bring out the meats. She feared the stew had scorched, but if she sold enough beer, her customers wouldn't notice. And later, she must dance again. She was eager for it, though she rubbed the small of her back, sighed, and wished she was younger.

It was nearly dawn when the last guest departed down the road toward town. Samidar stood in the doorway and watched the stranger stumble drunkenly toward the city gates. The spires and rooftops of Dashrani stood black and stark in the pale, early twilight. Soon the first rays of morning would lighten the stained windows and gold-tinged tiles. Though not a large city, yet, Dashrani was an important stop on the caravan routes, and the wealth of its citizens grew each year.

She leaned against the doorjamb as she did so many mornings and watched the last vestige of night fade away. A morose purple colored the sky. The evening's last hunting owl circled overhead, seeking prey, riding the light wind that stirred the branches of the few trees. As she stood there, the first rays of sunrise ignited the distant gentle swell of the land.

The doorjamb was worn smooth where Samidar leaned on it. Before the inn a road ran west into the hills and east toward the small town of Dashrani. Nothing moved along it as far as she could see, nothing but little dust-devils that rose and swirled in the wind.

"Mother?"

The floorboards creaked under Kirigi's tread as he came up behind her. She didn't turn or answer, just leaned on the jamb, stared down the road.

The weight of his hand rested briefly on her shoulder. He said softly, "You look so pensive."

"It's probably nothing," she told him, patting his hand. "Just a mood."

"Is it still Father?"

Samidar gazed off into the far hills, where only a few short months ago she and Kirigi had buried Kimon, her husband of twenty and more years. The rising sun lent the hilltops an amber halo. The peaks blazed with light, as they did every morning. So she had chosen them for his final resting place.

"No," she answered slowly. "Not Kimon. I grieve, but I no longer sorrow. The pain is almost gone, Kirigi, you needn't worry." It was a lie. She missed Kimon more than she could bear sometimes, especially in the quiet moments like this when the crowd had gone home to their own wives and husbands, when there was nobody to dance or cook for. She ran her hands along her arms, remembering, wishing for his touch.

But there was more, some sense of tension that wafted on the air. An eerie foreboding gnawed at her. Through the night she had occupied herself with her customers, pushing such worries from her mind, losing herself in furious dancing. But with the dawn and solitude she felt once again the strange apprehension.

"More clouds," Kirigi observed, stepping past her, pointing to the northern sky. "So many clouds of late, and this is the dry season."

He had stripped and washed clean. His skin glowed. His hair, nearly black as her own, shone with a luster. *He will break the ladies' hearts*, she thought to herself as she watched him stretch. Again, she wondered at his precise age. Ten winters with her now, and he couldn't have been more than six when Kimon found him and brought him home. Kirigi had grown tall and fair and hard in those years.

She glanced at her own body, still lean after so much time, kept that way by her dancing. In the light of morning, though, she could see what so many did not in the chiaroscuro of the inn's dim illumination: the network of scars that laced her forearms, the larger scar on her shoulder that was usually hidden under the strap of her halter, more scars on her ribs and thighs. Yes, she was lean enough, but her body was not pretty, not in the pure light of day.

"It's just not natural," Kirigi continued, studying the sky.

"It doesn't smell of rain, though," she answered. "It'll be bright and hot."

"You danced well last night," he said, turning, changing the subject, grinning. "Old Tamen's eyes were about to crawl out of their sockets. I'll be mopping up his drool all afternoon."

"And his wife will be scrubbing his trousers," she added with a wink, and they both chuckled. She turned her gaze to the west, toward the distant hills that were so green and misty in the dawn. "I feel good, Kirigi," she told him at last. Despite the odd sense of expectation that filled her, it was true. "I haven't felt this way for a long time—since we buried Kimon. But it's like I've come out of a deep cave and found the sun."

He followed her gaze into the hills, and his voice was softer when he spoke. "I'm glad." He swallowed, glanced sidewise at her. "I was feeling guilty because the pain had gone away from me, yet you grieved." He took her hand in his. "Let's walk a little way and celebrate a new day together."

They started down the road away from the city, giving no thought to Kirigi's youthful nakedness. Either of them sometimes walked that way in the early morning when no one else was awake to see, when the gentle wind and the new warmth felt good on the skin.

As they walked, dust rapidly collected on the hem of her skirts. Well, they were sweat-stained from her performances and needed washing anyway. "How much longer will they watch?" she wondered aloud without intending to speak.

"What?" Kirigi asked. "Your dancing?" He smirked as she traced one of the more livid scars on her forearm with a hesitant finger. "You worry too much about those," he told her. "They never bothered Kimon. Did you know your bed squeaks?"

She punched him playfully in the ribs. "And I'll bet you pressed your ear to the wall to listen," she accused.

"Every night," he confessed. "They don't bother anyone

else, either. Oh, they've caused a few rumors. I've heard folks wonder how you got them. Some think you were a slave, and some think you were tortured once. A lot of people think Kimon must have rescued you from some terrible life.''

The mist lifted from the hills as the sun climbed over Dashrani's rooftops. ''They'll never know how close to truth that is,'' she admitted. Memories came rushing at her, violent memories of another time and another life, memories and faces and images that haunted and tormented her. She caught her adopted son's hand and squeezed it, and somehow in that physical contact she found strength to shut them out.

She stopped walking and faced him. The barest hint of fuzz shadowed his cheeks, and his eyes were alive with a youthful innocence. His body, though, was that of a man, already swelling with thick muscle.

''I'm so proud of you, son,'' she told him suddenly, clutching his arm. Then she tilted her head and forced a little smile. ''Do you know what day this is?''

He nodded. ''The Spider.''

''The day of the Spider, the month and year of the Spider,'' she affirmed. ''When this night is passed, I shall have seen forty-three birthdays. Such a special triune occurs only once every twelve years. Let's hope it heralds good things for us.''

Kirigi licked his lower lip. ''But you told me the spider was sacred to Gath, the chaos-bringer.''

Samidar began to walk again. ''I've told you too many old tales from my past. Couldn't you have had the good sense not to listen? This is Keled-Zaram, and the gods of this country are not the gods of the West. Here, the spider is a symbol for artistry, not chaos. And am I not an artist?'' She danced a few steps for him and laughed.

''Forty-three,'' she said once more with a note of awe. ''I'll be too old for this, soon.'' She danced a few more steps and shook her hair. ''See,'' she said, pointing among the strands. ''You can see the streaks of gray.''

But Kirigi was not listening. He stared off into the hills again. No, she realized. Not into the hills, but beyond them. She studied the strong, high-boned features that seemed almost a sculpted setting for the precious sapphires that were his eyes. She bit her lip ''When will you go?'' she asked suddenly.

Kirigi started, and his gaze jerked back to her face. "Huh?" Then he blushed. "I'll never leave you, Mother." His arm went around her shoulder. The corners of his mouth twisted in a grin. "We're a team."

She leaned her head on his bicep. The blueness of the sky swirled overhead as they walked along. "Do you long for adventure, Kirigi?" She couldn't hide the worry in her voice. "Do you find Dashrani and the inn so dull?"

The hesitation that preceded his answer told more than any words. But finally he said, "You keep me too busy to dream about adventure, and between you and old Tamen things are never dull."

She closed her eyes, suddenly tired, ready to sleep, once more fully aware of that strange sense of impending—what?

"It's never so wonderful as we believe when we're young," she told her son as he guided her down the road. "Kimon and I learned the hard way." She stopped suddenly and peered back the way they had come. The dusty road seemed an appropriate metaphor for her life.

"We wandered most of the known nations and several lands marked on no map ever drawn by men," she said softly. "Lots of places, lots of adventures." She put her arms around Kirigi and hugged him, then leaned her head on his bronzed chest. "But after a while we discovered that the quiet times we spent together were far more meaningful and fulfilling than all the battles and exotic wonders. Then we began to worry and fear for each other. Adventure meant danger; the two go hand in hand like lovers. And danger meant that one of us could end up all alone again. We'd had too much of being alone."

"So you bought the inn and settled down," Kirigi interrupted.

"It wasn't easy at first. At least not for me, though I think it was what Kimon really wanted all along. I looked out the door every morning, just like I do now, and I saw this very road. It tormented me. Strangers came and went, afoot or on horseback, in carts and caravans. Gods! I thought. What cities had they seen that I hadn't heard about? What places were they going that I would never see?"

She drew a deep breath and kicked dust with her toe. "Gradually, though, we became part of Dashrani. And we found that all those times on the road paled beside the good times we discovered here." She folded her arms about herself, looked up, and surveyed the sky. It was purest azure except for the line of clouds in the north. They made a creeping advance. She rubbed the back of her neck as she watched them, reminded yet again of a nagging trepidation.

"It wasn't enough for Kel," Kirigi said abruptly.

Samidar bit her lip and turned away so he couldn't see her face. Suddenly the sun didn't seem as warm or the breeze as friendly. The birdsongs of morning became a harsh, irritating noise. "Let's go back," she urged. "I'm worn out."

He touched her shoulder. "I'm sorry."

"It's all right," she answered shortly. "I'm just tired. We'll grab some sleep. Then there's a lot to do this afternoon before we open."

"If you're thinking about the cheese, don't. Khasta came in for a hasty drink last night. I talked with him, and he promised to drive out today with a wagon full of his best."

Actually, she'd forgotten about the cheese. All she wanted was to sleep and for the increasing throb in her head to go away. She scraped her nails over the back of one hand and frowned. The grease on her skin made white half-moons under the nails. She could use a bath, too.

"Any other tasks can wait," Kirigi continued. "It's your birthday, and you deserve a respite. Our customers will understand. They have wives to clean their houses, but do they stay home? No, they come to us for their pleasure. They'll survive a little dirt tonight."

"Maybe I should hire a few girls," she joked halfheartedly.

"I wouldn't object," he admitted with a leer. "There's a discouraging lack of anonymous young ladies around here."

"What's wrong with the girls of Dashrani?" she prodded. "Go court them. You have enough to offer any female." Indeed he had, she noted with a sidewise glance.

"When I have to face their fathers every night?" He moaned, rolled his eyes in mock alarm. "Fathers deep in their cups? I've little taste for *that* kind of adventure."

She smacked his bare rump playfully. Then, arms linked, they headed back toward the inn. The sun was warm on her shoulders and neck, and it glinted off the spires of Dashrani. It wouldn't last, though. The northern clouds grew steadily darker and they made swift advance.

"If it rains, Khasta may not come," Kirigi said.

"If it rains, he won't need to," she answered. "Those look bad. A big storm's coming." She ran a hand through her long hair and frowned. Why did she feel so tense, suddenly so full of unknown fright? "Bad for business," she muttered, staring at the sky, hugging herself.

They went the rest of the way in silence. The smell of leaves and new grass floated in the air. Within Dashrani's wall, the townsfolk would be awake and about their early chores. Farmers would be heading for the fields. Samidar gazed down the road. It ran right into the city through the gate and beyond. In her memory the gate had never been closed. It was one of the things about the city that had convinced her to settle here. Everyone was welcome. There had been a garrison once, but little crime to justify it. Dashrani was a fat, lazy town, and its people were friendly. There was a saying known all over Keled-Zaram: "There are no strangers in Dashrani."

It took her eyes a moment to adjust to the inn's gloom. Coming behind, Kirigi bumped into her when she stopped abruptly.

They hadn't closed the door when they'd left. One of Riothamus's soldiers leaned on the farthest table, his back to them, drinking from an earthenware mug.

"We're closed," she said stonily. "Come back later, but be sure you lay down a coin for what you've helped yourself to."

The soldier rose to his feet, turned slowly around.

Samidar's jaw dropped. She blinked, stared. Kirigi's face split in a big grin, and he rushed forward to embrace the intruder exuberantly. Then he stood aside. The rapt look on his young face told Samidar he was as surprised as she.

A mixture of emotions trembled through her, rooting her to the spot where she stood.

Finally, the soldier extended a hand and spoke. The voice was almost exactly as she remembered it, a little deeper, but otherwise unchanged, tinged, as always, with mockery.

He said, "Dance for me, Mother!"

Chapter Two

His eyes were greener than a stormy sea, more striking even than her own, mysterious eyes full of secrets. They seemed to drink her soul's vitality. She studied his face, so young yet so rugged and weathered, beardless. He regarded her over the rim of his mug, sipping his beer, waiting for her to speak. She felt clumsy and tongue-tied, wanting to hold her son, but afraid to hold him.

"I've missed you," he said, leaning on his elbows, bringing his face a little closer to hers across the rough table.

She squirmed uneasily on the hard bench. There was a faint foulness to his breath, but it wasn't quite unpersonable. She forced the barest smile in response to his lie. Had he missed her, he would have found opportunity in the past five years to visit or, at least, to let her know he lived. So young when he ran away, just Kirigi's age, without money or weapon or farewell.

Her lower lip trembled with a mixed anger and joy. "I didn't know if you were alive or dead." She swallowed hard and looked away to the inn's farthest corner, cursing an inward chill. "Why have you come back, Kel?"

He blinked, set down his mug. "To see you, Mother, of course."

Her eyes sought all the dark corners and distant places. "Just me?" she said. "Not your father and your brother?"

"Father, yes, I want to see him, too!" He took another drink of his beer. "Kirigi's not my brother."

She avoided his eyes no longer but sought them out, fixed

13

him with a hard look. "He is your brother!" she hissed under her breath. "As much a brother as you'll ever have!"

"We're not the same flesh!" he answered sharply, glancing around to be sure Kirigi was still out of earshot.

"Your father and I loved him!" She was nearly on her feet, bending over the table, her knuckles white as she gripped the edge for support. "There could be no more babies after you. We thought you were the last and the only until Kimon found Kirigi."

He slammed the mug down, sloshing the contents. "Wasn't I enough? Didn't I love you enough? Couldn't you love me?"

She ran a hand through her hair, shook her head. "Oh, Kel, we did love you, with all our hearts. Taking in Kirigi didn't lessen that love. He was a little boy left behind by one of the caravans. There was more than enough room in our lives for two sons."

Kel got up and walked to an unshuttered window. "You didn't need me around. He took my place."

"No, he never." She went to him, put her hands on his shoulders, laid her cheek on his broad back. "He never took your place, son. He made his own place."

He turned. Their arms went around each other, and sudden tears streamed soundlessly down her face. "I'm so sorry," she managed, looking up, stroking his cheek with one shivering hand. "I spoke too harshly. I know how hurt you were; that was why you left." She stepped back and wiped her eyes. "But let's be kind now. We won't talk about it anymore."

She hugged him again, glad at last to hold her son after so many long years.

The back door opened, closed. Kirigi bounced in, exuberant and grinning, smelling faintly of the stables. He'd taken time to dress in short pants and a belted tunic. A few pieces of straw and manure clung to the soles of his boots. "A beautiful mare!" he exclaimed to Samidar. "White as the mountain snows!"

Kel forced a grin and said to his mother, "When did he ever see snow in the mountains?"

She shrugged, matching his grin.

Kirigi disappeared into the kitchen and returned moments later with a platter of cold meats left from the previous night's roasts, some slices of bread, and a pitcher of cool water. He placed it all on the table and beckoned them to breakfast.

"What's it like in the army?" he asked Kel, stuffing a chunk of beef into his mouth, sputtering as he added, "I'll bet it's great. We didn't know you were still in the country. Are you stationed close? Can you come home more often?"

Kel's grin widened. He looked tolerantly at his mother and helped himself to bread. He chewed quietly until a glance from Samidar warned Kirigi to silence. "Give your brother a chance to answer," she chided.

Kel leaned back, chewed a mouthful, washed it down with beer. "Riothamus is a madman," he said at last, "a butcher. He suppresses the people. Keled-Zaram trembles under his hard rule, and his soldiers commit horrors in his name."

Kirigi leaned forward. "What are you talking about? You serve in his army. What suppression?"

Samidar touched her younger son's shoulder, and he was quiet once again. "You wear Riothamus's uniform," she pointed out.

"A man must eat." There was harshness in his words. "I've known hunger, Mother, and felt its claws rake my empty belly. The king pays his men well. That's why we obey him." He took another drink and set the empty mug aside.

"We're touched little by affairs in the capital," she told him. "Dashrani is a quiet town, and for the most part ignored by Riothamus. There's no longer even a garrison in the city. The gates stand open and no sentries walk the walls." She looked down at her hands, then into his eyes. "Still, we've heard rumors, and there've been soldiers prowling around lately."

"Searching for the rebels," he confided. "Their leader is reported to be in this area, a sorcerer called Oroladian."

Her brow furrowed. "A sorcerer?"

Kel filled his mug with water from the pitcher. "Not much is known about the leader. We don't even know what he looks like." He shrugged. "Riothamus hunts anyway. It's all madness."

"Why don't you quit?" Kirigi asked innocently, reaching for another slice of meat.

Kel regarded him through narrowed slits. "Maybe I will soon," he said, then drank deeply.

"Mother?" Kirigi's hand halted before the meat reached his mouth. "You're pale! What's wrong?"

Samidar got up, crossed the room to the door, and gazed into the distant hills now crowned with the glory of the full sun. "You said a sorcerer?"

Kel turned on the bench. "Kirigi's right. You look like you've just peered into hell itself."

She wrapped her arms about herself and leaned against the jamb, her eyes squeezed tightly shut against a very private dread. "I've seen into hell before," she said, "and it didn't frighten me as much as your news." She opened her eyes and stared through a fine moisture at her son. "You haven't asked about your father."

Kirigi rose slowly. "I assumed you told him," he said gently. "That's why I left you two alone so long."

"Told me what?" Kel asked. "Where is Father?"

Time had healed the pain, but there was still a scar, hard and swollen and tender. She thumped a fist against the wall. "Dead. Kirigi and I buried him out there." She pointed toward the hills. "He used to hunt there. He said it was the most peaceful place he'd ever known. When he was troubled he'd go there to be by himself. He always came back in a better mood." She turned and met Kel's gaze. There was ice in her voice. "He won't be coming back anymore."

"He was murdered," Kirigi said, taking up the tale. "Mother and I had taken the wagon to town. A metal rim had broken free from one of the wheels." He got up, walked to the center of the room, and stood between a couple of tables. "We found him right here on this spot. See how smooth the floorboards are? I sanded for days to get rid of the stains." He stared fixedly at the place he indicated, then suddenly he seized up a small bench. His muscles rippled as he heaved it through the air. The wall shivered at the impact.

"Kirigi!" Samidar cried.

The bench lay broken on the floor. A deep gouge mark showed how forcefully it had struck. Kirigi trembled all over, veins and muscles bulging with tension. "I thought I was over it," he said harshly.

Samidar went to him, took him by the arm, but he shook her off and returned to his seat at the breakfast table. He stared morosely into his mug and said no more.

"I didn't know," Kel said lamely.

"You weren't here." She bit her tongue. She hadn't meant that to be an accusation; it just came out that way. She went to stand by an open window and looked out. A caravan was just leaving through the gates of Dashrani. It would pass her inn, so she went to shut the door. That was enough to tell them she was closed.

"You mentioned a sorcerer," she said, turning again.

"Oroladian," Kel said with mild irritation. "You keep coming back to him."

"There was more to your father's murder," she explained, steely voiced. "He was mutilated. The four fingers of his right hand were cut off. The murderer must have taken them, for they were never found."

"By all the dark gods!" Kel covered his face with his hands.

"Perhaps," she hissed, "it was the dark gods. Or rather, one of their servants. I wondered then, but this land was free of sorcerers and wizards, I thought. It must have been a madman, I told myself, because nothing of value was taken." She paced among the tables and benches. "Now you tell me there is a sorcerer, after all."

"But why would he do it?" Kel persisted, staring at his own fingers. "Why would any man do that?"

"There are rites," she answered darkly, "that require parts of a human corpse. The art is called necromancy, but I didn't know there were such practitioners in Keled-Zaram. This land's people know little of magic."

"What rites?" Kel said. "How do you know about them?"

She looked away, unable to meet his gaze. "You know I'm Esgarian. You know what that means."

"But you have no powers," he pressed. "You told me you lost them long ago."

"Still, I was taught!" She glared at him. "I have the knowledge. I remember!"

"I'll kill him," Kirigi muttered, interrupting them, his voice chilly and bitter. "This Oroladian must be mine."

"Kirigi . . ." Samidar began, but the youth did not listen. He rose, stalked out the rear door without another word.

Kel watched him leave. "You've raised him outtempered," he said when the door slammed shut.

"Like his father and brother."

Kel lifted his mug. "No, Mother, not like me and Father. I'm the calculating one, and Father was fierce, but gentle." He sipped his water. "No, Kirigi is yours; he's your son."

She came up behind him, massaged his shoulders through the red silk of his tunic. "You're my son, too, Kel." She hugged him, wrapping her arms around his neck, pressing her cheek next to his.

"I can't drink," he said at last.

She let him go. "Sorry." She came around the table and sat down. For the first time, she ate a bite of meat, chewed it thoughtfully. "Tell me more of this Oroladian."

He shook his head. "Nothing more to tell. Reports say he leads the rebellion, but the reasons are unknown. His supporters are like foxes, impossible to catch." He scratched his chin. "Truthfully, we're here only on the strength of a rumor."

She sipped water from Kirigi's mug, then lifted a tidbit of beef that dripped grease and juices down her fingers. After a while she set the meat aside uneaten and licked her fingers clean. Kel went into the kitchen and refilled his mug from the beer keg.

"There's something on your mind," she said when he had resumed his seat.

Their gazes met. Looking at him was like seeing a masculine version of her own face. He had the same eyes and dark hair, same chiseled features. Kel was tall and lean like his father, not as heavily muscled as Kirigi. Five years had made a different man of her son, though. There was something in those emerald eyes she could not fathom, some hint of mystery. She wondered, did she really know him at all?

"You used to tell me stories," he answered finally. "I don't remember them all clearly. I was very small. But you talked about a dagger, sometimes, and you called it by a name." His gaze seemed to burn right through her. "Demonfang."

She sat perfectly still, her fingers interlocked so he couldn't see her hands tremble. "What about it?" she said. "They were stories."

He leaned closer. "But were the stories true?"

She wanted to look away, break the eye contact, but she knew she mustn't. Instead, she put on a condescending smirk. "Of course not."

Kel half rose from his bench so she was forced to look up at him. The black raven embroidered on his silken tunic seemed to spread its ebon wings upon his chest like some evil bird of prey. The irony of it struck her, how that same bird had been her father's emblem long ago in Esgaria and how all the family warriors had worn it. Now, his grandson wore it as well, the ensign of a distant king.

"You're lying, Mother," Kel accused. A sardonic grin split his face, making a thin slash of his mouth. "I think the dagger was real. I think you still have it somewhere."

She rose and turned her back to him. "You're wrong," she answered, keeping her voice calm. "Demonfang was just a story, a tale to entertain a baby, to hush your crying." She faced him again. "You were always crying about something."

He stalked around the table, caught her wrist suddenly in a grip that would not be broken. She hadn't realized how tall he was or how strong. "I want that dagger, Mother." He twisted her arm cruelly, making her wince. "I know you have it."

"No!" she said through clenched teeth.

He twisted harder. Pain shot through her elbow and up to her shoulder. She glanced at the rear door and thought of calling to Kirigi. Yet if she did that, the brothers would certainly fight, and all of Kel's original fear and accusations, the sense of being driven out by the younger child, would become true. The breach would never heal.

"I thought you'd be reasonable," Kel whispered in her ear. "I'm the warrior now. I've need of such a blade and its power. Or did you plan to give it to Kirigi someday?"

She brought a foot up, smashed the heel down on his toes. It wasn't hard enough to break any bones, but it startled him, and his grip loosened enough to let her pull free. She spun and backed away a few steps.

"Your jealousy has warped you!" she snapped, keeping her voice low for fear of alerting her younger son. Now, she recognized the light in his eyes, and it made her shiver. "Get out!" she demanded. "Would that I had died before seeing you come to this! Leave while my sweeter memories are still intact!"

He set his hand on the hilt of the sword at his hip, but he didn't draw it. Still, the threat was clear. He loomed over her. "I'll leave when the dagger is mine!" he said. "You'll tell me where it is, or I'll carve your precious brat and hang his heart on a thorn!"

A bitter cold fell over her. Her fingers curled into fists, and she drew herself erect. "Kel, listen to me and believe what I say." She fixed him with a look and crept closer. "By

Orchos and every demon in the nine hells"—she shook her fist at him—"if you *ever* harm Kirigi, I'll kill you. He doesn't even know how to use a sword. Kimon never taught him." Her hands curled in the fabric of his tunic and she pulled his face to hers. "Even if I'm dead and you try to hurt him, I swear I'll rise up and strike you down!"

Kel roared. His hand crashed down against her cheek. She reeled, fell to the floor. His sword glittered in the faint light, free of its sheath. "So you prove with your own foul mouth that you love him more than the flesh of your loins! Sterile bitch! You couldn't give me a true brother!"

"You would have hated him, too!" she spat back. "Kirigi would have loved you as much as your father and I loved you. But jealousy perverted your heart and made you a sick thing!"

His sword descended until the point hovered at her throat. His face twisted into something she no longer recognized. "You almost push me too far," he said thickly, "but your time hasn't come yet, Mother. Not quite yet." The point moved down between her breasts. She felt the cold steel through the thin material of her apron tunic. "Just give me Demonfang, and I'll leave you for now."

She forced a laugh. "I told you, fool, that was a story."

He leaned ever so slightly on the sword. A spot of warmth trickled on her skin. In moments it would stain her garment. *Another scar*, she thought with a sigh, almost grinning at such a ridiculous worry.

"You push me with your lies," he warned.

She looked down at the point against her body, trailed her gaze up its gleaming length until their eyes met again. "We can never be friends after this," she told him dispassionately.

Obscenities burst from his lips. The sword flew up, crashed down, and carved a slice from the edge of the table nearest her head. It was the breakfast table, and mugs overturned from the impact. One rolled off, clattered on the floor, and stopped near her hand. She picked it up, ran a finger along the inside of the rim, licked it, tasted beer. Making a face, she cast it away. "Yours," she said disdainfully.

"I'll find it," he raged. "I have the means, if only you knew! You can't keep it from me."

Her head inclined toward the door. "Get out, Kel."

A sickly smile spread over his face. Then he threw back his

head and laughed. "Demonfang will be mine," he assured her, regaining his composure. "I'd hoped to save myself some effort by asking for it. I'd hoped that out of guilt for what you'd denied me as a mother you might be generous. I'd thought you might worry about my safety when you learned I was a soldier and give me a powerful weapon." He sighed and sheathed his sword. "Guess I was a fool to think you cared."

She got slowly to her feet. "Good-bye, son," she said sadly. "I did love you. Some part of me still does even after this." She touched her swollen cheek. "But I know you don't believe it."

Kel strode to the door, seized the iron ring, then hesitated. For a moment he looked as if he wanted to say something. Then his shoulders sagged, and his head drooped toward his chest. She resisted an impulse to go to him; something in her heart wouldn't let her make the gesture. Kel had chosen his road. She couldn't walk it with him. Perhaps he had realized that, too, for he straightened wordlessly and pulled open the door.

There was a shout and the briefest glimpse of someone outside.

Kel slammed the door with a force that shook the walls. In one smooth motion he slid the bolt home. His sword leaped from its sheath again, and he ran for the rear door. Before he reached it, someone kicked it open. New sunlight flashed on ring-armor and ready blades. Window shutters around the inn burst open, revealing helmed and armored troops. The front door shivered on its hinges, splintered, and broke.

A huge soldier filled the entrance, one massive arm locked around Kirigi's throat, a short-bladed sword braced against the youth's ribs. Samidar could see more men behind him, and the wagons of the caravan she had spied earlier. It was a trap, then, a planned ambush. But why?

Kel's sword described a shining, humming arc and stopped suddenly, gripped in both hands. His eyes raked around the inn. Enemies on three sides, the kitchen behind him. There was another door through there, but it was always bolted with three bolts. Troops would be waiting beyond it, anyway, she was sure.

"Drop that sticker, rebel," the big soldier commanded. He gave Kirigi a violent shake. "Or this one gets it clean."

"Mother!" Kirigi croaked, his wind nearly choked off.

"Quiet, son," she said quickly. "Be still."

The big man nodded, apparently in charge. "She's a smart one," he said to Kel. "Now, you be just as smart. Thirty men surround this pigsty. And I know you wouldn't want any harm to come to your little brother, here."

Kel's smile was purest evil. He threw a swift glance at his mother. "Send him to hell for all I care," he answered. Then a bloodcurdling cry bubbled from his throat, and he ran straight at the men who blocked the rear exit.

"Get him!" the giant roared, and before Samidar could move or cry out, she saw the muscles of his sword arm bulge. Half the blade's length slipped between Kirigi's ribs. The youth's eyes clenched tight; in a spasm he bit his lip and blood ran down his chin.

His murderer jerked the blade free and cast the boy aside.

Samidar screamed and flew across the room to her son. She sank beside him. Kirigi managed to roll over. He looked up, and his eyes were moist with pain and confusion. "Son!" she cried. "Don't die, don't leave me!" She wrapped him in her arms, pressed his face against her body, and rocked him back and forth.

His hand came up weakly, brushed her cheek. "Mother." The words were feather soft, dry as dust. "Don't cry." He tried to swallow, but more blood welled between his lips. She wiped it away. "It hurts," he moaned. "It . . ."

He went limp in her arms.

She screamed again, shook him, then brought her lips down on his. "No, no," she moaned, and kissed him again. He stared at her, but there was no sight in those sea-blue eyes. Gently, she closed the lids.

The sounds of fighting penetrated her grief. The clang of steel on steel rang hollow in her ears. The crash of overturning furniture, the shouts, the huffing, and the screams of the luckless reached her with a dreamlike ethereality. Kel fought like a demon, using the skills his father had so arduously drilled into him. The attackers got in each other's way, their unorganized numbers actually a disadvantage. Kel had only to swing at any movement.

She couldn't tell the death he had done already. The only one that mattered rested in her arms.

Kel forced a way into the short hall that led to the back door. That made sense if he could get to the stables and his horse. But, of a sudden, he twisted and disappeared through the door to her own small sleeping room. It slammed shut.

"Break it down!" the big commander ordered, and a pair of shoulders leaned to the job. "Smash it!" he shouted, sneering at his own men. "Put some muscle to it!"

"He's barred it on the inside!" someone called in response. But an instant later wood cracked, and the door sprang back on wrenched hinges.

"What the hell?" one of the soldiers shouted.

Another bellowed, "He's not here!"

"Search the grounds!" The commander shoved a couple of his men. "You two, tear this place apart! There must be a trapdoor. Find it! If he gets away, I'll have all your miserable hides!"

He left his men and came toward her then, kicking a broken stool out of his path. "Where'd he go?" he demanded hotly. "Show us how he got out of that room, or I'll wring your disloyal neck!"

She stared at the raven on his chest, the emblem of King Riothamus. Damn him to the blackest hell! She laid Kirigi's head easily down to the floor and stood.

"Pig!" she answered him. "Murderer!"

His huge, meaty hand seized her by the hair, and he jerked her head sharply back. He shook the fist that held his sword before her nose, and she could smell his breath as he bent close to her.

"None of that now, you old whore. You're going to tell us where that son of yours has gone and everything else you know about the rebel scum he runs with."

"Murderer!" She spat in his face and brought her knee up with all the strength she could muster. It slid off the inside of his thigh, doing little damage, but her nails scored a trio of crimson streaks near his left eye.

"Filthy, traitorous bitch!" he roared. Stepping back, he wiped the blood and spittle with his sleeve. She flew at him again, raking with her nails. But the fight ended quickly when he introduced the pommel of his sword to the bony ridge above her temple.

The last thing she saw as she fell was the not-quite-faded rose of Kirigi's cheeks. She reached out to touch her son.

Chapter Three

Samidar woke slowly, completely blind. Her head throbbed desperately. She rubbed her eyes, wishing vision into them, and discovered an area above her left eye where the pain was worst. She touched the spot and winced. It was tender, very swollen. The floor beneath her was rough stone, and cold. Carefully she sat up, fighting nausea.

She rubbed her eyes again, uselessly.

The air was cool and stale, her tunic thin. If only there was some water to quench her thirst. She sat quietly for a time, holding her aching head, fearing her new blindness, reliving Kirigi's murder again and again in her mind. She cried until the tears stopped. After a while, she cried again. The sound of sobbing rose all around her, echoes of despair and loneliness and grief.

She slept a little, or passed out. Thunder continued to roll inside her skull when she woke, and she was sick on the floor. Disoriented, she tried to stand but settled back on her rump in her own vomit. Doggedly, she tried again and found a precarious balance on her feet. She held her hands out, searching for any obstacle, and she took a few hesitant steps.

The effort cost her in pain. Her head was a drum, Kirigi's drum, she thought dully. An incredible, frantic tattoo beat at her temples until she nearly screamed. But a moan was all that escaped her lips, and she forced her legs to move.

It might have been one of the nine hells, a road of darkness through a land of darkness where she would wander blind until the stars burned out and the fires of time burned out and

24

the souls of the gods themselves shriveled into black husks. She gritted her teeth and kept walking, fearing at any moment she might trip and fall or the pain in her head would overwhelm her. The scuffling of her feet on the stones rasped in her ears, and the rustling of her skirts was the only other sound.

She broke a nail when at last she encountered a wall. She sagged against it, sucked the tip of the injured finger. A tiny laugh gurgled in her throat at the new, insignificant pain. She felt a sudden dizziness, realized she was breathing much too fast, and forced herself to a semblance of calm.

The wall was rough stone, the mortar between the crudely cut blocks old and crumbling. She ran her hand along it, hoping to pace out the size of her prison, exploring for a door or window.

When the throbbing in her head became too unbearable, when her legs would no longer move where she willed them, she sank down, leaned her back against the wall, and drew a long breath. Only when she rested did she begin to guess where she was.

The walls had no angles. She knew now she had been walking in circles. There were no doors, no windows. The answer should have been obvious sooner, would have been if not for the fog that shrouded her brain.

It was the oubliette at the old garrison, a deep pit used to hold criminals. It couldn't have been used in years, certainly not since the garrison was withdrawn by Riothamus. The citizens of Dashrani didn't bother with prisons or pits anymore. The few lawbreakers careless enough to get caught received more specialized punishment: either they made instant restitution or they forfeited limbs or life itself.

She fell asleep again and dreamed that Kimon came to rescue her. She saw him, shining with a soft light, descending from the center of the darkness, walking with bold strides on the very air. He bent with a broad, reassuring smile, extended a hand to help her up. But there were no fingers on that hand.

She woke with a start. The pain in her head had eased a little. She squeezed her eyes shut, opened them, still blind. A fine, clammy sweat filmed her skin. She should get up, she told herself, but to what purpose? Instead, she pulled her knees up to her chest, tucked the skirts around her ankles, locked arms around her legs, and rocked herself.

Time passed. She had no way of knowing how much. Sometimes the air seemed to grow cooler, and she shivered uncontrollably. Sometimes she felt stifled by the heat and the unending dark. She cried out, shouted for anyone within hearing. No answer came.

Her buttocks ached from sitting on the hard stone floor, and the dank cold crept into her joints. She finally rose, creaking and stiff. To warm herself she paced around the pit, then across it. Twelve steps from side to side, she discovered. She paced it several times until she was satisfied.

Thirst became a torment. She sucked on her sleeve to draw moisture into her mouth, gaining only small relief. Once, she even licked the wall where it seemed dampest, but the brackish limestone taste was too much to bear.

Despair slowly gave way to numbness, and she paced without purpose, waiting for something, anything, to happen. Little by little, numbness boiled into anger. She cursed her oldest son. *You'll answer to me, Kel,* she swore. All she saw with her visionless eyes was that sword in Kirigi's ribs. All she heard was Kel's voice taunting. *Send him to hell for all I care,* he'd told the commander. No more tears of grief, but tears of rage and bitterness stung her eyes. She thumped her fist repeatedly on the wall until her knuckles throbbed.

She must have dozed again. She wasn't sure. But suddenly there were voices somewhere above her. The words were muffled, indistinguishable no matter how she strained to hear. Then came a scraping of stone on stone.

A beam of sunlight stabbed down through an opened hole, illuminating the center of her prison. She blinked against the intense brightness. Then she clapped a hand to her mouth to stifle a cry of joy. She was not blind! It was only the blackness of the pit, the absence of any light at all. Yet the light was almost more than she could stand. She covered her eyes and peered carefully between her fingers.

A rope slithered down.

"Hey, down there!" a voice called. "Come into the light."

She hesitated. But when the same voice called again, she rose, leaned on the wall for support, then moved cautiously to stand in the pit's center. The sun warmed her face with a pleasing, welcome heat.

"Tie it under your arms," the voice told her. "We'll haul you out."

She looked up, trying to see the speaker, and jerked her gaze away. The light was a white pain.

"Hurry up!" a different voice ordered impatiently. "Or we'll let you rot down there."

Squinting, she stared upward again. Nearly twenty feet to the top, she judged. No stairs and no ladders, but she knew that already from her explorations. The rope was her only way out. She tied it loosely about her body, using a knot she'd learned in her more adventurous youth.

She tugged on the slack, calling, "All right!"

The rope snapped taut. They lifted her quickly, and hands grabbed her arms to pull her to solid ground. She squeezed her eyes shut again, unable to bear the direct light of day. But the fresh air smelled wonderful; she filled her lungs with it. Slowly, she began to tolerate the light.

There was a loud *whump* behind her, and the ground shook with a mild vibration. She turned. A tall tripod straddled the hole, but an immense flat stone now covered that opening. A heavy chain trailed from an iron ring set in the stone up through the tripod and to a rusty winch. Two soldiers bent over the crank that hoisted the stone, huffing with exertion. She glanced quickly around and recognized the compound where the old garrison once quartered.

"Move."

The two soldiers at her arms pushed her along. The two at the winch fell in behind. "Where are we going?" she dared to ask. Another push was her only answer, but they marched her toward a building she knew had once contained the garrison commander's offices.

But she wondered, *Where are the regular tenants?* When the garrison had pulled out years ago, the buildings had swiftly filled with squatters and vagabonds, the poor and homeless of Dashrani. None of those were in sight. Besides herself and her four guards, there were only a few other troops scattered around.

At that moment, though, the compound gates swung back. Gates? They'd been repaired, she noted. The old ones had nearly been off their hinges. A company of soldiers tromped in. They made formation as the gate closed after them, and a barked order from their captain put them at ease. An instant later, he dismissed them and they dispersed into the old barracks.

So the garrison had been reoccupied. Deep in the ground, she had heard none of it. What other changes had occurred? How long had she been in that hole, isolated?

"Could I have some water?" she asked civilly.

Her guards said nothing. What was it about low-ranking soldiers that their tongues seemed only for bullying and threatening? She licked her lips and silently cursed them.

They came to a halt outside the commander's offices. One of her guards advanced, rapped smartly on the closed door, and stepped back. It swung inward, and Samidar caught the flash of armor and more men inside. There was a quick exchange inside that she didn't quite understand, then two men strode out.

She bristled. The bigger of the two was the bastard who'd slain Kirigi. She felt scarlet heat rise in her cheeks as their eyes met. He made no gesture, his expression never flickered, but he mocked her with his gaze.

The other man seemed to study her with a curious amusement. She had never seen him before, but she put on an air of contempt as he paced around her, scratching his chin. She observed him from the corners of her eyes. By his dress she judged him rich, a man of importance. His tunic was cloth-of-gold over britches of black silk. His boots were quality leather, as was the belt and weapon belt from which hung a beautifully crafted sword. Sunlight glinted on the ruby pommel stone.

He took a position directly before her, and he swept back over one shoulder the scarlet cloak he wore. He was younger than she was, but no youth. "Where is your son, woman?" he asked her gently.

She folded her arms over her breasts and answered evenly, "Give me water. Your hospitality has been pitifully lacking so far."

"She has a foul mouth," Kirigi's murderer growled.

Her interrogator cut him off with a curt gesture. "After you answer my question you'll have the finest wine in Dashrani."

"Just water," she replied. "I'll take nothing else from butchers of children."

The giant grinned just as he'd grinned when he'd pulled his blade from her young son's body. "Let me take this rebel whore and . . ."

The scarlet cloak whirled. A finger pointed threateningly.

"Your mouth, Yorul, shut it or take it back inside." The tone brooked no argument. Yorul bowed his head to the other man, hiding a scowl, and said no more.

The interrogation began again. "Do you know me, woman?"

She cocked her head to one side. "I've known you in a score of countries," she said at last. "A bastard nobleman who puts himself above the people of the land, who climbs on the bloody corpses of comrades to grab another handful of power or influence, an orphan-maker and widow-maker." She met his gaze, an inward cold radiating to the surface of her skin, denying the sun's warmth. "You're the commander of this animal who killed my Kirigi. Your name?" She shrugged. "It doesn't matter. I'll see you both in hell."

His lips turned upward in mild amusement. He ran a hand through his thick black mane. "You're an outlander," he said, "despite the years you've lived in my country. I can forgive some insolence considering the circumstances." He crooked a finger at Yorul. "Tell her my name."

"Oh, let's not make a play of it," she snapped, and made an obvious guess. "And spare me the entire recitation. Your name is Riothamus, king of Keled-Zaram, and no doubt the Lord of the Sun and the Moon, the Scourge of Heaven and Earth, and all that rot, too, right?"

He made a slight incline of his head and smiled.

"And the commander of butchers of children," she added contemptuously, glowering at Yorul.

Riothamus made a small shrug. "We all have our faults," he answered without rancor. "Yours is that you spawned a rebel dog for a son."

"Kel wears your livery," she countered.

Riothamus's eyes hardened. "He and a band of his followers slaughtered one of my patrols. That was during the last new moon. They stripped the bodies and desecrated them. Then, dressed in my uniforms, they've terrorized the countryside, robbing farms and villages to raise monies to finance their illegitimate cause. Those who refused payment or resisted in any way were murdered. Whole villages have been burned." He rubbed his palms together in sudden irritation. "And because they wear my livery the rumor has spread that I am responsible."

She sneered. "For all I know the rumor is true. Maybe you want the extra money to fatten your own coffers, and you think you can get it and blame the rebels with a lame story like that. It takes coin to put down even a small rebellion.''

He stared coldly at her. An uneasy silence hung in the air. ''Are you really such a fool?'' he said finally. ''That kind of cruelty only breeds sympathy for the rebels, as I'm sure your son knows.'' He tapped his brow with one stiffened finger. ''My crown is not a prize in a contest, woman. I won't yield it up. As your son fights, so I must fight harder and harder. A lot of innocents will be hurt in the struggle.'' He took a step closer and placed a finger on her chest. He said evenly, ''Unless you prevent it by telling me where he is.''

She stared pointedly at the finger, then at him until he took it away. ''You speak as if you thought Kel was the rebellion's leader.''

''The leader is someone called Oroladian, a reputed sorcerer. But Kel na'Akian is his right hand.''

Kel na'Akian? Neither she nor Kimon came from lands where more than one name was tradition. She rolled the words in her mind. Na'Akian: roughly, ''cold blood'' in her native tongue. Yet she'd never taught Kel the language of Esgaria. How had he learned?

''We've hounded his heels for several days. His general movements indicated he might come this way, so I set out spies to watch. Your inn has been monitored for some time. We knew the instant your son rode up, and we disguised our troops as a harmless caravan to approach and surround your establishment.'' He cocked his head to one side. ''Yet somehow he eluded us. So I have to ask you again. Where is he?''

''I don't know,'' she answered.

His hand lashed out. Her head jerked unexpectedly and a trickle of blood blossomed on her lip. Still, his voice was soft and calm as he spoke. ''Your son is a rebel, woman, a traitor. By our laws, that makes his family traitors as well. Their lives and all their goods are forfeit. I can spare you, of course, but you have to tell me what I need to know.''

She wiped away the blood with the back of her hand. Her tongue licked the small wound, drew the bitter taste into her mouth. Slowly, a different thirst began to grow within her, an old thirst, one she had nearly forgotten.

''I can't tell you,'' she answered carefully, ''nor would I if I had the information. Your struggle doesn't mean a damn to me. Who cares which pig rules the trough?'' She tossed back her long hair and looked away from Keled-Zaram's king as if he were suddenly beneath her notice.

"Let me have the bitch!" Yorul rushed toward her, but Riothamus caught his arm.

"I don't know how your son escaped my encirclement," he continued, "but I mean to have him. He's caused too much trouble already. I don't even know *why* he seeks my crown. But he's looted and murdered and burned indiscriminately. How can you protect such a man?"

"He's my son," she answered simply.

"He's the bastard of an arrogant gutter-whore!" Yorul blustered, reddening. He turned to Riothamus. "Majesty, you cannot tolerate this foulness any longer. Look how the men are watching. They wait to witness your justice. Let me be the hand of that justice, and I promise she'll tell everything she knows about the rebels. Then I'll make a spectacle of her execution that will serve as a warning to anyone else who'd turn against you."

She glanced around. As Yorul had claimed, other soldiers were milling about the compound in twos and threes. A few leaned in the doors and windows. She and Riothamus were the objects of their barely concealed attention.

Riothamus looked thoughtful, as if considering Yorul's request. He scratched his beardless chin, looked her up and down, shifted his weight from foot to foot.

She turned her face away again, disdainful, not caring what words Yorul bent to whisper in his king's ear. Blood had begun to stream on her lip once more. She dabbed at it and regarded the stain of crimson on her fingertip. There was that taste still growing. She felt its urgency, recognized it, and hid a hateful smile.

"Curb your dancing bear," she said coolly to Riothamus. "You say the law brands me traitor by association with my son." She folded her arms, drawing the material of her tunic taut over her breasts. "Do you obey the law as faithfully as you quote it?"

"I am the law," he answered, raising an eyebrow curiously. "I am bound by it because it is my word."

She frowned. "I know nothing of your word. But I know of the rite you call *Zha-Nakred Salah Veh*. I claim it." She met his startled gaze, and their eyes locked.

Then his surprise turned to mirth. "Ridiculous!" He laughed. "No woman has ever invoked *Zha-Nakred Salah Veh*."

"I invoke it!" she snapped with a harshness that stilled his laughter.

"You're an outsider," he declared, clenching a fist. "You insult our laws by claiming such a right!"

"Can I be an outsider one moment and branded traitor the next?" She spat at his feet, inwardly pleased when Yorul reddened again. "I've lived in this land for more than twenty winters, run my business, buried a husband"—she looked at Yorul, letting him feel the hatred she bore him—"and lost a son here. If I'm an outsider, then let me go. Hunt my son if you will. But an outsider can't be subject to your stupid law by association." She indicated the four guards who still surrounded her. "But if I am a citizen, then you must grant the *Zha-Nakred Salah Veh*. These men have heard my request, and no doubt so have half the others standing in those doors and windows." She waved a hand to take in all the soldiers milling about purposelessly. "Those, too. They'll know your answer and the value of your law, your so-called word. It may not matter to them if you deny me. Then again, it might. Or if not to them, to others who will undoubtedly hear the tale." She gave him a salacious wink then and smiled broadly. "Besides, think of the fun it will be."

Riothamus stiffened. "The *Zha-Nakred Salah Veh* is not for amusement," he said soberly. "It is a solemn ritual, and time-honored in Keled-Zaram."

She pursed her lips and regarded him with an expression of boredom.

After a hesitation, he asked, "Whom would you choose?"

She looked at Yorul and spat on his boots. "Who else?"

Yorul's hand went to the hilt of his sword. His huge body shook with barely controlled rage at the indignity she had dealt him. "I accept." The words came out a snake's hiss.

But again, Riothamus hesitated. "He's nearly twice your size," he said to Samidar. "Few can match him with a sword. Choose him, and you choose certain defeat."

She closed her eyes. "Him," she repeated.

A bemused grin spread suddenly over his face. "Why, woman?"

She touched her lip again, held up the flower of blood on her finger to the light of the sun, showed it to Riothamus.

"On his sword is the blood of my son," she answered grimly, "my innocent son Kirigi, who'd wronged no man, who died a virgin, who had never lifted a sword in his short life." She turned and gazed directly into Yorul's eyes as she spoke. "This thing that wears your uniform is a pig, less than a pile of dung on the caravan trail, not worthy to walk the same earth where such a child dwelled. This thing beside you, Riothamus, is a bug, an ugly, blood-sucking bug, and all the rewards of the gods await the one who steps on it."

"But," Riothamus warned, "you're a woman. This rite is for men."

She shrugged. "A sword knows no sex."

Yorul drew himself erect, assuming his full, impressive height. "Allow this challenge, Majesty," he urged, puffing out his chest. "Despite the fullness of her breasts and the shape of her hips, this is no woman, but an unnatural whore whose thighs breed rebellion the way a piece of offal breeds contagion. This is spewl, a bit of vomit that rears up on legs to insult a monarch. Her presence befouls the land I love, and when I kill her it will not be a death that you witness, but a cleansing."

Samidar nodded. The *Zha-Nakred Salah Veh* had begun even without the royal permission. Ritual insults had been exchanged. Next, they would trade mock blows. Mock victories and mock defeats would follow for both foes. Only after that would combat begin in earnest.

If Riothamus allowed it.

"Are you set upon this course?" the king asked her. "I can prevent it. Just deliver me your son, Kel na'Akian."

She gathered her long hair in one hand, tied it in a heavy knot, and tossed it back so that it hung between her shoulders. "I don't want it prevented," she answered. "And one traitor in the family is enough. I can't turn on my son."

He shook his head. "Your own mouth damns you, then. Loyalty to Kel na'Akian makes you a traitor to your king."

Riothamus's voice was only a rustle in the distance, but she answered him steadily. "If you're my king, then I am a citizen of Keled-Zaram. I've made a legal request, which is my right under the law. You cannot deny it."

Riothamus shrugged and walked a few paces away. "I do not deny it," he said. "You know the ways of *Zha-Nakred Salah Veh*? The ritual is sacred, laid down by our ancestors,

and must be observed with great solemnity. Few men ask to
face this. It is the pinnacle of our civility.''

   She said nothing but nodded her understanding.

   He gestured to one of her guards. "Give her your blade,
then all of you stand clear."

   A sword was placed in her hand, and she drew a deep
breath. Good steel had a smell, a clean oiled scent that she
had not savored for a long time. Yet it was a familiar scent
that set her blood racing. Her fingers curled around the hilt.
She lifted the weapon, gripping it with both hands, careful to
hide the frown that tried to part her lips. The sword was
forged with a slight curve, after the fashion of Keled-Zaram.
How would that affect her two-handed style? For that matter,
did she still possess anything that might be called a style?

   "Insults have been exchanged?"

   Both foes agreed they had.

   "*Zha-Nakred Salah Veh,*" Riothamus intoned. He turned
to Yorul. "Demonstrate your skill and the method you will
use to dispatch your challenger."

   Samidar knew what was required of her. She lowered her
sword and stood absolutely still. Yorul drew his weapon. It
flashed suddenly in a shimmering circle above his head,
catching the sunlight, reflecting it in starlike beams on the
compound walls. Down it came, aimed at her skull, only to
halt a mere handsbreadth from her scalp. She didn't flinch
from such an obvious blow; it would have been too easy to
deflect, at least in her youth.

   Yorul backed a pace. His blade wove a dazzling pattern
around his body, flying from hand to hand with elusive
swiftness. With effortless beauty he displayed his skill, and
she was suitably impressed. The keen killing edge licked out
at her head, neck, ribs, each a potentially deadly strike.

   When a fine sheen of sweat appeared on Yorul's brow,
Samidar threw up her hands, feigned a soundless moan, and
fell back in the dust. She lay there a moment, listening to the
excited beat of her heart. Then, she rose.

   Yorul's mouth twisted in a nasty smile, and he sheathed his
sword.

   "*Zha-Nakred Salah Veh,*" Riothamus repeated solemnly.
"Demonstrate your skill and the method you will use to
dispatch the challenged."

   She drew another breath, raised her sword. Taking a step

closer to her opponent, she rotated the blade loosely in her grip. She tossed it clumsily from her left hand to her right, back to her left. Unexpectedly, she tripped on the hem of her skirts and nearly fell.

A chitter of laughter startled her. She had forgotten the other soldiers in the compound. They had gathered to watch. Nearly a hundred men, she estimated, all sent to trap and capture Kel. Now, though, they crept from the barracks, from the offices and other buildings, and it was she who felt trapped and captured.

But here is their captain, she thought, approaching Yorul again. She crouched low. No fancy swordwork remained in her, she realized desperately. The years had been too many; time had stolen her skills, yes, and even her strength. Her stamina was that of a dancer, not a warrior. The sword was already heavy in her hands, and it didn't help that she had been starved and left to thirst in the pit.

She stared at the man who had murdered her son, her beautiful Kirigi, and a red hatred filled her. The weight of the sword seemed instantly to lessen, and she knew she had but one chance.

Yorul waited stiffly, wearing an undisguised smirk on his face.

She swung with all her might. The glittering edge bit through the flesh and muscle of his neck. A scarlet spray fountained as he fell to the ground, and an obscene hissing was heard as the air in his lungs escaped through the ruin of his throat. Yorul's mouth rounded in a silent scream; one hand scraped spasmodically in the dirt. Then he was still.

An angry roar went up around the compound.

Samidar faced Riothamus, unable to repress the strange grin that spread over her face. A dizzy, light-headed sensation rushed through her. She raised her dripping weapon and her blood-spattered hands. "An old thirst is quenched," she shouted at the Keled king. "Kirigi is revenged, and that dancing bear"—she looked at Yorul's body and spat on it—"will dance no more."

Riothamus stared back, pale and disbelieving, his eyes full of accusation.

She had shamed the rite of *Zha-Nakred Salah Veh,* but she had avenged her son. His spirit could rest easier. But what of Kel? Her firstborn was as guilty of Kirigi's death as Yorul.

The sword tumbled from fingers gone suddenly numb, raising the tiniest cloud of dust that quickly settled again on the length of bloody steel. Just as suddenly, laughter exploded from her and tears of hysteria gushed down her face.

"Hang her!" Riothamus raged. "Take her to the gate and hang her! Leave her there until the flesh drips from her bones! Honorless whore!"

Hands seized her, dragged her unresisting across the compound. Her mouth seemed beyond her control, and words flowed forth in a torrent, curses heaped on Yorul. That he was dead was not enough. She damned him in every language she knew, to every hell she had ever heard of, in the name of every conceivable god, until she could no longer see his hated body for the soldiers that surrounded her.

They dragged her to the compound gate, then through.

It was over. She could do nothing more for Kirigi. Somehow, she got her feet beneath her and managed to walk with a peculiar calm. Her arms were twisted cruelly behind her, but she felt no pain. She felt nothing but a sweet detachment. The streets seemed familiar, and familiar faces leaned from windows and doors. She smiled at them, friends and neighbors, men she had done business with.

The city gate loomed. A broad wooden beam spanned the opening. They would toss the rope over that, she knew, and haul her up. But what would they anchor it to? She saw nothing that would serve. Would they hold the end themselves? No, surely not till the flesh dripped from her bones.

She gazed beyond the gate. Down the road she could see her inn, closed, no one at home.

The rope sailed upward, uncoiling, and draped like a strand of silk over the blunt, rough bar. She waited, filled with an eerie calm, for someone to tie it around her neck.

Then a short gasp sounded in her ear, and the hands upon her relaxed. She turned. Sun glinted on sword steel. For an impossible instant she was back in the compound facing Yorul. Sword sliced through soft throat, rose and fell again. Metal clanged on metal, a blow thwarted, then blood.

It ended very swiftly.

"Four," she said dimly, staring at the bodies of her guards. Two lay with their backs slashed open, swords undrawn. One of them gripped the end of the rope. Another lay bleeding from a throat wound. The last was split from groin to breastbone.

Someone grabbed her hand. "Come on!" a voice whispered urgently. "Hurry, damn ye!"

She let herself be pulled back into the city, around a corner, and down an alley. *Someone will find the bodies*, she thought to herself. *They won't be left to rot until the flesh drips from their bones.*

She stopped suddenly, jerked to a halt by her sleeve. Something was forced into her hands. Someone was pushing and shoving, trying to lift her, touching where they shouldn't touch. She didn't like it. Not at all. The guards had pushed her when they'd hauled her from the pit.

Samidar lashed out with the edge of her hand, made hard contact, and was rewarded with a loud grunt. With an effort, then, she fought free of the haze that filled her head.

"Tamen!" she cried, at last recognizing her savior. She peered at what he had forced into her right hand. Reins, she realized. Tamen had tried to mount her on a horse. She threw her arms about his neck and kissed the cheek that glowed redly from her blow. "What have you done, old man?"

"Given ye a chance," he answered shortly. "Now get on that beast an' get out o' here. I didn't gut them four without witnesses, an' even if they don't squeal, them's goin' ta be foun' pretty quick. Come on, woman, ride!"

"You've got to come, too!" she insisted. "You can't stay now!"

"I gotta wife," he said curtly. "An old buzzard wi' not a hair on her head, which is why ye never seen her. But I can't leave her alone. I'll trust the townsfolk not ta tell on me, then I'll get us both out tonight. She don' mind goin' out at night, long as she wears a hat."

"I'll pay you back," she promised hastily, mounting the horse. "I'll find a way." She arranged her skirts so the saddle leather didn't chafe her thighs.

"Just go fast," he told her. "None o' us like what them soldiers did ta yer boy. I heard 'bout that farmer they burned out a few days back. Didn't believe it till I saw what they did ta ye."

"There're two sides in every war, Tamen," she warned him. "Keep your eyes open and believe nothing. And be sure you get out of town tonight."

He slapped the horse's rump. The animal raced up the alley, took the corner so sharply she nearly tumbled from the saddle. She grabbed a handful of mane and righted herself and headed for the gate. She risked a glance over her shoulder. Incredibly, not a soldier was in sight, though a few heads poked from half-shuttered windows.

She had Yorul to thank, she realized. Keleds buried their dead as quickly as possible, believing if the sun rose or set on an uninterred corpse, the spirit would punish the living. Of course, most of his men would be preparing his funeral. Because of Yorul no one blocked her way. She smiled at the irony of that.

Past the four bodies she rode, through the gate. At the last instant, her hand shot out. She grasped the end of the rope that was meant to hang her, and she whipped it free, then discarded it, leaving it on the road in the dust of her passing.

Chapter Four

Dreams of our youth and memories past,
We who were first now we are last;
Though we are old still we are strong,
But who will remember when we sing the last song?

The rains that had threatened for days came that night. They fell in torrential sheets, battering the earth. The branches of trees, heavy with water, bowed to the ground. Rain pummeled the grasses flat, splashed in thick, muddy puddles, ran in swift streams down the slightest inclines. Flatland sheened with new lake surfaces.

Stark lightning flared purple, sometimes white, behind thick, dark clouds. Thunder shivered the air.

Samidar rode out of the hills, miserable. Her hair was plastered to her face; her thick skirts clung to her legs and to the sides and rump of her horse. Water dripped from her lashes. She wiped constantly at her eyes to clear her vision. The rain stung like icy needles, and her thin tunic provided no warmth.

The horse glopped along in the black muck that had once been a road. She could feel the poor beast tremble between her thighs. It carried its head low; water rilled through its sodden mane.

The weather forced her to follow the road. It was too dark, and the rain fell too heavily to let her see far ahead. At a better time she could have ridden unerringly across the open fields. On such a gruesome night as this, however, she feared the unseen hole or narrow trench that could break her mount's leg. She trusted, instead, to the road, which would lead her right to her doorstep.

She was soaked and shivering, but somehow the unrelenting downpour had beaten away much of her pain. The sinking sun had left her prone on Kimon's grave, and the first rain had pasted the earth of his burial mound to her face and hands. Yet, when she at last got up, the driving storm had quickly washed the mud away. Something inside her was deeply affected by that, and as she climbed upon her horse and departed the hills, she knew she had turned her back forever on the life she and Kimon had made together.

A bolt of lightning sizzled across the sky. Too late, she threw up an arm to shield her eyes, and afterimages of the bleak countryside burned behind her lids. A deafening blast followed, shaking her very bones, before she caught a breath.

The horse only looked up, blinked, lowered its head, and plodded on.

A peculiar odor touched her nose. She sniffed. It grew stronger, yet she couldn't identify it. She sniffed again. The wetness disguised the smell or muffled her senses. Still it lingered, more potent with each hoofbeat.

It was the odor of damp ashes.

Her inn was no more, burned to the foundation. The dimmest flicker of lightning illumined a piece of her kitchen fireplace. Here and there she made out something that might once have been a beam or part of a table. A roundish lump might have been her iron kettle. Nothing else remained. Even the stable was ashes; her horses, she assumed, would be in Riothamus's compound.

She slid from the saddle and wandered through the ruins, stirring the destruction with her bare toe. There was no fire left, not even a coal still glowing. The ash was cold and wet. Her feet and the hems of her skirts were quickly blackened. She made her way toward the fireplace. The brick was cracked and scorched. She gave it the smallest push, and it collapsed with a muted rumble.

Did they bury Kirigi first? she wondered. *Or are his ashes mingled here, too? If she dug around, would she find his*

bare, cooked bones? She peered around again, half expecting
a charred and mud-splattered hand to thrust up through the
debris. But fate or the darkness of night spared her that.

She returned to her horse and gazed back for one final look
at what was once her home. For a moment the air was full
with the sounds of laughter and lovemaking and birthing. Her
sounds and Kimon's and Kel's and Kirigi's. So much was
gone, lost in that pile of stinking ash, and no one would
remain to measure the loss when she rode away.

She took her horse's reins and led him across the muddy
road to the clean, rain-flattened grass. Carefully, she wiped
the ash from her feet.

She had waited until night to come back, hoping to reclaim
a few of her possessions, things she might need on a journey.
Too late, now. It was all too late.

She mounted up and set a course across the meadow, riding
north with her back to the ruin. To the east it was impossible
even to see the walls of Dashrani, and she didn't worry about
being seen, not on such a night as this.

There was no moon to chart the passage of time. She rode
hunched over in the saddle, the slick reins wrapped laxly
around one hand. The rain did not abate. Water ran thickly
off her face, down her throat, between her breasts, chilling.
She shivered again, and her teeth began to chatter.

She remembered such storms from her youth, storms conjured by the sorceresses in her homeland, far-off Esgaria. Her
mother had been such a sorceress, imaginative and full of the
power of her craft. Samidar had heard her mother speak the
words that turned sultry summer evenings into tempestuous,
frothing nightmares. She had seen the gestures that raised the
gentle whitecaps of the Calendi Sea into towering, smashing
waves and called down strange lightnings that encircled her
wrists like scintillating serpents obedient to her will.

But this was no arcane storm. It lacked focus or direction.
It was wild, lashing with fury and uncontrolled intensity. The
rain bit her flesh, lightning burned the vision from her eyes,
thunder roared in her ears. It raged without purpose, raw
nature as fierce and unrelenting as any guided magic.

Perhaps it was the gods who sent this rain to hound her.
She had offended a few in her time. Had they finally chosen
to bring her low, to spin the wheel of her fortune to this

dismal depth? Was it the gods that had turned one son against her and claimed the other's life? Was it the gods that had dragged her from her home and burned it to the ground?

She spat into the tempest. What could she not blame on the gods if she tried? *My fortune is in my hand,* she recalled. It was an old Esgarian saying, and long ago she had muttered it often. But now, there was no sword at her side to grasp as she remembered the words.

She had only the vaguest notion of where she was going. She rode mostly for fear that if she stopped, all the pain and grief would come back and crush her into the muddy earth, and she might never get up again. It didn't matter where she went, only that she keep going.

Still, when the steady, warm glow of a light appeared off to her right, she hesitated, then made slowly for it.

In the darkness and the storm she had almost missed her neighbor's farm. The glow was the hot, bright forge fire, and it illuminated the interior of the small stable barn. The doors to the barn were thrown open. She rode inside.

"Amalki?" she called.

A man whirled away from the forge, wielding a white-hot smoking coal poker as if it were a sword. His dark hair and close beard dripped with sweat; his naked chest and arms sheened in the crimson light. His eyes widened as he recognized her, then suddenly hardened. He cast the poker into a rim-charred water bucket. A cloud of steam hissed up as he hurried wordlessly by her and tugged the doors closed.

"Where have you been?" he said in a terse whisper. "The king's men have been searching everywhere for you. They found old Tamen and hanged him!"

She slid from her mount. "The bastards," she muttered, stepping closer to the forge. It gave off tremendous heat that promised to rapidly chase the storm's cold from her veins. "Tamen was my best customer and a good friend." She paused to reflect on a few of the times he had spent in her inn and to remember some of his more amusing antics. "That's one more corpse to lay at Riothamus's bloody feet," she said finally. "Perhaps these rebels have some cause, after all."

"Keep a courteous tongue in your head, Samidar," Amalki warned her. "That is my fire you warm yourself beside, and

you know I served in the king's army. Riothamus is no great
ruler, but he's no tyrant." He handed her a rough blanket that
had lain folded on an upended barrel. It was slightly damp,
and she suspected he'd worn it over his shoulders to come out
in the rain. She accepted it gratefully and made a reluctant
apology.

"What are you doing out here?" she asked, changing the
subject.

Amalki pointed to a stall where a thin-looking horse lay
with its legs folded under it on a bed of fresh straw. "Sick
mare. I feared the damp and cold would finish her if I didn't
light the forge to keep her warm."

"She should be warm enough," Samidar answered, finding a strange kind of comfort in such small talk. "With those
doors shut, this place will be a furnace."

He nodded, sitting back on the barrel to regard her. A
silence fell between them. She turned away from his gaze to
stare into the shining coals.

"I've got some of your things," he said at last.

She turned back to face him again, feeling a small surge of
hope.

"When you're warm and dry, we'll go over to the house."
He must have read the questions in her eyes. "I was on the
road when the soldiers started to burn your inn." He hung his
head, then a small grin parted his lips. "It seemed a shame to
let everything be destroyed, so I took the sergeant aside and
offered him a bag of coins to let me rummage." He wiped
sweat from his face with the back of his hand. "Of course,
you can have it all back."

If he had them, there were a few things she wanted. She
couldn't burden herself, though. Her life at the inn was
finished; there would be no point in keeping souvenirs. "What
did you get?" she asked.

Amalki shrugged. "I don't know, really. I had a wagon,
and I loaded it with everything I could get my hands on.
Then the rains started before I could get home. I dragged
it all inside before it was spoiled, but I've been out here
nursing that poor beast ever since. No chance to go through
it, yet."

"Was there a trunk?" she asked. "A wooden trunk about
this long and high with three metal bands and an iron ring?"

He looked thoughtful. "Yes, I think I got that."

She licked her lower lip. The heat was making her thirsty. "Everything is yours," she told him, "except a few items in that trunk." She moved back to her horse and tugged on the cinch. "I'll unsaddle him, if you don't mind. Just for a while. He's soaking, too, and the saddle blanket will chafe him."

Amalki shouldered her gently aside and hefted the saddle himself. He spread the small woven blanket near the forge to dry. "You've been a good friend, too, Amalki," she told him. "You know I can't stay long."

He didn't look at her but grabbed a curry brush and went to work on her mount. "Can't let this one get sick," he answered. Then he added, "No one's looking for you until the storm breaks. That's not going to be soon. You can rest here and eat something, then ride out in the morning."

She moved back to the forge's warmth while he brushed. "I can't wait that long," she said. "I'll take you up on the food, though. I'm starved. I still don't know how long they kept me in that damned hole."

"Two days," he volunteered. "The soldiers rode to all the farms announcing your arrest." He looked over his shoulder, and his mouth was a thin, tight line. "I'm sorry about Kirigi. He was a fine lad, always had a good word for people, and just coming into his full manhood." He shook his head. "A shame, but at least you got his killer. If only you hadn't bespoiled a sacred rite to do it."

She didn't want to talk about it, but the hint of accusation in his voice rankled. "Look at me, Amalki," she demanded. "I've seen forty-three winters! I'm old by most nations' standards." She swallowed before continuing. "A man killed my innocent son without even giving him a chance to defend himself. I took the only vengeance I could, ritual be damned! Yorul had more of a chance than he gave Kirigi. At least the pig had a sword in his hand."

Amalki made no reply. He concentrated on brushing her horse, making long strokes from withers to rump. Samidar watched him morosely, and she watched the tall, twisted shadow he made on the far wall.

"Could I see my things?" she asked, suddenly impatient.

Amalki set aside the curry brush, leaned on the animal's rump, and looked at her. "I didn't mean to offend," he said softly. "It's just hard for me to ignore the traditions of my own people. I sometimes forget you weren't born in this land. You did what you had to do.''

"And I'd do it again," she told him with a sad shake of her head. "You've never had children, Amalki. You don't understand what a parent will do for them.''

His face lit with an embarrassed smile. "Maybe I will soon, though.''

Samidar relaxed a little. "How is Teri?''

Amalki held his hands before his belly, and his smile widened. "By the next new moon," he said. "A descroiyo woman passed by with the last caravan. She told Teri's fortune.'' He beamed as he spoke. "It's going to be a boy, Samidar.''

She closed her mouth. No need to tell him what trouble sons could be. Besides, the descroiyo's power could never be trusted. For a coin they told what the customer wanted most to hear. Of course Amalki wanted a son, and Teri wanted to give him that son. But if it was a daughter, the descroiyo would be long gone, and the parents would be just as happy. That was always the way.

She wiped sweat from her face. With the barn doors shut the heat continued to build. Her tunic's fabric turned stiff and scratchy as it began to dry, and she squirmed uncomfortably. "I'd still like to see that trunk," she said.

Amalki nodded, led her horse into a stall, and scattered a handful of fresh straw for it to eat. Then he crossed to the doors and opened them a crack. He stuck his head out. "Just checking," he said somewhat sheepishly. "No chance anyone would be looking for you in this storm." He waved for her to follow.

The rain still beat thick and hard, and a wind had risen to whip it with stinging force. She ran after Amalki, mud splashing on her bare ankles, skirts flapping and tangling about her legs. Her wet hair blew over her eyes. She tried uselessly to brush it back and kept her sight on the dim outline of his small home.

Amalki reached the door ahead of her and pounded. The old wood shook visibly under his fist. She caught up with him just as it opened.

Teri moved back as they scurried inside. Her eyes widened when she saw Samidar, and her jaw dropped. Amalki took

the wooden bar from his small wife's hands and set it across
the door again.

"Blows open without it," he said. "Haven't got around to
making a proper lock."

Teri caught his arm, her gaze full of questions.

Amalki reassured her with a kiss. "Get a bag together," he
instructed. "Fill it with food that can stand a journey. Get a
waterskin, too." He paused, made a face at the puddle he had
left on the floor, mopped the droplets of rain from his chest
and arms. "Make it a wineskin. There's water enough."

Teri hesitated, one hand on her pregnant belly. She glanced
at Samidar, then at her husband, and drew a deep breath.
"Give her something dry to wear," she told her husband as
she headed for the tiny kitchen. "Does she have a horse?
We'll help her, but she can't stay here." At the kitchen
entrance she stopped and turned back to face Samidar. "If it
was just Amalki and me, I'd do anything I could for you.
You've been a good neighbor." She patted her tummy. "But
there's a child to think of now."

Samidar nodded. "You've risked too much already, and
I'm grateful." She looked to Amalki and reminded him again
of the trunk. The longer she stayed in this house, the greater
the danger to her friends.

"It's back through here," he said, picking up an oil lamp.

She followed him into a side room. The lamp suffused the
interior with an amber glow that flickered and danced as the
wind forced between the uncaulked boards that served for
walls and teased the slender flame.

She had not known Amalki was such a collector. Or maybe
"scavenger" would have been a better word. The room was
full of old tools and utensils, chests, scraps of leather, linens
and fabrics she didn't recognize, colored rocks the size of her
fists, garments cast in careless piles. There was no order to
any of it.

"No, I'm not a thief," he explained. "I wander the caravan roads. Amazing what they leave behind or what falls
unheeded from their wagons. Or sometimes I fix a wheel or
mend a harness, and they pay me with goods."

"You should open a shop in Dashrani," she said.

"Don't want to live in the city," he answered disdainfully.
"But when the baby comes I'll probably have to sell some of
it."

She spotted her possessions scattered about. There were her cook pots and a keg of her best beer. "Drink that," she advised. "It will spoil quickly back here." There were some of her skirts and Kirigi's *dumbeki*. She ran her fingers over that, remembering. There were other items of Kirigi's. She did her best to ignore them all. At last, she found her trunk half-covered by the carpets that had lined the floor of her small sleeping room.

"You didn't miss much," she said solemnly.

Amalki shrugged. "There was lots more, but the sergeant was impatient."

Samidar swept the carpets aside and lifted the trunk's lid. "Bring that light closer," she said, kneeling. "Then for Teri's sake you'd better leave me alone to change."

Amalki placed the lamp on a shelf where it could shine on the trunk's contents. "For Teri's sake," he said with a barely concealed smirk, "or for mine?"

She waited until he was gone. When she was alone she sank back with a sigh and leaned one arm on the old trunk. She felt like crying again, but there were no tears left. Instead, she listened to the rain as it smashed against the thin wooden walls, and she rubbed her arms and shoulders. It was cold in the drafty room.

At last, she gathered her courage and bent over the rim. She emptied the trunk item by item, memory by memory. Here was the shawl Kimon had given her years ago, with its bright embroidery and pearls sewn along the edges. Here was the blanket that covered them that first night in their inn. Another blanket followed, the one Kimon had wrapped so proudly around his newborn son. There were a few garments under that. She set everything aside with tenderness. Amalki had no conception how much she had given him or what she was leaving behind. He wouldn't treat these things with much care. Maybe that was why she took her time.

As she reached the bottom of the old trunk she found the things she sought. The clothes were worn, folded and bound into a bundle with a belt. She set them close at hand, separate from the other pile she had made of her memories, and reached back into the trunk.

Her sword lay within. The leather sheath was battered and scratched, but the lamplight gleamed on the keen edge as she exposed a short length of blade. The smell of oil touched her nostrils, a bit of lubricant to protect the steel from rust. She slid the blade back home and regarded the unadorned hilt; the wrapping was dulled with the clear print of her hand.

She cradled the weapon in the crook of her arm almost as if it were a child. A slow sigh escaped her lips as she leaned it against the trunk.

A pair of boots came out next, once supple but now stiff from disuse.

All that remained in the trunk was a circlet of twisted silver. The metal was tarnished with age and neglect, but nothing dimmed the polished moonstone inset. Long ago a good friend had given it to her. Samidar gathered her hair, put the damp mass through the circlet, and balanced it on her brow. She traced around the setting, recalling how much it resembled a third eye when seen in the right light or from the proper angle. It was one of her dearest treasures.

She rose, wincing at the tingle of returning circulation in her legs. Slowly, almost ritualistically, she peeled off her wet tunic and untied the strings that held her skirts around her waist. They fell around her feet, and she stepped free. She had no more use for them but to wipe the mud from between her toes. With a peculiar frown she realized she must have tracked filth over Teri's floor.

Lastly, she removed the jeweled halter she had worn all this time under her tunic. She'd had no chance to remove it since that night of dancing at the inn. So much had happened so fast. She laid it carefully aside, watching the light glimmer on the gems and gilt threads.

Samidar closed the lid to her trunk. She gazed then at the belted bundle at her feet and finally bent to pick it up. Unfastening the belt, she shook the folded items loose.

A sense of time distorted swept over her. She pulled on trousers of thin gray leather; the thighs were worn smooth from riding. There was a jacket-styled tunic; the belt wrapped around her twice and held it closed, and the sleeves fastened close at the wrists. It was also gray, but made of softer linen. She stamped her feet into the black boots; over twenty years unused, they were a bit tight, but she knew they would stretch with wear. A cloak remained, and a pair of gloves, all of fine gray leather. She tucked the gloves into her belt and draped the cloak over one arm.

She reached for her sword. The sheath had its own weapon

belt. She fastened it around her hips. After so long, the weight of it felt awkward. She adjusted it several times before giving up.

Suddenly she covered her face with her hands, overpowered by a sense of her own age. The sword was made for her by a man long dead. The friend who had given her the circlet also was dead. The garments belonged to someone else, another Samidar, a much younger and wilder woman.

Samidar with another name.

The name echoed in her head; her lips mouthed the word. She forced herself to utter it. Only the barest whisper came out, and she made herself say it out loud until she knew the name was hers once again.

She picked up the halter and gave a last look at her neatly ordered pile of memories. In a few days they would be mingled with the rest of Amalki's treasures, just more junk in a room full of junk. It was not easy to turn her back on twenty-three years of her life. But she did, taking the lamp with her, abandoning it all to darkness.

Amalki and Teri were in close conversation before the fireplace. The warm log fire seemed to create a crimson halo around Teri's belly as if to emphasize the femininity that Samidar was forever surrendering. They stopped when they noticed her. Amalki started to speak again, then stared at her garb.

"Samidar—"

She cut him off with a curt gesture. "My name is Frost." The name sounded distant to her ears, as though it drifted across a lifetime before leaving her lips.

Amalki swallowed. He pointed to her sword. "Do you have any idea how to use that?"

She peered at him, and an inner voice told her she should laugh. Yet a door had closed on her heart, leaving a void where her emotions had been. She felt his concern, and a part of her was grateful for it. But she couldn't respond to it.

"What are you going to do?" Teri asked uncertainly from the mantel.

Frost looked at her. The young woman's voice was silky and deep, and their gazes met unflinchingly across the room. Teri was beautiful. Had she been as beautiful when she was pregnant with Kel? By the next new moon, Amalki had said, they would have the child.

She approached Teri and held out the halter. "If you have a daughter, then this is for her. Teach her to dance, Teri. Nothing matters, but to dance. All of nature is a dance." She reached out gingerly with her other hand and touched the bulging tummy, feeling the life within. Teri allowed it with a kind of unshakable calm.

Frost looked over her shoulder at Amalki. "If it's a boy," she instructed, "then sell the jewels and buy him a sword. The best you can find. All of nature is a dance, but all of life is a struggle. Dancing and fighting—two sides of the same coin."

Teri touched the hand that still rested on her belly, drawing Frost's gaze back. "You talk as if you expect to die."

She smiled at that and pulled her hand away. "You're young, Teri. You don't like to think about it yet, but we all die. You and me, Amalki, even the child in your body. No, don't curse me with such a mean look. Ask your husband; he was a soldier. He knows what death is." She turned around. "Tell her, Amalki."

But he only shrugged, looked askance.

"Well, no matter. You still have a long life ahead of you." She pushed the halter into Teri's reluctant hands. "But not if I'm found here or if anyone learns you've sheltered me. So, it's time to go." She patted the sword on her hip and ran a hand over her clothing. "I've got what I came back for." She headed toward the door.

"Wait," Teri called. She lifted a small cloth sack from the floor near the fireplace. "Here's food. I hope it's enough to see you safely away."

Frost took the bag, then hugged the giver. "Never touch your man's weapons," she whispered to Teri as they embraced. "Grow old and wrinkled from motherhood and farmwork, and find your happiness in that. I did for a short time."

She broke away and shouldered her meager supply. "Don't follow me out, Amalki. Stay here and hold your pretty wife. I think I've upset her." When Amalki made to protest, she shushed him. "I can saddle my own horse. I've had more experience at this sort of thing than you can guess." She forced a smile. If only he knew what his neighbor had been in other times and other lands! "I'll close the barn doors tight so your mare won't get cold." She lifted the lock bar from its brackets, but she held the front door shut and turned back. "You've been good friends. I'm going to miss you." She pulled the door open.

"Would you mind if I named my son Kirigi?" Amalki called suddenly.

She froze, half-out into the night. "Don't," she answered in a near whisper. "Kirigi is dead."

She shut the door behind her then, before any more could be said, and ran out into the dark and the rain.

Chapter Five

For two days the hills and lowlands of Keled-Zaram rolled
before her, carpeted with lush, damp greenery. Here and
there patches of tiny yellow fireglows and white starflowers,
petals ashimmer with thick dew, filled the moist air with the
odors of early summer. Yet the weather was autumnal. A
wispy mist hugged the low places, stirred and drifted with a
ghostly grace, pushed by the currents of every random breeze.

The sky lay like a bleak shroud over the land, featureless
and oppressive. Even the sunlight seemed to shrivel into itself
until nothing shone but a pale, milky hole in the gray heavens.

Frost pulled her sodden cloak tighter at the throat, dropped
her head a bit lower between slumped shoulders, too miserable to curse. The constant drizzle soaked her to the skin; a
thin stream of water dribbled from the tip of her nose, over
her lip, off her chin. Her thighs were stiff, chafed from
rubbing on wet saddle leather. The chill breeze conjured
gooseflesh until she thought her entire body would finally
draw into one shivering bump.

Nor was her poor horse any happier. If possible, its shoulders slumped more than hers. It carried its nose nearly to the
ground, its matted mane thick and heavy and dripping. It
plodded along over the slick grass and mud, sometimes stumbling, sometimes stopping out of sheer despair until she
nudged or kicked its flanks to get it moving once more. She
pitied the beast as it trembled beneath her, yet there was
nothing for either of them but to keep moving.

No tree gave shelter, for the branches and leaves rilled with rain. She passed no farmhouse, no village. Water clung to her lashes, but she kept her eyes on the dim horizon.

When darkness at last fell, she dismounted in the lee of a hillock, gathered her cloak and hood about her as tightly as possible, and sat down in the wetness. With the reins wrapped securely about one hand, she rested her head on her knees, locked fingers around her legs, and waited, too numb to think, empty of emotion.

She dozed in fits. The first hints of another gray dawn roused her, and she rose and climbed in the saddle again. At least the rain had stopped. She took a strip of dried meat from Amalki's sack, chewed without tasting.

The sun held no promise of warmth; the clouds looked swollen and menacing as ever.

The sun's zenith found her at the bank of a treacherous, rain-engorged stream. Its waters churned, carving chunks of thick mud and tufts of grass, sweeping them swiftly out of sight. Yet it was not too deep, for a bubbling white froth marked where a trio of stones poked above the surface.

She chewed her lip; her thoughts turned back.

It had been a much smaller stream those twenty and more years ago, barely a trickle. With Kimon, she had stopped to drink here, perhaps at this very spot. Ashur had been with her then, that huge, beautiful black unicorn who had carried her through half a dozen wars and more adventures than she remembered. He, too, had once drunk from this stream. If she let herself, she could almost see Ashur's eldritch, unearthly eyes. They had not been true eyes at all, but twin sparks of flame that flickered, burned, yet gave no heat. . . . They haunted her, those eyes. She saw them in her dreams, in her nightmares. Even now she felt an emptiness, an unending ache, when she thought of them.

She stared down into the swirling water. A large piece of driftwood arrowed its way along the currents, passed before her, vanished downstream.

Perhaps, she reasoned, it would have been better never to have come to Keled-Zaram, never to have made a home and settled down. Kimon was dead now, and Ashur had disappeared long ago. One son was slain, and the son of her flesh had gone gods knew where.

It chilled her to realize how alone she was.

"It's you and me, horse," she said, giving her mount a pat

on the withers, urging him into the stream. That was the first she had spoken and the only voice she'd heard in days. "It's you and me," she repeated just for the sound of it.

The horse waded carefully to the center of the stream and stopped. It bowed its head to drink. The water came halfway to its belly, and though her boots were already wet, she freed her feet from the stirrups and held them high to avoid a further soaking. She knew enough not to let him drink his fill and tugged gently on the reins. A cluck of her tongue set him moving again, and they scrambled up the opposite bank.

She twisted in the saddle and looked back once more. Was this truly the spot where she and Kimon had once stopped? She was certain it was. But time and rain had long since washed away their footprints.

In the late afternoon the rooftops of a small town appeared suddenly in the south. Soushane, if she recalled its name properly. She and Kimon had passed through it, too. She stopped and sniffed the air, rich with the savory smells of cooking as wives and daughters began the evening meals. The wind blew the odors to her, and her stomach felt suddenly empty. She leaned forward, lifted her nose, inhaled deeply. Barely, she could spy the smoke curling high from the nearest chimneys. There was a tavern there, too, or used to be. She licked her lips at the thought of warm wine.

But she tugged the reins and turned her horse aside. Soushane was a stop for the border patrols, who were also fond of its tavern. She was a fugitive. Word of her crime might not have reached this far, but then again, it might. She took another sniff, filling her nostrils with a sweet, unidentifiable flavor, and sighed. A piece of dried fruit from Amalki's bag would make her supper tonight, and to wash it down there was water. Gods, how there was water!

She swung wide around Soushane to avoid being seen. Keled-Zaram shared a long border with Esgaria and the warrior-state Rholaroth. The border itself was a river called Lythe, whose source was somewhere far to the north of Rholaroth in the cold, forested land of Rhianoth. She had seen that distant country but did not know the truth of the legend that the river sprang wild and raging from the mouth of a vast black cavern that led down into hell itself. "Which hell?" she had asked innocently enough as a child. But her mother had only smiled,

arched her eyebrows in a way she had, and proceeded to
another legend.

The river Lythe was not far away. She and Kimon had
crossed it and arrived at Soushane in only two days.

She kept a sharper watch now. Where there was a town,
there would be farms. Where there were farms, there would be
farmers with tongues. She did not want to be seen.

And there were patrols to watch for. It was not likely they
would work this far from the border, but there was the chance
of a supply troop or a replacement detachment. Soushane was
not large enough to host a garrison, but a day's ride north and
west, at high-walled Kyr, it was a different story.

The weakling sun seemed not to set so much as to merely
fade from the sky. Night closed in quickly, but not before she
glimpsed remembered foothills in the far distance. Memories
chilled by the passage of years shivered through her. She
pushed on through the thick of darkness, ignoring the aches
of her body, the small voice that cried insistently for her to
rest. Not until the ground began to rise steeply under her
horse's hooves, not until it leveled and began to fall again,
did she stop and dismount.

It was cold, and she was hungry. She curled up on the
damp earth with her sack of provisions and her waterskin.
The reins still grasped in one hand, she worried what to do
about her mount. She had no hobbles to fasten his legs, and
she feared letting him wander free. Finally, she tied one rein
about her ankle. It was bothersome, but it freed her hands for
eating.

She sipped slowly from the waterskin. It bore the faintest
taste of the red wine Amalki had filled it with days ago, wine
she had quickly finished. Fresh stream water had taken its
place; it lacked the liquor's bite, but it was cool and welcome.

She unhitched her sword belt and laid it close by, then she
plunged one hand into the sack. It was too dark to see; her
fingers closed on the first thing they brushed. A sausage. She
broke it in half, returned part of it, and ate the rest. Next, she
found cheese, a bit of hard bread, several pieces of dried
fruit. She surprised herself. The bag was far lighter when she
finished than when she began, and her belly was contentedly
full.

The horse nibbled the grass near her feet, apparently too
weary to think of roaming off. She reached out and rumpled

its forelock. It looked up at her with soft, moist eyes and
went back to feeding.

Frost lay back, locking hands behind her head, and gazed
upward at the featureless night. If only she were dry; if only
the ground was hard and warm under her back; if only there
were stars to count or a fire to sit and stare into. She closed
her eyes.

But it's not so bad, she caught herself thinking.

After a while she untied the rein from her boot and stood.
She listened. The darkness was still. If the world turned, as
some philosophers insisted, it turned in utter silence. No
creature, no insect, made a noise, no limb or blade of grass
stirred. Even the horse had stopped its munching.

But there was something. A muffled beating, a far-distant
drum throbbed at the edge of her awareness. She strained to
hear it. Then her lips tightened in a thin, satisfied line of
recognition.

It was her own heart. The wild, triumphant sound of it
melted all through her, filled her with its affirming power.

She laughed suddenly, and the echo of it rolled among the
hills. The numbness that for so long had been part of her was
gone. She knew, at last, that she was still alive, fully and
vitally alive.

Dawn flamed in the east, pushing back the thick gray
clouds with wispy streamers of gold and vermilion. The air
was warmer than it had been for days. A steamy moistness
hung over the land as the sun exerted its strength.

Naked, Frost stretched, enjoying its touch on her bare skin.
Her clothes and cloak lay spread on the ground. Though she
knew they would not dry there, for a few moments she was
free of their cloying dampness. She shook back her hair; at
least it was beginning to dry. She combed her fingers through
it to smooth the snarls and tangles.

She ate from the sack again and drank half her remaining
water. From her vantage she could look back the way she had
come, across a flat, broad expanse. The sun was brightening;
she shielded her eyes. Nothing moved out there, not even the
one scraggly tree that broke the steppe's monotony.

She turned to look the other way. The peaks of high,
rolling hills rippled the horizon. They might have been mountains in the first ages after creation, but time had worn away

their majesty. *Shai-Zastari*, the Keled people called this range: the Barrier Hills. On the other side was the river Lythe, and beyond that, Esgaria.

She saw her purpose at last. It had festered within her, hidden and secret, from that moment in Amalki's home when she'd donned garments untouched for so many years. She had strapped on her sword. She remembered clearly how it had felt when her fingers had curled around its familiar hilt. Yet her other hand had closed on emptiness, grasping for a weapon that hadn't been there.

The empty hand had brought her on this path. Through rain and miserable cold it had led her. She had fooled herself, believed she had wandered merely to avoid capture. But all the while that empty hand had known.

She stared at her palm. Soon, she would fill it with what it longed for.

Bending to retrieve her sword, she drew it from its scabbard. She was long overdue for a hard workout. Twenty years overdue.

Her fingers curled around the hilt. The leather wrapping was damp, but orange fire flickered along the steel as she slowly exposed it to the sun. The blade gleamed, smelling of fine oil. Kimon had cared for it with the ritual precision of his Rholarothan heritage. The edges were keen, the point perfectly honed. Light danced along its entire length, rippled like dazzling water as she turned it.

In all the intervening years she had not touched it, fearing the memories it stirred. But now, that fear was gone and her past came rushing upon her. In an instant she relived her life, every great sadness and every overwhelming joy, every adventure and every quiet moment. They had been locked up, those memories, in her sword, and she had set them free. She didn't try to resist or shut them out. She welcomed them. A long sleep had been lifted from her, and Frost was Frost once more.

But when the memories were past, a vague sense of emptiness still lingered and, at the core of that emptiness, some darker emotion. It nagged, and she probed it as she would a sore tooth.

It worried her, but she began the first tentative steps of a barely remembered practice pattern. The movements came back slowly. Little by little, though, they became a dance.

She swung her sword in familiar two-handed drills, cutting, thrusting, blocking. Still, some sensation gnawed at her like an itch demanding to be scratched. She whirled, dodged imaginary blows, sidestepped, and parried.

Suddenly she stopped. The sword trembled in her hand, plunged to the hilt in a foe that had no face. She held it there, sweat running into her eyes. Then, slowly, she twisted and twisted it.

At last she knew what emotion hovered at the heart of her emptiness.

Revenge.

Kimon had been taken from her. Murdered and mutilated. Samidar had wept and grieved, but Samidar had done nothing more. She bit her lip, tasting shame. Well, Samidar was gone now, and there was Frost.

Kirigi, at least, she had avenged. His murderer screamed in hell while the soul of her young son rested a little easier. But what of her husband? What of his soul?

Kimon would have no peace until she gave it to him.

But could she give it?

She took careful stock of herself. Already her breathing was ragged. Sweat streamed thinly down her throat, rolled down between her breasts. Her shoulders throbbed, promising sharper aches to come. She reviewed her performance; rusty would be a kind word. Slow and clumsy were more accurate.

She might practice for a long time and never regain her old proficiency. But if she didn't have her sword to count on, what did she have?

She shook her head, then began to work again, moving through her paces with careful deliberation. She studied herself, making small corrections, discovering weaknesses, *remembering*.

Her mouth formed a grim line when she finally rested.

She sheathed the blade, but she held it by the scabbard for some time, considering the sweaty mark of her hand on the hilt wrapping. She laid it aside, finally, and reached for her clothes.

It took some effort to stamp into wet boots, then she strapped the sword around her right hip. Her cloak was still thick with moisture. She left it spread on the ground while a bit of cheese and the last piece of bread made her hasty breakfast.

In the first gray of twilight she had spied a gnarly bush, invisible in the night. She'd tied her horse to it and freed it from the weight of the saddle. Already it had eaten half the leaves.

She grabbed up her cloak, saddled the weary beast, and began a long, gradual descent into a narrow valley. A steep climb led out of it and into another. At the bottom she found a small stream of run-off water and let her mount drink.

It didn't take long for the sun to dry her garments. Its warmth beat down upon her bare neck. For the first time in days she enjoyed a measure of comfort. On the summit of the next hill, though, she saw the clouds that lingered still far in the east. No matter; if it was a storm, she was riding away from it.

All afternoon she picked her way carefully along the increasingly treacherous slopes. The horse was tired; she didn't push him but let the animal choose its own pace. The ground was mud slick; a wrong step would be dangerous.

Ahead, one tall peak rose over the others. *Sha-Nakare*, the Keled soldiers called it: Watchers' Hill. From its pinnacle a man could spy across the Lythe into Esgaria. In the early days of the Keled kingdom, there was always an encampment of troops atop *Sha-Nakare*. But war had never come between Esgaria and Keled-Zaram, and the soldiers were long years gone.

She made her way toward that highest hill, forgetting to eat until her belly rumbled. She took something from the bag, not even noting what it was. It eased her pangs, and she pressed on. *Sha-Nakare* loomed over the other peaks. It alone might be called a mountain, but only by men who had never seen the Creel Mountains of Rholaroth or the sharp, impossibly jagged Akibus chain in the haunted land of Chondos.

Softly the sun sank from the sky. The palest golden nimbus crowned the summit of *Sha-Nakare* as she approached its lower slope. Night crept up behind her. In the shadow of the mountain she felt the jaws of darkness close.

She debated whether to continue. Somewhere, she knew, there was an old trail leading to the top. If she could find that, it wouldn't be a difficult climb even in the night.

She gazed up at the sky. For the first time in many evenings there were stars. Soon there would be a moon, a

waxing gibbous moon, if she remembered correctly. That
meant light to see.

But when was moonrise? She twisted in the saddle, searching the heaven for some indication, finding none. She chewed
her lip. Patience was not one of her virtues. The moon might
appear any moment or not until very late.

She paced her horse slowly at the foot of the *Sha-Nakare*,
straining to see some trace of the upward trail. In daylight she
wouldn't have bothered, just climbed the slope. But at night
she wanted safe footing. The horse was dear to her right now,
and her neck dearer still. She wouldn't risk either on an
unseen hole or a loose stone.

The moon, at last, floated over the rippled crests of the
Shai-Zastari. Frost sighed, cursed gently to herself. She must
have ridden past the trail half a dozen times in her blindness.
She sighed again. A wash of ivory light showed the way.

It was a narrow path of hard-beaten clay packed down by
the feet of centuries. Nevertheless, clumps of grass and a few
pathetic shrubs encroached on its boundaries, reclaiming inch
by inch as time crawled by. Few men came here anymore;
only the occasional hunter or a weary patrol in a mood for a
view.

It had been twenty years and more when she'd first climbed
this trail with Kimon at her side. He'd sung to her as they'd
ridden. She couldn't remember the song.

The summit of *Sha-Nakare* was broad and flat, windswept.
A lonely tree stood there, a dead and rotting hulk. Its bare,
splintering limbs shivered in the stiff breeze, and she shivered, too, not from the breeze, but from the awesome sense
of time and age the tree exuded. *Nothing lives forever,* it
whispered to her, and the thought seemed to echo among the
worn, eroded hills. *Nothing, nothing. . . .*

Frost stepped out of the saddle and rubbed her stiff back.
Moonlight limned everything with a pale shimmering. Rings
of small stones marked where campfires once had burned.
Larger stones indicated where men had leaned back and gazed
into those fires. She led her mount to a stake some traveler
had planted in the earth and tethered him.

The rich, sweet smell of water wafted on the air. She drew
a deep breath, shut her eyes for a quiet moment, then walked
to the western edge.

A tightness squeezed her chest.

The moon made a winding silver ribbon of the Lythe. The scent of the river rose upward like the perfume of the world. The shadows of the hills only slightly dappled its sparkling, rippling surface. But she turned her gaze beyond that beauty.

Esgaria.

The thought flickered briefly through her mind of what she had come here for. *In time,* she promised. But there was time, too, to stare over the river into her homeland, time to remember its wildness and its wonders, time to reflect.

She had seen but seventeen summers before that last fatal night in Esgaria. It had been late spring when the forests around her father's estate were heavy with foliage, teeming with game. Often, she had stood on the parapets and listened to the owls calling. Then, when her family, the servants, and all her father's soldiers were finally asleep, she would sneak to the lowest levels of the castle, where she kept a sword and shield hidden. For long hours she would practice in secret with her teacher all the skills and techniques that made a master warrior, then a few hours' sleep before dawn.

It had had to be done in secret. In Esgaria it was death for the woman who touched a man's weapons.

Frost pulled back from her memories. The wind that blew at her back rushed on across the Lythe to her homeland. It shook the tops of the trees that drew almost to the water's edge. In all her travels she'd seen no nation with forests as dark and majestic as Esgaria. She wrapped her cloak tighter about herself to stop the noisome flapping.

Her brother had found her that last night, her jealous and hateful brother. As she was denied the right to touch a sword, he was forever forbidden, as were all males, to study the secrets of sorcery. They'd each had what the other most wanted, and he'd despised her.

He'd found her that night, and he'd tried to kill her. It had been his right. But her teacher had taught her well. Very well. Fighting had been a game until then, an exercise, a game like any other.

She still remembered vividly her brother's body, his red blood dripping down the length of her blade, spattering the floor. That had been the beginning of her nightmares. Her father, unable to punish her as the law demanded, killed himself for shame and grief. Her teacher, Burdrak, had then confronted her. Her father's close friend, he had blamed himself and sought revenge.

She hadn't known why she'd fought back. She recalled how her thoughts had churned; fear had raised turmoil inside her. Her sword had seemed to work of its own will without her participation. Later, of course, she had realized it was her will to live that had driven her.

So Burdrak had died.

"Though your tears mingle with his blood, foolish daughter, you will never be redeemed!"

For a thousand nights those words had echoed in her dreams, and she remembered the look of grief and anger on her mother's face as she had screamed them. That tormented visage haunted her even to this day. And though Frost had made a kind of peace with herself over the many seasons since, still, in the long, empty nights she sometimes heard her mother's voice. *"You are a thing of fire and frost,"* her mother had cried, taking the wet blade from her child's hand. *"Frost, that should have been your name. And I curse you, you cold and unfeeling creature!"*

And it had been an evil curse, but not so evil as her last act. To follow her husband and her son, she had plunged the sword deep into her breast. Only a hint of pain had creased her features. Instead, her expression had betrayed a malicious glee at the black guilt she had laid on her daughter. She'd actually withdrawn the blade and given it back into Frost's hand before falling down by her husband to sleep at his side forever.

It had been long ago. Time had eroded the sharp edges of memory, the nightmares no longer tortured her. All that remained was a deep, sorrowful regret and an abiding homesickness.

Frost stared out across the Lythe. The Waters of Forgetfulness, some called the river. In a vain hope, she once had drunk of those waters. But she had not forgotten.

She turned away. Another purpose had brought her to this high summit, and it was time to be about it.

She went to the old tree and put her back to it, facing west. On her right was the first of several long-unused firepits. A small boulder rested near it. She walked to it, placed her palms on the cool rock surface.

Twenty years ago Kimon had helped her. Could she move it alone?

She leaned her weight against it and strained. The stone didn't move. She stood back a moment, rubbed her hand where the rough rock had abraded the flesh. This time she put her shoulder to it. Her muscles trembled and popped; a rushing roar filled her ears.

The stone rocked slightly, then settled back in its familiar place.

She backed up and kicked it, cursing, breathless. The moon seemed to laugh at her. She cursed it, too.

She peered around. Nothing to use for a lever but her sword, and she would not risk that. She got down on her knees, braced her shoulders, dug the toes of her boots into the earth. Slowly, inexorably, she pushed, straining until her joints cracked. She sucked for breath, but she didn't stop.

The stone moved. She eased and let it roll back into the depression where it had rested so long undisturbed. She pushed again, blowing air to concentrate her effort. The stone rolled again a little more and settled back.

She rolled it back and forth, each time gaining a bit of ground. Finally, with a furious determination that ripped a raw-throated yell from her, she straightened her body, every muscle taut and burning. Her toes carved furrows in the moist earth before finding purchase. A red haze filled her vision.

She fell flat on her nose. The stone rolled an arm's length away and stopped.

Frost sputtered, wiped dirt from her mouth, sat back to catch her breath and let the heat in her cheeks cool. Her hands felt raw; she licked them, rubbed them gently together.

When she was rested she crawled back to the depression and began to dig. The point of her sword broke the earth; she scooped it out with her hands. It surprised her how easy it was. The ground was not packed at all, but loose and easy to turn.

In only a short time the sword scraped something metallic. She arched an eyebrow. Hadn't she buried the box deeper? Perhaps time had dulled her memory. Or perhaps excitement had made her dig faster. She brushed the last of the dirt aside and lifted out a small iron box.

She leaned back against the boulder and balanced the box on her lap. Her fingers hesitated at the catch.

When she knew that her adventuring was over those long years ago, she had buried the dagger. Demonfang was too dangerous, its power too unpredictable. An innkeeper and a dancer had no use for such a weapon. Here, deep in the earth, she knew it would be safe.

But now she was a warrior once more. And if it was truly a sorcerer who had murdered her husband, then she wanted Demonfang at her side.

She twisted the catch and threw back the lid.

The dagger was not there!

She tilted the box until moonlight limned the bottom. She shuddered. It was full of dead insects! Even with the moon she could not see clearly. She pinched one of the creatures between thumb and forefinger and lifted it onto her palm for a better look.

To her surprise a tiny amber light winked at her. Startled, she shook her hand. The light winked again several paces away and hovered in the air.

A firefly! It hadn't been dead after all.

Suddenly the box was filled with a pulsating amber glow. All the insects were alive! By twos and threes they sprang into the night. A chill raced up her spine; her free hand closed on the hilt of her sword. With the back of her hand she knocked the box back into the hole and leaped up.

Her horse gave a fearful whinny and stamped the earth.

Hundreds, maybe thousands of fireflies blinked in the darkness. She spun about and quickly noted the unbroken gloom that shrouded the crests and valleys of the lesser hills. She shivered again, seized by a single thought.

Sorcery!

One of the insects landed on her hand. Its small light flared, and Frost screamed. Her left hand shot out and squashed the bug to a pulp. A blister showed where the firefly had burned her!

They came for her then, swarming, diving, seeking her bare flesh. She flailed at the air in a vain effort to drive them away. They lit on her face, on her hands, bringing searing pain.

Straight for her eyes one flew. She caught it reflexively, crushed it, and screamed. A blister rose in the center of her palm.

She smelled an acrid odor of singed hair. They were in her hair!

She ran blindly for her horse, throwing up her hood to cover her head, clutching it around her face. Even the fabric of her clothes smoldered where the fireflies touched it.

She snatched the reins and leaped into the saddle. Before her feet found the stirrups the beast gave a bellow of agony and reared, nearly unseating her. The unholy insects attacked both mount and rider with unrelenting malevolence.

A sudden intense heat on her back warned her that her cloak had caught fire. She ripped at the clasp with one hand, fighting to control her horse with the other. The flames raced up her neck, and she let go a terrified shriek. Then the clasp came free; she flung the blazing garment away.

A fireflash on her hand; a sob tore from her, and the reins slipped from her tortured grip.

The panicked steed seized its chance. Frost could only grab for its mane to hold on. It fled from the insects, carrying her along, over the western rim and down the precipitous incline.

The fireflies pursued mercilessly, flying with an unnatural speed.

A horrible sound filled her ears, the horse screamed as only an animal can. It smashed forward, falling on its neck. There was a loud, sickening snap as she pitched over its head, weightless for a dizzying instant before she hit the ground. She rolled, tumbled downward, unable to stop. The bulk of the horse crashed behind, threatening to crush her.

How she managed to find her feet she never knew, but suddenly she was up and running, not daring to look back. The Lythe swept below, shining in the moonlight.

With a cry of triumph she flung herself into the river and swam until she thought her heart would burst. Water filled her mouth and eyes and ears. Her sodden clothes weighted her arms and legs. The current battered her.

Just when she thought she was too weak for one more stroke, her feet touched the soft silted bottom. She scrambled ashore and collapsed, gasping for air.

On the far side of the river the fireflies had stopped. They flitted furiously along the bank, but they advanced no farther. Their arcane flashing illumined the night, reflected on the silvery river surface, tiny, sharp firespots far more brilliant than nature allowed.

Frost bit her lip, watching, thanking her gods. Water often proved a barrier to the supernatural. Ghosts could not cross it, and some demons could not. Sorceries faltered or dissolved completely for all but the most adept conjurers.

She had gambled rightly that the Lythe would be her salvation.

The winking grew dimmer and dimmer. One by one the fireflies apparently vanished until the night was dark and calm once again, and the moon was the only light.

Frost rose shakily to her feet on the grassy bank. A sweet smell rode the wind. Behind her, the leaves of great trees rustled. An owl hooted ominously. She caught her breath and listened.

It was home soil she stood on. For more than twenty years she had dreamed of Esgaria, and here she was.

Esgaria.

In renewed fear she leaped back into the Lythe, driven by ancient guilts and nightmares. She had not dreamed of this land—it had haunted her dreams like a vengeful specter.

Again she swam, desperately beating the water. But this time fatigue and the pain of her burns proved too much. Before she could reach the Keled shore the last strength went out of her arms.

She squeezed her eyes shut, tried to gulp one more breath. The river sucked her helplessly down.

Chapter Six

Forms of the future, shapes of the past
—the sea reflects the land—
Scattered shards on the leaves of the cards
Made whole by the knowing hand.
Turn, turn, turn them card by card,
All faces to the sun,
And fate be known to us alone
When all are turned and done.
When dreams and hopes are turned to troth—
Reveal them if you dare!
No chance to flee what eyes may see—
Dark angels of the air!
Wands and coins and cups may lie,
But ebon swords beware,
For truth is found when there abound
Dark angels of the air!

The Broken Sword was full of cooking smoke, the odors of
stale bodies and stale wine, vomit, and worse. The floor was
sticky with sweat and grease. Smoky oil lamps suspended
from the ceiling beams provided illumination bright enough
for customers to see their drinks, dim enough to hide the filth
on the cups.

It was a crowded night in the tavern. Imric, the owner,

turned his perpetual scowl around the room as he filled mugs with a dark, frothy brew from an immense stained keg. His one good eye gleamed as he watched the purses shrink and his cash box fatten. His wife, Bela, a noxious sow of a woman, pushed her way among the tables and standing customers, rolls of gross fat quivering, mouthing the lewdest suggestions to her regulars, spilling drink indiscriminately on anyone luckless enough to block her path.

If any were so foolish as to complain about the oafish service or the burnt victuals or the flat beer, or if any were so bold as to refuse payment, there was Orm. The giant kept constant guard by the front door; his eyes continually swept the tavern for any hint of trouble. He bore no weapons; he didn't need them. His fists were as lethal as any mace.

Frost shut her ears to the deafening noise of the crowd. Too many drunks and braggarts tonight. Not much chance to listen in on the individual conversations. Instead, she leaned over the table close to the small candle she herself had brought along, picked up her cards, and turned over the first one.

The Sword-soldier. She frowned. Twice tonight that one had turned up when she'd made a random deal. A dark-haired man, romantic, courageous, domineering, a bringer of change. She turned up the next card.

The Ace of Swords: strong love or hate; conquest and strife. She chewed her lip, studied the first card again, then exposed the next.

She peered at the painted eyes of the High Priestess, mysterious eyes that saw everything and nothing. Unknowable future, she interpreted, unforeseeable change, hidden influences. It clouded the meanings of the other two cards.

Frost shrugged, picked up the three, and shuffled them back into the deck. The readings never made sense; the cards did not work for her. She had no power over them. They were just part of her show, essential to her descroiyo disguise.

She dealt the cards to pass the time or for the amusement of any customer who dropped a coin in her palm. She told them what they needed to hear. It was easy. The faces on the cards made no difference. The poor man in rags wanted to hear of wealth. The wistful-eyed soldier sought love. The merchant, licking his lips and leaning forward so aggressively, craved influence. No, it wasn't the faces on the cards, but the face of her mark that composed her tale. She had only to look carefully at them and study their telling gazes to know which lie to speak.

As she spoke, she also listened. Sometimes they told her of Riothamus, of troop movements, of unrest in the countryside. Never directly, of course, but among the gossip and the complaints there was usually some item that piqued her interest. She learned news of the rebels whose activities had increased of late. Villages had been burned, guards murdered, supplies raided. She learned, too, of retaliations and counterattacks. As the nights went by, a picture of cruelty and savagery formed with blame enough for both sides.

The city of Kyr was buzzing with rumors, and sooner or later all rumors found their way to the Broken Sword. So, Frost kept her descroiyo fortune-telling guise and listened.

And waited for her son. Kel was coming. She could feel him like a hardness that grew in the center of her breast, a cold stone where once her heart had been. The rebel attacks were all in the south and west these days. He had to be near.

She drew a card from the deck, turned it, smiled at the irony. The Prince of Demons grinned at her from the table. Truly, tonight the cards mocked her.

The tavern door opened. A gust of wind blew dust through the entrance. The lamplight flickered wildly, then settled again as the door softly closed. She looked up, expecting another soldier come for a drink with his comrades. Kyr was full of soldiers, and more arrived every day as the rebellion fomented.

But the newcomer was no soldier. His face was hidden beneath a dust-caked hood, and a heavy cloak concealed much of his form. He was tall, though, tall as Orm, who stood warily on guard at the entrance. The stranger gave a nod of greeting to the bare-chested giant but said nothing. He paused to survey the faces in the tavern before he took the three short steps down to the floor level, wended his way through the press of bodies, and took the stool directly opposite her.

He leaned his elbows on her small table. Her tiny candle failed to penetrate the shadow under his hood, and he did not look up. Suddenly a silver *minarin* appeared magically between two of his gloved fingers.

She leaned back on her seat. "I am descroiyo," she said disdainfully. "Sleight of hand does not impress me."

A second *minarin* appeared beside the other. He placed them on the table beside her cards.

"Now I'm impressed." She swept the coins into her purse. "How do you come by Rholarothan money? Are you a traveler?"

He still had not thrown back the concealing hood; his face remained a mystery, but his voice was full and throaty. "Ask those." He indicated her deck. "Let them tell you what they will."

"Then it's a reading you seek," she said, taking up her cards, shuffling them carefully. "For two *minarins* I'll tell you a wonderful future."

"The truth will be sufficient," he whispered, raising his head enough that she saw his mouth move. A close-trimmed beard of black and gray dressed his chin.

"Lay your fingers on the top card," she instructed. "You must remove your gloves." The stranger did as she requested, and she began the traditional descroiyo chant. "Forms of the future, shapes of the past—"

A little boy tugged on her sleeve, interrupting her. "Mistress, would your gentleman like some wine or ale while you divine his fortune?" In the lamplight and shadow his face looked small and innocent, wide-eyed. His name was Scafloc; he was the tavern owner's only son. A meaner brat did not live in the city.

She scowled at him. "Go away, or I'll turn you into a toad. We're busy."

Scafloc stuck out his tongue. "You couldn't turn a trick on the busiest corner in town, you old fraud."

A huge hand closed around Scafloc's head, twisted it back until the child was off balance. The stranger lifted him up, bent him over a knee, raised a hand to strike.

Scafloc never cried out, but his desperate gaze sought Frost's. "If he dares," the little boy hissed, "I swear I'll forget the message old Dromen Illstar told me to give you! I swear!"

"Wait," she said, and the stranger stayed his blow. "Not that your backside doesn't need a good beating. If you've got a message from Illstar, then give it to me."

Scafloc put on a false smile. "It'll cost you one of those silver coins I saw him give you."

The customer raised his hand again, but again she stopped

him. She took out one of the *minarins* and laid it on the table. When the child reached for it, she snatched it back. "No fair!" he squealed, eyes burning with fear and anger. He squirmed on the stranger's knee.

"First, the message."

Scafloc swallowed. "Meet him in the Rathole tonight. He's got news you're after."

She thought about that. Two months had passed since she'd come to Kyr, hoping to find a trace of the forces that fought King Riothamus. Find the rebels, she figured, and she would find her son, Kel. Find Kel, and she would find Oroladian.

She had questions to ask that sorcerer.

"How much did Illstar pay you?" she said to Scafloc.

The child shrugged. "That rotten old fart? Not a brass *quinz*."

"Little liar." She tossed the *minarin* over her shoulder. It disappeared among the scuffling feet of the inn's customers. Scafloc freed himself and dived for the coin.

"I'll pay you another," the stranger offered.

"No need. One *minarin* is already twice what most of these pig-faces will pay." She picked up the cards once more and reshuffled.

Before she could deal the first card, Scafloc reappeared with a tray and goblet of wine. "Compliments of the house," he announced. He took the goblet from the tray, swallowed a great gulp of it himself, then placed it before the stranger. He grinned, showing all his teeth, held up the *minarin* for Frost to see, then faded back into the crowd.

"Someday," she said across the table to the hooded man, "some rat will do the world a great favor and eat that child's heart while he sleeps. Of course, the rat will die, but what a worthy sacrifice it will have made."

She turned up the first card and placed it between them. A frown caused her brow to furrow. Again, that same card. . . .

"The Sword-soldier," she said with some irritation. "It must represent you." She looked across at him, still unable to see much of his face for that hood. "Swords are the cards of conquest and adventure, cards of strife and battle. Their element is air, for conquest may be as elusive as air, and the object of a quest may be as nebulous and ungraspable." Almost, she reached across the table to sweep back his hood, but she resisted the impulse. "Beware the suit of Swords," she warned. "Unlike the other cards, they never lie. This is a card for a strong, dark-haired warrior."

He leaned closer to study the card but said nothing. She turned up the second and laid it over the first.

"Another Sword," she said quietly. "The Queen. Sometimes, the Swords are called dark angels, and the Queen of Swords is the Dark Angel. She represents a widow, or perhaps a woman unable to bear children. She represents mourning or longing for someone far away." Again, she sought the stranger's gaze, trying to measure his reaction. He sat steadfastly, fingers interlocked, regarding the cards. She fished for some clue that her interpretation was pleasing him. He had, after all, paid good coin. "You have a wife somewhere, perhaps? And she misses you?"

He didn't answer, but from beneath that hood she felt his eyes upon her.

She turned the third card and placed it upon the others. "The Silver Lady," she intoned. "The moon." She hesitated. It was an ill card foreshadowing danger. A descroiyo bearing bad news made no money. How should she phrase the lie? "This is a card of the imagination," she started, "of intuition." She looked up; for the briefest instant, the flickering of the lamplight reflected in his gaze. "Unforeseen perils mark your path," she blurted. "Foes you do not know wait ahead."

Now why had she said that? It made it harder to turn the reading around and give it a more positive interpretation. He'd said he wanted the truth, but truth could have lots of shadings.

"The Six of Cups," she said, revealing the next card. "The element of Cups is water. This card represents an old acquaintance, someone in your past."

His hand came across the table, settled on hers as she reached for the next card. She paused. There was warmth in his touch, a gentle fire that startled her. Without intending it, she leaned forward and brushed back his hood.

"Do you remember me?" he whispered. "Have I changed so much?"

She leaned back, slowly covering her mouth with her hands. She did know him; there was familiarity in that tousled dark mane now streaked with gray. She knew those eyes, so black and intense and challenging, that mouth, the shape of the jaw, those beautiful cheekbones. It was an older face, a reminder of how much time had gone by, but an unmistakable face.

"Telric," she answered with a soft sigh. "By all the gods of all the nations . . ." She shook her head, suddenly weighed down by the press of her own years. She sighed again. "How did you ever find me?"

He took both her hands in his, leaning forward. "How could I tell you everything and make you believe me?" he said. "I've searched for you, woman, since that day when you left me alone on the steppes beneath Mount Drood."

She regarded him across the candle flame. "Then you mean to finish the feud your father began. You've come to kill me."

He shook his head, and there was sadness in his eyes when he looked back at her. "Lord Rholf died years ago in some petty war along the Rhianothan border. My last brother, too." A sheepish grin lifted the corners of his lips. "After you spared my life on that mountain, I tried to convince him to leave you alone. He disowned me for it."

She pulled her hands away, feeling uncomfortable under his gaze. The goblet of wine looked so inviting, but she refused to drink after that whelp Scafloc.

He unfastened his cloak, shook the dust from it, folded it, and laid it aside. "I tried to find you on my own," he continued. "I traveled a lot, sent out spies, gleaned rumors and stories from the places where you passed. But I never seemed to catch up with you."

He looked down into the small flame. "After my father and brother died, I returned to Shazad and reclaimed my inheritance. I could have had the governorship, too. That's hereditary. But I didn't want it." He paused, then their gazes locked. "Father never forgave you for killing Than and Chavi, you know? He even sent assassins to find you."

"I know." She smiled. "I married one of them."

Telric raised an eyebrow.

"Kimon is dead, now," she explained. "But how did you manage to find me after so long? Why did you bother?"

He squirmed, then picked up Scafloc's goblet and sipped from it. "Although I turned down the governorship, I'm still a blooded nobleman, and I spend a lot of time at the imperial court." He sipped again. "A story came to Rholaroth that the lover of the Keled king had been slain by a woman."

"Lover?" she said.

Telric shrugged and set the cup aside. "His name was Yorul. According to the story, the woman was a real demoness with a sword."

She smiled at the exaggeration. The truth, of course, had been lost as the story passed from mouth to mouth. Or perhaps the Keleds themselves had altered it to make Yorul's death more glorious. She remembered a piece of advice her father once had given her: "Never let truth stand in the way of a good story."

"I left immediately for Dashrani," he went on, "and asked a few questions, enough to determine that it was indeed you." He reached once more for the wine cup, then paused. "I couldn't believe my luck after so many years." He reached out then, as if expecting she would put her hand in his. "I heard about your husband and son, and I'm sorry for you. I made a crazy guess you might decide to go home to Esgaria."

She looked down at the unfinished reading. Telric showed no interest in continuing it. Slowly, she picked up the cards and began to shuffle absently. "Kyr isn't on the way to Esgaria," she pointed out.

"It's on the way to Shazad, though," he answered. "My hometown, where you first appeared when you crossed the Esgarian border. I had some idea that maybe I could trace you back from there."

She swallowed, eyeing the wine. "I can't go back to Esgaria," she confessed.

"Then it was purest luck that I chose this tavern to quench my thirst. I rode all day. I was thirstier than a desert weed."

She broke down and sipped from the goblet. The liquor burned a warm, welcome trail all the way down her gullet.

She had chosen to work the Broken Sword because it was the closest inn to the city's main gate. Most travelers found it before any other tavern, and they all had tales to tell.

"I couldn't believe it when I saw you sitting here." His eyes burned into hers, gleaming with the candle's steady light. "You haven't aged a day!"

She laughed at that. "Flattery will get you many things in this world, Rholarothan." She wagged a finger under his nose. "But an outright lie only gets you trouble." She leaned back on her stool until her back rested against the wall and regarded him for a long moment. "Why?" she asked finally. "If you've forgotten the feud, why did you bother to search for me?"

Telric took the deck of cards from her, thumbed through them, examining the faces. Then he shuffled and executed a slick one-handed cut. He set the deck back on the table. A look of sad longing filled his eyes as he looked across at her. His palm covered the deck. When he lifted it, the top card clung as if by magic; it was impressive trickery.

He turned his hand, showing the card.

The Lovers.

A warm pain knifed through her heart. She blinked and stared at the man across from her. His face was guileless, his heart open. There was no lie, no pretense, no deception. She saw in his eyes what he felt, and a terrible sorrow overwhelmed her.

"For twenty years?" she whispered.

"More," he answered. "I've counted the years, every season, every month and day, hoping to find you. When hope finally stopped—and it did stop—I counted those days."

Frost bit her lip. Slowly, she reached out and touched the back of his hand. "I don't know what to say, Telric."

She had killed two of his brothers in a tavern brawl in a sleazy border city called Shazad. That had been a long time ago, right after she'd fled from Esgaria. She hadn't known then they were the sons of Lord Rholf, Shazad's governor. A hard, vindictive man, he'd chased her over the breadth of Rholaroth to slake his thirst for vengeance, and his two remaining sons had ridden with him.

She'd eluded them, but shortly after that she'd saved young Telric from a tribe of diminutive cannibals who dwelled in the high peaks of the Creel Mountain chain. She'd set him afoot along the main caravan route as soon as they were safe. He'd been arrogant and bold, but a certain mocking charm had graced his speech.

She remembered now that he had promised they would meet again someday. She had paid him no more attention than she paid the whispering of the wind, but he had proved himself a prophet.

Had he loved her at that moment when they'd parted? Had he *known* he loved her?

She pulled her hand away, took the goblet of wine, and drained it. Then she set the empty vessel aside, picked up the card Telric had shown her, returned it to the deck, and placed the pile neatly between them.

Telric bore an odd resemblance to Kimon. They were of a similar age, both tall and thin, dark of hair. They spoke with the same Rholarothan accent, shared an earnest intensity that reflected in their bearing. Only the eyes were different. Kimon's had been full of the sky, blue as the day. Telric's eyes were black as the longest, deepest night that ever cloaked the world.

But there was more, something that both surprised and shamed her. Telric stirred her in the same way Kimon had. She felt the heat rising in her cheeks from a fire she thought had gone cold long, lonely months ago.

She picked up the deck of cards, tucked it in her purse with her coins, and started to rise. "I have to meet someone. . . ."

His hand caught her wrist. "Don't go," he said. His voice even sounded like Kimon's as he pleaded with her. "Twenty years and more," he continued. "Can't you give me a little time, now?"

She shook her head, fighting the fear and confusion that swelled inside her. He had no right to look so much like her husband, to make her feel things a widow should not, no right to sit there and say he loved her. She jerked her hand free, but he quickly caught it again. His grip was more urgent.

"Please!" he persisted. "Will you rip out my heart and walk away?"

"Stop it!" she hissed. "Let me go, Telric, before you regret this chance meeting." She pulled free once more, but this time he rose and grabbed her by the shoulders.

His face clouded with anger and hurt. "Is your heart so full of ice? Is that why they named you Frost? What kind of bitch must have spawned you, woman?"

A huge fist crashed into Telric's jaw, sending him sprawling backward over the table and to the scum-covered floor.

"Orm!" Frost called desperately, catching the giant's arm. Once or twice before, he'd come to her aid when a dissatisfied customer complained too loudly or tried to take back payment for an inglorious fortune. "That's enough!"

But Telric found his feet and leaped for his attacker. Orm only grinned and swatted him aside effortlessly as he might a bothersome fly. Telric tumbled helplessly into a group of soldiers, jostling their drinks.

She watched it happen with a surreal awareness, as if she were reliving an episode from an earlier life. Fists began to fly, then cups and platters, chairs, benches, stools. She watched it all, unable to move or call out, terrified.

Then a fist crossed the edge of her vision. Her arm came up of its own will, deflecting the blow. She stepped in close, lashed out with the heel of her hand. Someone stumbled back, clutching a ruined nose.

It had been so easy; she'd just let it happen.

A blade scraped from a sheath, a sound immediately echoed as others cleared steel. The brawl turned deadly now. Blood began to spill.

She lifted the hems of the many descroiyo skirts she wore. Strapped to her ankle was a small, sheathed dagger. It would be of little use against swords; still, it was better than nothing at all.

A loud roar caught her attention. To her right, Orm heaved two men up by their tunics and smashed them together until their foreheads ran bright with blood. He cast them aside. Frost caught her breath and let it go, relieved that neither of them was Telric.

A soldier grabbed her around the waist and tried to force her backward. His breath was stale with beer as his mouth came down savagely on hers. With one hand he gripped the material of her blouse, but it refused to tear. She considered plunging her dagger into his belly. Instead, she brought up her knee with all the strength she could muster. From the expression he wore as he stumbled back, she decided he would have preferred the dagger.

She looked around for Telric. The Rholarothan hadn't drawn steel yet, but he was making effective use of a short wooden bench. As she weaved her way to him, one of the town's fat merchants slashed at his throat with a slender, glinting knife. Telric caught the point in the bench's broad seat, twisted, snapping the metal, then jabbed the rough end into the merchant's face.

Scafloc blocked her way momentarily. His cherubic face turned up toward her, wearing a wide smile. "Great fun, isn't it!" He laughed, then disappeared again, quickly lost in the turmoil.

Ducking and dodging blows, dealing a few of her own, Frost made her way to Telric's side. "Let's get out!" she shouted over the din, tugging at his sleeve.

"Too far to the door!" He planted his foot against some stranger's backside and shoved. The man propelled into another, and both bounced off the wall.

"Over the bar," she suggested.

He followed as she slid along the edge of the fighting. A piece of crockery shattered above their heads, accompanied by a high-pitched giggle that could only have been Scafloc's. A soldier crashed to the floor at her feet. She paused long enough to pick him up and push him back into the brawl. "Give 'em one for me," she mumbled.

Then she was rolling over the counter, running through the kitchen at the rear of the tavern.

Bela leaned her huge bulk against the larder, chewing a chicken breast. Grease stained her mouth, her heavy jowls. "You folks having a good time?" she called jovially.

"The best," Frost answered, flashing a smile, ushering Telric through the rear door. A three-legged stool flew back into the kitchen and splintered on the cooking hearth. Bela made a face and chewed another bite of bird.

Frost pulled the door behind them, drawing a long breath. The night air was cool and refreshing, a welcome change from the tavern's smoky atmosphere. "This way," she said, taking the Rholarothan by the elbow, leading him up the gloom-filled alley to the street.

As they turned into the broader lane, a beggar rattled his cup. She ignored him as she did all who walked the nighted streets. Kyr never slept; the avenues and alleys were never deserted.

"Stay to the middle of the way," she instructed her companion. She indicated the high apartments on either side. "They dump their slops at all hours."

"Where are we going?" he asked as they turned into yet another street. Tavern signs hung at every corner, illuminated by suspended oil lamps. Other businesses, too, remained open to catch the late shopper, to suck in the last coin. "Where?" he repeated when she didn't answer.

"The Rathole," she answered shortly. "Now shut up and stay close. And better keep a hand on your purse."

The streets grew narrower, the people fewer. The ones they did encounter had a seedy look and darting eyes that watched everything. Soon, even those were gone, and the only footsteps that sounded were their own.

Frost made a series of turns into lanes that were little more than muddy alleys. Garbage and filth lent an awful perfume to the air. A dog growled in the shadows. She knew this route by heart and had never before found trouble along the way. Still, she carried her dagger unsheathed in her fist. More than one kind of dog could hide in shadows as thick as these.

"This is the oldest part of Kyr," she whispered to her companion. "Only the very poor live here, or criminals seeking to avoid capture. Even by daylight few soldiers come here."

Telric leaned close; his breath tingled warm on the side of her neck. "Then what are we doing here?"

Her lips drew back in a tight grin. "I live here," she answered. "We can't all wallow in Rholarothan luxury."

She made another turn. The alley was completely black. No light penetrated from any apartment window. Not even the faint starlight relieved the gloom. The street was not paved, and the slime and sewage seeped over the toes of their boots.

"It stinks," Telric muttered, holding his nose.

"The smell of poverty," Frost said, slapping his hand, forcing him to breathe the full, sour aroma. "A flavor you've never known, I'll wager."

He grunted, inhaled once, then pinched his nose again. She chuckled mirthlessly.

They came to a crossroad of alleyways, and she hesitated.

"Lost?" His tone was mocking.

She ignored him. Each night the Rathole moved. One night it was down the alley to her right. Another night, to her left. Some nights it was straight ahead.

"Wait here," she ordered, and chose the alley on her right. After ten paces she stopped and waved her hand cautiously up and down before her. The way was clear. She went a little farther, waved again, then backtracked. She said nothing to Telric but took the alley straight ahead. Again, after ten paces or so, she stopped, waved her arm slowly, and encountered nothing. *It's always the last one!* she thought indignantly.

"This way," she said to the Rholarothan, taking his arm. "But slowly until I tell you otherwise."

They moved down the remaining alley. At eight paces she pushed Telric behind her. She took the ninth step, started to take the tenth.

A jolt rushed through her, some instinctive warning. She brought her hand up and found the wire she knew would be there. It was a bare finger's width from her eyes. She backed a step and called Telric.

"Feel," she told him, low-voiced. She guided his hand to the wire. He ran it gently over the razor-sharp barbs that spiked its length. It stretched completely across the alley at just a height to rip out a man's throat.

"Now bend down," she said, showing him a similar trip wire at a level meant for ankles and shins. At the ends of both wires small bells dangled.

"No strangers come to the Rathole alone," she warned. "And nobody comes here in a hurry. It's no place to elude a pursuit."

"Not much of a trap," he whispered with veiled contempt.

She smiled secretly but said nothing. Perhaps he didn't understand what barbed wire could do to a running man. She hoped he never found out the hard way, or even by witnessing the result, as she had when a particularly stupid thief had tried to rob the Rathole, run away, and forgotten about the wire. Stupid, and very messy.

She stepped between the strands and waited for Telric to follow. Down the alley she made a last turn. It looked like a dead end in the darkness. Only someone familiar with the alley, as she was, knew that between the two buildings that appeared to block the way there was space for a man to squeeze through sideways. Of course, there was a wire there as well.

The way was dark except for the faint gleam of light that leaked under an old wooden door. She rapped lightly with her knuckles and waited. The door opened a crack, spilling a shaft of amber brightness into the narrow street, causing her to blink. A grizzled face peered out at them, then threw the door wide.

A big voice bellowed across the tavern, "Captain! Welcome, welcome, welcome! An' ye brung us a friend. Got a good purse, has he?"

The door closed softly behind them. Frost lifted the hems of her skirts and sheathed her dagger. These were acquaintances—if not friends—of hers, and she trusted them as much as she trusted any in Kyr. She straightened and faced the grinning, whiskered old rascal who had called to her. He had a mug in one hand and a dirty but very buxom wench in the other. He sprawled drunkenly over a massive, wood-carved chair that might once have belonged to a wealthier nobleman.

"Dromen Illstar," she said, her voice gruff, "take your hands off that sweet piece of baggage and come give a real woman a kiss."

Illstar grabbed his stomach and convulsed with giggles. Then he swatted the wench's rump and sent her off to a corner, leaped up, and clapped his hands. "Now, Captain," he moaned, clearly putting on a show for Telric's benefit, "ye know it jus' wouldn't be right to kiss my superior officer, me bein' of lower rank an' all."

She braced her hands on her hips, gave him a hard look as if scrutinizing a soldier whose uniform was awry. He promptly snapped to attention—or a vague semblance of it—and looked appropriately terrified.

She rubbed her chin. "Well, seeing as how you smell like you haven't bathed in a month, we'll forgo the kiss this time."

They regarded each other for a long moment. Then both broke into a bout of laughter, flung arms about each other, and traded kisses on the tips of their noses.

"Woman, it's damn good t' see ye!" Illstar wheezed, freeing himself from the embrace. He caught his chest, looking for a moment as if breath would not come. Then he straightened and smiled, and all seemed well again. "I missed ye!" he added.

Some illness was wasting the old man away, she knew, but Illstar refused to speak of it. She remembered him strong and vigorous as he had been years ago when she'd first met him. She kept that image in her mind. It helped her to smile and laugh with him.

"I missed you, too, Dromen," she allowed. "You were gone far longer than expected."

"All in the service o' my captain." He bowed grandly, sighed, and returned to his chair. The wench returned to his side again, and he took a sip from the mug he had never put aside. "But first, something to drink for ye." He wagged a finger. "And you've been damn rude not t' introduce yer comrade."

Frost turned to Telric and compressed her lips into a crooked grin. The Rholarothan's hand was clamped to the hilt of his sword. His eyes swept continuously around the tavern. The look on his face was both challenge and warning. She followed his gaze.

The Rathole was the closest thing to a private club the city's known criminals could claim. For some, it was simply too dangerous to venture into the public places where the lamplight might reveal them to the soldiers. They were creatures of the shadows, to whom the light was a sure enemy. When they needed wine or a woman, or when the need for a friendly human voice grew too great, they came here or to one of the two other Ratholes to be with their own kind.

And a scruffy-looking lot they were, too. It wasn't nearly as crowded as the Broken Sword, but the air of menace was far more palpable. She counted only nine other men at tables pushed back against the walls. They regarded Telric with hungry gleams in their eyes and caressed their blades, but because she was with him they kept their distance. She had Dromen's tales to thank for that. There were three other women as well, besides the one in the old man's arms. They served the beer and wine and saw to any other need, too.

It had been a lucky day when Dromen had found her. In the descroiyo disguise, she had angered some of the local beggars who thought she was cutting in on their territory. They had complained to Dromen. The old man pretty much ran Kyr's criminal elements. What a surprise when he had confronted her on the street with two of his thugs!

One of the serving women pressed a cup of wine into her hands. Another served Telric. Frost tasted it and nodded. "A good vintage. Where did you steal it?"

Illstar giggled drunkenly and winked. "From the garrison cellars, o' course. Rotten officers get all the best wine." He winked again. "Then I get it from them."

"Of course," she agreed, raising her cup to him in salute. She pulled Telric up beside her as she took another drink. "My friend's name is Telric, Lord Rholf, formerly of Shazad. He's Rholarothan, but you must promise to forgive him for that. It was the luck of birth and no fault of his own." She nudged the embarrassed nobleman in the ribs. "He's also an old friend."

Telric declined to bow, but he did at last remove his hand from his weapon.

"And this," Frost continued, waving her arm in a grandiose manner, "is the Sun of the Underworld, the Lord of Liars and the Prince of Thieves . . ."

Illstar stamped his foot indignantly. "Only the prince?" His roar was quickly smothered in another fit of giggles.

"Sorry," she said. "The King of Thieves. No coin leaves the city but by his generous mercy." She tossed down a gulp of wine and smacked her lips noisily. "This is the Emperor Rat who rules the Rathole." She raised her cup again, then lowered it and added with mock contempt, "This is my former supply sergeant, Dromen Illstar." She drained the last of the wine and tossed the empty cup at the old man's feet, grinning.

Illstar blew her a kiss.

"Why do they call you Illstar?" Telric inquired rudely.

" 'Cause it's bad luck for you to cross him, bub."

Frost turned to the fellow who had answered, a rather handsome lad who sat in the corner between two lamps. A couple of days ago, he'd skewered two guards in a street brawl. "Evening, Raul," she hailed him politely. "How are the wives?"

He grinned over the rim of an earthen wine bowl, showing one broken tooth. "Gone," he answered slowly. "I divorced 'em." He lifted his bowl, and the sound of his slurping reached across the room.

"All?" Frost let go a long sigh. "A sign of the times. No fidelity left in the world."

Telric touched her shoulder. He looked uncomfortable. Clearly, he was ready to get out of here. It amused her, somehow. Telric was a warrior, but he was also a rich man, a lord in his own land. Unless he was a very dishonest one as well, he probably had never seen such a place as this in his entire privileged life. Still, she thought as she cast another glance around the tavern, she could understand his disgust. She wondered why it was that such places no longer bothered her.

"Did the captain tell ye how we served t'gether in the army back in Korkyra?" Illstar said conversationally to Telric.

"She was my captain before she went to guard the young queen. Slept right along with us in the barracks, she did. A meaner fighter ye never saw. I tell ye, the things she could do with a blade!"

"Dromen was my supply sergeant," Frost repeated. "Anything our company needed he could supply. Didn't matter who he had to swindle." She made another mock bow. "You were a master even then, Dromen. If there was a sheep to fleece, you had the shears in your pocket."

"I never saw a man who could match her!" Illstar exclaimed. "Like a demon she was, or a witch!" He leaned forward suddenly, spilling his wine. Breath rattled in his throat; his eyes bulged with fearful consternation and the knowledge that death made a slow, creeping approach.

But it was not yet the old man's time. At last, withering lungs responded; life-giving air swelled his chest, and he sagged back into his seat. The wench at his side tried desperately to hide her look of worry. No doubt her security hinged on Dromen's well-being. Who would look after her if he died? She stroked his brow with the tips of her fingers and tried to soothe him.

Illstar brushed the hand away and leaned forward again. Beads of sweat sheened at the corners of his eyes, but it seemed the spasm had passed. "Now you're goin' out t' fight again, aren't ye, Captain?" He pointed a finger at her, a finger that slowly traced little patterns in the air as if some message were being written there. "But we'll not ride t'gether this time, Captain." He shot a hard look at Telric. "Ye go with her, Rholarothan, an' ye take care o' her. Hell, she'll probably take care o' you, come t' think on it. But ye mind what I say. I got a long arm if ye let anything happen t' her."

A distant gleam lit his eyes, a gleam that misted over strangely. "You're older now, woman," he said with a low, passionate fire. "An' ye say ye been settled for a good long time. No fightin' and no hard ridin'. But ye listen t' me." He got to his feet, drew himself tall as he once had been. "It all comes back. It comes back easy, if ye let it." He smiled, and the gleam returned, clear of mist. "I know. I just spent the past month out there findin' somethin' out for ye. An' it comes back, all the old habits, all the old skills. Like the taste o' meat, ye never forget it."

She went close to him, took his hands in hers. "Scafloc said you had news."

"I'm the supply sergeant," he reminded her with another of his sly winks. "I never let ye down, did I?" He squeezed her hands. She clung to him, waiting. "Tomorrow night the rebels will attack Soushane. Your son will lead them." Dromen glanced sharply up and snapped, "Sit down, Raul, and have some more wine. I've already sold the information t' the garrison commanders." Raul scowled but returned to his seat.

She pulled her hands away. "You sold my son?"

"I saw no reason not t'," he said frankly. "Turned a nice profit from it. My sources were on their way t' do the same. I only beat them t' it." He paused, swallowed, then went on quietly. "Soushane is a peaceful little town; farmers, mostly. No reason for the rebels t' strike it, an' they'll burn it, too, if they follow their pattern. No reason, woman, jus' meanness."

Their gazes locked. His intensity was plain. But he had told the garrison commanders, and she didn't know if she could forgive that. For a fistful of coins, he had betrayed her son. Worse, he had betrayed her.

There was no time to waste. Tomorrow night she would meet Kel. "Is that all your news?" she asked icily.

Dromen shrugged. "They say strange things follow the rebels. Terrible things happen. They say there's a sorcerer behind it all."

"No more?"

The old man shrugged again.

She turned to Telric. "Give him your purse," she said.

"What?"

"Give him your purse. He's earned his gold. Pay him and let's get out of here."

Telric frowned but loosed the strings at his belt and tossed a jingling leather bag at Illstar's feet. His wench scooped it up in a smooth, swift movement.

At the door, Frost looked back at the man she had called friend. An empty, hollow feeling spread through her. Dromen Illstar was not long for the world, and not all the gold in Kyr could buy him an extra day. She blinked and headed out into the darkness, following Telric.

"We had good times, didn't we, woman?" she heard the old man call as she tugged the door closed.

Chapter Seven

The tall, sharp grasses whispered in the winds that blew in fitful gusts over the broad steppe. Tattered clouds raced low in the darkening sky, black and threatening, stripped with rents and tears that allowed brief, tantalizing glimpses of the twinkling stars and the thin, pale moon. The air bore the peculiar sweet scent of pollen and fine dust.

In Soushane, far from Frost's vantage point on a small swell of land, lamps were beginning to shine in the windows; smoke curled upward sleepily from the chimneys. There was little else to see as night descended.

A horse whickered. Frost rose wearily on one elbow to see what disturbed the mounts. Telric's bay stood quietly beside the excellent black he'd purchased for her with coins from a second, secret purse. War-trained, neither beast required hobbles or tethering. They remained saddled, patiently waiting.

"It was nothing," Telric assured her, and she lay back down.

To reach Soushane in time, they had ridden all night, all the long, scorching day, and into the twilight of evening. There had been no time for sleep. Now the wind lulled her, and the gentle rasp of the grasses was a potent lullaby. Stretched on the earth, which had grown warm with the heat of her body, she had trouble keeping her eyes open. Only the conversation kept her awake, and that had become a low, dangerous drone.

"Twice across?" Telric said. He turned over on his back and watched the clouds speed by. "You're lucky you didn't drown. The Lythe is a wide river."

"I nearly did," she confessed. "I thought I *was* drowning." She paused, chewed the tip of her thumb as she remembered the cool waters closing over her, the leaden fatigue that had numbed her limbs. "In fact, I even thought I was dead." She hesitated again. Telric said nothing but waited for her to continue. "I know I quit fighting the water and just gave up." She stared beyond Soushane to the far horizon. "I saw my husband, then, and he called to me. I thought I'd made it to the nine hells." She forced a weak smile. "Or one of them, anyway. He kept calling my name over and over. I remember how much I wanted to go to him, and somehow I found the strength to answer his call. I started moving toward the sound of his voice, but I couldn't seem to reach him no matter how hard I tried." She tilted her head curiously, feeling a chill. "I must have passed out. When I woke up I was on the shore. Of course, my husband wasn't there. It had only been a dream."

"The mind can play strange tricks when we're under duress." His hand flicked out, and he tickled her nose with a blade of grass.

She looked at him with a sudden wistfulness. He reminded her so much of Kimon. Then, aware she was staring, she averted her eyes. There was still a dull ache when she thought of her husband, a sore that the Rholarothan's presence forced her to pick and prod.

"And your son, Kel," Telric continued. "How did he come to lead this rebellion?" He tickled her nose again, then her ear.

She brushed him away. "I don't know," she admitted. "There's a lot I don't know about Kel. He ran away a long time ago. A few months back, he turned up again, and Riothamus's troops were after him." She bit her lip. "It was the first I'd heard about a rebellion."

He raised an eyebrow. "You *must* have been isolated. Even in Rholaroth we'd heard rumors. Nothing specific, just little incidents that indicated something bigger might be afoot."

"I didn't think I was isolated," she said defensively. "I just thought I was . . ." She searched for the right word. "Content."

There was nothing more to say after that, or so it seemed. Telric rolled to his back again to watch the clouds. Frost gave her attention to the windows of Soushane, wondering what went on behind those curtains and closed doors. What of the men and women eating their suppers or curling up for the night down there? Farmers and shopkeepers and herdsmen, mostly. Were they content? Or did they pass their lives in isolation and ignorance?

She would never again sit down before a fireplace for a quiet evening. Those times were behind her; she felt that in the deepest part of herself. Sadly, she shook her head. Her life had been filled with adventure and terrible events that had shaped and molded her and led her to a philosophy that had all but worshiped the sword.

But somehow, with Kimon to guide her, she had found a sense of innocence again, some tiny, dormant piece of herself that had not been drowned in the bloodshed or trampled in the adventuring. In her inn with her husband and children, she had nurtured that little piece and allowed it to grow until she had nearly forgotten what she once had been.

Her hand strayed to the sword lying on the ground at her side. It had a cold, ugly feel, a utilitarian feel. It knew what it was for.

What I once was, she thought darkly, *and what I am again.*

It hurt to realize that innocence was lost. Far, far worse to find it and lose it a second time.

"Look!" Telric interrupted. He had rolled over onto his belly. Her gaze followed where he pointed.

On the eastern edge of the sky, a long, dull streak of violet lightning illumined the lowest clouds. She groaned. It hadn't rained for two months. Now, here she was again in the open with no hope of shelter. She hadn't even a cloak this time.

Telric sat up. "Could Illstar have lied to you?" he asked. "Or could he have been wrong?"

Her fingers dug in the cool, moist earth. She rolled a handful of soil on her palm, tossed it upward, watched as it scattered on the wind. "Dromen served me well in the Korkyran Wars," she answered. "I don't think he lied."

"He sold your information to the garrison commanders," Telric reminded her.

"I only paid him to find my son," she explained, "not to keep quiet about it. My error. Illstar has a very literal mind."

Telric crossed his legs and tugged at the grass. "Why are you doing this?" he said finally. "Why chase Kel? When you talk about him there's such bitterness in your voice."

She shut her eyes as memories engulfed her. A thin, acrid smile parted her lips. "Let me tell you a story." She sat up suddenly beside him, so close their knees almost touched. "Before Kimon and I married, we were part of an adventure which caused us to ally ourselves to an old sorcerer and his demon familiar. Near the end of that, the demon broke his pact with the sorcerer and deserted our fellowship." She hesitated, then looked straight into Telric's black eyes. "But not before . . ." Her shoulders bunched up around her ears then sagged. "Before he raped me. For a brief time I was pregnant with his unwanted spawn. Fortunately, Orchos, the lord of death himself, saw that the child never developed in my body."

Telric started to speak, but she waved him to silence. It was hard enough to tell the story without answering questions. "When Kel was born, Kimon insisted on choosing his name. I always thought he took it by shortening Keled-Zaram, as if he were trying to emphasize our ties to our adopted homeland."

"Kel," Telric repeated to himself. "That makes sense."

She bit her lip. "But Kimon always had a rather bizarre sense of humor. That demon I mentioned? Its name was Gel. Kimon used to tease me that he'd named the baby after the demon." There was a sharp bitterness in her voice. "In fact, when Kel misbehaved, Kimon often claimed some part of the demon seed had survived and infected our child." She planted her hands behind her and leaned back. "In the past few months I've often wondered if he wasn't right." She shook her head and closed her eyes again.

The Rholarothan pulled another blade of grass and brushed her knee with it. "That doesn't explain why we're sitting out here in the weeds."

She watched the clouds. They made strange patterns, fantastical shapes that raced across the night. A star winked briefly through, as if an eye had opened and closed. Occasionally, the wan moon peaked through.

Talk of demons has warped my fancy, she thought caustically. All the clouds seemed to her the shades of lost souls. They flew with frantic speed, searching for the peace of the afterlife.

A long, emerald streak lit up the eastern sky. Heartbeats later, distant thunder echoed.

"I don't know my son anymore," she confessed. "Something has touched him, twisted him into a cruel mockery of my Kel." She met Telric's gaze once more and sat up straight. "I need to know if it was something I did," she said forcefully. "Or something I didn't do. Or if something did it to him." Her fingers curled into tight fists. She rubbed her knuckles together in her lap. "I've got to talk to him," she stressed. "I've got to know."

Telric scoffed. "You think you can change him." He tossed the blade of grass over his shoulder. The wind caught it and carried it tumbling away. "Well, forget it. Sometimes, woman, people just go bad and nothing can be done about it. You met my brothers, Than and Chavi."

"But there's more," she said, leaning forward until their faces almost touched. "The four fingers that were cut from Kimon's hand. Only a sorcerer, a necromancer, would do something like that. Kel is involved with a sorcerer, someone called Oroladian. Supposedly, the two of them lead this rebellion."

"It could have been a madman who killed your husband," the Rholarothan argued. "I've seen cruelties that had nothing to do with magic."

"I've been to lands," she said thoughtfully, "where the warriors take trophies from the men they kill. Bits of hair or an earlobe or something." She leaned away from him, fighting the tension that knotted her shoulders. "But what I found on *Sha-Nakare* was purest magic. Someone stole something that belonged to me. In my hiding place they left a mystic entrapment that could only have been arranged by an adept of considerable power."

Telric tore a handful of grass from the earth. The dirt that clung to the roots spattered them both as he cast it away. "And you want to tangle with that kind of power?"

Frost reached inside her tunic and extracted a small leather bag that hung on a thong about her neck. "I haven't shown you this," she whispered. "It isn't pretty." She opened the bag and reached inside with thumb and forefinger. Telric moved closer, then jerked away, eyes wide with disgust.

She held up the finger for him to see. It had been severed between the first and second joints. A bit of the bone and torn vein could plainly be seen even in the dark. It had a very faint odor, though the flesh appeared almost petrified.

"Gods," he grumbled. "You carry that with you?"

"I think it belongs to Kimon," she answered. "After I woke up on the bank of the Lythe, I climbed back to the top of *Sha-Nakare*. In the daylight I found this in the hole where I'd buried a box years ago. The empty box was still there; this was under it."

"It might not be Kimon's," Telric cautioned.

It was her turn to scoff. "I think Kel's sorcerer used it in some way to find what I had hidden on that hill." She looked away, turning cold all over. "There are things," she explained in a reverent voice, "necromantic things a sorcerer can do with parts of corpses." Her hand strayed to the hilt of her sword. She laid the blade across her knees, ran a finger along its edge. "I think this Oroladian killed my Kimon; then, with the fingers in his possession, the sorcerer commanded my husband's spirit to betray the location of my dagger."

"A dagger?" the Rholarothan interrupted. "That's all you had hidden?"

Alizarine lightning crackled, nearly blinding, tracing a frightening lacework over the sky. Thunder shook the steppe. A wind howled and whipped at them. Frost felt her hair lifted straight behind her, and dust stung her eyes.

"It doesn't matter what was hidden," she snapped. "It was mine!" The sudden wind died, and the world turned eerily quiet. Frost listened for a moment, then continued in a lowered voice. "I'm going to find my son. He came to the inn that day asking about the dagger. That wasn't coincidence." Her lips compressed into a thin, taut line. "Then I'm going to find Oroladian." She looked upward again at the racing clouds. *Lost souls all, searching for the peace of the afterlife.* She had thought that earlier, and the image still remained with her. "Then, I'll put Kimon's spirit to rest."

"Vengeance?" Telric prodded.

"Vengeance," she affirmed coldly.

He leaned back and casually stretched, but his gaze fixed her intently. "Vengeance poisoned my father," he reminded her. "It consumed him until the day he died, cursing a woman he never found."

She put the finger back into the leather bag and returned that inside her tunic. Her hands fell upon her sword again. It

seemed to radiate with its own life, and it cried with a
hunger.

"You're like that card in your fortune-telling deck," he
said at last. "The queen of Swords—the one you called the
Dark Angel."

She shut her eyes and rocked herself slowly upon the earth.
"The Dark Angel," she repeated. "The bringer of retribution."

"No," he replied heavily. "Only the gods bring that." He
stared out across the landscape, then rose suddenly to a half
crouch. "Still, maybe you didn't come all this way for nothing. There come riders."

She leaped up, fastening her sword belt around her waist,
sheathing her blade, staring where he pointed.

A small forest of torches marked the riders' progress. She
made a vain effort to count them, but the wind fanned the
flames too wildly. She settled on fifty as an estimate. It was
impossible to distinguish the riders from her vantage, impossible to spot Kel among them.

Telric whispered to himself, but loud enough that she
overheard, "Why bother with such a sleepy, harmless town?"

"I've got to get closer," she said, moving toward the
horses. "They won't see me in this dark." She grabbed the
reins of her mount and swung up into the saddle. "You don't
have to come. Kel isn't your problem."

Telric didn't waste breath answering. He mounted and
started down the low grade, leading the way.

The riders stopped before they reached the edge of the
town. Soushane had no walls for protection, no gates, no
guard towers. Candles and lamps continued to shed pathetic
light through the windows, and smoke poured guilelessly
from the chimneys.

On the far side of Soushane an orange glow began to color
the sky. Frost sniffed. A thick smoke rose on the wind. It
rolled over the steppe like a gray tide.

"They're burning the fields," Telric said needlessly.

She stopped her horse. "Something isn't right," she muttered. She stared toward the rebels. Still fifty by her best
guess. Another force, then, had sneaked around to set the
blaze while their comrades waited to advance. *How many
altogether?* she wondered.

But something else troubled her more.

The streets of Soushane remained empty. The doors stayed

shut; candles burned innocuously as if nothing were happening. Yet the fire in the fields was too high, the air too full of the smell of smoke. No one in the town could be so unaware.

"I'd run to the door to see what was happening," she said aloud to herself. "I'd try to save my crops. I'd warn my neighbors. I'd shout and scream and try to wet my roof."

Telric caught her meaning. "They must know," he suggested. "They're afraid and hiding."

"But who warned them?" she countered. "It's supposed to be a surprise attack."

Her companion raised an eyebrow. "We found out."

His words were not lost on her. She rubbed her chin, considering. Every hair on her head tingled with the wrongness of what she saw. Had Illstar warned them? She scoffed at that. Not a farmer among them would have had coin enough to pay his price.

"Gods!" her friend screamed suddenly. "What in all your nine hells is that?" Then, in a much lower, sober voice, he added, "I laughed at your talk of sorcerers."

Beyond Soushane, an immense pillar of fire shot roaring into the sky. It writhed, twisted among the clouds, splintering and taking new shape. It burned with a terrible, shining intensity, feeding on nothing, burning just the same.

It reflected strangely on the rugged clouds, turning the heavens into a shifting tapestry of crimson and shadows.

"A hand!" Telric croaked. "A hand to smite Soushane!"

It was true. The fire coalesced, transformed, and took its final shape, a huge and horrible hand that flexed and curled unholy fingers. It moved malevolently, reaching for the city, trailing smoke and sparks. It poised for an instant above Soushane's heart. Then, it smashed down.

Rivers of flame swept through the streets, swelling outward, igniting anything that could burn. Wooden dwellings exploded in red-orange fireballs, scattering sparks and brands that settled on the rooftops of other buildings, spreading the destruction. The demonic hand was no more, but the arcane fire raced with heartbeat quickness through every lane and back alley.

At last, the doors of houses and shops flew open. Armed troops ran screaming with terror into the streets, beating fire from scarlet cloaks and plumed helms, fleeing like panicked rodents. The flames that burned all around lit up their faces, illumined their fear.

"The garrison," Frost cried. "They got here before us!"

The townspeople streamed out behind the soldiers, women with children in their arms, men sheltering their wives with blankets or curtains.

Stable doors sprang open. Mounted cavalry poured into the streets. Fire-panicked steeds trampled anyone in their path, crushing child or soldier indiscriminately. Wails and shrieking, sounds of agony and despair lifted from the town, mingled with the roaring of the flames, the collapse of stone and lumber.

All the while the rebels waited, watching. Then, as one mighty voice they gave a triumphant shout. Brandishing torches, they spurred their mounts and charged toward helpless Soushane.

"Kel!" The name tore from Frost's throat. Dread and fury churned within her, fear of the power she had witnessed, red rage for her merciless son. She drove her horse toward the rebels, toward Soushane, cursing the seed that ever gave Kel life.

The rebels hit the town with terrible force, flinging torches through doors and windows, using them as fiery clubs on the nearest townsman or soldier. As soon as a rebel let go his torch, he drew his sword. The flames reflected mesmerically on the glittering steel edges.

The screams and crying were terrible to hear: frightened people, wounded people, dying people. Over that rose the crash of charging horses, the clash of metal on metal, the tear of flesh and the snap of bone. And over it all the crackling of the fire. It brought back all the horrors of all the wars Frost had ever seen. She tried and failed to shut her mind to it; her soul cringed. Hell had claimed this little piece of earth.

She steered her mount through the tumult, searching for one face. Without warning the horse leaped sideways and wheeled as a burning wall collapsed beside her. She heard a child's scream too late to help. The fiery timbers crushed the life from a father and his young son. Her horse snorted, stamping in protest and fear. The heat of the flames seared her face and the backs of her hands. She fought the reins, striving to control the beast.

Barely in time, she saw the sword whistling toward her

head. She ducked, spurred her horse in a tight circle, and freed her own blade. Her foe glared at her, and her heart nearly stopped. Human eyes gleamed with battle lust behind a skull mask. But it was more than a mask. Firelight shone on the dull white bone, revealing the jagged crown where the braincase had been sawed away. She raised her sword to counter his next blow with the gut-wrenching knowledge that she had hesitated too long.

It never struck. Another horse rammed into the rear of the rebel's mount; half a length of steel slid into his ribs, and he fell backward with a muffled cry, tumbled from his saddle, and sprawled in the street. His own horse trampled him as it ran off.

She had nearly forgotten Telric, but there was no chance to thank him. The fighting swirled around them, sweeping them apart.

The garrison soldiers had found some measure of courage at last. They began to fight back with a fury. But the skull-faced rebels renewed their press, smashing at anyone who did not wear their black jerkins and hideous death masks.

She found herself in an unpleasant position. With neither the mask nor the scarlet cloak of a soldier, both sides regarded her as the enemy. A shadow crossed the edge of her vision. She crouched suddenly in her saddle, twisted, and raked her blade through the middle of a Keled regular. His face warped with pain, and he spilled from his horse.

Frost stared, numbed, the fire and the battle momentarily forgotten. Blood oozed down her blade, dripped on her hand as she lifted it.

It had happened so quickly, without thought. She gazed down at the dead man. Her hand trembled, and the trembling spread upward through her arm and all through her.

Then she let out a breath and drew another one, getting control of herself. She hadn't come to fight, but to find her son. She kicked her horse forward, skirting the thick of the combat, avoiding engagement, searching the rebels' faces.

Even through the skull masks she would know his eyes.

But what the raging light of the fire revealed sickened her. Never in her youthful years had she avoided battle this way. There had been no time—or she had never taken time—to observe and study the horror of it. But now she *saw* the men who fought and died. The range of their expressions appalled

her. The terror in the eyes, the hatred; the grim set of mouths
or the gnashing teeth; the narrowed lids that flashed suddenly
wide; the grunting and the sighing and the wheezing.

It was madness, unreasoning and ugly, devoid of purpose.

The sky exploded with a series of rapid flashes. Thunder
shivered the air with resounding force. Instants later, a sharp
rain needled earthward, hissing as it joined the fire. Swiftly,
the streets turned to mud.

It made no difference to either side. Rebel and garrison
regulars hacked at each other, cut each other down while the
rain and the fire made twisted, demented shadows that nipped
at their heels like demons.

Frost wiped the water that collected on her face, at the
verge of laughter or tears.

Then, she spied him. She wasn't sure how she knew him.
The battle raged like a barrier determined to keep them apart.
And he wore the same skull face as his followers. But she
knew.

The sky lit up with another jagged bolt, and it framed him
for her eyes. She called his name, but Kel didn't hear. He
leaned from horseback and plunged his sword through a
soldier's throat.

"Kel!" she shouted over the din.

Thunder was her only answer.

She spurred her horse toward him, knocking aside an un-
wary rebel who stumbled into her path. After months of
seeking, she had found her son. She dared not pause or take
her eyes away for fear of losing him again.

She was witness, then, when a soldier leaped and caught
Kel's arm and dragged him from his saddle into the mud. Her
son's sword went flying away as the two of them disappeared, scrambling in the furious tumult of clashing bodies.

She screamed, heart hammering, unable to reach his side.

Then, as if all the hells had opened, a soul-freezing shriek
rose over the other noises. Sudden fear took a bite of her
heart. All through the streets the fighting stopped as that
horrific sound strained to a higher pitch and abruptly ceased.

Frost knew the sound. Gooseflesh rippled on her arms; a
chilling tingle crawled up her spine. A circle widened around
her son as he rose from the mud. Warriors lowered their
weapons, uncertain. An instant's pause, and the shrieking

returned. It poured from the mouth of the man at Kel's feet, a man already dead.

A desperate stillness fell over Soushane's streets, interrupted only by the thunder, the pelting rain, the hissing fire.

Kel laughed, a dry, hysterical sound like the breaking of old bones. From the heart of his dispatched foe he bent and plucked a dagger and held it high for everyone to see. He shook with his mirth.

It was a small weapon, but the flames and the lightning reflected brilliantly on its silveriness. It shone in his fist like an arcane jewel.

Demonfang!

Something deep in her soul called out to the blade even as she remembered its curse: *Once drawn it must taste blood, either your enemy's or your own!* It was far more than it appeared, far more than any common dagger. She had possessed it, experienced its power, felt it move like something alive in her hand, felt its hunger.

She shouted again to her son, but her voice was drowned as Demonfang's shrieking began anew. It was a malevolent sound, the lamentations of souls in torment, and every warrior cringed away as they realized it was the blade itself that screamed. It filled their ears, blasted their courage.

"Sheathe it!" But her shout was insignificant, overwhelmed by Demonfang's strident fury. For long years it had lain buried on *Sha-Nakare*, forgotten and silent. *Starved,* she thought, but that was only fright worming through her. Still, it was free again, and it heralded the fact with a vengeance. The shrill anger of its cries tremored through her head.

"You fool!" she cried, fighting to control her horse. It stamped and bucked, sensing Demonfang's power. She feared for her son. Kel didn't know what he held in his hand. "Sheathe it, quickly!"

Sheathe it he did. Kel jumped upon the closest soldier and thrust the blade with all his strength through the Keled's breast. Demonfang squealed with glee, then went silent, satiated for the moment. A heartbeat passed, and the soldier's mouth opened. Not with his own voice did he scream, but with the dagger's.

The garrison's courage shattered. The battle turned to a rout as the rebels recovered and sprang on their foes. The skull faces did a relentless, bloody work, moving like wolves among rabbits.

The clouds erupted with red lightning, and bolts boiled across the sky until the heavens blazed as brightly as Soushane.

"You fool, you fool!" Frost shouted, forcing her mount through the battle, intent upon reaching her son.

Then, the world spun crazily. A burning beam fell across her path, throwing up smoke and sparks. Her horse shied, reared, slipped in the mud, and teetered backward. Too late, she tried to jump clear, but her foot caught in the stirrup. The beast's weight crashed on top of her, and fire and lightning were smothered by an engulfing wave of darkness.

She woke slowly, clawing her way toward consciousness. The acrid smell of smoke filled her nostrils. Cool mud pressed against her face. She was soaked to the skin, though she could feel the heat of the fires. The flames had burned low, but they still crackled with hungry avarice. A constant drum boomed in the back of her head. She moaned softly, tried to sit up. Pain shot through her right shoulder and down into her breast. After several attempts, she managed to right herself.

The fighting was over. Bodies lay everywhere, rebel and Keled side by side. She wiped a hand over her eyes to clear her vision but only smeared her face with mud. There was no sign of any townspeople. Either they were all dead or hiding out on the steppes.

Kel had not even noticed her. She had come so far only to fail. It was her own fault, though. She should have waded into the thick of the fighting as she would have in her youth. He would have noticed her then. Instead, she had hugged the walls and shadows, avoided the conflict. Why should he have noticed her?

She cursed herself, driving a fist against the shoulder where her pain was greatest, fitting punishment. She'd proven Soushane's citizens weren't the only ones who knew how to hide! She had just managed to hide in the battle itself.

Now Kel was gone once more, and her chance was lost.

She struggled to her feet and looked around. Despite the heavy rain, the fires still burned. By morning, nothing would be left of Soushane but a few pitiful, smoking ruins. She remembered the terrible hand of flame that had smitten the town. The sorcerer's fire had done a merciless work.

Oroladian.

The name floated unbidden into her thoughts. Perhaps she hadn't failed at everything, after all. Suspicions had been confirmed, at least. Only a sorcerer could have obtained Demonfang and given it to her son. Only a sorcerer could have conjured that fiery apparition. Frost felt for the thong about her neck and for the leather bag with its sad content. Her mouth set in a grim, tight line.

Oroladian.

The sorcerer had Kimon's soul. Only her husband had shared the secret of Demonfang's resting place. That made the sorcerer Kimon's murderer as well.

Oroladian.

She knew her enemy now. There was suddenly a focus for all the anger and hatred that boiled within her. There was purpose to her life again. To free her husband's soul, to free her son from a vile influence, to kill Oroladian.

A horse whinnied in pain, a wounded beast that lay on its side in the mud, thrashing uselessly. A deep sword gash in its belly oozed dark blood. She glanced around for her own mount. It was gone, of course. She imagined some wide-eyed, frightened Keled clinging to its back, running for the end of the earth. *And off it,* she prayed, cursing the faithless animal.

Her sword was half-buried in the mud. She bent stiffly to pick it up, wiped the blade along the fabric of her breeches, and sheathed it.

A sound made her turn. A figure slogged through the watery soup that had once been a street, weaving a way toward her. She touched the hilt of her weapon. Even that small motion reminded her of her aches and bruises. Yet there was something familiar about the approaching shadow.

"Telric?" she whispered hopefully. She hadn't seen the Rholarothan since the beginning of the fight. At the sound of her voice the figure halted, turned in her direction, took another step, and stopped again. A hand rose in supplication, and there came a low, desperate moan. Knees buckled; the man fell face forward.

She limped to his side, rolled him quickly over, and squeezed the mud from his nostrils. The light of the fires showed the tatters of a Keled uniform. Not Telric, then. Nevertheless, something about him stirred a memory.

She knew him, yes. Off duty, he'd been a frequenter of the Broken Sword. She'd seen him often, even told his fortune once. He'd laughed and paid her an extra coin for the amusement. He'd laughed again, but politely, when she'd declined his next offer.

Three deep slashes had exposed his entrails. His wide brown eyes flickered with fleeting life, and she wondered if he remembered her, too. Then they were vacant, reflecting only the flames. He had laughed his last on this side of hell. She prayed he had reason to laugh on the other when Orchos passed his judgment.

She laid his head down gently and rose again, wincing as pain blossomed through her shoulder. One by one, she began to search the bodies that littered the streets and the spaces between the few buildings that yet stood.

Telric was not to be found.

Behind her, a wall crashed down. Startled, she jumped and screamed at herself when her shoulder protested. Sparks and smoke streamed upward and settled again, a scintillant rain within a rain. From beneath the burning rubble she saw the feet of the two corpses she had last examined.

That, she convinced herself sadly, was why she couldn't find her companion. Somewhere, under all the fiery ruin, Telric must also be buried. She didn't know him well enough to shed tears. Or maybe she was just too weary, too sore. But something hardened and turned cold within her. Telric had loved her, he claimed, and now he was gone.

One more debt to collect from Oroladian.

The anger swelled within her like a palpable force. *I'm coming for you, sorcerer.* She moved through the street, picking her way among the dead. The rain beat mercilessly on her face; the odors of charred stone, burning wood, and flesh cloyed. She drifted through the town and out over the dreary steppe. With each trudging, shambling footfall, she swore, *I'm coming for you! I'm coming!*

Ahead, she spied the low ridge where she and Telric had shared the quiet time before the battle. The sky crackled suddenly with brittle thunder and crackled again. Over the ridge, the night split open as a cobalt bolt of frightening power ripped the darkness, illuminating the land with a blue flash.

Frost threw her arm over her eyes to spare her vision, but afterimages lingered.

Then, through the ground came a beating. An unearthly cry trumpeted in the distance, a cry she knew. Her heart raced; she stared wildly, seeking the source. It came from the ridge! She began a limping run, ignoring her pain.

The cadence in the earth grew stronger, closer.

She stopped, brought up short and breathless by a fantastic sight. Two spots of fire raced in the night, trailing red-orange tongues. *His eyes,* she knew, *or what served him for eyes.* Her spirit leaped; she rejoiced, shouting and calling his name, measuring the swift advance of those eyes and the steady pounding of his great hooves.

A black silhouette moved against the deeper blackness. A streaming mane lashed the wind. An ebony spike long as her arm gleamed between the eerie light of those eyes.

The beast crashed to a halt before her, kicking up mud and chunks of grass. It reared, and again sounded that call like no other creature of this world ever made.

Then he calmed, gazed at her, and snorted. With an almost playful timidity, he moved closer, slipped his horn under her arm, and nuzzled her side. It hurt, but she didn't care. Frost flung her arms about his neck and hugged ferociously, shedding tears into the tangled mane.

The unicorn stood completely still, and the fires that were its eyes dwindled to a softer incandescence.

"Ashur!" she murmured, disbelieving, afraid to let him go. So much had been taken from her of late. At last, something lost had returned. "Ashur!"

Chapter Eight

Ashur.

She did not know what Ashur was. He might have been a demon. He was violent and deadly. But there was no evil in him. A god, she once wondered, could he be a god? But there was no ego in him. An elemental, perhaps, a spirit of fire. That might explain those strange eyes that burned with eldritch flame but gave no heat. Or a wind spirit. That could account for his unnatural speed and endurance.

Her hair whipped and streamed behind her as she bent low to his neck. The land passed beneath his tireless hooves as they ran. The rain had ceased; the clouds had broken apart. A pale, luminous moon lit their way.

She laughed to remember how she had teased herself with guesses about the unicorn. Ashur had been a gift to her years ago, a wizard's gift. The dagger Demonfang had been another gift. The same wizard, Almurion, had given her both. Weapons, he had called them.

After a time she had come to understand Demonfang. But Ashur defied reason. There was a subtle power in the unicorn, a mystery about him she had never fathomed. But there was a bond between them, also, a love that made the mystery unimportant. If he was a demon or a god or a spirit, she didn't care. If he was a beast and nothing more, it didn't matter. Ashur belonged at her side, and he had come when she needed him.

How had he known, though?

If Kimon had risen from the grave, it could not have been a more wondrous miracle.

Frost bit her lip and leaned closer to Ashur's neck. His mane lashed her face as she urged him to greater speed. The heat of his muscled body radiated all through her.

Kimon had not risen from the grave, nor had Kirigi. Kel was not free from a sorcerer's charismatic influence. She rejoiced at Ashur's return, but as she rode the anger grew in her again. Oroladian, damn his venomous heart, had much to answer for. And there was Telric's name to add to the tally. All of Soushane as well.

For an instant she was weightless, wide-eyed. She hugged the unicorn with her knees, gripped his mane tighter as he leaped a broad ravine. They struck the far side with a bone-jarring force that sprayed mud and earth. Ashur rushed on, smooth, powerful muscles rippling beneath her, the slick lather of his efforts moistening her thighs. She gave herself to the swift motion and the furious tattoo of those crashing hooves.

The dark silhouette of Kyr rose before her, limned in the moon's ivory radiance. There was no hint of dawn yet in the eastern sky, but it couldn't be long away. Atop the high, solid walls of the city, lights burned in every watchtower. Shadows moved within them.

Frost rode up to the gates only to find them closed. She had ridden fast, but apparently news had already reached Kyr.

Above the gate, a voice challenged her. She looked up. A torch flared. In its brightness she could not make out the man who held it. But she could see the pike he bore and the red gleam of his helm. "Who's below?" the sentry called again.

She thought quickly. The gates were sealed only in times of danger, but once shut it was Kyran law they remained sealed until sunrise. No one was allowed in or out while they were closed.

She must get inside, though. Once the sun colored the day there would be little chance of finding Dromen Illstar until the darkness gathered again. The man had bat blood in his veins, and sunlight was unnatural to him.

"Just a frightened old woman!" she lied, putting a tremor in her voice. Hurriedly, she unstrapped her sword, clutched it in both hands. "Our farm was attacked and burned, my man and sons murdered. For mercy, let me in!"

The sentry leaned over the parapet. "Your farm burned, you say? Rebels?"

"Some men!" she cried, hoping she sounded desperate and convincing. "I didn't know them. Please, open the gates. They might be following, and I have only my poor husband's sword for protection." It was an impulse, but she threw back her head and waved the sheathed weapon clumsily. "What can I do? Help me, please!" She set up a loud wailing, rubbing her eyes with the back of a fist.

"You've got a good strong horse, by the look of him," the sentry called back. "Ride fast and stay ahead of them. You can come back tomorrow."

More torches and more guards clustered above and looked down at her. "Please!" she begged, lifting an outstretched hand in supplication. "I'm only a poor woman, and I'm so tired. I've ridden far, and the horse is worn."

She smiled at that lie and thanked the gods for whatever power it was that made ordinary men see a horse when they looked at Ashur. What would they do if they saw, instead, a beast from the myths of ages past?

"Let her in," someone mumbled.

"She's alone," another whispered. "There's nobody else out there."

"Please!" she screamed. Her anxiety was not entirely false. She had to get inside and find Illstar before the sun rose. No one knew where the wily old man spent his daylight hours. But already she began to hate the role she played to achieve entrance. "I have relatives within who will take care of me. They might reward you!"

"You know the law," the first sentry grumbled to his comrades.

"Damn the law!" someone bellowed in response. "We can't leave a woman out there. Not if rebels are about. You heard what they did in Soushane. We've had the report not more than an hour. Let her in, I say!"

There was a short general buzz atop the wall. Then, a loud creaking drowned that. Gears ground noisily, and huge chains clanked. Ponderously, the heavy gate parted, but only a crack. "Get inside and be quick about it, or the officers will have our heads!"

It was wide enough for Ashur, but Frost slid to the ground.

Most men saw only a horse when they gazed at the unicorn, but there were a very few men with better instincts. She seldom had ever taken him into a large city, and there was no need to do so now. She whispered in his ear, then slapped his rump. A thick lump filled her throat as he sped back into the night.

He would be close when she needed him. She knew that now, as she should always have known it. All those years of worrying and wondering about his fate had been pointless. Ashur would always be close.

"Get in, woman!" a voice hissed.

She hurried through the narrow gap. Three men met her, fully armed. She noted the quality of the polished leather armor, but it was too soon to abandon her role playing. She threw herself at their feet, hoping she had never met them in her descroiyo guise. "Thank you, lords! You have spared me. My family lies dead, but I am spared. Your gods are gods of goodness and mercy. Bless you, lords!" She kept her head low, her face covered with her hands, and she lavished them with praises until they looked away in embarrassment.

"That's quite a sword," one sentry observed, trying to bring an end to her flattery.

"I plucked it from my husband's body while they burned our crops." She rubbed at her eyes as if brushing away tears and hugged the blade closer to her breast. "I'll give it to his brother, who lives on the street of tanners. He'll have to look after me now. That's Keled law." She pretended a sigh and started to leave them.

"Wait," one of the sentries called. She stopped but did not turn around, still fearing recognition. The sword slid partly out of the sheath. "There's unrest in the streets tonight. Soushane was also burned. Most of the garrison was slaughtered trying to defend it. Honest folks have shut themselves in their homes, but without soldiers to patrol the city, criminals have run riot." The sentry came up beside her, and she quickly put the sword back in its sheath. The man's voice softened somewhat. "You've been through enough tonight. Two of us will accompany you to the house of your husband's brother."

She thanked them profusely, suppressing a scowl, and led them through familiar streets to the Broken Sword. A few of the local urchins knew the city better than she; it had been her first task on coming here to learn the maze of roads and alleys. Possibly one or two of the garrison regulars knew it as well. A couple of gate sentries, though, barely offered her a challenge.

At a certain corner she turned quicker than they and melted into the shadow of a doorway. They passed her, unseeing for a brief moment, then stopped in confusion. She was out of the shadow and running soundlessly back the way she had come before they even turned around. It was impossible to suppress a grin as she slipped away from them.

If there was turmoil in the streets earlier, the lateness of the hour had quelled it. Nothing but an eerie quiet greeted her as she made her secret way to the Rathole.

The streets began to narrow; a familiar stench spilled from the alleys. Twice the hush of night was disturbed by some small animal's digging in the garbage. Behind closed shutters she glimpsed the dim dancing of lamps and tapers, but no voices strayed without. She wondered at news that could send an entire citizenry cowering in the gloom of their private dwellings. The garrison, the city's police force, might be slaughtered; thieves might roam the streets unhindered; rebels might storm the countryside. But the walls were high and strong, and a courageous heart had no reason to fear.

Yet Kyr was tomblike.

She reached the crossroad formed by the alleyways where the night before she had stood with Telric. The memory of him made her shiver, then steeled her with a fierce hardness of purpose.

She stole down one way, feeling with her sword for the expected wires. She followed that course until it opened into another intersecting alley and knew she had chosen wrong. She retraced her steps and decided on another way. It, also, was the wrong choice.

Patiently, she prowled along the third path. Her weapon suddenly scraped on the thin, deadly barrier. She paused for a moment and thought, then fastened her sword belt around her hips and drew the blade. The metal made a silver blur as it rose and fell. The barbed wire snapped with a cold *ting* that was instantly smothered in the jingling of the warning bells. She took her time, though, located the lower trip wire, gave it similar treatment. Sparks flashed as her sword's point struck a cobblestone.

The way was clear if she needed a quick retreat.

She knew, now, where the Rathole was this night. She crept silently along until she arrived at the door. Light showed beneath the jamb; the sound of merriment echoed softly within. Perhaps they had not heard the bells. It was a night for thieves, the gate sentries had told her. They must be celebrating their pickings.

The alley was narrow, the opposite wall close. Frost leaned her back against it, felt the strength swell within her. She sucked her lip, reached out, and rapped firmly on the old wooden door. Muscles tensed; her body fired with purpose and power. Her fingers flexed around her sword's hilt.

The door opened a crack, spilling light into the alley. Illstar's doorman peered out with one eye. Frost's booted foot lashed out with terrific force. The door smashed inward, crushing the doorman's nose, sending him sprawling in a spray of blood and squeals of pain.

"Illstar!" She stepped over the threshold. The firelight from the lamps rippled along the length of her bare blade. She counted them at a glance: eleven men, a handful of women, and Dromen on his throne, King of Thieves. Her voice rolled through the room, chilling. "You owe me, Illstar!"

Raul reached her first. More bluster than brains, he had never been much of a thief. Despite his impressive build, he was even less of a warrior, and she wondered how he had ever managed to kill two of the soldiers. His sword hissed free of its sheath, carved an arc through the smoky air toward her head. She gave him barely a notice, dropped to one knee, and raked the edge of her weapon through his taut gut. He staggered, his mouth forming a wide, round hole, with scarcely time to acknowledge the spreading red wound before her blade slashed again upward and through his throat.

She stepped away from him, her eyes locked on Illstar. Two more men attacked her from either side. The flash of metal in the corner of her eye warned her. She spun, bringing her sword up and across, to intersect not her foe's blade, but the hand that held it. A scream of shock and agony ripped from the unfortunate fool as he collapsed to the floor, groping for his severed limb.

She turned to meet the third attacker. His sword went up. So did her foot, ruining his manhood. His weapon tumbled from numbed fingers; he doubled, clutching between his legs. Her sword bit deeply through the exposed back of his neck.

A rush of motion on all sides, and the Rathole was suddenly empty. Only Dromen Illstar remained and a whimpering wretch curled in a corner insanely trying to rejoin hand and wrist.

Dromen gazed at her, outwardly calm, but the blood had drained from his face. "I told you," he said, unable to keep a slight quaver from his voice, "it comes back. No matter how old you get, it comes back." He lifted his cup to her and drank.

"It comes back," she agreed. She strode up to him, gathered a handful of his robe, and wiped her blade clean. "You cheated me, Dromen," she said. "You told the garrison, and they were in Soushane before me, waiting for my son. I never even got near Kel. Your information was useless!" She took the wine cup from his hand and drank, watching him carefully over the rim, almost daring him to try something. When the vessel was empty she cast it over her shoulder. It clattered on the floor.

"Now you're going to make up for that by giving me different information." Dromen started to protest, but she pushed him backward into his seat. "Don't tell me about keeping confidences or privileged sources, either. You were gone more than a month searching for word of my son, and I'll bet you know a lot more than you told me." She waved the point of her blade under his nose. "I know you, Dromen Illstar, and you always keep something back for yourself." She caught his hand in an irresistible grip and began to squeeze. "Well, this time you're going to share, old friend."

Dromen said nothing, just stared at the blade and licked his lips when she slowly set the razor edge on the delicate webbed flesh between the two smallest fingers of his captured hand. "Oroladian cut off my husband's fingers from his right hand," she told him coldly. "But I'm not going to cut yours off. . . ." She smiled grimly, a cruel smile full of dark promise. "I'm going to saw between your bones until the edge of my sword meets your wrist. Then I'll separate the next two fingers."

A bead of sweat rolled on his temple. "You're not in a very good mood, are ye, Captain?"

She shook her head.

Dromen's pink tongue darted out, dampened the corners of his mouth. "Of course, I'll tell ye everything."

She didn't free his hand or even remove her blade. "You were always a reasonable man," she admitted grudgingly.

"That wasn't very reasonable of ye." He gestured to the several bodies whose blood had spoiled his floor. "If ye needed somethin' more than what ye laid out in the original agreement, ye shoulda known ye only had t' ask."

Her sword nicked his flesh. A tiny drop of scarlet welled and seeped down the back of his hand over his wrist. Dromen's eyes widened fearfully; he tried to pull away, but she held him firmly. "I thought it best to impress you, old friend," she said. "You betrayed me, and I lost another friend because of that. The garrison must have known hours before you told me. They were already hidden and in position when Telric and I arrived." She twisted the blade a little, drawing another cut on the inside of his smallest finger. "And I'm very mad about that, Dromen. You'd better tell me where I can find Kel again, or give me the name of someone who can. You have contacts who can find out if you don't know yourself." She smiled, fixing him with a hard look. "Though I suspect you do know."

Illstar sat stiffly, tense, though he put on a broad grin. With his free hand he pointed to the corpses. "They've gold on 'em," he said lightly. "Do ye plan to take it?"

Again, she shook her head.

"In that case, let me pour us some wine," he suggested with uncertain calm, "then I'll sing ye a song and tell ye a tale. Anything t' please my favorite captain." He waved at the dead men again. "There's the coin t' pay my fee."

Frost glanced slowly around the Rathole. The man whose hand she had severed lay unconscious, very pale, bleeding freely from the wound. He would be dead shortly. She backed to the entrance, stepping over Raul's body, threw the lock bolt, and dropped a security bar across it. She glared at Dromen, folded her arms, and waited, still grasping her bare blade.

Illstar affected an air of calm, poured wine from a sectarius into small vessels that rested nearby on a side table. He offered her one, smiling, and relaxed on his throne.

"You taste it first," she ordered.

Dromen cocked an eyebrow and frowned. Then his smile returned. He raised the cup he'd extended to her, placed it to his lips, and drank delicately.

She crossed the room and took the wine from him. She sipped a little. Dromen Illstar stocked only the best for his customers—the best he could steal, anyway. The wine's heady bouquet filled her senses. She sipped again, savoring the nectarous delight. The point of her sword came to a rest on the floor; she leaned slightly on the hilt. "Sing me your song and tell me your tale," she ordered her unwilling host, "and the melody better please me."

A racking cough shook Dromen before he could speak; his wine sloshed from his cup, soiling his sleeve. A sound rustled in his throat like dry leaves in a wind. His hand trembled violently. But finally, he managed to control himself and he downed a swallow of liquor. That seemed to still his seizure. The old man sagged back into his seat.

"The wages of sin . . ." he said with a sigh. He drank more wine, then with a smirk gave a wry twist to a popular saying of philosophers in his Korkyran homeland. "Are fun, frivolity, and joyful self-indulgence." He waved a hand at nothing in particular and smacked his lips. "The lung rot gets the pious man and the profligate. Best t' fill life's cup t' the brim while ye can, right, Captain?" So saying, he refilled his vessel and raised it in a silent toast.

Her sword's point rose from the floor, came to rest on the inside of Illstar's thigh. She ran the flat of the blade suggestively back and forth as she spoke. "Don't stall me, Dromen. You'll make me irritable."

His gray head shook. "You've been in the streets tonight, Captain. You've seen how empty they are? People are scared. Your son did that t' them." He took another drink. A dribble rolled down his chin, and he wiped it away with his sleeve. "Ye know how many garrison troops made it back from Soushane?" He waited until she shook her head. "Only two," he informed her. "Two men out o' more than a hundred. And they sang such a song, ye should know. All o' magic an' sorcery an' such." Suddenly, he threw back his head and laughed. "An' it spread like fire through the streets an' taverns."

"A different kind of fire spread through the streets of Soushane," she said. "The garrison never had much of a chance. It was magic all right, and a goodly number of soldiers burned to death before they got the chance to draw steel."

Dromen regarded her with cool respect. "I've known ye, Captain, an' because ye say it, I'll believe ye. I remember that dagger ye used t' carry. Beautiful thing, but horrible, an' reekin' o' sorcery. Still, it made the difference in many a fight." He pointed to her weapon belt, where Demonfang used to ride her hip. "What became o' the thing?"

Her sword's point slid higher along his thigh, more eloquent than words.

Dromen lifted the blade carefully between thumb and forefinger and placed it on a less threatening part of his anatomy. When he released it, he smiled. The smile vanished as the blade slid right back.

"Well, no matter," he admitted. "I digress. Ye want t' know about your son." He winked over the rim of his cup. "An' you're right. I know somethin' that might help."

Dromen paused and refilled his cup yet again. His eyes betrayed a fine, alcoholic glaze as he lifted the beverage and drank. Frost wondered if it calmed his fear. Did he think she meant to kill him? Did he know how close to hell he was? She felt the leather wrapping on her weapon's hilt, suddenly damp with the sweat of her palms. Her eyes met his, and she saw something there. *Yes, he knows*, she realized, *and he plays with it, dares it and invites it*.

"Ye know, the Keleds are like naive little children in matters o' magic. There isn't much o' it in this land. Gods know why. The steppes just don't seem t' breed wizards the way mountain country or forest lands do. When the people o' Kyr heard it was magic that crushed the garrison, they went running for their homes and bolted the shutters. It was almost funny t' a more experienced man o' the world like myself."

He winked at her again, sipped his wine, and continued. "I did wonder why ye ever named your son after this land. Keled-Zaram is a nation o' sheep. But he's no sheep, that one. Your Kel is a wolf."

She removed her sword from the old man's thigh and reached for the wine sectarius. She didn't want Illstar drunk before he completed this meandering tale. She raised her own cup to her mouth and downed some of it. "Do you speak Rholarothan?"

"Never had your gift for tongues," he confessed.

"Funny you should mention it in just that way." One hand strayed to the leather bag suspended on the thong under her

tunic. She felt the outline of Kimon's finger, and a chill
passed through her. "His father named him," she explained.
"It's a Rholarothan tradition for the father to name his sons,
and the mother has no involvement at all. He didn't insist on
many of his homeland's traditions, so I gave in on this
matter, and never questioned his choice. But in the language
of Rholaroth *Kel* means 'wolfling.' I honestly don't know if
my son is named for Keled-Zaram or for a wolf cub." *Or,*
she thought grimly, *for the father of the demon baby I once
carried in my body.*

Illstar nodded. "He is aptly named, then. Your wolfling
has grown, however, an' he leads a mongrel pack of misfits
and malcontents, mercenaries no respectable army would hire."

"But why?" she pressed. "To what purpose?"

He shrugged. "That's the mystery, Captain. The obvious
answer would be that he wants the throne. But he goes about
it in a peculiar way. His attacks have no focus. He strikes at
random from one part o' the kingdom t' the other. Lately,
he's been workin' these parts." He tapped his chin with a
finger. "It makes no sense, though. Soushane, for example—
jus' a small town with only their fields and flocks t' support
'em. No industry, no armory, no garrison. No threat o' any
kind. Why even bother?" He stared down into his cup, but he
didn't drink. "Some say your son is the chaos-bringer himself, Gath, the god o' madness. He kills and pillages for the
pleasure in it." He waved a hand and looked away from her.
"He's your flesh and blood. Maybe ye can understand him."

"I can't," she admitted. "But I intend to get some answers."

Dromen twirled his cup between his hands and smiled.
"Then your supply sergeant will supply ye one more time.
But I'll warn ye, Captain. The man who gave me this information has long since departed Keled-Zaram. Fail this time,
an' I can do nothin' more for ye." He drained his cup and
gestured for the sectarius. Frost held it away a moment, then
relented and surrendered it. "My informant gave—or rather,
sold—the names o' two towns unfortunate enough t' have
attracted your son's interest. Soushane was one." He filled
his cup again, talking as he poured. "In three nights you'll
find him again at Dakariar." He set the sectarius aside and
fixed her with a sharp gaze. "I've a daughter in Dakariar,
Captain. That's the real reason I told the garrison about
Soushane. I wanted him stopped." Dromen peered into his

cup, then suddenly tossed it away. Red wine splashed on the walls, staining them. "Damn stuff has made me maudlin," he rumbled, scowling.

"What about this sorcerer, Oroladian?"

"Can't help ye," he answered curtly. "Nobody's ever seen him. People's seen his powers, but never him. An' nobody knows where he came from. There's a story, though, about a tower down along the Keled-Esgarian border. Stood empty for most o' a hundred years, but some say it's been occupied lately. Some say it's your son an' this Oroladian."

"Where is this place?" If Kel planned to attack Dakariar, she could find his tower and wait for his return.

"Don't know," he confessed. "Just somewhere along the Lythe River far to the south."

Frost bit her lip. There was no choice, then, but to go to Dakariar. She prayed for better luck than she'd had in Soushane. She had to find Kel.

And when she found him, what then?

She sheathed her blade at last. "Did you tell the garrison about Dakariar?"

Dromen Illstar closed his eyes briefly. "Always hold somethin' in reserve," he answered softly. "Ye never know when a piece o' information might go up in value."

She raised an eyebrow. "Your information isn't worth a *minarin* now. There's nothing left in Kyr to send against my son but a handful of gate guards."

The old man glanced down at his hands. "Riothamus has patrols searchin' for him."

She shrugged. Riothamus and his patrols had been scouring the countryside for months. They still hadn't caught up with Kel. She took little pride in the fact, yet it was hard to count the king as much of a threat.

There was nothing more to learn here. Frost gazed at Dromen, once her friend, recalling him as he had been when they both were younger. Time had marked them in different ways, and though they both strove to hide their scars, his, at least, were plain to see. She wondered, were hers?

She moved to the door, unbarred it, unbolted it. Neither she nor Dromen said good-bye. He rose from his seat but didn't approach her. He went, instead, to the bodies of his slain customers, kneeled, and began to strip them of their valuables.

It was not the Dromen she once knew, she told herself. Quietly opening the door, she passed into the alley and into the night.

When the Rathole was far behind her, she drew a slow, weary breath and let it out. No chance to leave the city until dawn, she knew. A lie and the compassion of nervous sentries had unsealed Kyr's gates and gained her entrance. Nothing but the sun itself would open them to let her out.

Her footsteps echoed on the paving as she retraced her course through the squalid alleys. She squeezed between close walls and made her way up a narrow, filth-littered street. Apartments loomed on either side, stacked one atop another, all dark and silent, so old and ramshackle a good wind often set them to swaying.

She stopped abruptly and listened. Only her breathing broke the unnatural silence.

Kyr was one of the largest cities in the kingdom. It teemed with life, throbbed with energy. Even this slum possessed a vitality of its own. But nothing stirred about tonight. Where were the street people, the imbibers, the beggars, prostitutes?

It filled her with a kind of awe to suddenly realize how profoundly shaken the citizens of Kyr must be. Their garrison had been destroyed, a neighboring town burned.

But it was more than that, she knew. It was the sorcerer. A pungent fear nestled within the city's walls now, stifling. It was magic that drove them cowering into their homes.

It occurred to her that she might be the only soul abroad in the darkness.

No lamp lit the streets, yet she knew her way. At last she arrived at the foot of a high stone stairway that led steeply up the side of one of the oldest dwellings in this section of Kyr. The steps were small and crumbling, barely wide enough for two people to pass. Often, they were made more treacherous by the flakings of stucco that fell from the deteriorating wall.

She paused on the second level's landing and put her ear to the apartment door there. No sound stole forth; no candlelight spilled under the jamb. At the third level she stopped before her own door and pushed it open.

It had been all she could afford when she came to Kyr, a spare room with a hard rope bed and a few sticks of scratched furniture. The lamp she normally kept burning had gone out, its oil spent. There were candles, but she had nothing to light them with now. A little moonlight seeped through the room's sole window. She closed the door and threw the inside bolt.

Sitting on her bed, she unstrapped her sword and leaned it against the wall. Next, she removed her boots with a soft grunt and cast them into a corner. The skirts of her descroiyo disguise were strewn around her on the bed. She gathered them into a bunch, then dropped them on the floor.

A twinge of sadness caught her in that unguarded moment. Across the room by the small table, Telric had stood with his back turned while she had changed from the skirts into her riding leathers. She imagined she could see his tall shadow there now waiting and watching.

She bit her lip. Confidences had been shared along the road to Soushane. Telric had proven easy to talk with. They had shared a brief time together long ago, and now another very brief time. Yet his deep, gentle voice had warmed a spot inside her.

That spot was cold again. There was nothing she could do for Telric. There was nothing she could do at all but sleep and when the sun finally rose start out for Dakariar.

She stripped and lay back naked on the coarse blanket. Though she closed her eyes, sleep eluded her. She turned her face to the wall, then rolled onto her back. The woven ropes felt like hard stones through the thin bedclothes. She rolled to her stomach.

But it wasn't the ropes that kept her awake.

The room was full of Telric. It echoed with his voice, his footsteps. He moved half-glimpsed in the shadowed gloom. It wasn't the breeze through her window that kissed her bare skin, but Telric's scented breath.

She sat up suddenly and seized the skirts she had dropped on the floor. Among them was the purse she wore as a descroiyo and inside that her deck of cards. She took them out, untied the leather thong that bound them together, spread them on the bed beneath the window where the moon illumined them best.

It was impossible, insane.

She searched through the cards, finding ones she had turned up before, combing her memories. She had sat at the Broken Sword. Telric had not yet come through the door. . . .

The Sword-soldier, the Ace of Swords, the High Priestess. Yes, she remembered. Then, the Prince of Demons.

The door had opened, then, and he had come, cloaked and hooded, into the inn and straight to her table. She turned the cards, remembering, scattering them over the blanket.

The Sword-soldier again. The Queen of Swords—the Dark Angel herself. Then, the Silver Lady. Frost glanced out the window at the moon, then back at her cards. The Six of Cups. Yes, there it was! That meant an old friend.

The reading had gone no further. Telric had stopped her and pushed back his hood. "Do you remember me?" he had asked. Those words reverberated in the air, tormenting her.

Finally, she shook her head. For a long time she stared at the faces and symbols on those particular cards, denying what they suggested. She rose and paced the room, then returned to the bed to stare at the cards again.

It was impossible.

She could not tell the future. Even the simple magic in the cards was beyond her. The witch-power had been stolen from her long years ago by her own mother's curse. The fortunes she told at the inn had always been lies.

But those cards . . .

It had to be coincidence, she decided. Such things could happen with the cards. Even for a fraud they were unpredictable. Many people—especially street people—tried to earn a *quinz* or a *minarin* by telling fortunes, and few had any idea at all of what the cards truly meant.

Her breathing slowly calmed; the rapid beating of her heart slowed. She put away the cards and sat back on her bed with her back against the wall, her knees drawn up so the moonlight could not touch her.

Coincidence, she repeated to herself.

But there was a nagging element of doubt.

It seemed through the cards she had predicted Telric's coming.

Chapter Nine

When I was young
The sea rose up in ire at my command.
When I was young
The Gift of Tongues
Was mine, wind and fire flowed from my hand
And every lie was golden, each illusion grand
When I was young.

Frost passed through the gates of Kyr as the first morning light crept into the east. The sentries hesitated when she approached. The sight of a woman bearing weapons was no common thing in Keled-Zaram. She wondered briefly if they recognized her as the kohl-eyed descroiyo who worked the Broken Sword. Or did they recall the story of the woman who killed the lover of King Riothamus and shamed the rite of *Zha-Nakred Salah Veh*? She strode ahead, and wordlessly they cranked back the massive doors.

She was tempted to laugh as she walked away from Kyr. The events of the previous night had left deep marks on the gate guards. The blood in their veins had turned to milk. It was never the cream of the garrison that drew gate duty, but men of uncertain courage, oldsters or the very greenest of recruits. There was only a handful of them now to guard Kyr; the slaughter of all their comrades had plainly shriveled their spirits.

117

But they were good men in their own way, she allowed. Frightened they were, but they stood their posts. And out of compassion they had allowed her inside last night. Nor could she forget that it was her son, flesh of her flesh, who caused their fear. Any temptation to laugh died within her, replaced by an angry shame.

She moved across the plain, one hand gripping the hilt of her sword. Quick, purposeful strides took her away from the city until the high walls were only distantly perceived and the smells of industry no longer spoiled the air.

Then Frost put two fingers to her lips and blew a long, piercing note. Instants later she spied the unicorn. He raced from the east out of the sunrise, charging toward her over the hard ground. His black mane lashed the wind, tail streamed straight behind him. The earth churned up beneath his heavy, pounding hooves.

A flash caught her eye—the morning light rippling along the ebon spike upon his brow.

It didn't matter what kind of creature he was, she told herself again. It was enough that they belonged together.

The unicorn stopped suddenly, then paced up to her with lowered head. His deadly horn slipped past her ear as he nuzzled her shoulder. She smiled, drew a hand through his tangled forelock, and scratched his ears.

"Time to ride, my friend," she said, grabbing a handful of mane, swinging onto his broad back, "just as we did in the old days." Ashur snorted, tossed his head high. She touched booted heels lightly to his flanks.

The ground flowed past, an endless and undistinguishable series of gentle slopes and rises, grasslands and barren fields. She lost herself in the rhythm of her ride, forgetting time, oblivious to the scorching sun that burned the exposed flesh of her neck and face, to the wind that chapped and cracked her lips. Ashur's mane tickled her as she leaned close; his muscles and hers worked as though they were one, together in sleek, swift harmony.

She could not draw breath enough to sing for the rush of the air. Yet music swelled within her, filling head and heart, powerful melodies that set her blood to singing. Old tunes from her youth sprang unbidden into her memory. Potent, stirring lyrics lost over the years suddenly returned. The thunder of the unicorn's hooves and the beating of her own heart set the cadence. It was the wind that blew the tune and the sun that sang the high notes.

She could have ridden forever like that; Ashur could have carried her off to whatever land of myth he came from, and she would not have cared. Instead, they reached the peak of a low crest that suddenly was familiar. She jerked gently on a handful of mane, and Ashur stopped.

She looked down at the ruins of Soushane. The music within her abruptly died. She slid to the ground, took a few steps down the slope, and stopped. Ashur came quietly to her side.

A host of carrion birds circled over the rubble, artfully winging among the wispy tendrils of smoke that still curled upward into the blue sky. Beyond the town, a small sea of black ash extended nearly to the horizon, marking how the field fires had spread into the grassland before the heavy rain that must have finally extinguished it.

The smell of burning still lingered in the air, but it was the scent of charcoal and ashes, old smoke. There was another scent, too. She knew what it was. In the town it would be stronger. Stronger yet as the sun grew hotter and hotter. Tomorrow, no man who wandered by would dare approach Soushane's ruins. The air would stink with rotting and contagion.

What had become of the citizens? she wondered. Surely some had escaped. She had seen them flee. Would they not return to mourn their dead? At the very least, wouldn't they come back to scavenge what remained of their belongings? Hoe blades or rakes, even eating utensils, were all expensive and could be salvaged from the aftermath of fire.

She walked slowly down the hill, and Ashur followed. The odor of death was not yet too strong to bear. The earth, however, was slick with mud; she picked her way carefully and didn't hurry. Once she nearly slipped but caught herself by stumbling into Ashur. "Thanks," she mumbled. He only regarded her with those weird, flickering eyes.

Soushane's people would never come back, she realized. Ashur's unnatural eyes had given her the answer to that puzzle. The fire that burned their homes had been unnatural, too, sorcerer's fire that came in the shape of an immense, evil hand, that spread with impossible speed, leaving no building untouched. To Keleds who had little traffic with sorcery or wizardry it must have seemed that all their gods had deserted them, and that all the hells had come to claim their pathetic world. She recalled the terror of the gate guards in Kyr and how that city's people had shuttered themselves inside their homes. Kyr had not experienced the fire, nor the slaughter that followed. How much greater must be the terror of the farmers and herdsmen who had survived those events!

She found the first body before she reached the outermost buildings. A sword wound cut deeply through the man's chest and up through his shoulder. His attacker, then, had been mounted. An expression of pain and despair made a frozen mask of his once handsome face. A shock of sandy-brown hair peeked out from beneath his garrison-issue helm. His lifeless hand still clutched the hilt of his weapon.

Frost swallowed hard. Whoever held the sword that killed this soldier, here was her son's handiwork. Kel na'Akian, he called himself. Kel Cold-blood, born of her loins. She cursed herself, and she cursed Kimon, though he was dead, for they were responsible for their son.

The soldier on the ground was not much older than Kirigi.

She swallowed again and thought of Soushane's people, who would never return to this damned place. With a sigh, she took out the gray leather gloves that were tucked into her belt and slipped them on. Gently as she could, she pried the sword-hilt from the young man's grip, though his fingers were stiff and reluctant to yield. Next, she took his hands in hers, cringing inwardly at the touch of his icy skin, and dragged him into Soushane

As she passed the smoking remains of the first building, a shrill cacophony and a sudden rush of pinions made her jump. Inadvertently, she dropped the dead soldier and whirled, reaching for her sword. Startled carrion birds climbed for the safety of the sky. There were far more of them than she had imagined from the crest, and they scolded her furiously for disturbing their feast.

The carnage had been horrible to see in the darkness of night when only the uncertain fires showed the faces of the men who fought here. In the full light of day it sickened her. The sunshine stripped away the falsehoods of war. Here were no heroes or villains, here were no soldiers, no captains, no veterans, no recruits. Here was no victory or defeat, no glory.

Here were only dead men, dead women and children. The

sun shone on their cold faces, on the hopeless and disbelieving expressions of people who knew with an instant's surety
that there would not be another breath, another heartbeat, that
death's hand had shut their eyes forever. There was pain, the
agony of a sword thrust written plainly in the twist of a
mouth. The searing touch of the fire reflected in the gleams of
unseeing eyes—if the faces were not charred beyond recognition, and if the birds had not gotten to them yet.

Frost couldn't help herself. She braced her hands on her
knees and vomited. She had eaten no breakfast, and there was
little in her stomach, but what was there she surrendered.

She could not leave them like that. The birds were already
settling back to resume their banquet.

There was no dignity in death. How many times had her
teachers taught her that, and how many times had she taught
it to others? Dead was dead. Once dead, then dead forever.
Yet there was no dignity in living—not for her—if she walked
away from this.

It was, after all, her son's handiwork.

Ashur plodded along beside as Frost went through the
streets. One by one she dragged the bodies to the center of the
town and placed them in neat, close rows. Citizen, soldier,
rebel, it didn't matter to her. The children she placed in the
women's arms with extra care. There was no way she could
always match parent and child, but she hoped that somehow
their souls understood the gesture. She sweated as she worked,
and the sweat ran in rivulets and dripped onto a cold lip, an
unfeeling cheek, a fear-wrinkled brow.

When she could find no others in the streets, she searched
the town's grassy perimeter, then the remains of the fields.
Some of the bodies were cooked so badly she could barely
bring herself to look at them, let alone to touch them. Still,
she swallowed the bile in her throat and bent to her task.

It was dangerous to search among the smoking ruins. There
were wall remnants that promised to collapse in the next good
wind, half-fallen roofs that were instant traps. But she moved
purposefully among them. Somewhere in all the smoking
rubble there had to be a flame yet burning, some small spark
of fire to ignite the pyre.

A low, creaking groan caused her to look up. She leaped
back, feeling heat close to her face. A lone standing beam,
scorched and char-blackened, crashed to the ground. Sparks

and ash and smoke rose in a tight, choking cloud. A hot ember caught on her sleeve, and she hurried to beat it off.

A small blue flame quivered ephemerally along the center section of the beam, then threatened to die. Quickly, she fell to her knees and blew a thin stream of air. The tiny flame brightened. She blew again, nursing the flame. The beam was too big for her to drag, and it was too hot. She glanced around desperately for some piece of rubble and found a broken, half-burned board. It took fire from the beam with only a bit of coaxing.

She had her brand at last. Cautiously, she made her way back to the rows of bodies, cupping one hand to protect her lambent treasure.

Among the corpses she had scattered bits of wood and charred materials that had cooled enough to touch. She doubted it was sufficient fuel, but there was nothing more she could do. She lay her torch to a pile of sticks and splintered boards. Slowly, the fire took hold. From that pile she took more brands and placed them among similar piles until a ring of small fires burned around the bodies. It was not enough, she saw. She took some of the brands and tossed them among the corpses, gratified when the clothing began to burn.

An odor rose thick in the air, a smell that made her sick once more. But her nausea only made her angry, for she realized that despite her efforts this was no decent funeral pyre, that the flames were not hot enough to accomplish their task.

Ashur nuzzled her shoulder, but it did not console her. The anger built as she watched the grisly, futile scene. The fires popped and crackled. Here and there, limbs seemed impossibly to stir, faces turned away. Strands of hair waved and floated on the shifting currents of heat. Garments flapped grotesquely.

The little woodpiles began to collapse, already half-consumed, their purpose unfulfilled.

Frost cursed again. She cursed herself and she cursed Kel. She cursed Kimon and the seed he had planted in her body. She cursed the night they had joined and the day of her son's birth. Clenched fists beat on her thighs. She ran to the closest ruin, drove her fist through the remains of a wall, and tore savagely at the thin, fire-weakened boards. The heat of them scorched her gloves; heedless, she hurled them with a manic strength into the midst of her pathetic pyre and returned for more. Her hands ached until she could barely curl her fingers. But it didn't matter. She cursed, and the cursing drove away the pain.

Then, a howling rose mysteriously in the east, a screaming that chilled her to the bone. She dropped the board she held and stared out beyond the town, uncomprehending.

A sweeping wind of terrific force flattened the last remaining structures. She uttered a choked cry before it blew her off her feet; she hit the ground hard, gasping for breath. An unearthly trumpeting filled her ears, sounding loud even over the whining of the gale. She rolled to her side, searching for Ashur. The unicorn stood face into the wind, head lowered, mane and tail streaming, fighting the element's unrelenting power.

But there was more yet to see and greater cause to wonder.

The sudden wind fanned the pyre, driving the flames higher, hotter, creating a swirling maelstrom of incinerating fury. The stench nearly strangled her; the heat toasted her skin until she covered her face with her hands and peered between her fingers. She could not see the bodies for the obscuring, shimmering blaze.

She fought up to her knees and crawled to Ashur's side. Her hands clutched around his legs and in his thick coat as she pulled herself to her feet. Dark smoke spiraled into the heavens. She clung to the unicorn, locking arms about his neck for support.

As suddenly as it began, it ended. The wind died, the screaming ceased. Only the fire continued as it fed efficiently on flesh and bone. It would burn for hours, perhaps even through the night.

She spat the dust from her mouth, quivering. The steppe winds were unpredictable, often devastating. They appeared without warning and dissipated as swiftly. But never had she experienced one of such force or seeming purpose!

She stared at the pyre. The wind had come, accomplished what she could not, and faded. Had it been a wind at all, or the breath of some god who favored her?

She covered her mouth and nose. The odor was too much to bear, and she was nearly sick again. She swung up onto Ashur's back. "Away!" she managed, coughing as the smoke swirled her way. She leaned close to the unicorn's ear. "By the god of all the hells, away!"

She rode long into the evening. The setting sun tugged the curtain of night over the earth, and the colors of day surrendered to gray shadow and gloom. The night breezes blew upon her face with a growing chill. Yet even the sharp gusts could not keep her eyes from sliding shut.

She caught herself as she started to slip from the unicorn's back. A voice somewhere in her head urged her to ride on. *Your son is doing mischief*, it said, *and mayhem. Ride on! Ride on!* But her strength was gone. Her lids were heavy from the need to sleep. Her limbs felt like great weights. She dropped to the ground, feeling the shock through her knees and thighs. An outcropping of rocks to her left was the only shelter; she curled up among them, hugging her legs to her chest.

She had no cloak to ward off the cold, but her discomfort was short. Sleep claimed her almost at once.

The sunrise brought her gradually awake. Every part of her cried in miserable pain. She feared she couldn't move at all. Every muscle resisted her, stiff and unbending. Her legs burned as if they were on fire from gripping Ashur's saddle-less back. Her hips felt bruised; her back and shoulders were unyielding knots of tension and fatigue. Her breasts throbbed, her arms cracked and popped when she tried to lift them. The cold of the hard ground penetrated her bones, made joints inflexible.

She rocked slowly on her back, rubbing the sorest places. With no one to see, she allowed quiet tears. Not since that night when she'd fled Dashrani had she hurt so! She'd toughened herself, she'd thought, made her body stronger.

Had she only fooled herself, or had age imposed some limitation on her?

She refused to accept that. She had pushed herself hard in Soushane, then had ridden much too long without rest. Of course her body protested and punished her.

Nearby, Ashur nickered suddenly and stopped chewing the mouthful of grass he'd been working on. Unmoving, he looked out over the steppe. The flames that were his eyes seemed to burn brighter. Frost forced herself to rise, ignoring the torment that movement brought. From the unicorn's side she gazed out and discovered what had startled her mount.

Far out on the flatland a patrol rode by. The red cloaks of Riothamus's soldiers fluttered against the blue morning. The king himself must be close, she reasoned, and with him a larger force. She grabbed Ashur's mane and urged him back into the shelter of the rocks. She was in no shape for an encounter if she was spotted.

Patiently she waited until the patrol was out of sight. Then, biting her lip, she tried to leap astride Ashur, but grating joints failed her. Instead, she clambered onto a low step where two rocks supported each other and called the unicorn close.

"Hold still, or I'll smack your nose," she told the beast as she leaned out and gingerly swung one leg over his broad back. A twinge shot through her knee.

She'd been lucky, she thought as she started across the plain. She had few doubts about the king's memory; if the patrol had found her, she would have hanged. With Riothamus in the area her problems were doubled, and time was running out.

She rode stiffly, and each jounce brought a new kind of torture. There was nothing to do but endure it.

By noon, however, her aches and pains had eased a bit. Ashur ran a swift, straight course across the featureless land. Though he showed no other strain, a creamy lather slicked his glossy hide and saturated her breeches. It was but one more discomfort to annoy her.

But the frown she wore had nothing to do with such little complaints. She thought of her son. Five years had not dimmed her memories of him. Even as a child Kel had been calculating and methodical. There'd always been some purpose to his actions, and she was sure that had not changed. Why had he burned Soushane? Why all the other towns and villages? There had to be a pattern; she racked her brain to see it.

Yet what if it was not some purpose of Kel's? What if it was a plan of Oroladian's formulation? It might be the sorcerer who directed her son's actions. But again, to what end? All she felt sure about was that nothing had been done at random.

Unless, of course, Kel or Oroladian was mad. She knew nothing of the sorcerer, but she had talked with Kel. There had been anger in his eyes and hatred and cruelty. But she had not seen madness in them. And unless the years had changed him, her son was too shrewd to become ensnared in the machinations of a lunatic unless there was something tangible in it for him.

But again, there would have to be a purpose, some pattern. If only she could see it!

By chance, she glanced to her left. A huge cloud of dust drifted on the horizon. Riothamus's army, she was certain. To judge from the patrol and the direction of the cloud, the king was on his way to Kyr. That put her safely out of their path for now.

How long, though, would it be before Illstar sold the information she had squeezed from him? How long before Riothamus followed her to Dakariar? She should have killed the old thief and shut his mouth. But there had seemed no need when only a handful of frightened gate sentries remained to guard the city.

Well, there would be plenty of soldiers to man the garrison now, and with Dromen's tongue to point the way, plenty more to come after her.

But they would come too late. Unless Dromen lied, Kel would be in Dakariar tomorrow night. Ashur would carry her there in plenty of time. Riothamus and his army would only just be arriving in Kyr.

She almost laughed. Maybe in his disappointment, Riothamus would do what she should have done and put an end to Illstar's miserable existence.

That single thought made her feel better than she had all day.

Approaching evening found her on a narrow road that wound among the fields of Dakariar. A small band of workers leaned on their hoes and gazed at her as she passed, but none hailed her, and she did not want to stop.

Dakariar was larger than Soushane, but too small to warrant a defensive wall. The road led straight into the town. She passed shops that were beginning to close for the night, yet the merchants hesitated in the hope she might see something to buy. They smiled warmly at her and indicated their wares. She smiled back but rode on.

Potters cleaned their wheels; tanners folded hides; a blacksmith continued to hammer a piece of glowing metal. They looked up from their tasks as she went by, curiosity lighting their faces.

Frost turned a corner and knew at once this was not the street she wanted. A young woman with heavily kohled eyes and rouged cheeks stood in a doorway with a red lantern in hand. Plump breasts strained against the tight material of a scarlet gown as the whore reached up to hang the light on a peg beside the entrance.

"Looking for work?" the woman asked with a wink.

Frost started to ride by, then changed her mind.

"You're older than I first thought," the whore said when Frost stopped and looked down at her. She thrust out a hip and leaned lewdly against the doorjamb. "Still, I could clean you up a bit—"

Frost interrupted. "I need to talk with your elders."

The whore grinned. "I'm not so young, either, dearie. Never knew my father, and Mama's long dead of the pox."

Frost allowed a thin smile. "The town elders," she corrected. "Your governor, or whoever is the authority around here."

The whore let go a sharp laugh and slapped her thigh. "A governor, now? As if that boy-lover king in his fine palace would bother to look our way and say, 'Here's a fine noble or one of my favorite relatives come to watch over you.' A dirty little pig-town like this?" She chuckled boldly, staring Frost right in the eye. "I won't hire you as a whore, but as a fool to entertain us with your fancies!"

Frost forced another smile and clung to her patience. "Who do the merchants go to for settlement of disputes?"

Kohled lashes batted, painted lips pursed thoughtfully. "Sure you don't want a job? Can you dance?"

"Not a step," Frost lied.

A loud sigh. "Lost our dancer last week. Some crazy farmer cut her up." Another sigh, then the whore pointed down the street. "Look for the priests at the Temple of the Well." She turned to go back inside. "Come see me if you need that job," she added before closing the door. "I'll make a woman of you."

Frost shook her head, amused, and rode on. She turned another corner and found herself on a broad lane, Dakariar's principal thoroughfare, she guessed. Only the taverns were still open this late, and she licked her lips, suddenly thirsty.

But she had business. The Temple of the Well was her first duty. She looked up and down the street, wondering which way to go.

A pedestrian came her way, a clerk to judge from his inkpots, and she begged direction. The temple, he told her, was at the very heart of the city. The avenue would take her to it. She thanked him and nudged Ashur onward. "A beautiful horse," he called after her. She grinned, stroked Ashur's neck, and nodded.

She had seen many temples to many gods in her time, and this one was plain by comparison. A single story of white cut stone, it gave no clue as to the god it honored. Yet, as the clerk had said, it stood at the very center of Dakariar, and the road made a circle around it, a hub that all lesser roads joined.

A series of slender pink columns made a half circle before the temple's unornamented entrance. Within them stood the low rock wall of a well.

She dropped gingerly from Ashur's back, expecting the pain that shot through her knees. She gritted her teeth, then drew herself erect and walked past the columnar ring to the door. The wood, though plain, was polished smooth and without scratch or nick. She knocked and waited.

Moments later, the door eased open and a pleasant face peered out. The man regarded her blankly, then his expression lit up. "A stranger!" he shouted back into the temple. "The gods have sent us a stranger!"

Four more men joined the first in the doorway. As one, they spilled out, forcing her back to the well. She leaned against the rock wall in stunned silence. Strangers couldn't be all *that* uncommon in these parts.

"She's thirsty," one of them exclaimed. "Give her a drink from the well." Another hurried to obey. A crank turned and a bucket rose on a rope. She could smell the water's cool sweetness.

Yes, she was thirsty! A clay goblet appeared from somewhere, was filled from the bucket, and passed into her hand. They waited eagerly while she drained the vessel. The last drop oozed down her throat. She wiped her lips with one hand and gave the goblet back.

"Another?" asked the one who had answered the door. "I can tell by the dust on your clothes that you've come a long way."

She nodded and gratefully accepted the cup when it was refilled. She drank it more slowly, studying the five men.

They were priests, obviously. They wore similar robes of ordinary white linen, and their feet were bare. Their heads were not shaved, but the hair was cut to little more than a blunt stubble. None wore facial hair. The ages of the five varied, but the youngest had met her at the door and urged the second drink upon her.

He had a nice look, she noticed, and soft blue eyes.

"Thank you." She handed the empty goblet to him. "I'm told you're the authority in Dakariar."

One of the oldest grinned. "What fool told you that?"

She nearly told him, then thought better of it. Perhaps the whore had lied to her. "You're the priests of the temple?" she asked warily.

"I am Lycho," the youngest said. "These are Cleomen, Pericant, Jemane, and Oric." Each bowed in turn. "We are the priests of the well, but we're no kind of authority."

"I'm told you settle disputes and that sort of thing."

Lycho shrugged.

"We help some of the townspeople solve their problems," Cleomen said. "They usually abide by our judgments, but we have no power to command them."

"They come to us for water from the well," Jemane said. "Maybe they think we would not give it to them if they didn't heed our advice."

"But we would never do that," Pericant added. "The water is for everyone."

"To deny water would be to lose the blessing of the gods," Oric explained.

"What gods?" Frost asked, noting again the plainness of the temple. "Who do you worship here?"

"All the gods of goodness," Lycho answered, "those who made the water that eases pain and ends suffering . . ."

"The water that heals sickness . . ." Cleomen said.

"And restores vitality . . ." Jemane said.

She waited for Pericant and Oric to add something to the litany and was mildly amused when they folded their hands and regarded her silently. Apparently, they believed the water in their well had some properties. If so, two cups had done nothing for her. She could still feel the ache in her bones.

"I must talk with someone," she said finally. "Dakariar is in danger."

"Danger?" Pericant raised an eyebrow. It seemed to be his turn to speak. They were a chorus, these five, each waiting graciously to give his line.

"The rebel Kel na'Akian is on his way here with an army." Five faces stared back impassively. "Surely you've heard of him," she persisted. "Dakariar is not that secluded."

Oric nodded. "The townspeople have more dealings with strangers than we do. Not many outsiders are interested in local temples. But we hear tales, and we know of Kel na'Akian."

"Perhaps you should come inside," Lycho offered. "A little food and rest would do you good while you tell your news. There is more water, of course. It will ease your fatigue."

"And I'll see that your mount is stabled and curried," Cleomen said. "I once fancied myself a judge of horseflesh, but I've never seen his match."

Frost would never stop wondering at the power that disguised her unicorn. It surprised her every time someone called Ashur a horse, and she pitied them for their blindness. What beauty they missed. Yet it often made her think. What other beauties in the world might be hidden from *her* eyes?

"Approach him slowly and stroke his nose a few times," she instructed. "He's a sucker for a pat on the nose. Then he'll follow you."

She watched as the old priest obeyed. A few moments later, Cleomen started down the street with Ashur close behind. Lycho touched her shoulder, and she and the remaining priests went into the temple.

It was as plain inside as out. There was a fair-sized hall, but it contained only a long table with benches on either side. The walls were unadorned. No paintings decorated the ceiling. Two slitted windows in the east and west walls let in light, though there were also sconces with candles and oil lamps on two short pedestals. A door on the right presumably led to other chambers.

"I don't understand," she remarked casually. "A temple without an altar? Where is your idol? Who do you worship?"

"We do not know the god or goddess we serve," Jemane answered. "But a divine presence blesses our well. That is all the altar we need."

"We do not need the deity's name to do homage," Pericant said.

Oric caught her gaze. "To any who ask we give water from the well, and whatever their affliction they are made better." He gestured to the table and the mysterious door in the opposite wall. "A few of the very ill must stay with us for a time and drink regularly. Those we feed and house until they are healthy." He made a short bow. "I myself was such a one, but I elected to stay and join my brothers in service."

"As I did," Lycho confessed.

"I see no women among you," Frost observed. "Are they not welcome?"

The priests grinned. "Very welcome indeed," Jemane said. "We are not a celibate order. But they go home to their fathers and husbands eventually. There aren't many like you who dare to travel without a man."

Lycho led them to the table. Frost unstrapped her sword and leaned it close at hand against the bench as they all sat down. Only Pericant disappeared through the doorway. He quickly returned with a tray. On it was a pitcher of water, vessels for everyone, and cool slices of pork.

"Is this all you drink?" she asked as Pericant poured for her.

They nodded in unison, each lifting a cup to his lips. She did the same, silently toasting whatever strange god they served. Water, after all, was better than nothing, and she could still taste the dust of the road in her mouth.

"You've got to warn the citizens," she said when her cup was half-empty and a piece of meat had softened the grumbling in her belly. "Tomorrow night Kel na'Akian will burn Dakariar." She watched their eyes, trying to gauge their reactions. "Your people can fight him, or they can run away while they've time."

A deep furrow creased Lycho's brow. He leaned forward on one elbow. "Why Dakariar? What could we have that he possibly wants? This is a poor city."

Jemane also leaned forward, yet outwardly he was calm as he asked, "How is it that you come bearing this message? I might have expected a herald from Kel na'Akian, come to

strike some bargain, perhaps. Or a messenger from the king."
He fixed her with a steady gaze. "But you are neither."

She didn't look away, nor did she hesitate to answer. "Kel
na'Akian is my son."

Jemane arched an eyebrow and spoke out of turn. "Then
you must have some idea what he wants from us."

She shrugged and gazed down into her cup. "I wish that
were true." She swallowed hard and looked at each of them.
"But I haven't the slightest guess what he's up to. I don't
even know where he's at at this moment."

"Can you stop him?" Pericant asked.

"I don't know," she answered truthfully.

"You're going to try, though," Oric observed.

"I don't know that, either." She shook her head, reached
for another strip of pork, then changed her mind. Her hunger
was not really so pressing, after all. "I don't know what Kel
is planning," she told them. "I'm not even sure what I'm
planning."

A quiet fell over the table. The rest of the platter went
untouched. The last light dimmed beyond the windows as the
sun outside faded.

Finally, Lycho got up. He drained his vessel, then spoke to
the others. "Jemane, would you please light the candles?"
Jemane rose with a nod. To Pericant and Oric he said, "Will
you warn the citizens? Go door to door, to the taverns, any
place where there are people. Our guest has provided the only
options; tell them they must prepare to fight or to run away.
But tell them to make their plans quickly. Cleomen will join
you when he returns from the stables."

Pericant and Oric finished their drink and left silently.
More than Lycho and Jemane, her news seemed to have
affected them most grimly.

"Pericant, Oric, and Cleomen were born in this town,"
Lycho explained as if he had read her thoughts. "That's why
I thought it best to send them."

She looked up at him curiously. He was obviously the
youngest of the priests, yet he had given instructions and the
others had obeyed. "Are you the first priest?" she asked.

"First priest?" He tilted his head quizzically. "Oh, I see."
He shook his head. "We have no leader or any kind of
hierarchy. This time, I saw what had to be done. Next time, it
could be Cleomen or Jemane." He folded his hands and put

on a weary smile. "Let me show you a place to rest. You look like you could use a decent sleep."

She started to protest. "But Kel . . ."

He raised a stern finger. "You said he wouldn't come until tomorrow night."

She thought about it and remembered the hard ground that had been her bed last night. She still ached from that and from her long ride. She said no more but picked up her sword and followed Lycho.

Once through that dark doorway, they passed down a long corridor. The candles mounted on the walls were unlit, but enough light spilled from some of the smaller side rooms to let her see. There was a narrow kitchen, and next to that a chamber empty of anything but kneeling cushions. An inner prayer room, she decided. She passed another room whose center was occupied by a large wooden tub; several white garments hung on lines and dripped on the grooved floor.

Beyond that were the sleeping rooms. Lycho opened a door and motioned for her to enter. A single lamp filled the small room with a warm amber glow. Her gaze fell at once on the bed. It was not plush by any standard, yet she could see that the mattress was soft. A beautifully dyed linen cloth lay folded at the foot. Lycho spread it over the mattress and tucked it under the edges.

"This is your room," she said with sudden realization.

He nodded and winked. "Between us, it's the most comfortable in the temple." He opened a chest beside the bed and took out a large pillow. It was dyed with a different but equally beautiful pattern. He placed it on the bed and fluffed it. "I'll use one of the other rooms. There's little sickness in Dakariar this time of year, and we've no other guests."

"I can't take your room," she protested.

"You're not taking it," he said with a grin. "I'm giving it. Would you like more light?"

She wanted nothing but to crawl into that bed and grab some sleep. She leaned her blade against the wall close enough to reach if she needed it. Then she sat down on a stool and removed her boots.

Lycho watched her. "I'm going to bring you a pitcher of drink," he said. "Your fatigue is plain to see. The water of the gods will chase it away."

"Will it chase away my confusion?" she said softly, surprising herself. She looked at the man standing across the room. He was younger than she was; his face was still unlined and his hair untouched by gray. Yet he had been generous, and there was something about him she trusted. It seemed a long time since she had trusted anyone.

"You are troubled in your mind," Lycho said gently.

She leaned back against the wall and let go a sigh. "I don't know what's happening," she confessed, finding it easy to talk to the priest. "I don't know what my son is plotting. I don't know if his will is his own, or if a sorcerer has entranced him." She looked at her hands and began to massage the stiffness from her fingers. "I hate him with all my heart for what he did to his brother," she said distantly, "and yet, I love him, too. How can that be?"

Lycho said nothing, but he listened, and she found she could not stop talking.

"I want to kill him for the things he's done, but I don't know if I can." She sat forward, rested her elbows on her knees and her chin in her palms. She closed her eyes, and faces swam in her memory—Kimon and Kirigi and Kel— each wearing the expressions she remembered best.

Her heart felt like a lifeless stone in her chest.

"I don't know what's happening," she repeated. "I don't know what I'm doing."

Lycho kneeled down before her. He tilted his head and smiled when she met his gaze. "Follow your spirit, woman." His voice was a comforting whisper, and he placed a hand on the side of her knee. "It will tell you what to do when the time comes."

"You didn't see Soushane," she insisted. "I gathered the bodies. . . ."

"When the time comes," he said again, "you'll know what to do. You're Kel's mother. No son can forget the one who gave him life." He stood slowly, squeezed her hand, lifted her to her feet, and pointed to the bed. "Now rest. I'll bring you the water."

"I'm not really thirsty," she said, starting to unfasten her tunic.

"Drink anyway. It won't end your confusion, but when it eases your aches and pains, you may see things more clearly."

He left her alone; she listened to his footsteps recede down the corridor. He'd been kind, she reminded herself, so she resolved to drink his water and not offend him. Every town and village had its local superstitions. But priests without a god? She scratched her head at that.

By the time Lycho returned, she was naked between the sheets. He set a pitcher and cup on a small stand and poured for her. With a word of thanks she accepted and drained the cup, then handed it back. "You haven't asked my name," she said at last.

He tucked the topmost sheet close under her chin. "It wasn't important," he answered. "You came to do a good deed, to warn us about your son." He moved her sword within easier reach.

She bit her lip. "No, I just came to find him."

Lycho bent over the lamp, prepared to extinguish it. But he paused long enough to wink at her again. "But you warned us first. You see? It's just as I told you." He blew out the lamp and darkness filled the room. "When the time comes, you'll know what must be done."

She heard him move toward the door, though she could not see him. "It's Samidar," she whispered quietly, "though most people call me Frost."

She didn't know if he'd heard.

A lonely kind of fear stole over her as she lay there in the dark, listening for any tiny sound that might break the silence. But, little by little, the softness of the mattress and the cool of the sheets dulled her senses and swept her to the borderland of sleep. She turned onto her side and listened to the distant muffled thudding of her heart. A wetness damped the corners of her eyes, lingered on her lashes.

Her last thought set the tone for her dreams.

She felt so old.

Chapter Ten

When Dark Angels sing
The wings of Night enfold
The souls of men,
And melodies of wind
Whistle down in sharp arcs
To wake the land.
Crimson notes blow,
Spreading music in a flow,
And last songs are heard one time
Then never again.

Frost woke with only a vague memory of the strange songs that had filled the night's dreaming. Yet some of the lyrics stuck in her head, and she lay on her back for some time trying to decipher their meanings, piecing them together with other bits she remembered as if they were parts of a puzzle.

But if she could not remember the words, it was impossible to forget the singer. His face hovered in her memories, untouchable, beyond her embrace. "Kimon," she moaned softly, clutching the thin sheet to her breasts. His voice was a haunting echo, distantly heard, fading.

She sat up slowly and swung her feet over the edge of the bed. The sky beyond the room's only narrow window was still dark, nor was there anything to light the lamp. She

listened for some sound, anything to indicate if anyone else
stirred.

Nothing.

She wrapped the sheet around herself and stood. The floor
stones were cool against her bare feet. She padded noiselessly
to the door and out into the corridor. A thin beam of amber
light stole under a door farther down the hall, but she didn't
approach it. Instead, she turned the other way and emerged
into the temple's main chamber, where the priests had fed her
earlier. She passed the table, went outside into the night, and
leaned upon the well. A gentle wind blew down the empty
streets.

All Dakariar must be asleep, she thought, *but me.*

"Are you all right?"

She whirled, startled, then relaxed when she recognized
Lycho standing in the entrance. She leaned back on the well
and thought before giving an answer. Slowly, a wan smile
parted her lips. Her aches were gone; the soreness had left her
muscles; all the stiff spots from sleeping on the ground had
melted away.

"It's the power of the water," he told her. He came to her
side and began to haul the rope. She could hear the water at
the well's bottom and smell it as he drew it up. He produced
a small cup from a pocket in his robe. "Drink, Samidar," he
said quietly. "It has more work yet to do."

She looked at him strangely, wondering what he meant.
She didn't really believe in his well. She had needed sleep,
that was all.

"Your body's pain is soothed," Lycho continued, "but I
can feel the heaviness of your spirit. Drink of the well." He
pushed the cup into her hands and lifted them to her lips. "In
time, it will ease all your burdens."

She hesitated, then tossed the contents down with a quick
gulp. She was thirsty, after all. She gave him back the vessel
when it was empty. "I haven't got time," she said. "Kel
comes tonight."

Lycho was silent for a long while. He dipped his cup into
the bucket and sipped. "It is a wonderful night," he said,
gazing at the stars that twinkled overhead. "But not long
before dawn."

She looked at him, finding some measure of strength in his

tranquillity. His mouth shone with moisture, and his eyes were full of a soft glow. "You are kind," she told him.

He smiled. "You are lost," he answered, touching her bare shoulder lightly. "At least, you think you are. But you'll find yourself."

She turned away and her gaze wandered up and down the street, then up to the night sky. The moon was already down, it seemed. The breeze kissed her cheek. "I don't know, Lycho. There's so much I'm afraid of, so much I don't know." She took a few steps out into the lane and said wistfully, "Can you understand? I'm standing in shadows and staring at stars."

He folded his arms and sat back on the well's edge. "If you can see the stars at all, then they'll fill you with light."

Such guileless words, she thought. How could she help but grin? She realized suddenly just how little Lycho knew of the world. He had said he was not from Dakariar. From the next town, then, she guessed, or the next city over the hill, or maybe the next farm. She couldn't laugh at him, though. His innocence touched her.

"We both should have been poets," she said, "with our sweet words and clever phrases."

Lycho shook his head. "What do you mean?"

"Never mind." She went back to the well and sat beside him.

The night was silent, a world of grays and blacks, of shadows and deeper shadows. Yet the air was cool and refreshing. She was glad she had awakened so early. The water's smell so close was almost a perfume, and Lycho beside her smelled as clean and sweet. She studied him out of the corner of her eye. Their arms brushed, and she made a quiet decision.

"Would you make love to me?"

Lycho looked down at her slowly, and she could not read his expression. His hand covered hers, a soft caress. "I don't love you," he said honestly, "though in time I think I could."

Love didn't always matter. It was his warmth she needed. Her arms had been empty for too long, and for too long there had been no one to hold her. More than anything she wanted to touch him and to be touched, to forget everything but what they could share together for a short time.

But he kept his silence.

"I'll say please, Lycho," she offered. "I'm not above that."

There was the slightest tremor in his touch when he rose. He clung to her hand. "I'm the one who should say please," he answered. His fingers interlocked with hers. His flesh was warm as fire.

She took a deep breath, then led him back into the temple and to her room. She needed no light to find the bed and wanted none. She unwound the sheet from her body and draped it over the bottom of the bed, then watched as Lycho lifted the hem of his robe, pulled it over his head, and let it fall to the floor. He wore another garment of linen around his loins. He unwound that and dropped it by the robe.

She thought of Kimon, mildly surprised to find she could do so without any sense of guilt. This was no act of betrayal. She needed arms to hold her, and Kimon's arms were dust and death. Her love for her husband was not weakened, nor was her grief diminished.

But Lycho had arms of flesh and blood, and her flesh and blood cried out for his touch. It would not have been different for Kimon had he lived and she died. It wouldn't have been different for any man or woman.

"Samidar . . ."

She shook her head, touched a finger to her lips. No words were necessary. He came to her then, and she slid her arms around him. He did the same. She laid her head on his chest to hear the pounding of his heart, and a welcome contentment settled upon her. She hugged him close.

They did not need love to make love. The sun found them curled in each other's embrace, peacefully sleeping.

Later, when they had breakfasted, they walked through Dakariar. Pericant and Oric went with them. The town was subdued, the streets filled with a ghostly silence.

"They're afraid," Pericant said ominously. "They hide behind their shutters."

"Many left in the night," Oric informed them. "Nearly half the town was gone by midnight."

None of the shops were open. Not a single wagon rolled down the roads. To all appearances Dakariar was dead. An anvil lay abandoned in the gutter, and farther down the way a trunk with a broken lid spilled its contents in the dust. Those who had fled had wasted no time.

Frost went to the nearest door and pounded. No answer. She pounded again and called out. Nothing stirred or answered from within. She tried her weight against the door, then, and wasn't too surprised to find it barred on the inside.

She turned back to Lycho and frowned. "I guess the smart ones ran away. We're left with the mice."

He gave her a tolerant smile. "We're left with the women and the children and the old ones." Then his smile vanished, and he shrugged. "Maybe a few mice."

They walked the circuit of the town. Now and then, they caught a frightened gaze peering through the crack of an upper-level shutter. No one else braved the open streets. Even the gutter-grazing animals had disappeared.

"I don't understand," Pericant said. "These people know us. Why won't they answer when we call?"

Oric wrung his hands; a deep furrow creased his brow. "They think your son serves a demon. They've heard about the magic that follows him and the destruction he's brought to other towns." Thick tears rolled suddenly down his cheeks. "These are my neighbors and kinsmen," he said. "I don't want to see them die."

Frost gripped the hilt of her sword, but she had no reassurances for the priest. The memories of Soushane were still too much with her. If she was confused about her son's motives, she could not deny he was to blame for that carnage.

She gazed around at silent Dakariar and wondered if tomorrow it would also lie in black ashes. Her hand clenched tighter around the hilt. Not if she could do anything to prevent it.

But could she?

There was no hope of raising a force to combat Kel. Plainly, Dakariar was a town of farmers and merchants, not warriors. It would do no good to barricade the streets. The rebels' numbers were too overwhelming. And, she admitted, no barricade at Soushane could have withstood that mystic hand of fire.

"There was a young woman living here," she told the priests, "a daughter of Dromen Illstar. I don't know her name or residence."

Lycho, Pericant, and Oric exchanged glances and shook their heads. "No name?" Lycho frowned.

"It's no great matter," Frost continued. "Her father asked me to see about her. Probably she's left already. She had a husband to look after her." But as she spoke she peered at the shuttered windows and wondered if Dromen's offspring cowered behind one of them. Her former sergeant had dwelled in Keled-Zaram for eighteen years; his daughter was sixteen.

A pair of pigs rounded the corner ahead, snouts close to the ground, sniffing. They stopped at sight of the humans, glared with smallish eyes that gleamed in the sunlight, and ran back the way they had come.

"The first ones we've seen," Pericant observed. "Even the beasts sense trouble."

Frost rolled her eyes but kept her mouth shut. How could they not sense it? It was midday, and normally busy streets were completely empty.

They returned to the Temple of the Well without further conversation. Oric drew up a bucket of water, and each priest produced his own cup from the pocket of his robe. Lycho shared his with her. Magic or not, it tasted cool and washed the dust from her throat. She asked for another, received the cup, and drained it.

Jemane came out to meet them. "We have guests," he said quietly. "Two families. They believe the gods of the well will protect them if Kel na'Akian comes."

Frost looked at Lycho. She had reason to believe in gods more than most men, and she believed in their power. But she had learned never to rely on their willingness to help. It was possible these priests were on better terms with the divine. The expression Lycho wore, however, did not encourage.

"Where are they?" Lycho asked of Jemane.

"Cleomen is feeding them. They haven't been here long."

Oric sighed. "We must offer what comfort we can."

Pericant held the door open, but Frost touched Lycho's arm. "Shouldn't you think of leaving, too?" She kept her voice low so the others wouldn't hear. "No one in this town will fight against Kel. You priests should think of your own lives."

Lycho brushed her cheek tenderly, smiled with patience, and went inside.

She followed and caught his elbow again. A group of

twelve sat at the long table, and Cleoman poured water for them as they ate from heaped platters. Oric joined in the serving. Frost turned her back to them and forced herself to whisper, "I don't know if I can stop my son. He may not even listen to me! You run a terrible risk if you stay here."

The young priest laid a hand gently on her shoulder, but his gaze went past her to the families and his brother priests. "This is our temple," he answered solemnly. "We've pledged ourselves to caring for it and to caring for the people of Dakariar who come to the well. Before, you might have convinced us to go." He nodded to the refugees. "But now they've come. We can't turn them away."

"Take them with you!" she urged. "They're no safer here than in their homes."

Lycho shook his head. "Look at them, Samidar. That man and woman—'ancient' would be a kind word. And those two are mothers with suckling babes. The rest are children." His hand slid up to her chin and he made her look into his eyes. "How far could any of them run?"

She pulled his hand away from her face and squeezed it in a hard grip. "Go to the fields," she said. "Hide in the wheat. Go anywhere, but go as far as you can. I saw Soushane, Lycho. I'm telling you, nothing was left!"

Lycho was adamant. "We serve the gods of the well," he said simply, freeing himself from her grasp. "We are needed here." He left her and went to aid his brothers.

Frost threw up her hands in exasperation and finally returned to her room to await the coming of night—and the coming of Kel.

At Soushane he had come from the east under the mantle of deepening darkness. So, as the sun's last rays cooled on her shoulders, Frost tied back her hair and waited just beyond the town.

She spotted the torches first, a wave of flickering light. From the south a thick cloud of smoke roiled into the sky as the fields began to blaze.

The rebel force drew nearer until she could make out individual riders in the front ranks. Rows of skull faces grinned back at her. She drew her long blade and gripped it in both hands, then turned the point down and leaned on it. *Wait,* she told herself. *Be patient and see what will happen.*

The northern fields began to burn, too. The smoke rose into the sky like an offering. How, she wondered, had they gotten around her? Then the thought shivered through her mind, Was it a human hand that set those fires? Or was it sorcery?

The advancing rebels stopped, and she knew they had seen her. At the center of the line, barely close enough for her to see the gesture, a figure beckoned two men forward. She stared; the skull mask was not enough to disguise her son.

The two riders paced ahead of the ranks, then suddenly spurred their steeds straight for her. Their weapons caught the gleam of firelight and flashed redly. Through the earth she felt the thundering of their horses' hooves.

With a calm detachment, she realized it would have done no good for Lycho to hide in the fields. Perhaps she should have sought him out before she left the temple, but only Cleomen had been in the main hall with the families, and she had said nothing to him. Still, she found herself recalling Lycho's soft embraces. Indeed, they had not needed love to make love.

She lifted her sword in a two-handed grip and balanced herself to meet the riders. They charged side by side. The man on her right brandished a double-edged sword like her own, a fierce cry on his lips. The one on her left leveled a stout spear. She thanked her gods and her luck that he braced it under his left arm.

Their battle shouts might have filled the night, but all she heard was the beat of her heart and the rush of her blood. The spear was the principal threat with its longer reach. It was also her foe's weakness. As they rode down upon her, the rider with the spear would try to impale her. The other would try to cleave her in two.

She could almost feel the labored breathing of the mounts, the heat of their lathered, sweating hides. The skull faces bore down upon her. An arm flung back, and the spearhead gleamed, flew to claim her life.

With a smug grace she leaped to her left, and the point whistled through empty air. Simultaneously, she dropped to one knee and raked her blade over the horse's legs. The beast screamed and crashed headfirst into the ground. Its rider tumbled head over heels and hit the earth with stunning force.

The second rider's momentum carried him past his comrade. By the time he stopped and wheeled his horse to face

her, Frost had snatched up the spear. Their eyes met for just
an instant, then she hurled with all her might, sending the
shaft deep into his unarmored chest. The rebel fell sideways
from the saddle, snapping the spear in half with his own
weight, driving it even farther through his body.

She returned to the first rider and stood over him. His horse
was dead, its neck broken from the fall, but he was in better
shape. He struggled to catch a breath, to draw his sword
when he looked up at her, but she put a boot on his hand and
ground his knuckles into the dirt. A cry of pain and fear
ripped from his throat, and he cringed into a fetal position in
expectation of the death blow.

She hooked the point of her sword under the edge of his
skull mask and stripped it off. A thin stream of blood welled
along his cheek where the point had scraped his flesh. "You're
not dead yet, dung-ball," she said evenly, gazing down at his
dirty, youthful face. Odd how he reminded her at that moment of an adult Scafloc. "You're going to take a message
back to Kel na'Akian. Tell him he's a bad boy, and his
mother wants to talk to him."

The soldier paled and stuttered, "M-mother?"

"That's close enough," she assured him. "The exact word-
ing doesn't matter. You just tell him I'm here." She kicked
him until he scrambled to his feet.

"M-my horse . . ." he wheezed, rubbing his bruises, backing away from her cautiously.

"Take that one." She nodded to his comrade's mount. It
stood uncertainly near its dead rider. "Don't make me wait."

The nervous steed shied away as he limped toward it but
finally allowed him to climb stiffly into the saddle. He seemed
to find some of his courage when he loomed over her. But
she glowered at him and brought her heel sharply down upon
the skull mask. The brittle bone splintered with a loud *crack*.
The subtle threat was not lost on the rebel, and his courage
faded again. He jerked on his reins and started back toward
Kel's army.

The entire front line rode a few paces forward to meet him,
and Kel na'Akian held a short conference with his soldier.
Moments later, the man took his place in the ranks, and Kel
continued forward alone.

He sat his saddle proudly, the reins of his mount, a huge
black, grasped lightly in one hand. The other hand rested on

the pommel of his sword. His garments were of a shiny black cloth, and he wore a breastplate, greaves, and vambraces all of black lacquered leather. Even in the darkness he gleamed. The rising wind caught his black cloak, and it billowed behind him. A reflection of firelight told her it was lined with cloth-of-gold.

Shining and deadly, she thought bitterly, *like a rabid angel.*

He stopped before her, pushed back his hood, and removed the skull mask. A thin, amused smile lifted the corners of his mouth. He leaned forward and looked down upon her. "During my five years of wandering I picked up quite a few tales about you," he said with a touch of pride in his voice. He gazed at the corpse with the spear through its chest, at the horse with the broken neck. "But I never dreamed you were so good."

She stared up at her son, rested her sword's point on the ground, and leaned once more upon it. "You've shamed me, Kel." The wind rumpled his dark hair as the wide ebon pools of his eyes fastened on her. Green eyes, she remembered, but full of the shadowed night. "You've made me sorry I ever bore you."

He slid from the saddle and stood beside his horse. "I'm glad to see you, too."

They regarded each other for a short moment, then he came to her. Their arms went around each other, and she forgot all her anger and fear and confusion. They were mother and son locked in a warm, overdue embrace.

But the instant passed. The smell of smoke from the burning fields wafted over her, evoking memories of Soushane.

She stepped away from him. "Come with me, son," she pleaded suddenly. "Ride away with me, now. We can leave all this behind and start over in another land."

Kel's smile returned. He looked at her with a strange tolerance that sent a chill up her spine.

"We can start over," she repeated, desperation creeping into her voice. "We can forget about your sorcerer and forget about Soushane!"

His eyebrows went up. "Soushane?"

"I was there," she told him. "I fought. I saw what you did to the town. I only went to look for you, but I was forced to fight."

"I didn't see you," he admitted, "but how gratifying. Tell

me, Mother, did you see me use this?'' He pushed back the folds of his cloak to reveal the dagger on his belt.

She caught her breath at the sight of Demonfang. The dagger belonged to her. She knew its power better than anyone, and yes, she remembered how he had used it. Then she recalled *Sha-Nakare* and those demonic fireflies. She recalled the purse around her neck and its contents—and she recalled her suspicions. A vein in her temple began to throb; she clenched her empty fist.

"Your sorcerer obtained that for you," she hissed. "Only magic could have found where I buried it long ago." She fumbled for the thong about her neck and pulled the small purse from under her tunic. "Only your father and I knew where it was hidden." Her breaths came quicker and shorter as she tugged it open. She fixed her son with a hard stare as she rolled the severed finger into her palm and tried to keep a grip on her sword at the same time. She held her grisly prize for him to see. "You tell me, Kel, and tell me true. I know the ways of magic. I know what magicians do to power their spells." She paused, swallowed, half-afraid of the answer he might give her. What then would she do? This was her son! She trembled all over and raised the finger closer to his eyes. "Is this your father's?"

The smile faded from his lips. Otherwise, he didn't move, nor did he make any effort to lie. "Of course."

She stared at him, and her own eyes suddenly burned. She shook so violently that the finger rolled from her palm and fell into the dust at her feet.

A cry tore from her, a sound full of hurt and misery and rage. Her sword moved, powered by all the fury and strength she could summon. It cleaved an arc through the air, whined straight for Kel's unprotected neck.

It halted a scant handsbreadth from his flesh as if invisible demons had caught the blade. A peculiar numbness spread into her arm and upward to her shoulder. She tried to strike again, but her limb would not obey, nor could she uncurl her fingers from the hilt or even lower her arm. Swiftly the sensation flowed through her until her body was no longer her own to rule.

Kel's eyes glowed with an arcane inner fire that flashed around the black rims of his pupils.

"It's you!" she gasped, still capable of speech. A terrible

understanding flooded her. "You're the sorcerer. There is no Oroladian!"

He shook his head, and his eyes glittered, alive with power. "I am the sorcerer, Mother." He laughed. "But there is an *Oroladian*. Have you forgotten your own native tongue after so many years in foreign lands? It is a title. It means 'Triumphant over the Earth.' "

"You killed your father?" Rage made her strain uselessly against the spell that held her.

He shrugged. "I didn't plan it. I came to talk with you. I needed answers to questions only an Esgarian would understand. But you were gone. Father and I argued, and he said things I couldn't forgive."

She clenched her eyes shut; she had that much control of her body. "You murdered him!"

"And I took the fingers of his right hand," he affirmed coldly, "in strict accordance with the ancient texts. His spirit would serve me four times while I had them." His mouth twisted in a sick grin. "He was never so much use to me while he lived."

Frost cursed her helplessness. Her steel still hovered a mere hand's width from Kel's neck. So close to revenge! "He loved you, but you were too blind and selfish to see it," she shouted. "Kimon gave you everything!"

His eyes flashed, and an unseeable power seemed to squeeze the very air from her lungs. "He never loved me! Nor did you! You replaced me with that little piece of gutter-garbage and dared to call it son!"

"Kirigi was a brother to you!" she cried. "I couldn't give Kimon another child!"

"Shut up!" He held out his hand. For the first time she saw the glowing object he had concealed in his gloved palm. It was an amulet of some sort, the source of his magic. "Shut up!" he screamed again, and the numbness that gripped her spread into her throat until she could say nothing. "You've shown your love well enough." He ran one hand down the length of her bare steel and pulled the edge closer until it touched his flesh just below the jaw. "You came out of vengeance, Mother, to punish me. It was Kimon and Kirigi that drove you here just as surely as if their souls had laid whips to your back! Don't speak of how you loved me!" He squeezed the amulet in a tight fist, and sparks of scintillant

fire shot between his knuckles. "Because this time I've replaced *you*, Mother. What I could never get from you another
is more than willing to give."

He turned his back to her and waved an arm, leaving her to
wonder at his meaning. His soldiers rode forward at his
command, torches sputtering and leaping and staining the
darkness with a destructive light. He faced her again, his
features warped with a beatific malice.

"You've kept me from what I came for long enough. Stay
by my side, Mother. We'll claim the prize and destroy this
town together." He lifted his gaze to the sky; it had filled
with smoke from the burning fields. "Can you hear the gods
singing?" He barked a short laugh. "We'll make an offering
of Dakariar."

The amulet's power commanded her, and she took a place
by Kel's right hand. They waited for his army to catch up,
then walked side by side into the town. She could not even
turn her head to see if anyone peeked through the shuttered
windows. *Don't!* she begged him wordlessly. *Not another
town. Not Lycho and Pericant and Oric, not Jemane and
Cleomen. Not more lives on my conscience!* Whatever Kel
did, she was to blame. He was her son!

As they walked Kel began to mutter. The sound was
Esgarian, but only a few of the words were clear. With his
free hand he reached under his tunic and lifted a chain from
around his neck. A small golden fish dangled from it. As he
chanted, it began to spin faster and faster, though his fingers
remained absolutely still. At the first crossroads the fish
abruptly stopped.

Kel chose the way the fish pointed. As soon as they
moved, it began to spin again until another decision was
required.

Frost would have trembled were it not for the power that
controlled her. She knew the route, and more, she recognized
the motive that compelled the chain. What else would a fish
seek but water?

It led them straight to the Temple of the Well.

The five priests emerged from the doorway and stood
protectively around the source of their sacred water. Lycho
spoke first. "I see you've found your son," he said to Frost.

Kel deposited the fish and its chain down the front of his
garment. "My mother is at a loss for words, so joyful is she

at our reunion.'' He regarded the five with a cool, disdaining grace. Then he went to the well and drew a bucket of fresh drink. He dipped his hand, tasted, then spat.

The priests did not react. "Whatever you want from us is yours,'' Pericanț said. "Dakariar is a peaceful town. We'll not resist you."

"Oh, I promise you won't resist us," Kel answered with a smirk. He turned his back to the priests as he gave the bucket a push. The rope made a sharp hiss as it rushed through the pulley, and a soft splash rose from the depths.

Lycho's gaze sought hers. She hoped he could read the fear she felt or know some small part of her mind. But she could say or do nothing. By her silence, he might even believe she had joined her son against Dakariar!

She strained to reach the sword Kel had ordered her to sheathe. Her muscles would not obey; her son's magic was too strong. Still, she tried, and sweat beaded on her brow as proof of her effort.

"We have innocents within," Jemane cried suddenly, taking a step forward. "We beg you not to harm them!"

Frost saw the bloodless color of the old priest's cheeks. He quivered visibly, and he wrung his hands. Lycho put an arm about his shoulders and pulled him back to the well. They stood there, closed in that embrace, and waited to learn what Kel wanted of them, the younger man consoling and soothing the older.

But Kel demanded nothing. He waved a hand limply over his shoulder.

The air sang suddenly with the twang of bowstrings. She couldn't see the archers behind her, but a flurry of arrows smacked sickeningly into the five priests. The impact of four shafts carried Jemane backward over the well's rim. Oric and Cleomen barely had time to scream before they fell, clutching at multiple wounds. Pericant, perhaps swifter than the others, tried unsuccessfully to run. Three quick barbs brought him down on the temple's threshold.

Lycho sank to his knees and stared in horrible surprise at the seven shafts that sprouted from his chest and belly. He reached out, hands trembling and hesitant as if uncertain which shaft he might touch. He looked at her in his last moment, then, and her heart nearly broke. He tumbled for-

ward, splintering the wooden arrows with his weight. A dull
mist swiftly veiled his open eyes.

Metal points protruded redly from his back. The white
cloth of his robe slowly dyed with the spreading stain.

She could not scream. Her mouth would not open. But a
soft moaning vibrated in her throat, the only vent her grief
could find. Tears rushed from her eyes and trailed down her
face. In all other respects, she was Kel's puppet.

A cold wind whistled down the street. The sky clouded
over, blotting the sun.

Kel disappeared from her field of vision and returned a
moment later bearing objects from his saddlebags. He set
them on the ground beside Lycho's body. "Drag this away,"
he ordered his guards, giving the priest a kick. Two soldiers
seized the body by its heels and pulled him behind the well.

Frost cursed both their souls. Rage began to replace her
pain, and since it was all she could do, she observed her son
carefully.

The objects were a goblet of gold, a small emerald exposed
on a wrapping of clean black silk, and an intricately carved
dagger. Kel bent over them and muttered something she could
not hear. A guard handed him a canteen, and he filled the
goblet. Next, he picked up the jewel and rolled it between his
palms. This time she heard his intonations. The language was
Esgarian.

"Eye of Skraal," he chanted over the gem, invoking the
name of the goddess of wisdoms. There was more, but the
words changed to a tongue she didn't know.

He set the emerald back on the silk square and picked up
the dagger. He rubbed a smooth place in the dust with his
forearm, then began to write glyphs there with the dagger's
point. She recognized the symbols. They all made reference
to Skraal.

Why, she wondered, *does he invoke Esgarian gods in this
land? Why Skraal? Why not her god-husband, Lord Tak, who
is patron of witches and sorcerers?*

Kel rose carefully, stepped around his markings, and nodded to a couple of his men. "You know what I need," he
said. "Any one of them will do."

Two rebels picked up Cleomen's body, climbed on the
edge of the well, and held the old priest upside down. The
hem of his robe slid over his face, exposing the feeble flesh.

When Kel tugged out the arrows it slipped even farther down. Kel cut it away with the same dagger he had used to make his glyphs.

An athame, she realized. A ceremonial knife. She struggled again to free herself from the spell that held her, fearing what her son intended.

The dagger flashed down and up, biting deep into Cleomen's belly. Kel made a sharp ripping motion, opening the old man as if he were a pig to be butchered. Blood, warm and steaming, spilled out in a rush, spoiling Dakariar's sacred well.

Frost's rage hit a new peak, and a true scream escaped her lips. Kel jerked around in surprise. His hand dipped into a pocket of his left sleeve, and he extracted the amulet. It flared at his touch, and she felt her breath taken away. He came toward her, grinning.

A brilliant flash of lightning split the western sky, followed instantly by tremendous thunder. The clouds turned even darker.

Kel stopped in midstep, his attention drawn to the sky. His annoyance was plain, and he frowned. Another wind wailed down the street, destroying the patterns of his glyphs. He cursed savagely and hurried back to them, forgetting her.

But she smiled to herself, an inward smile full of hatred and loathing for her son. He had her, yes. But there was weakness in his magic. She had broken his spell for just an instant, long enough to cry out. And if she could break it once . . .

Kel hastily redrew the symbols the wind had ravaged, chanting as he worked. The two men on the well's edge were growing weary of holding Cleomen's weight, but he ignored their complaints. The old priest seemed nearly empty of blood; still, there was enough for Kel to catch on the blade of his athame. Those few precious drops he scattered among the glyphs.

"Dump the carcass and get away," he ordered the two. They tossed Cleomen callously aside and jumped clear.

A new note rose suddenly on the air, a sound that made Kel start and look around in consternation. A crash followed it, then another. Her son cursed and picked up the goblet, returning to his task.

Yet Frost knew that sound and what the crash indicated.

Still another crash echoed, and yet another. A high-pitched trumpeting called to her.

"Gods!" Kel cried angrily. "Is this damned town haunted?" He shouted orders to his men. "See what that noise is and put an end to it. A painful end."

From the corner of her vision she watched a handful of rebels rush up the street toward the stables. *Hurry,* she wished them. *Hurry to your own painful ends. Set him free before he kicks down the walls.*

Kel returned to his magic. He approached the edge of the well bearing the cup and the dagger. He raised both high and called in a loud voice. *"Skraal, ninima a Tak, sunima a Timut o Siakun, jamal o ansa Kel na'Akian."*

She knew the language, and she knew the invocation. But how could Kel? He was male, and no male was allowed the knowledge of these spells. A coldness gripped her heart. His magic was Esgarian. Only an Esgarian could have taught him. And that was against the Way!

The sky shattered. Jagged lightning streaked the night. Thunder nearly deafened her. A heavy rain began to pour, drenching her in an instant.

Ashur's cry rose again over the loud splintering of old boards.

Kel ignored it all as best he could. *"Skraal, jamal o ansa Kel na'Akian!"*

He turned the goblet upside down, and a white powder streamed into the well. He stepped back and waited expectantly.

A gusher of fire exploded from the depths of the well. It soared, crackling and hissing, high into the air, giving birth to mad shadows with its furious orange light. Heat blistered the front of the temple, and the eave of the roof began to glow.

"Damat, Shinimi Skraal, Damat!" Kel cried with glee. He approached the pillar of flame with a look of purest ecstasy on his face, his fists raised high, the dagger clutched in one hand. *"Damat, Shinimi Skraal!"*

A tumult of shouts and squeals drowned him out. His scouting party ran back down the street, colliding with the ranks of other rebels. Ashur charged right behind them, venting that terrible battle cry. The unicorn lowered his head and impaled the nearest man. With a mighty toss, he flung the body back over one shoulder. In the light of Kel's strange fire, Ashur's black horn gleamed wetly, incarnadined.

Frost could not move, but her heart leaped.

Lightning crackled wildly, fracturing the darkness.

Kel stared in utter confusion at the beast, the lightning, at his own magic. "Stop that animal!" he ordered his troops, recovering himself. "Don't let it close. Kill it!"

But panic swelled quickly among the soldiers. Frost couldn't move, yet the turmoil around her was easy to see. Kel's men tried to ring the unicorn. They jabbed at him with spears and swords. But those who ventured too close died beneath vengeful hooves, were bitten to the bone or pierced by that fatal spike. Ashur slammed into horses, knocking riders from the saddle to be trampled by their own comrades.

Still, they harried him, and the unicorn could not reach her side.

Kel turned his back to the turbulence. Once more he called on the goddess of wisdoms. Then, he thrust his hand deep into the blazing pillar. It did not burn him, and when he pulled his hand out again he held an immense, dazzling emerald. Nearly the size of a human hand, it cast reflections of the fire like stars upon the earth.

The pillar of flame subsided and died. The well's wall, scorched and weakened by the intense heat, collapsed inward, leaving nothing but a hole before the temple's charred entrance. Frost listened to the multiple splashes of the stones with a deep regret.

Kel rushed to her, holding his treasure. His black hair was plastered to his head and rainwater streamed from his lashes and nose and chin, lending him a hellish countenance. "The second of the Three Aspects," he told her proudly, "and this will lead me to the final Aspect." He beckoned to the guard who seemed always near his elbow. "Get my horse," he ordered, "and find one for my mother. Hurry!" He stared toward Ashur and his embattled warriors with just a hint of fear. "I've never seen such a horse. They don't seem to be hurting it much, and I haven't time to see to it myself."

His servant brought their steeds. The screams of men dying and the enraged cries of her unicorn overwhelmed his next words, but she felt herself compelled to mount beside her son. With the greatest effort she strained to turn her head, to catch the barest glimpse of Ashur. She caught him just in the corner of her eye. His hide shone thick with blood. But was it his? Or was it the blood of Kel's soldiers?

"Now ride!" Kel shouted, gripping his amulet, leaning close to her ear. "And you'll do nothing but what I tell you, Mother."

He put the reins in her unresisting hands. With another shout he forced his way through the confused ranks of his men, clearing a path for her. "Ride!" he called back.

Obediently, she nudged the horse's flanks with her bootheels. Because she couldn't turn her head, she didn't know how many of the rebels followed. But when Ashur tried to chase them her son gave orders.

"If it takes every one of your lives, keep that beast away!"

As they left the city behind, she glimpsed the fires that still raged in the fields. Smoke sailed high into the air, thick and black, growing thicker as the rain fell. Perhaps some of the crops would be spared.

Then she realized also that Kel had not taken time to burn the town. A sense of relief stole over her for that. Kel rode swiftly, pushing his horse to the utmost. She followed, watching as from time to time he cast glances back over his shoulder. *Almost in fear*, she thought. *Fear of Ashur?*

And what of the unicorn? There had been blood on his coat. . . .

She sighed, unable to do more.

Perhaps Lycho's spirit and those of the other priests would rest easier. She couldn't take much credit for it, but Dakariar, at least, had survived her son.

If only she could wipe the damnable rain from her eyes. . . .

Chapter Eleven

Frost stared sullenly from the high window of her prison. On the plain below, Ashur paced angrily, stamping the muddy earth. The flames of his eyes sizzled and flared, casting pools of rich amber light in the supernatural darkness. A half score of bodies lay scattered on the wet, cold ground, men who had tried to drive the unicorn away. Their screams still echoed in her ears.

A large piece of wind-driven fabric flapped across the plain, one of the many ruined tents the storm had flattened. She watched until it disappeared in the distant wood that surrounded Kel's tower.

The sky flashed again, momentarily blinding her. Her vision danced with afterimages. For three days since Dakariar, the lightning and thunder had raged. Not even Kel's sorceries had been able to halt the rain. They had ridden in sodden garments and slept—or tried to sleep—in high places that were not likely to flood.

She was sure some of the horses would die of sickness, and more than a few of the rebels were coughing and spitting.

She hugged a blanket around herself for warmth and leaned outward. Rain pelted her face and wind blew her hair into her eyes. The river Lythe cut a wide, silver-gray scar on the dark landscape. If she leaned just a little farther, she could gaze across it into Esgaria. She shivered to know her homeland was so close.

Below, Ashur let out a cry as if he had seen her. The unicorn pranced beneath her window, then charged the huge wooden gates. His hooves smashed uselessly at the iron-banded beams. A rain of arrows filled the air in response, and he wheeled about on his hind legs and raced away out of range.

Frost bit her lip sharply. A crackling bolt ignited the sky, revealing a shaft that jutted from Ashur's right flank. Perhaps it was not embedded too deeply, though, for the creature stamped and pranced as ferociously as ever, kicking up sprays of mud and water, venting his frustrated war cry.

A key grated in the lock at her door. She didn't need to glance over her shoulder to know it was Kel. The door opened. A ray of light poured in before the door closed again. The light remained to brighten the room.

"If you promise not to burn us down, I'll leave the lamp," her son said gently.

She said nothing, just continued to stare beyond the window. The rain upon her skin seemed the only piece of reality she could cling to.

"You wouldn't think of jumping, would you?"

Was that sarcasm in his voice or genuine concern? She couldn't tell anymore, and dimly she realized she didn't care. She didn't know this Kel at all.

"You're such a fool, son." She turned and leaned heavily on the cool stone wall, regarding him as she hugged the blanket closer around her nakedness. "You won't be rid of me that easily."

He went to the window and looked down. "What in the nine hells is that beast? It doesn't quit. It runs around out there as if it were waiting to kill us all!"

She smirked, recalling the bodies below. "I'd say he's made a pretty good start." Then she fixed her son with a mocking gaze. "What do you think he is? What do you see when you look at him, mighty sorcerer?"

Kel leaned outward, bracing his hands on either side of the window for support. "A horse, you stupid woman!" But he licked his lips. "Sometimes, though, I almost see more. As if there were another shadow laid over its shape." He shook his head and continued to stare.

"He frightens you, too," she said, voicing her suspicion. Kel didn't tremble or blanch or betray any outward sign, but she could taste the fear he exuded. "What do you really see, son? Do you see your death?"

He moved back to the center of the room. "Don't you wish it was," he scoffed.

"With all my heart," she answered, meeting his accusing gaze unflinchingly. "If it's true that you killed your father, yes, then I wish it. And because your cowardly action caused Kirigi's murder, yes, I wish it." She watched him pace the room. By the look on his face she knew that her words hurt him. She wanted them to hurt. "You're my firstborn child, and you've made me hate you. Can you feel my hate, Kel?"

He stopped in midstep. "You're a cold bitch," he said softly. "You chose your name well, Mother. *Frost*. There was never anything motherly about you. You're a creature of frost and fire."

She started. Years ago, someone else had spoken those same words to her. But her mother was long dead; strange to hear them again from her son's mouth.

A series of jagged bolts split open the darkness beyond her window. The thunder that followed shook the tower to its foundation. The wind abruptly changed direction and blew the rain into the room. A puddle quickly formed on the floor.

Kel moved to close the shutters. "Damned storm," he muttered.

"Leave them!" Frost ordered. She edged him aside and stood at the window, welcoming the storm's fury. Another cobalt flash silhouetted her in brief glory. The rising gale whipped the corners of her blanket, and the rain swiftly drenched her. She opened her wrap to feel the storm upon her bare skin.

"You'll die of sickness," Kel warned.

"We all die," she answered. "But some die with honor, some like beaten curs that just roll over in the ditch and give up." She made no effort to hide her scorn. "How will you die, mighty sorcerer?"

His bootheels rang on the floor stones as he came up behind her. She could feel the warmth of him, his breath on her neck as he spoke. "Did you ever wonder," he said bitterly, "in all those five years, where I had gone, what I was doing, if I was alive or dead?"

"Every day that passed I thought of you," she answered truthfully, folding the blanket about her body again. "So did your father. He hunted everywhere for you at first. Your leaving nearly killed him. Apparently, your homecoming did."

"He shoved me aside!" Kel shouted. "He brought home that brat!"

Frost moved away, unable to bear his nearness. "We've sung this song before, Kel," she said dully. "No more verses about your jealousies. Your father loved you." She rubbed her eyes with thumb and forefinger. "Gods, how can you stand there and confess you murdered him without tearing out your own tongue?"

"What is death to me?" he snapped, anger coloring his cheeks. His eyes seemed to glow, or was that a trick of the lamplight? "You say you wondered about me? Maybe you did. With Kirigi to keep you happy, though, I doubt it."

He wore a thin green robe with two large pockets. He extracted something from the left one, but his fist remained clenched tight. "You told me tales, Mother. Remember those wondrous stories of magical deeds, of gods and fantastic adventures?" He waited as if expecting her to nod. When she did nothing he went on, "Well, I found no adventure—at least, not at first—but I did find knowledge."

A cruel smile blossomed on his lips. "Watch, and see what I learned."

He held his fist out and shut his eyes to concentrate. A soft incantation issued from his throat, so low she couldn't hear the precise words. Pale wisps of smoke began to waft between his fingers, tenuous vapors that drifted a few paces away and began to congeal. At first, the form was a mere shadow. But the shadow thickened.

It stepped forward into the lamplight.

"Kimon!" She caught her breath. Then, she leaped to embrace her husband.

"Stop!" Kel's arms locked around her, lifting her off her feet, pulling her back. "If you touch him, he will return instantly to whatever hell he dwells in. Nothing will ever call him back." He set her down again. "No living human may touch a spirit."

Kimon regarded her. There was a chilling depth to those blue eyes, a fearful wisdom that had never been there when he lived. She found it difficult to look at any other part of him. Yet her arms reached out of their own will, powered by her longing, as if to embrace him from across the room.

Sadly, he answered with a shake of his head.

"Necromant!" Though she whispered, the word echoed around the room, both curse and accusation.

"I confess it," Kel said with quiet pride. "Necromancy. Death magic. I met an old man in Rhianoth; he taught me the rudiments. That was my sixteenth summer, and not long after I left home. In my seventeenth, he died." He looked at her and at the ghost of his father. "But I had his skills by then, and I knew how to seek out others to help me hone them. You see, I had a talent for this blackest of the black arts. Perhaps I inherited it from you, Mother. I know the stories about you were true—that once you were a witch."

She walked carefully to her husband's side and stood as close to him as she dared. Deep inside she cried to hold him, touch him, kiss him. Yet she dared not. "You're my beloved," she told him thickly. "Still and forever, my only beloved."

Kimon made no answer, and she could no longer read the messages in those piercing eyes.

"He can say nothing on his own," Kel explained, "but only answer one question when I ask it. One finger, one question."

"You hold your father's spirit prisoner." There was no disguising the grief and contempt that mingled in her voice. "And though you're my son, I'll hate you forever for it. Open your fist, I know what you hold."

His hand uncurled. On his palm rested one of Kimon's severed fingers. "I hate you," she whispered again. In her heart where once she had kept Kel's name, she imagined a gulf that grew ever wider. "I hate you forever and ever and ever." She stared from the mutilated digit to her husband's hand, noting with small satisfaction that he had regained two fingers.

"So this is your third question," she said to her son. "Ask it, then, and let him go."

Kel came to her side. "Four fingers, four questions. For the first, I asked if the stories of Demonfang were true. For the second—after you denied my request—I asked where the dagger was hidden." He laid a hand on her shoulder.

She moved away from him again. "Why? What made it so important?" She could not peel her eyes away from her husband. She feared that if she looked away for even an instant, he might be gone when she turned back. Then she would be once more alone with her monster son.

Kimon's eyes, too, followed her wherever she moved.

"I needed objects of power," he answered. "I am a sorcerer, not a witch or a wizard. I must have sources of magic to tap, words, runes, and talismans whose energy I can channel to my ends. Demonfang possesses incredible energies. I tell you, in the past few months I've collected many such things, but none so potent as your dagger."

"And for these objects you ransacked Keled-Zaram?"

He nodded. "One day soon I'll rule Keled-Zaram and its neighboring nations. I've gathered my treasures from many lands, but the Three Aspects were hidden only in this kingdom. I've searched everywhere to find them. Once they are in my possession, and with Oroladian's help"—he peered intently at her, and his eyes gleamed—"my power will extend far beyond necromancy into unexplored realms of true sorcery."

Frost hugged her blanket for warmth against a sudden chill. Kel resembled her so much, yet she wondered if there was truly anything of her in him. Her son was a stranger. It occurred to her that he might be right, that she had failed him in some way. Had she *ever* known him?

"Oroladian." She repeated the name again. "Who is he?"

"Not a *he*," her son answered grimly. "Oroladian is a great sorceress, and I will sit at her feet to learn many things. Already, she's taught me much. But to continue my lessons I must bring her the Three Aspects."

She advanced slowly on her son, finding a measure of satisfaction in the way he gave ground. "You've mentioned those before. What are they? Part of some spell?"

"It doesn't matter if you know," Kel answered haughtily. "Generations ago, the ancient priests of Chondos hid three objects in this land. They chose Keled-Zaram because of all the nations of the world this one bred the fewest magicians. Here, they thought the objects would be safe from discovery."

He folded his arms into his voluminous sleeves as he talked. "The objects were the Three Aspects of a spell capable of returning life to the dead. You've heard that a Chondite adept at the height of his power might wrestle with the death god and win new life?" He waited until she admitted she had. "Well, this particular spell was much easier. Anyone possessing the Three Aspects could work this magic. It was dangerous knowledge, for it set the different priestly brotherhoods at each other's throats. Finally, to prevent full-scale civil war in Chondos, one priest from each faction smuggled an Aspect into this land, concealed it, and took his own life so that the secret could never be torn from him.''

He paused, then began to pace about the room. ''The Aspects themselves are the stuff of legend: the Lamp of Nugaril, the Eye of Skraal, and the Book of Shakari.''

Frost had heard vague tales about the objects. That they were the components of a great conjuration, though, was news. Each was reputed to be a source of power in its own regard, and wizards and sorcerers for generations had tried and failed to find them.

''You've promised these things to some whore?''

Kel spun and raised a hand to deal her a savage blow. Barely, he controlled his temper. ''Mind your foul tongue!'' After a moment, he lowered the hand and forced a weak smile. ''I have two of the objects already. The lamp was hidden in a hollow stone that made the cornerstone of a house in Soushane. The eye was at the bottom of Dakariar's well. The resonations of any single Aspect can be traced by sorcerous means to the next. With two now in my possession, I can find the third, and I'll claim it in three days' time.''

She couldn't hide her interest. ''And then?''

His smile widened; he wagged a finger under her nose. ''Ah, Mother. There's so much more to tell, things that would chill even your cold soul.'' He feigned a pout and clasped his hands in front of his chest. ''But I've promised to keep some secrets, so content yourself with what I've told you.''

Frost wished she could hit him, and the wish spawned the act. She drew the back of her hand almost casually across his mouth. A spot of blood welled at the corner of his lips.

Kel glared. He touched the cut and looked at the blood she had drawn. His expression betrayed his hurt and anger, and that made her smile. He had spread so much pain and suffering through the land. It pleased her to know he could suffer, too.

Kel turned his back to her and addressed the ghost of his father. Kimon still waited patiently, silently, at the room's center. ''I have no question for you,'' he said bitterly. ''Return to the—''

Robin W. Bailey

"Wait!" Frost snapped, interrupting him. "You wouldn't want to waste one of your precious questions, would you? You've only got one left after this. Surely there is something you should ask your father?" She caught her son's arm and shook it encouragingly. "Here's your chance, Kel, if you've got the guts. He has to tell the truth. Go on, coward, ask him."

Her words were full of cruelty, taunting. She never dreamed she could hate as much as she hated at that instant. It didn't matter that Kel was her son. She wanted to hurt him and to twist that hurt until he bled inside.

"Ask him," she urged. "Ask your father if he loved you."

Kel stood frozen, staring at his father. "No," he said, his voice a choked whisper.

"Ask him!" Her rage finally found vent. She smashed her fists against his chest, nearly toppling him. He caught her hands and pushed her away and retreated to the far corner. She shouted at him. "Now's your chance! Learn the truth and see what madness your jealousies have wrought. He loved you! Ask him!"

"No, damn you!" he cried angrily. He waved a hand wildly at his father. "Spirit, back to hell. Leave!"

But before Kimon was gone, Frost leaped and flung her arms around her husband's neck. She pressed her lips to his in a desperate kiss.

"Stop!" Kel ordered uselessly.

Joy leaped in her heart, but the blood seemed to freeze in her veins and the breath turned brittle in her lungs as she sealed the embrace. Then, the sensation passed. Her arms held nothing but empty air; Kimon was gone.

She ached with the burden of her grief, but she also knew a spiteful gladness.

Kel glowered at her.

"He's beyond your power, now," she said, rejoicing. "No matter how many parts of him you have, you can never call him back. I've set him free."

Kel's countenance was purest malice. He strode to her, seized her hand, and forced it open. Then he laid Kimon's severed finger on her palm and wrapped her fist around it. "I don't need him any longer," he hissed, squeezing her fist until she thought her joints would pop. "And I don't need you! Blood has blood, and I have someone to care for me as you never cared. Stay here, you cold bitch, sealed in this tower. Let your damned steed pound at the gate. There's another way out, and the Third Aspect lies waiting for me to claim it.''

He pushed her aside and went to the door. "When my true blood wears the mantle of true life, perhaps then I'll come back for you—if I think of you at all.''

Kel slammed the door behind him, and the key grated in the lock. She tried it, nevertheless, and beat her fists on the wooden planks when it refused to open. At last, though, she gave up and went back to the window. The wind and rain were strangely soothing. She squeezed Kimon's finger in her palm, pressed it to her heart, then set it lovingly on the damp sill.

"Look to the storm.''

Frost whirled. Kimon's ghost stood once more in the dim circle of lamplight. She moved toward him impulsively, but he held up a hand to stay her. His right hand. He had all his fingers again.

She cast a surprised glance back to the windowsill. The severed digit still lay there, but even as she watched, a wind swirled strangely into the room. The finger rolled about and teetered precariously near the edge. Then, against all logic, the wind swept *out* of the room, sucking the precious limb into the night.

Frost clamped a hand to her mouth, choking back a small cry.

"Find your soul in the storm, my wife,'' Kimon said, his voice soft as a lover's touch. "You are the thunder and the lightning.'' He pointed beyond the window; another sizzling bolt seemed to emphasize his words. He lowered his hand, and for a moment his eyes became the same gentle blue eyes she had loved before.

"You are my beloved, still and forever.'' His words echoed in the small room as though a vast gulf separated them and he spoke from a great distance. "Forever and ever,'' he repeated.

Not all her anger and hatred for Kel could hold back her grief. She sank to her knees and wept, aching to hold him in her arms, unable to tear her gaze away as he faded slowly.

When Kimon was no more than a pale shadow, she heard

his voice again. "Farewell, Samidar, Samidar, Samidar. . . .
I loved my son. . . ."

Outside, the wind wailed a high, lonesome note.

She sat there on the floor and waited for the tears to end as
she knew they would. She had cried enough to learn that. The
blanket had slipped from her shoulders; the cool air raised
gooseflesh on her arms, yet she made no effort to warm
herself or to rise. All she knew was a deep weariness of body
and spirit flavored with a deeper sense of loss.

But slowly something stirred within her. Kimon's words
played over and over in her head. He had returned one final
time to bring a message. What was it? She climbed to her
feet, trudged to the window.

The lightning made a brilliant lacework against the ebon
clouds. Thunder crackled and boomed.

You are the thunder and the lightning, Kimon had said.
What did it mean? She leaned on the sill, stared into the
tempest. The rain beat on her face. Bolt after searing bolt
dazzled her vision. Every rumble of thunder spoke with Kimon's
voice: *Look to the storm, find your soul in the storm.*

She stood there until her legs began to cramp and water ran
from the tip of her nose and from the thick ropes of her hair.

Then, far below, Ashur came racing out of the woods and
over the dark plain. She hadn't even noticed his absence.
Where had he gone?

With a wild cry the unicorn attacked the tower gate again.
She held her breath, but this time there was no answering hail
of arrows. He pounded the stout beams with his hooves, but
the iron-banded gates held.

The sound of Ashur's fury rose over the storm. The unicorn pranced, snorting and stamping uselessly as if daring
archers to draw mark upon him. He bellowed, but no answering response of any kind came from the tower.

He saw her then as she leaned out the window, and he
stopped. Absolutely still, he turned those unearthly eyes up to
her. Suddenly he reared, sped back to the middle of the field,
turned, and gazed expectantly at her again.

The heavens exploded with renewed violence. A radiant
bolt speared downward and struck the gate.

Frost shielded her eyes with a corner of the blanket. The
thunderclap nearly hurled her to the floor, and the very air

strove to crush her. Her hand found purchase on the sill as the tower shivered. An acrid smell filled the night.

Ashur ran back and forth, shaking his sodden mane in a maddened frenzy.

But the gate still held.

Impossibly, a second bolt shot from the sky. The tower rocked under its impact. Ashur reared and screamed. The flames that served him for eyes flared with an intensity that reflected the entire length of the great spike on his brow.

Frost pressed a hand to her mouth; her teeth bit the soft flesh of her palm. Kimon's words roared in her mind, loud as the storm itself. *You are the thunder and lightning,* he said.

It couldn't be true, yet it was. It must be!

So much became clear to her in an instant. At the Broken Sword her cards had foretold Telric's coming. At Soushane the steppe wind had come unnaturally to fan the pyre. Now, this storm had come. Was it an unconscious manifestation? She recalled the other storms, so many of late, each when she was upset or angry. . . .

She leaned as far out the window as she dared. The gate was immediately below. She couldn't see the actual entrance for a parapet and, below that, an overhang of jutting stone blocks. Her gaze wandered skyward uncertainly. She drew a deep breath.

Yes, she could feel it now, the storm raging through her. It was a tingling, a slowly building symphony barely heard at the core of her soul, growing louder with each beat of her heart.

She reached beyond the window out into the storm and made a clawing motion with her hand.

A violet shaft lanced downward, shattered the overhanging stones and blasted a gaping hole in the parapet. An awful odor swirled up in thick, vaporous clouds. Bits of wood and stone exploded outward.

Though scorched and blackened, the gates still sealed her in. Again she reached out and pulled lightning from the sky. For an instant the darkness was transformed to painful white. The tower lurched fearsomely under the force of the blast.

A black crater yawned where the gates had been, and the surrounding earth burned and smoked.

Ashur bellowed triumphantly and raced for the opening.

Her witch-powers were back. Frost sagged against the wall

and squeezed her eyes shut. After so many long years how could that be? She could feel the energy swelling like a potent song in her soul, straining for release. She turned back to the window, stared into the storm with an awful trepidation. Then, just to prove she could do it, she sent another bolt hurtling earthward.

"Witch!"

She repeated the word over and over, shaking her head in denial. Years ago her own mother had stolen her powers, and truly Frost had never missed them, had almost been grateful when they were gone. Now, by some trick of the gods they had returned. She was a witch again. More, she had been for some time without knowing.

Ashur's cry echoed up from the bowels of the tower, shaking her out of her reverie. He was down there alone against all of Kel's soldiers! She ran to the door, forgetting it was locked.

She backed up a few paces. The tiniest portion of her power surged forth, and the lock clicked. The door eased inward.

She glanced at the wet pile of her clothes near the door. There was no time to dress if Ashur was in danger. Her bare feet slapped on the floor stones as she ran along the narrow hall to the tower's only stair.

Halfway down she met a guard. His face was pale, his breathing labored as he ran up the steps. He stank of terror. Yet he dared to reach for the sword he wore. Clumsily, he drew and lunged at her.

The song at her soul's core crescendoed in response. She lifted her finger. A spark leaped from her to the tip of the soldier's weapon. The guard gave a short scream as blue fire raced up his blade and touched his hand. His hair stood on end, eyes and mouth snapped horribly wide. He collapsed then and tumbled back down the rough stairs, his sword clattering beside him.

She didn't know what she had done to him. Was he dead or just unconscious? She had only wanted him out of her way. The music had done the rest.

But she had no more time to waste. She hurried down, leaping over the body where it had come to a crumpled stop. There was no sound from below, and she feared for her unicorn. Halfway down the winding stair she began to run.

Kel's tower was a simple, ancient structure. Its many levels were all serviced by the single stair. The topmost level was her son's private quarters and study. Other levels housed his officers and their aides. Another level was the kitchen and dining hall. There were storage levels and levels whose rooms were empty. The very ground level was a huge open space. During attack or storms, men and horses were sheltered inside.

By the smell of dung she knew she had nearly reached there. Still there was no sound. Was it over? Had Kel killed her beautiful creature? She took the final steps three at a time.

Ashur greeted her with a nicker. Her heart nearly cracked when she saw him. His hide was slick with blood from what looked like sword cuts. There was a deep wound in his right shoulder that looked several days old. An ugly, oozing scab had tried to crust over it. An arrow jutted from his flank. Cursing the archer, she seized the shaft and jerked it free. The point had not embedded deeply, but fresh blood poured.

Despite his injuries, the fire had not dimmed in Ashur's eyes, nor apparently from his heart. She spied two more guards on the earthen floor. A huge hole gaped in the chest of one; the other's skull had been crushed by the unicorn's hooves.

She threw her arms about his neck. "I'll take care of you," she whispered soothingly. "I'll get you clean, and you'll be well again."

Moments passed, and she realized they were alone. Kel had gone, and all his men with him. A huge trapdoor in the rearmost area of the floor revealed a long, sloping tunnel large enough for mounted men to ride single file. No doubt it emerged far into the woods.

She had seen such a design once before in Rhianoth. A lord trapped in his castle and under seige sent half his men through a similar tunnel. His warriors also emerged in a wood, returned, and attacked the enemy from the rear. It had been a marvelous victory.

She rumpled Ashur's forelock and stroked his nose. "Did you think they'd taken me along? Is that where you ran off to?" Of course, he couldn't answer, but he must have followed the rebels until he'd realized she wasn't with them.

Kel must have left right after their argument. She almost pitied his men; they'd had no chance to rest. But then she remembered Soushane and Dakariar, and her pity faded.

This was an excellent chance to look for some clue to Kel's plans. He'd told her part of a fantastic tale, but he'd left other parts dangling. She wanted to know more of Oroladian and the Three Aspects, and she wanted to know where Kel had gone.

She returned to the stair. It descended to deeper levels below the earth. She would explore those, too, but first she wanted a look at Kel's private rooms. She'd grab her clothes on the way.

"I'll be back," she told the unicorn, patting his cheek. "If anyone comes, you get away. You're hurt already. Understand?" She almost expected him to nod. Of course he didn't. He just regarded her quietly, and the flames of his eyes made a soft flicker.

She took the stairs two at a time. The guard still lay unmoving, awkwardly bent. She paused long enough to examine him. His breathing was shallow, irregular, but he lived. If bones were broken, she couldn't detect them.

She scratched her chin and stepped over him. She didn't even know what she had done to him. The magic had simply sprung from her and taken its course without any conscious effort. But he showed no sign of getting up soon, so she put him out of her mind.

Her garments were still soaking wet as she retrieved them from her room. They had arrived at the tower only a few short hours before her argument with Kel, and there had been no time for them to dry.

His men had been bone weary after the grueling, storm-driven ride from Dakariar, and Ashur had harried them all the way. Yet Kel had dragged them out again already, heedless of the rain and wind. She took that as a measure of how she had hurt and shamed him. Somehow, she found little joy in that now.

Perhaps it was, instead, a measure of madness.

She wrung as much water as she could from her garments and pulled them on. They were cold and clammy. She had to stamp into her boots. Her weapons had been taken from her; she had no idea where to find them. She rubbed her left hip where her sword should be. Without it, she still felt naked.

She went back to the stair and climbed to the next and highest level. One by one she opened the doors, finding rooms much like the one she'd been locked in, airy and sparsely furnished.

But one room was very different. Even as she reached for the hand ring, the lingering sensation of occult power prickled on the edge of her awareness. Carefully, she stepped inside. Even without the glyphs and symbols that decorated the walls and ceiling, she would have known it was here that Kel practiced his sorceries. She studied the markings as best she could in the faint lamplight that spilled in from the corridor. They were Esgarian, and she recognized some of them. She repressed a shudder, crossed to the window, and gazed out. The room had a western view. It looked directly across the Lythe River into her homeland.

She could no longer hold back the shudder, nor fool herself that it was the chill wind that caused it. Years ago in that land she had dared to touch the weapons of a man, to learn the use of sword and shield. It was the greatest crime for an Esgarian female. Worse, she had been forced to kill her brother when he'd discovered her at practice. The penalty for either crime was death. Instead, she'd run, choosing life and exile.

Weapons had been a game to her, little drills and dances to perform in the dark haunts of her family's manor. But fate or the gods had intervened, and the game had suddenly become a way of life. She had wandered homeless from land to land with only her sword between her and an early grave.

Then, she had met Kimon. He, too, had lived by his sword as an assassin, the hireling of a Rholarothan lord. He had loved her instantly, and with time she'd found she could not help but return that love. Together, they had put away their swords and sought a better way.

That was so many years ago. She had been what, nineteen? twenty?

But fortune's wheel had turned. Kimon was gone, and the sword was her way once more.

And across the Lythe another Esgarian woman had dared to break the law. Only women could study magic in that land, as only men could wear weapons. One taboo was as strong as the other. Yet that woman had taught her son.

The damp clothing chafed her flesh. Frost considered for a moment; then, with a small exertion of her own magic, she dried them. It was so easy. Why did it send a shiver up her spine?

She forced the question out of her thoughts and continued her exploration. In one wall was a connecting door to the next room. She found it double-locked, but it opened for her as effortlessly as all the others had. The power surged within her, eager to serve her needs. It had been dormant so long; now it seemed she could barely contain it.

She stepped across the threshold. Instantly she jumped back, letting go a short scream of surprise. Was it some ward or guardian spell that set her skin to tingling? She reached out delicately with her own psychic senses. No, it was not a spell.

She returned to the corridor and took one of the lamps from its wall sconce. With light to guide her, she stepped over the threshold again. A terrible sensation gripped her, but she gathered her courage, refusing to be forced out. There were more lamps mounted on this chamber's walls. She went to each of them in turn, igniting the wicks. Behind each lamp hung a mirror of burnished copper. The room was quickly aglow.

Still, the vibrations were nearly overwhelming.

A case of books stood against the nearest wall. A portion of the disturbance emanated from those volumes. She scanned the titles, slipping each one carefully from its shelf and replacing it. They were grimoires and books of power. Some were written in Kel's familiar hand. Had he copied them from older works, she wondered, or had he authored them himself? They were not dusty; to judge from the worn pages, he used them often.

A table and a modest chair occupied the center of the room. She approached it, ran her hand lightly over the smooth wood. A bowl of clear water had been placed there. She leaned over and gazed into it, seeing her reflection.

But the face was not quite hers. It was younger somehow, familiar, but different. She blinked, startled. When she looked again it was her own troubled expression. She bit her lip. Had it been an illusion? She doubted that. Kel's magic was real, not fakery. Then what had she seen in the bowl?

She peered into it again expectantly, but nothing happened. Yet she knew she hadn't imagined it. She stirred the water with her fingers. It was only water, nothing more, and finally she turned away.

There was a cabinet against the opposite wall. It was from

there the strongest sensations came. She approached it, cringing with every step, yet forcing herself closer.

The cabinet doors opened invitingly.

Frost stopped. Her witch-powers had not done that. There had to be some magic in the cabinet itself. Unconsciously, she reached for a sword she didn't have.

The lamplight illumined the cabinet's recesses. She made herself creep closer, fighting the vibrations that beat at her like a wave. She looked inside.

There was the chalice and the athame Kel had used to conjure the Eye of Skraal at Dakariar. Each resonated with potent, evil influences. There was a blood-red crystal she had never seen. Some subtle power compelled her to reach out and touch it. At the last instant she jerked her hand away, warned by her own witchcraft. Two amulets lay on golden chains beside it, carved with figures she didn't recognize. Like the chalice and the dagger, they reeked of foulness.

She examined each of the cabinet's five shelves, touching nothing. There were many other objects, all infused with varieties of occult energies.

These were the treasures, then, that Kel had collected or stolen in his wanderings. Some were the tools of the necromant: the silver spade, a severed hand whose flesh had not decayed, a vial of powdered skin. But there were other things common to sorcery. The shelves were heavy with jewels, small idols of nameless gods, rings, strange talismans. She bent closer, hoping against hope that Demonfang was also there, but the cabinet did not contain her blade.

She backed away, and the cabinet doors closed without even a squeak of hinges. Never had she seen such a collection. She shivered again. Sweat had beaded on her brow; she wiped it with her sleeve. How had Kel amassed so much in five years' time? she wondered. What price must he have paid to obtain them?

She feared she knew the answer.

Taking her lamp, she went back out into the corridor. The only other room proved to be Kel's sleeping quarters. She took her time searching his trunks, rummaging through his desk, rifling his closets.

When there was nothing more to interest her on the top level, she searched the others. But she paid them only cursory attention. Her mind wrestled with greater problems. Kel had told her much about the Three Aspects, but not all. He intended them as gifts for the sorceress Oroladian. He had obtained the Lamp of Nugaril from a cornerstone in Soushane and the Eye of Skraal from the well in Dakariar.

She weighed that. Gemstones were thought to have special powers sometimes. According to legend, emeralds in particular possessed certain healing properties. Could the eye have been the source of the magic Lycho had attributed to his water?

No matter, that wasn't part of the larger puzzle.

Kel had two of the Aspects. He had gone to obtain the third. The Book of Shakari, he'd called it, and it was hidden three days away. But where? Knowing the time it would take, she could guess the distance, but in what direction had he ridden?

She worked her way back to the ground level. Ashur stood watch at the ruined gate. He snorted and twitched his ears at sight of her.

"Not yet," she answered. "I want to get out of here, too, but we're not finished."

There were the dark sublevels to explore. Her lamp, though, was nearly empty of oil. There were torches in sconces near the gate. She took one and extinguished the lamp. Holding her new light high, she descended.

The first sublevel was an armory. Steel glittered in the orange lambency of her torch. Racks of pikes, spears, and swords; row upon row of shields hung on the walls. Pieces of armor lay scattered about. There were greaves, vambraces, and breastguards, all of the finest lacquered leather, a few sewn with metal ringlets for extra protection. Frost thanked her gods and went straight to the rack of swords. She searched until she found one that suited her, a fine length of double-edged steel in a quality sheath and weapon belt. Its hilt was wrapped in rough leather as her old one had been. All it lacked was the time-worn print of her hand.

She would miss her old blade. It had served her well for years and through many adventures. But there was a delicious irony in the fact that Kel had provided her with a better one.

There were more rooms on that same level: a surgery, stores for grain and kegs of beer, a tack room. She hesitated there. A saddle and bridle for Ashur would make riding more comfortable. But what of his wounds? At last, she chose the

lightest equipment and carried it back to the stair. She was
still uncertain about using it but could decide later.

She went down to the next level. It was the last. She
allowed a thin, tight smile. The superstitious part of her had
almost expected nine—like the levels of hell.

The final step disappeared under water. The corridor was
narrow, dank, and flooded with seepage. The water rose over
her ankles as she sloshed her way through the dark confine.
The first door she found was locked with a heavy iron bolt.
She noted the small, barred grill at eye height and realized at
once where she was.

This lowest level was Kel's dungeon. Perhaps her analogy
to hell had not been so far off the mark.

She put her face to the next door's bars and peered inside,
but her head blocked the torch's light, and she could see
nothing.

"Is anyone down here?" she called softly.

The lapping of the water against the walls was the only
sound. Her torch sputtered dangerously, and she discovered
she had lifted it too close to the low stone ceiling. Scorch
marks streaked the rough-hewn blocks where the flames had
touched. She bit her lip, suddenly aware of the immense
weight above her head and of the age of the tower's stone and
mortar. She turned to go.

A low, cautious voice crawled out of the blackness beyond
her torchlight. "Hello?" it whispered. "Who's there?"

Reflexively, she went for her sword. Even though her
witch-powers had somehow awakened, she found reassurance
in curling her hand around its hilt. She stared uselessly ahead
into the stygian tunnel. Crouching, she moved forward, trying
not to splash too noisily. *That's stupid,* she told herself. *If it's
an enemy, he won't listen to the sound—he'll see the torch.*
Still, she proceeded as quietly as possible.

"Are you there?" the voice called again. "Hello?"

Frost stopped. There was a quality to the voice that she
almost recognized. Her pace quickened. She passed a third
door and a fourth, pausing at each, peering inside. They were
empty.

"Where are you?" she shouted back. The echo reverberated in the dank passage, and she waited for it to fade. "Are
you a prisoner?" The very stones hurled the question back.

"Down here," the voice answered. "The last cell. Who are you?"

She didn't answer. How could she tell him his captor was her son? She hurried on, found the last door, and pressed her face to the grill. Another face appeared there suddenly, and noses bumped. She leaped back in surprise.

The prisoner recoiled from the light, then turned back and squinted through the bars. He whooped with weak delight. "Gods of Rholaroth, woman, I thought you were dead!"

Her mouth fell open, then snapped shut. The dirty, stubbled face with the wild hair and blood-reddened eyes was barely recognizable. "Telric!"

"I didn't know your voice for that damned echo," he said through clenched teeth. "Get me out of here."

There were pegs on the wall, but no key ring. It didn't matter. "Just push it open," she told him.

"It's locked, damn it! Find the key. It must be around somewhere."

She grabbed one of the bars, freeing a small part of the strange song in her soul. "It's not locked. See?" She pulled and the door swung open. "Come on out."

He gaped in confusion that swiftly turned to consternation. "How'd you do that?"

She chewed the tip of her finger. "I'm afraid you'll find out soon enough." She changed the subject. "You look awful. What are you doing here?"

His clothes were filthy, and he smelled. Yet he took her in his arms, hugged her and rested his head next to hers. She could feel the need in him. She wanted to yield, to soothe his fear. Instead, she stiffened at his touch.

He seemed not to notice. "I thought you were dead," he repeated. "I saw you fall. I think I took the flat of a blade on the head myself right after that. I woke up in the mud just as your son and his mercenaries were leaving."

"Kel took you prisoner?"

"The place was an inferno. I managed to grab a riderless horse and followed him." He hung his head sheepishly. "I had some idea about avenging you, but he must have spotted me. A couple of his men hid in the tall grass and jumped me as I rode between them. They brought me here, and I haven't seen anyone since." He wiped his mouth with a grimy sleeve. "They haven't even sent food or water."

His voice was hoarse and raspy. That was why she hadn't known him when he'd called out.

"I drank some of the seepage, just enough to wet my lips. But it tasted of lime and mud. I was afraid to swallow much. I don't know why they bothered to bring me here when they could have killed me quicker."

She eased out of his embrace. "Let's get you some food, then, and get out of here. There are plenty of supplies, and everyone's gone."

"I'm glad you're alive," he said, trying to embrace her again.

She put a hand on his chest to stop him. "I'm glad you're alive, too," she said honestly. "But we've got to hurry. I know part of what Kel is up to. I've got to learn the rest." She frowned; then an idea occurred to her. "In fact, I've got to go back up. I saw a map in Kel's study. It could be useful."

She made her way up the stair, and Telric followed.

"What happened to him?" Telric asked, stepping over the unconscious guard who had suffered her magic.

"Bad luck," she answered tersely. She pointed when they reached the kitchen level. "Find something for both of us. I'm going on up."

She left him and went straight to her son's quarters. The map was where she had remembered—a small side drawer in one of his trunks. It had been drawn on a folded square of tanned leather. It appeared surprisingly complete and accurate, and she wondered briefly at the hand that had made it. She stuck it down the front of her tunic and left the room.

One level below, she paused on the steps and stared the length of the corridor toward the room that had been her cell. Without knowing why, she returned there. A puddle had formed on the floor beneath the window where the rain had blown in, but the storm's fury had abated. She went to the sill and looked out.

A sickly, gray-green pallor hung over the world. The wind had died. An unnatural silence reigned. *No*, she reminded herself. *It was a natural silence, completely natural.* The song in her soul was muted now.

"Let me help."

She spun and almost fell backward. "Kim—!"

But it wasn't Kimon, only Telric standing in the same

place, bathed in the same amber lamplight. Gods, how it hurt to look at him! So much like her husband. She bit her lip hard.

Could it be? They were both from Rholaroth. Kimon had even worked for Telric's father. A bastard son? Were Telric and Kimon brothers?

Her hands curled into fists, and she cursed herself. *No, you foolish woman, no!* Her husband was dead and, at last, put to rest. It was no good looking for him in another man. A mere trick of light and positioning had caused her to see Kimon in Telric. That, and her own grief. But it was an illusion, no more. Only an illusion.

"I said, let me help," he repeated. "I don't know what you're planning, but you've got a peculiar look. Whatever it is, count me in."

His offer sent another pang through her heart. Kimon once had told her about three words that meant even more than "I love you" because they were words of action instead of declaration. Those words, he had said, were "let me help."

She smiled, tight-lipped, forcing herself to look at Telric, to see once and for all that he was not Kimon. At last, she grew somewhat calmer.

"Thanks for your offer, but this time I need more. I need an army." She took his arm and pulled him into the hall, pausing long enough to shut the door behind her. "There's only one place to get it," she added.

Chapter Twelve

Who are you, Gentle Stranger,
A wizard or a clown?
You caught me in your magic
When I thought I'd fallen down.
Do you know your own beauty,
Like a spark of the evening star?
In the shadow of your passion
Can it matter who you are?

Together they walked away from the tower. The mud squished over the toes of their boots as they passed among the storm-flattened tents where the main body of Kel's soldiers had resided. She almost smiled at the way canvasses were strewn over the landscape.

She shifted the weight of the saddle she carried and glanced at Ashur as he plodded beside her. She would have to ride him soon. It was the only way to reach Kyr in time. But there was another thing to do before she had to slap leather on his poor back.

"I can carry that for you," Telric offered.

She shook her head. "You've got enough with that sack of supplies." She gave him a look from the corner of her eye. He, too, had armed himself from Kel's store of weapons. With some food in him he looked stronger. If only he'd had time for a bath. She looked away again and tried not to inhale too deeply.

The land had been cleared to form a wide, circular plain around the tower. She knew they must be near the edge of the Keled steppes, though the terrain was still relatively flat, but the hills of *Shai-Zastari* could be no more than another day's ride to the north. She shuddered, recalling *Sha-Nakare* and the terrible fireflies. Had she followed the Lythe River south instead of to Kyr after that night, she might have stumbled upon her son's demesne.

When they reached the first struggling shrubs and saplings of the surrounding forest, Frost stopped and set aside her burden. "Wait for me," she told Telric, and he set down his sack and gave her a quizzical look. She turned and stared back across the immense clearing. The tower rose like a black and menacing column that held up the bleak gray sky.

"It's clear to me now," she said at last. "I was confused, but now I see. It's like I've awakened from a long, troubling dream." She rubbed her hand along Ashur's sleek neck and tangled her fingers in his mane.

She filled her lungs with a deep breath and drew herself erect. "I've accomplished things. Kimon's spirit is free to find rest." She forced a tiny smile. "And I've avenged you, Telric, though perhaps it doesn't count since you weren't dead."

Telric interrupted with a surprised grin. "You came to avenge me?"

She shrugged. "You'd have done the same for me."

He scratched at the stubble on his chin. "I did try," he reminded her.

Their eyes met, and she saw the depth of his feeling for her. He had said he loved her. She didn't need her witchcraft to know it was true. Perhaps all her confusion had not ended. Kimon was dead, and Lycho, who had been kind to her, was also dead. What would become of Telric if she dared to let him get so close?

All men die, she reasoned. Then she made her own argument. *But must I be the shear that snaps their thread?*

She thrust such thoughts behind her and returned her attention to the tower. She had stopped for a purpose, and there was little time to waste.

I've seen into my son's heart, she thought regretfully.

Though he serves this Oroladian, this sorceress, his will is his own. He is not controlled; that was a silly hope. There's no influence to free him from except his own evil, and there's nothing for me to do but stop him, to hunt him down and put an end to him before he spreads more death and destruction among innocent farms and towns. I brought him into this world—the responsibility is mine.

The power surged within her, a song of fearsome potency that filled all her being. Her very soul opened, pouring out its music. But this time she held it inside, shaping and bending it to her will.

The tower stood imposing and lifeless, a construct of coldly chiseled stone. It seemed the very antithesis of Soushane, a town full of children's laughter and the smells of cooking fires, a town nestled contentedly in the heart of its fields, a community where simple folks lived and grew old in each other's arms.

Frost had hoped for such a life with Kimon. Kel had ripped that from her.

He had ripped it from the people of Soushane, too.

Her son had trampled dreams into the mud—her dreams and Soushane's dreams—and he had laughed about it.

But Kel would laugh no more, and he would trample no more dreams.

With every thought the song within her swelled, growing into a chorus of shattering intensity. She stretched out her hand toward the tower; her fingers clenched spasmodically.

The heavens erupted with arcane fury. Bolts of terrifying power split the clouds and stabbed earthward, striking Kel's fortress again and again, battering, smashing it on all sides. Stone exploded outward, showering the plain with fragments. Still her fist clenched and clenched, and still the lightning flashed until nothing remained but a scattered pile of rubble.

An acrid stench wafted through the night. Frost opened her hand, lowered her arm, and let the music subside. The tempest ceased. The last deafening thunder rumbled away into the distance, and the world was quiet again.

"It doesn't begin to repay Soushane's people," Frost said bitterly, her mind full of the memories of the burning town. "But maybe they will rest a little easier."

Telric gaped at her with a mixture of fear and awe. Words formed and died on his lips. He backed a step, stumbled on a root, and caught himself. He held his ground, but his knitted brows and open mouth betrayed his uncertainty.

"Yes, I did that," she confessed, answering his unvoiced question. "I commanded the lightning. All the storms of late have been my doing, though I didn't realize it until tonight. They were reflections of my moods, unconsciously conjured by a power I didn't know I had."

"You're a sorceress, then," he accused, "just like your son."

"I'm a witch," she corrected, "and there's quite a difference, as Kel will learn. I'm nothing like him."

"Witch, sorcerer, wizard," he spat. "What's the difference?"

She regarded him coldly, wondering how she could have befriended such a stupid man. "My power is my own," she snapped. "It comes from within me; it's part of what I am, as natural to me as my arms and legs. I don't have to leech it from something else. That's what a sorcerer does. He finds an object—a talisman or an amulet—or he finds a word or symbol that contains magic. Then he channels that power for his own purposes. There are wizards, too. They're served by demons or granted power directly from the gods—"

"You're a witch," Telric broke in rudely. "Is that how you managed to kill my brothers?"

An icy anger overwhelmed her. She closed the distance between them in two quick strides and dealt the Rholarothan a stinging slap. "You heartless bastard! Your brothers were pigs who tried to gut a harmless old man. I stopped them with steel. Do you understand? I didn't have any witchcraft then, nothing but a blade and my skill, and that got me by for more than twenty years. Don't try to flatter your brothers—I didn't need magic to butcher those pork-faces."

Telric glared. Then, slowly, his anger began to ebb. He looked down at his hands and rubbed them together. "Were you really coming to avenge me?" he said, subdued. "Against your own son?"

She relented a bit and nodded. How could she explain to him the atrocities Kel had committed? "You and too many others," she answered. "I haven't told you; there hasn't been time. But Kel murdered his father." It was her turn to look at her hands, but then she raised her head and their gazes locked. "For that act alone I would hunt him down even if I had to follow him through all the nine hells. Add to that crime his part in Kirigi's death, and you begin to see what a monster I've spawned.''

Telric regarded her strangely. "Can you kill your own son?"

She swallowed hard. It was a blunt question, and her answer was equally blunt. "Yes."

His shoulders sagged. He came to her and laid a hand consolately on her arm. "Your gods have dealt you evil cards, woman. I guess you have no choice but to play them, and I'll be with you until the final draw."

He put on a weak smile. More than anything he could have said, that reassured her. She didn't want Telric to fear her witchcraft. He had said he loved her, and in this moment when she had decided on a fateful course, that suddenly meant a lot to her.

She caught both his hands and squeezed them. She would never love the man as he wanted her to love him, but she could feel a swiftly growing bond. "If our friendship had been a long one," she said gently, "someday you would have made that charge. It's best to have gotten it out of the way." She gave his hands an extra squeeze, released him, and bent to pick up the saddle she had set aside. She straightened with her burden. "I'm sorry about your brothers, Telric, but they gave me no choice."

"You were right," he said, taking the saddle from her. "My brothers *were* pigs. I spoke in anger. Will you forgive me?"

She pursed her lips and nodded.

They stood quietly and the world seemed to pass around them in the short space of a heartbeat. Then Telric turned and went to Ashur. "Careful of his back," Frost warned as he adjusted a small quilted pad on the unicorn and lifted the saddle into place. She moved to his side and stroked Ashur's nose, and the beast stood patiently still while the cinch was strapped tight.

Telric went back for the sack of supplies. "Do you know," he said, facing her over the saddle, jerking a thumb back at the ruined tower, "when you did that, you glowed all over with a weird light." He paused, but his gaze never left hers. "Like an angel," he added.

"A dark angel," she mused aloud, thinking of all the

twisted meanings of that phrase. "I was born in the year of the Spider, in the month and the day of the Spider as the Esgarian calendar is reckoned," she told him. "That tiny creature is sacred to Gath, the god my people call chaos-bringer. Well, my life has been full of chaos." She glanced away toward the ruins, and the blackened, broken stones seemed to mock her. "My peaceful years with Kimon were no more than a brief intermission." She bit her lip sadly. "And now the tragedy resumes."

She mounted Ashur carefully, mindful of his injuries, wishing she had power to heal. But it was easier to destroy with magic than to mend or create. She could bring a tower down upon its foundations with far less effort than it would take to repair the unicorn's flesh. It troubled her, and she considered bitterly that perhaps it was the natural impulse in man to spoil and destroy and that the act of creation might be as unnatural as magic itself.

She took the supply sack from Telric and lashed it to the saddle. Then she extended her hand to pull him up behind. He hesitated, eyeing the unicorn's wounds, but finally he swung a leg up, balanced himself, and locked his arms about her waist.

She patted Ashur along the withers and silently apologized for making him carry both their weights. There was no choice, however. Even if they could find another horse for Telric, it wouldn't be able to keep up. She had to ride hard for Kyr. She apologized for that, too.

The clouds broke as they rode. The sun shone down upon them, and the late afternoon sky turned a cheerier blue. It did not last long, though, before the purple hand of night began to stretch over the land.

In the northern distance loomed the peaks of the *Shai-Zastari*. They had made good time, yet she knew they had to make better. The ground turned rocky as the first bright stars appeared in the heavens. She brought Ashur to a stop and called for a brief rest.

The unicorn's wounds were crusty and oozing. She winced to see them and uncinched the saddle to free him of its weight. She pulled it off. Then, taking the waterskin from the supply sack, she set about cleansing the worst of the injuries.

"I'll only use my share," she told Telric when she noticed him watching. "You won't go thirsty."

"I'm not worried," he answered gently. "Use it all if you need it." Then he quipped, "Your storms have made the ground so wet we could suck the stones."

She used it sparingly, anyway. When she was done she slung the saddle over her shoulder and took the reins in one hand. "We'll walk awhile," she said.

But Telric blocked her path. "Not until you eat something." He held the sack out to her and pointed to the saddle. "And not unless that is on my shoulder."

She sighed, too weary to argue, and dropped the saddle on the ground. She rolled up the quilted pad and sat on it while her companion rummaged in the supplies, finally handing her a chunk of pale cheese and a piece of bread.

"Too much," she said, breaking the cheese and returning half of it to him. "A full stomach would slow me down; let's just settle for easing the rumbles."

She wolfed her portion, then got to her feet. Impatiently, she waited for Telric to finish. He ate at a deliberately casual pace, eyeing her all the while, smiling between every bite.

She knew he did it only to prolong her rest. But she had no time to waste. There was yet a long way to go. Feigning a reluctant submission, she let her shoulders droop, drew a breath, and sank down beside him. When next he lifted the cheese to his lips, she leaned quickly over and slapped the back of his hand.

Telric's eyes widened in surprise, and his cheeks puffed out. His jaws worked frantically. He swallowed hard twice. Then, he wiped away the crumbs that had stuck to his stubbly chin. He licked his lips and rubbed his throat.

Frost rose and took the reins once more and started for the *Shai-Zastari*. They were only shadows in the deepening darkness, but she knew the direction. Behind her, she heard Telric's scramblings as he hastily retied the supply sack, hefted the saddle, and hurried after her. She grinned secretly to herself. The expression on his face when she'd shoved in the cheese . . . !

They traveled through the night. The morning sun found them on the far side of the hills. Telric's head bobbed on her shoulder, and his arms clung loosely around her waist. She ached all over from too much time in the saddle, but she was grateful for their progress.

Ashur's wounds had scabbed over, and the bleeding had stopped. He had carried them without rest through the hills, picking his own way when there was no path to follow. As a result, the worst terrain was behind them. Only the flatland steppes lay ahead. If she rode a straight course to Kyr, she could bypass Dakariar and the ruins of Soushane. She had no desire to see those places ever again.

"Wake up, sleepy." She nudged Telric in the ribs with her elbow. "You want to fall off?"

He jerked upright as if awakened by his direst foe. "Whaaaa? . . ."

His arms tightened about her reflexively as the unicorn bolted forward. His head snapped back, and his chin came down hard again on her spine. He muttered a low, grumbling curse in her ear. She only smiled and tickled Ashur's flanks with her heels, urging him faster.

"You'll run him into the ground at this pace, woman!" Telric called over the rush of the wind when they had gone some distance. He spit the strands of her hair out of his mouth and pressed his cheek harder against her shoulder.

She realized the Rholarothan didn't know what Ashur was, and how could he? Like most men, Telric thought he rode a common horse. She had power to show him, though, and she used the smallest effort to widen his perceptions.

Telric let out a howl and stiffened against her. His arms nearly squeezed the breath from her, and his heels rose to lock over her knees. His cry rang in her ears, and she laughed wantonly.

She leaned forward in the saddle until the unicorn's thick mane lashed her face, until she could feel the glittering tongues of cold flame that gushed from his eyes. That great black horn rose and fell, lunging with the motion of the gallop, ashimmer with the light of the sun.

The heat of the day kissed her neck, and the warmth of Telric's body wrapped around her like a sweaty new skin. Between her thighs, Ashur's smoothly pounding muscles built another kind of heat. She tingled all over, and her senses filled with a vibrancy.

Convulsive laughter rushed from her, and Telric's howling echoed on the wind.

                              *   *   *

That day passed and the next.

At twilight of the third day, the walls of Kyr made a shadowy stain on the far horizon. Frost stood in the stirrups to gaze at it. Telric slid to the ground, but the feeling had gone out of his legs, and he stumbled awkwardly, falling, too weary even to curse. He sat up slowly and began to massage sensation back into his limbs.

She paid him no attention. It had been at dusk when Kel had worked his evil at Soushane and dusk again at Dakariar. *Three days*, he had boasted in his tower. *In three days he would claim the Third Aspect and his spell gift to the sorceress, Oroladian, would be complete.*

"The Book of Shakari," she mumbled aloud.

Telric looked up from the ground and waited for her to say more. When she didn't he shrugged and returned to rubbing his legs.

Even now, as the sun sank behind the distant trees and the evening gloom gathered in the east, she imagined her son reaching out with a hand of fire to claim his bloody prize. The Book of Shakari was said to contain all the wisdom of the gods of light. It was a book of enchantments and of philosophy for divine beings that man could understand but very little. Why, she wondered, did Kel require such a book?

To give life to the dead, her son had told her. But whom did he intend to resurrect? Not Kimon, surely, and not Kirigi. Who? Perhaps it was someone Oroladian wished revived.

So many questions and so few answers.

So little time, her every instinct screamed.

Night's hunger had swallowed half the sky. If Kel had not already gained the book, he would have it soon. She felt for the map inside her tunic. It was warm against her flesh, damp with her perspiration. Where, she wondered, was Kel at that very moment?

"What if he's not there?"

Frost blinked, then realized Telric hadn't meant her son. She eased out of the saddle and stood over him. "Riothamus will be there. Kyr is the only major city in these parts, and by now news of Dakariar will have reached him. He'll be too angry to leave this area if he thinks there's a chance of capturing Kel."

"But we haven't seen any patrols," he reminded her.

"Dakariar is to the southeast. Soushane is nearly in a line between that town and Kyr. Riothamus's men will be searching in that direction."

"So you think he'll still be here?"

She nodded. "He's a king. I very much doubt if fieldwork suits his tastes. Kyr has few luxuries, but its entertainments are vast and sparkling compared to a hard day in the saddle or a night spent on the ground."

He rubbed his backside and grimaced. "Perhaps he's a wiser man than you give him credit for, then." He rose stiffly to his feet and went to Ashur's side. As he had before during their brief rests, he passed his hands near those flickering eye-flames, amazed that they did not burn. He scratched the unicorn's nose and smoothed the tangled mane. It amused her how Ashur nickered softly and allowed the attentions.

Telric took the waterskin from the sack. It was nearly empty, but he sipped from it, then poured a dollop into his cupped hand. The unicorn made short work of it. The Rholarothan didn't even flinch as that mighty horn moved so close to his body. He poured a second, more generous quantity and held it for the creature to drink.

"In all my days my only experience with magic has been the dull prestidigitations of court fools." He drew one hand down Ashur's broad face and passed the waterskin to Frost. She drained the last of it. Kyr was close at hand, and there was no longer a need to conserve. "But in a matter of days I feel like I've walked to the brink of hell and looked down. Kel's hand of fire, your lightnings, things I thought only demons could do . . . ." He swallowed, frowning, and Frost realized he was avoiding her gaze. He had made this speech already, almost defensively. Now it poured out with a sincerity that touched her.

"When I looked over your shoulder and saw"—he hesitated and put a hand near Ashur's face again—"these strange eyes, I thought I'd been a fool to trust you, that my reward was to be carried to damnation by a witch and her witch steed." He ran his fingers through the unicorn's forelock, then up the long length of that ebony spike. "Later, though, I thought maybe this was just an illusion, some trick you were playing with my mind." He drew a deep breath and straightened his shoulders. The fatigue seemed suddenly to leave him. "But he's real, isn't he? I want him to be real."

Frost didn't answer. There was no need to tell him what he already believed. And she saw in his eyes that he did believe. She remembered when Telric first approached her at the Broken Sword. He had made two *minarin* coins appear and placed them on the table. An insignificant feat of sleight of hand, but it revealed something to her now. She watched him stroke the unicorn, and she knew.

Telric had wanted to believe for a long time.

"What did you call him?" he asked over his shoulder.

She told him again. "A unicorn."

He repeated it. "A beast from your oldest Esgarian legends, you said. But how did you come by him?"

She let her thoughts wander back. Once, such memories would have been too painful; she would have turned away rather than call them up. But with the balm of time they had become the stuff that gave life meaning. In her day she had done great deeds and songs had been sung about her. One song that came to mind would have answered his question.

But it was not a time for songs.

"I was much younger," she started, "and there was another book of great power. Two wizards, Almurion and Zarad-Krul, vied for it. By chance I stumbled into the midst of their battle." She stared up at the brightening stars as if she were staring back through the years. "Just before the demons of Zarad-Krul struck him down, Almurion gave the book into my keeping, instructing me to carry it into the shadow-land of Chondos."

Telric suddenly paled. "I first saw you at Zondu near the Chondite border." He looked up sharply. "Gods of Rholaroth! I thought it was a diary or a journal."

She arched an eyebrow and smiled patiently. "You couldn't have known you'd stolen the Book of the Last Battle, a grimoire that contained all the spells and words of power the forces of light will use to defeat the forces of darkness in the Last Great Battle."

He stared at his hand. "Our priests speak in awed whispers of that book. I've touched it? No wonder you came after me."

"And you thought that court fools were your only experience with magic." She smirked, then added wistfully, "Magic is everywhere, Telric. It brushes all our lives. We just don't always recognize it."

"You must have missed your powers when they were stolen from you," he said gently.

She shook her head. "I was glad they were gone. It's one thing to glimpse the magic in the world—it's something else to hold it in your hand. There's always a price to pay, no matter how good your intentions. And the worst price is the gulf it carves between the adept and the rest of humanity." She looked at him, and their gazes locked. "It becomes very lonely."

He reached out for her hand. Their fingers intertwined. "You were telling me about your unicorn," he reminded her after an uncomfortable pause.

She almost didn't hear him, but slowly the words sank in, and she let go of his hand. "Almurion was a servant of the lords of light," she continued. "He knew that Zarad-Krul would try to follow me, so he gave me two special weapons. The first was the dagger called Demonfang, which Kel has stolen."

"Ashur was the other?"

She chewed her lip. "I've always believed that. He came along after the wizard had died. I'd run into a problem with some outlaws, and he charged down the road like some improbable nightmare. Only it turned out to be the outlaws' nightmare."

"He helped you against this wizard, Zarad-Krul?"

She reached out to stroke the unicorn along the withers. "Yes. We were together for years after that. Then, when Kimon and I finally settled down, Ashur just disappeared. I'd given up any hope of ever seeing him again, of ever learning what had happened to him." She threw her arms about the creature's neck and buried her face in his mane. "But that night when Soushane burned"—she eased away from Ashur and let him lick her hand—"I just looked up and there he was."

"Magic," Telric said with contained awe. "As if he knew you were in trouble."

She thought about that. "I can't explain it," she admitted. "I can't guess where he went during those twenty years and more." She patted Ashur's nose. "Truthfully, I don't even care as long as he's with me again."

"You can't explain magic," Telric said, putting his hand

beside hers on the unicorn's nose. "You just have to accept it."

Frost gazed at her companion, trying to see the young boy-man she'd met so long ago. He'd been hot-tempered and foul-mouthed then, and reckless, in every regard the spoiled son of nobility.

How time had changed him! The slender youth had grown tall and strong. The temper was gone, or at least under control. Telric had turned quiet and gentle in a way that did nothing to dilute his manliness. She wondered at the experiences that had changed him, that had lined his face and powdered his hair with gray, that had turned him from a brash fool to a man she felt she could trust.

She looked at her own hand. The flesh did not betray all her years, but there was stiffness in her joints when she made a fist. Twenty years ago there had been no stiffness.

Time had changed them both. Time and experience. She looked again for traces of the young Telric, but it was easier to see what he had become. She could almost love the difference.

She turned away suddenly, ashamed of the thought.

The night closed in swiftly. Frost stared toward the dimming silhouette of Kyr, then climbed into the saddle. She stretched a hand down for Telric. "We've got to hurry," she said sharply. "Since the slaughter of the garrison at Soushane, they've taken to shutting the city gates at night. If we don't ride now, we'll be locked out until morning. I lied my way inside once, but I doubt I'd get away with that a second time."

Telric swung up behind her and settled himself with a grunt. His arms went around her waist. "What if you're recognized?" he reminded her. "You didn't part company with Riothamus on friendly terms as I recall your story."

"He tried to hang me," she quipped as she touched her bootheels to Ashur's flanks.

"Great," was all he had time to answer before they were racing away.

Kyr swelled rapidly as the unicorn's strides ate up the distance. Frost's gaze swept the countryside, alert for any sign of a patrol that might intercept them. She had no cloak to hide her face or her weapons. She prayed that darkness alone would serve as her disguise. Darkness and boldness and luck. It was late, and hopefully the guards' minds would be on supper and bed.

"What if the gates are already locked?" Telric called when it appeared they would not make it in time.

"We'll open them," she shouted in reply.

"More lightning?" There was a mocking note in his voice that somehow lightened her spirit.

"Credit me with some subtlety," she scolded.

"Oh, subtlety." He leaned close to her ear to be sure she heard clearly, and he took the opportunity to flick her lobe with the tip of his tongue. "Was that what flattened Kel's tower?"

She jabbed him in the ribs and heard him chuckle. His arms tightened around her playfully.

But the walls of Kyr loomed and there was no more time to play. "If the gate guards question us, answer in Rholarothan," she instructed. "I remember enough of your language to fake it. We're travelers. If they hesitate, remind them of your nobility. Use just enough Keled—and use it poorly—to get your meaning across. If they're still difficult, then threaten and bully, make them sweat. Keleds have a tremendous respect for rank and station, and they'll finally give in."

"You're my wife," Telric said quickly.

She called over her shoulder, "Your what?"

"They'll ask who you are," he said with certainty, giving her another squeeze. "You're my wife."

"A wife with a sword?"

He made an exaggerated shrug that she felt even over the harsh rhythm of their ride. "What the hell," he said. "We're from another land. Our customs are a little different."

"Right," she agreed doubtfully. "Don't try to consummate anything."

"Sounds like a challenge to me," he muttered under his breath.

But all their planning was for nothing. The gates of Kyr were still open. Four sentries watched with disinterest as they rode by, then went back to their dice game.

Chapter Thirteen

Blood to make your garden grow,
Blood to make it flourish;
Blood-red drops the seeds you sow
That all your magicks nourish.
Blood to color all your dreams,
Blood to make you shiver,
Blood to gurgle, froth, and steam
And flow in crimson rivers,
Blood to bathe a warrior's blade,
Blood—the coin of war;
Blood for those who, finally paid,
Lie bloodless evermore.

"You!"

It had taken valuable hours to find Dromen Illstar. The
Rathole had been moved again to a totally new location. All
the previous spots had been abandoned. It had taken some
effort to find a thief she recognized and to beat the information out of him.

Illstar had hired some protection since their last meeting.
On either side of his throne stood a pair of giants, naked to
the waist, wearing huge daggers in their belts. They moved
toward her, reaching for their weapons, but Illstar himself
called them back.

"No point in wastin' good flesh," he grumbled with a weak smile and a shrug of resignation. "What in the nine hells d'ye want this time, Captain? I thought I was rid o' ye."

Frost strode to the middle of the room, ignoring the dozen customers standing or sitting about. She knew some of the faces, but she had no words of greeting for any of them.

"You owe me, rat-catcher," she said to Illstar. "I saved Dakariar from burning. Your daughter's alive somewhere."

The old man's eyes narrowed suspiciously. "She's here in the city with me. I owe ye nothin'."

She smiled grimly. "You owe me all right. And you'll pay. You're going to show me the tunnels into the governor's palace."

Dromen Illstar leaned forward, genuinely surprised. "What tunnels would that be, Captain?"

She moved closer, put the toe of her boot on his chest, and eased him back into his chair. The bodyguards again moved to interfere, but again the old man stopped them. "No games," Frost said smoothly. "I haven't time. Every thief in Kyr knows the tunnels exist. I'm gambling you know what they don't, though—namely, the entrances. You're going to show us." She gestured over her shoulder to Telric, who stood guard by the door.

Illstar pursed his lips, scratched his chin. "An' if I don't?"

Her expression turned to purest malice. "Then I'll find your daughter and serve her heart to you in a cup of wine."

Dromen glanced down into the cup he held in his hand, then back at Frost. His eyes gleamed with fear and hatred.

But she knew she had him.

The wall that surrounded the governor's palace was not so high as the city wall, but it was a formidable barrier. It had four gates. Each was guarded and sealed against intruders.

A wide thoroughfare separated the palace from the shops and businesses that thrived in its shadow. The shops were closed now. Dromen Illstar and one of his lackeys led them from one cloistered doorway to the next, always keeping to the darkness.

On the rear side of the palace compound, a row of grain silos loomed like an immense palisade. "The fourth one," Illstar said, pointing. They moved quietly, swiftly, through the street, with their goal in sight.

"No guards?" Telric whispered.

The lackey snorted, but Dromen Illstar thumped him in the chest to shut him up. "Why would they guard one silo? That would only draw attention to it."

When they reached the first silo, Dromen stopped. "I've done my part. I'll leave ye here."

Frost brushed his elbow meaningfully. "Let's go," she said.

Dromen didn't move. "I've brought ye this far, an' I've showed ye the silo. Ye don't need me anymore."

"Let's go," she repeated, touching her hilt for emphasis.

There was a huge iron lock on the silo door, but Dromen's bodyguard had brought a crowbar at the old man's suggestion. He slipped it through the lock and leaned on it. Metal groaned, but the lock held. Telric lent his strength, and the two men strained together.

The lock snapped with a sound so loud they all spun around to see if anyone else had heard. But the street remained empty, and the palace gate nearest them stayed shut.

Dromen gathered up the pieces of the lock, and they moved inside and shut the door.

The blackness within was complete. Someone struck flint and steel. The sparks were dazzling, and Frost turned her eyes away. Then an orange glow banished the darkness as the naphtha-soaked torch Dromen produced caught fire. He grinned and put the flint and steel back in a pouch on his belt.

The dust was thick enough to choke, but no grain had ever been stored here. Frost turned in a slow circle, arching her neck. The torchlight did not illuminate the highest recesses. "I thought the tunnels were abandoned," she whispered.

"Not used is not abandoned," Illstar answered. "I'm sure the governor knows about the tunnels. Otherwise, we'd be ass deep an' more in grain right now. Nobody comes here, though. The tunnels were made a century ago just in case the governor ever needed a hasty exit." He glanced contemptuously at Telric, then thought better of it. "But Rholaroth has expanded in other directions, an' things around here have been peaceful enough."

"Count your blessings," Telric said with a wink.

Dromen snapped barely under his breath, "Eat my dung."

"So where's the entrance?" Frost interrupted. She saw nothing that looked like a trapdoor, and she had no time to

waste while two men exchanged insults. Illstar wasn't a
native Keled, anyway. What were old quarrels to him?

The old man walked to the wall opposite the door. He
tapped it with his knuckles. "False," he pronounced. "The
trapdoor is just between this an' the real wall."

She went to his side and rapped experimentally. "How
does it open?"

He spat. Apparently, Dromen was feeling more in charge
of the situation now that they were off the street. The arrogance showed on his face. "Hell, Captain. Who knows if it
opens at all? The wood here is thin. Break your way in." He
folded his arms and stepped back.

She gave him a withering look and was gratified to see a
small part of his arrogance fade. Perhaps he was telling the
truth. Certainly she spied no seam where a door might slide
open or swing upward, but she refused to let this camel turd
take pleasure in her confusion. She rapped the wall once
more, judging its thickness. Then, gritting her teeth, exhaling
hard, she drove her fist through it.

The wood splintered noisily. Carefully, she drew her hand
from the jagged hole. Blood trickled down her knuckles, and
there was a scratch on the back of her hand where the skin
was thinnest. The shock of her punch still shivered through
her bones, but she let nothing show on her face. Instead, she
leaned forward and calmly wiped the blood on Dromen's
tunic. He didn't move, nor did his eyes leave hers while she
did it. They reflected his fear.

Telric's boots made short work of the rest of the section.

Frost turned her back on her former sergeant, ducked her
head, and stepped inside a narrow cubicle. From the outside
of the silo such a small room would be undetectable. The
trapdoor took up most of the floor. She bent and lifted it by
its heavy metal ring and peered down into darkness. She
could barely see the beginning of an old staircase.

"We'll take the torch," she said. Telric pulled it from
Illstar's grasp, then he squeezed in beside her, took the ring,
and held the door open for her.

But she moved back to face Dromen again. She reached
out to flick a bit of dirt from his shoulder and made a
pretense of straightening his garments for him. "If it crosses
your mind that I'm becoming bothersome, and if you think
you could get rid of me by going straight to the sentries"

—she smiled maliciously and tugged his beard—"don't. You fought beside me long enough to know me." She patted his cheek. "Dead or alive, Dromen, I'd come for you."

He caught her hand and pushed it away. "Just stay away from me, woman. I've paid everythin' I ever owed you now."

"You owe," she said with a shake of her head, "anything I care to collect."

She turned her back to him again and returned to the tunnel entrance. With her foot on the first step she took the torch from Telric. "Tell the nice men good-bye," she said.

Telric put on a crooked smile. "Good-bye," he muttered, and he followed her down into the earth.

The passage had been designed for a quick escape in times of trouble. There were no confusing side tunnels, no false ways, no traps or barriers. According to Dromen, there were at least five others like it, all providing swift retreat from different parts of the palace. Dromen claimed to know the locations of all of them.

Unless he had lied, this tunnel would take them to the governor's hall, where all state functions were held. Somewhere near the hall they would find the exit from the governor's private quarters.

"What is it you have over that man?" Telric whispered as they crept along.

She led the way around a corner and down a long, straight section. By now, she suspected, they were inside the wall and moving beneath the grounds. She almost imagined she could hear the rhythmic thump of the sentries' feet through the earth.

"Dromen's a superstitious man. He's never quite known whether to fear me or worship me." She paused and listened as her echoes raced ahead. "Never in his life had he seen a woman use a sword until he signed on with the Korkyran army, and he had a tough time accepting me as his captain. It didn't take long before he challenged me. I humiliated him," she said lightly, "beat him into the ground without even having to cut him." She smiled at the memory. "Some men would have hated me for it, but afterward Dromen Illstar was practically my slave."

She was silent for a moment, savoring remembrances of

distant days. "There was another thing, too. Once, a soldier double-crossed me at the expense of numerous men in my command. It was Dromen who tied and held the traitor while I cut off his head." She stopped abruptly and turned to look at Telric. The torchlight threw strange shadows over his face; she couldn't adequately judge his expression. "Does that bother you?"

The Rholarothan shrugged. "The man betrayed you," he answered simply.

She nodded, repressing a grim smile. In Telric's land they also would have beheaded the traitor—and then hunted down his family.

"I gave him no trial," she went on. "It was a field decision. Korkyra was at war with Aleppo, and the soldier's guilt was undeniable." She bit her lip. Her last word bounced on the walls and faded into the gloom. "But I've never forgotten the look on Dromen's face when he released the headless corpse. He kept looking at the body and at me, and I knew something had been on his mind. He'd always been a bit of a swindler and an opportunist, even then. I recall the thought flickering through my mind as I watched him that maybe he'd considered a similar betrayal. A clever man can make an easy fortune in times of war if he's willing to sell his friends." She sighed softly and continued up the tunnel. "But if that was in his mind, the execution frightened it out."

The tunnel made a sudden bend. She took the torch from Telric and lifted it higher, peering ahead. "When we ran into each other in Kyr, I took him to the Broken Sword to share a brew. That incident was one of the first things he brought up."

The torch revealed a set of stairs at the tunnel's end. She hesitated only briefly, then started up, pressing a finger to her lips for quiet. According to Dromen, this passage went up into the palace and continued behind false walls that were built years ago when Keled-Zaram and Rholaroth had been in constant conflict. She had no way of knowing how thick those walls were or who might be on the other sides of them, so she would risk no more whispering.

She took the steps two at a time and reached the top. She pivoted then to give Telric the benefit of the light and nearly struck him in the face with the fire. He had come noiselessly behind as quickly as she and barely blocked her arm before

she burned him. He shook his head sternly, warning against
her apology. He also knew they were in the palace, where
silence had a new value. He motioned for her to move on.

A little farther ahead they found another flight of steps.
They ascended and followed the passage to still another flight.
At the top of that, the way ran straight as far as the small
torch allowed them to see.

Telric sneezed. The air was stale and smelled of damp must
and age. Frost glanced at him, then turned her attention to the
floor. In the light of the torch their footsteps showed plainly
on the thick carpet of dust, but before them the pounce was
undisturbed. No one had walked these corridors in years.

The tunnel ended suddenly. On the terminating wall she
found a wooden lever and smiled with satisfaction. Of course,
there was no need to disguise it on this side. She passed the
torch to Telric and pulled the lever down with both hands. It was
stiff, but a section of the wall slid open with a stony rasp.

The heavy folds of a tapestry stirred gently in a sudden
draft. Frost eased it aside just enough to peer out, then she let
it fall back into place.

"Damn that Dromen Illstar!" she hissed. "That's the governor's hall. We've come too far." She ground fist and palm
together and chewed her lip.

But Telric poked his nose through the open door and
around the concealment. Then he peered back down the way
they had come. "Illstar only said it was somewhere along
here," he reminded her. "But I think I can help. The governor's private quarters should be back this way." He began to
retrace their steps carefully, running his hand along the wall
on his right.

Frost followed him. "How do you know that?"

"A long time ago," he answered quietly, "I came here
with my father on some affair of state. I was quite young, and
it was my first taste of the world beyond Shazad. In those
days, the governor's rooms were just off the main hall so he
could get away for a few moments between his various public
duties."

Frost knew the current governor was young and had taken
office since she had arrived, so it couldn't be the man Telric
had met. Yet there was every chance the new man would
keep the same quarters. Such rooms were always built large

and comfortable as suited a nobleman or a member of the royal family.

She grew excited again. They had only to find that room and her plan could still work.

Telric stopped without warning, and she bumped into his back. His hand curled around another lever. With only the flickering torch to guide them, they had passed it without noticing. She wondered how many others they might have passed and cursed herself for carelessness.

This time Telric gave Frost the torch, and he tugged on the device. He stopped before the secret panel had opened even a handsbreadth. Another tapestry concealed the opening. A dim light trickled under the edge and oozed into the passage.

"Someone's home," she mouthed soundlessly, and Telric nodded.

She pointed and moved a little way down the tunnel while Telric waited. The floor and walls were made of stone; she had no qualms about laying the torch down. It wouldn't do to let its light bleed through the tapestry and give them away, but she didn't want to extinguish it yet. It would come in handy if they had to beat a hasty retreat.

At Telric's side once more, she took a deep breath, drew her sword, and nodded. The Rholarothan leaned on the lever slowly. She prayed the old mechanisms wouldn't grate and warn anyone in the room beyond.

The door opened halfway and jammed. Try as he might, Telric could budge the lever no farther. No matter, she indicated, tugging at his sleeve. It was enough; they could squeeze through. She felt for the edge of the tapestry and eased it back. Several candles burned on a table, but the room was empty. She beckoned to her companion and stepped inside.

Telric stole softly around the left perimeter of the huge chamber. She went to the right. On either side of the room were archways leading to other rooms. They crept soundlessly over the plush carpets, listening for any clue that they were not alone.

A few chairs of antique design and a delicately carved table were the only furnishings. A mirror of burnished copper hung upon the east wall. Frost glanced at herself as she passed by it. She hesitated, winked at her own reflection, and turned away. *No great beauty,* she told herself. But then, she had never been a great beauty.

Telric snapped his fingers just loud enough to attract her
attention. He had reached the archway on his side. A nod of
his head warned her the room beyond it was occupied. She
moved quickly to her own archway and peered around. A
glance was enough to tell her it was empty. There was a large
door, however, that opened into the palace's main corridor. It
was bolted from the inside, though. She wondered if there
might be a guard on the other side.

Another soft snap from Telric made her turn. He stood in
his archway, gazing into the occupied room without bothering
to conceal himself. He looked back over his shoulder, and
there was a thin-lipped grin on his face. He crooked a finger.

A couple of easy strides took her to his side. She cracked a
smile of her own. It had been as easy as Dromen Illstar had
said it would. She might even leave the old thief alone after
this.

This was the governor's bedchamber. They crept to opposite sides of the expansive, quilted bed with its high-backed
frame and draped veils of transparent gauze. A single fat
candle burned away the hours on a slender pedestal in the
corner of the room. Its light fell on two sleeping faces and on
the exquisitely embroidered coverlet that hid their forms.

Telric raised his eyebrows in a silent question. Slowly, so
the steel would not rasp on the leather of the scabbards, they
drew their swords.

Frost looked down at the two sleepers. Their arms were
wrapped about each other, a lovers' embrace. They lay in
peaceful, fitless repose. She despaired of ever knowing that
kind of sleep again. Perhaps for that reason she hesitated to
wake them.

Telric tilted his head impatiently, waiting for her to make
the next move. It was, after all, her plan that had brought
them here.

With the point of her sword she indicated one of the two.
"Riothamus," she mouthed. Then she pointed to the other
and made a fist over her heart. "The governor." Her lips
moved in the barest whisper.

Here was a discovery. Many in Kyr had wondered how so
young a lord had earned the right to govern so important a
city. Well, she had found the answer, and she remembered
the old saying: It matters whom you sleep with.

But the people had accepted him. He had proved himself

more than merely an adequate administrator by restoring fair trade with the smaller agricultural villages around Kyr, by filling the granaries and siphoning part of the grain into the bowls of the city's poor, by stamping out the corruption that had riddled the garrison's ranks. And he had proved himself a fair judge as well by acquitting nearly as many men as he had hanged. It was an excellent beginning for one of such tender years.

Frost had no wish to harm the young governor. He was innocent of any part in her business with the king. She hoped things didn't get messy in the next few moments.

The flat of her blade came to rest upon Riothamus's chest. She sat down gently on the bed by his side. When he didn't stir, she leaned close to his ear. "Boo, I'm a demon from your darkest dream," she whispered. "Wake up you silly, sleepy jackass."

The king of Keled-Zaram let out a single snore, turned on his side, and draped an arm over her knee.

Frost sighed, gazed over at her companion, whose sword point rested on the governor's shoulder. Telric's expression was full of tension. He chewed his lip, a habit he was picking up from her, and bent closer, ready to clap a hand on the younger man's mouth if he should wake and call out.

She gave him a sly wink, then whispered into the king's ear again. "I know how to wake you," she threatened. She eased the coverlet down until his ribs were exposed. Then, she began to tickle him.

Riothamus bolted awake, eyes wide with surprise, his mouth forming a broad oval. But her palm cupped tightly over his lips, and she brought her face nose to nose with his.

"Hello again," she greeted him lightly. Her sword came up so that he could see it. The candlelight rippled up and down the polished edge. After she was sure he had seen it, she laid it across his knees, letting its weight serve as a reminder of its presence.

The governor woke up, too. He saw the sword, tried to sit up, but Telric pushed him firmly back down on his pillow. The Rholarothan's sword came around to the poor fellow's throat, and her friend wagged a finger to underscore their preference for silence.

They regarded each other then with furtive glances, and an understanding was achieved. Frost gripped Telric's blade between thumb and forefinger and eased it away from the youth. "I don't think there's any need for that." Her voice took on a little more volume as she spoke. "We're all good friends here, aren't we, Your Majesty?" She took her hand from his mouth and placed it on Riothamus's shoulder. She gently kneaded his bare flesh.

Riothamus gazed at Telric, at the blade across his knees, and back at her. The fear in his eyes transformed to smoldering anger, but he nodded slowly.

"I'm sure neither of you will call for the guards," she said, running a hand over the expensive coverlet. "You wouldn't want us to stain all this fine embroidery."

"How did you get in here?" Riothamus hissed.

The young governor started to speak, then thought better of it. Probably he knew about the tunnels. Apparently, his king did not.

"Good evening, Lord Sarius," she addressed the youth. "You were sleeping so peacefully. I regret the need to wake you."

Sarius eyed the sword that Telric still waved in the vicinity of his naked chest. His fist clenched when he answered, "Then take what you came for and let us get *back* to sleep."

She could almost hear the unspoken *bitch* that was implicit in his tone. She smiled tolerantly and gave her attention back to Riothamus.

"I need your help," she told him calmly.

His eyes narrowed, and he pushed himself up on his pillows to sit stiffly. "You desecrated the *Zha-Nakred Salah Veh*," he snapped. "You murdered Yorul—"

Frost interrupted. "His last lover," she explained for Sarius's benefit. To Riothamus she said, "We're never going to get anywhere if you insist on discussing old times."

The king glared, and there was nothing particularly royal about the rage that burned in his eyes. "You have the balls of the gods themselves to come and ask my help. I'll help you straight to hell!"

She raised her sword from his lap and let it settle on his shoulder. The cold steel edge rested right next to the large, throbbing vein in Riothamus's neck. "That's an unreasonably uncooperative attitude," she chided. "Let me put my proposition in terms closer to your heart. Work with me and listen to my advice, or my son will take your crown and your kingdom, probably your life as well, before winter arrives.''

Riothamus paled.

"She's lying," Sarius scoffed.

The king stared scornfully at his bedmate; then he looked back at Frost. "Why would she lie?" he said slowly. He swallowed as he searched her face for hidden meanings. Their gazes met and locked. "Why would you even come to me at all? Kel na'Akian is your son."

Frost rose from the bed, stepped back, and sheathed her sword, noting that Sarius, at least, breathed a little easier for that. Telric, however, refused to follow her lead, and the wary young governor watched the Rholarothan from the corner of his eye.

"I won't debate my reasons with you," she said. "You probably wouldn't believe them, anyway. But my son's got to be stopped, and I'm the only one who can stop him. I need your help though."

"You killed Yorul," Riothamus accused her again.

Telric's deep voice startled them all. "She gave funeral rites to every last citizen of Soushane. They were your people, not hers." His words were venomous, and he glowered angrily at the two men in the bed. "She did your duty, you foolish excuse for a king. There wasn't a Keled around to do it."

She had told him that story on the way to Kyr. A certain sense of regret washed over her as she listened to him relate it to Riothamus. He made it sound as if she had done a heroic deed, when she had only attempted to atone for some small part of her guilt and shame.

Yet part of her thanked him for coming to her defense.

"Is that true?" Riothamus asked, amazed.

"If it is, what could be more fitting?" Sarius snapped. "She whelped the butcher responsible for their deaths."

Telric reached down, tangled his huge hand in the governor's thick hair, and dragged him out of bed. Sarius's face twisted in pain and surprise, but his wide eyes locked on the blade that suddenly hovered before his nose. "You need a lesson in how to respectfully address your elders," the Rholarothan said. He dragged the naked young man from the sheets and sent him stumbling into the adjoining room. "We'll

just have a talk by ourselves,'' he called back over his
shoulder to Frost.

Riothamus watched them go. "Did you really do what he
said for Soushane?'' he asked when they were alone.

Her lips drew into a thin line. What should she say to him?
"I've lived in your land for more than twenty-two summers,"
she started, folding her arms. "My husband and I settled
here, made a business for ourselves, tried to raise two sons.
Your father was king when we came to Dashrani; you were
only a young boy." She paced to the far side of the room and
regarded him from the shadows. "You think I am Esgarian."
She fixed him with her gaze. "But Keled-Zaram is as much
my land as yours. I buried my husband in this earth, and
Kirigi's ashes are scattered on its winds or beaten into its
mud." She made a fist. "Keled-Zaram is my home!"

Riothamus eased his feet over the edge of the bed and
wrapped a sheet around himself. He stared at the floor, then
up at her. "But your older son has raped Keled-Zaram. He's
still raping her and laughing at us while he takes his pleasure.
Nine towns he's burned, and countless farms. No one ever
knows where he'll strike next. I can't defend my own people."

"It wasn't entirely your fault," she said in a consoling
voice. "Kel was searching for certain objects. When he found
the first it became a little easier to locate the next. When he
had both it was easier still to divine the third. At this very
moment he rides to claim it. He may have it now."

Riothamus stood, but he remained by the bed. "What are
these things—these objects?"

Frost considered. She needed his cooperation and his trust,
so she held nothing from him. "Objects of magical power
concealed in Keled-Zaram by Chondite sorcerers of centuries
past."

The king rubbed his palms together. "Then the stories of
this Oroladian are true? There is sorcery involved?"

"The stories are somewhat true," she acknowledged, "but
twisted in the telling. Oroladian is a sorceress, a female, but
she's not in Keled-Zaram. She waits for Kel across the Lythe
River in Esgaria. My son intends these objects as gifts to
her."

Riothamus began to pace, though he kept a safe distance
away from her. "But the tales we've heard from the few
pitiful survivors," he insisted, "stories of fire that appears

from the heavens, tales of shrieking skull-faced demons that follow your son—''

"The demons are only men in death's-head masks," she interrupted. "But there is magic at work, too. Kel is also a sorcerer." She leaned back against the wall; the cold stone sent a shiver up her spine. "That's why you need me. That's why only I can stop him."

He stopped his pacing and looked at her suspiciously. "What do you think you can do that my army can't?"

"In time, you will see what I can do," she answered cryptically. She reached inside her tunic for the map she had put there. It was warm with the heat of her body, damp with her perspiration. She carried it to the bed and unfolded it.

"Wait," the king requested, and he went into the next room, where Telric and Sarius had gone. She heard voices, muffled and indistinct, then the sharp sting of a royal command: "Shut up, Sarius!" Riothamus returned bearing several candles, which he lit from the lone candle by the bedside. He placed them around the room, caring nothing for the hot wax that spilled on the floor and furnishings. He came to her side, then, and leaned over to study the map in brighter light.

"I've had time to think about this as we journeyed here." She pointed out Soushane on the coarse leather surface. "Kel found the first object—he calls them Aspects—here. Three days later"—her finger shifted to where Dakariar was marked—"he claimed the second Aspect."

Riothamus broke in. His finger jabbed at several other sites on the map. "What about all these other places he's attacked? Here, here, here. . . ."

"I told you," she said patiently. "He was searching. He had to find any one of the objects. It would lead him to the others." A sudden inspiration flashed into her mind as she thought about Dakariar. "Did any of those other towns have peculiar legends or tales told about them? Special wells or temples, sacred groves, or anything like that? Maybe some fantastic thing from your history happened there?"

The king scratched his chin and thought. Then his eyes seemed to light up. "These four," he said, pointing. She noticed immediately when he failed to indicate Dakariar. Perhaps he didn't know about the well and its reputed healing properties. And if he didn't know about Dakariar, then maybe he didn't know about the rest.

Still, it was enough to convince her that Kel's attacks had never been random. She thought of the cabinet she had seen in his sanctorum in the tower. No doubt some of those obscene objects had come from Keled towns. With her own eyes she had seen him conjure Skraal's emerald jewel from the well at Dakariar. If Chondite priests had hidden such a thing there, what might other, darker priests have concealed in this innocent land?

A movement in the doorway caught her eye. Telric and Sarius were standing there quietly. The Rholarothan's hand rested paternally on the younger man's shoulder. The governor tolerated it with a subdued expression. She half smiled. Whatever they had talked about, it seemed Sarius had gotten the message.

Riothamus brought her attention back to the map. "All right," he said. "You say he found two objects here and here. Where's the third?"

She chewed her lip thoughtfully, praying she had guessed right. By the nine hells, she had to be right! She bent closer and spoke in a near whisper. "Kel gave me the clue himself, when he told me that Chondite sorcerers had buried the objects. Still, it took a little time for me to put it all together. I wouldn't have done it without the map." She traced an imaginary line between Soushane and Dakariar. "Do you know anything about Chondos?"

Riothamus shook his head impatiently. Of course he knew about that haunted country. No educated monarch could be ignorant of the powerful brotherhoods of Chondos. She explained, anyway.

"The triangle is their most sacred symbol. It is the form and focus of all their arcane power. That's what they believe, at least." She drew an imaginary circle around Soushane and Dakariar. "These two are on a straight line. There's only one place on this map that, set with them, will illustrate a triangle."

Riothamus stabbed his finger down before she had to tell him. "The Plain of Kings!" he exploded. "All my ancestors! . . . Not even Kel na'Akian would dare!" His eyes narrowed in grim fury. "Of course he'd dare." He whirled away from her, headed for the door. "I'll send a force at once."

"No!" Her voice stopped him in midpace, though she had used none of her magic to compel him.

He turned on her. "My father is buried there, and my

grandfather. All their fathers before them lie there, too. What sacrilege does your son commit while we stand here talking? Do you expect me to do nothing?''

Frost knew about the Plain of Kings, where all the rulers of Keled-Zaram were entombed. Immense sculptures, accurate to the last living detail, marked the final resting places of the men who slept beneath them. As Riothamus had said—there his father lay, and there he would someday also lie with his own likeness preserved in carven stone for all time.

No, she reminded herself. Not for all time. The oldest of the sculptures was already battered and beaten by the blowing sand and dust. Features had been worn smooth, and a face had been forgotten. Nothing, but nothing, stopped the slow crawl of time.

She rubbed her face with her palm as she spoke. "It would do no good to send men there. Whatever Kel plans, you could never reach him in time. But look closely and take my advice." She bent over the map again and waited until he joined her. She listened to his labored, angry breathing. His fists clenched in the bed coverlet until his knuckles turned white.

"After a raid Kel always returns to his tower." She ran her nail along a stretch of the Lythe River. "Somewhere in here. There's no reason not to assume he'll do so this time." She glanced over her shoulder at Telric and shot him a knowing glance. "He'll find it somewhat changed and worse for wear, however."

"But that's nearly a week's ride from Kyr," the king complained. "About three days for Kel na'Akian. Are we to attack him in a fortified tower?"

Frost shook her head and indicated another area on the map. "We'll be ahead of Kel, waiting for him. You see, he and his men must travel through this narrow pass and through this range of hills. During a storm it would be very dangerous for a man to ride through there. Sure death for a large movement of troops."

Riothamus nodded in agreement. "Flash floods and mud slides. You're right about sure death, and it's been raining a lot lately." He straightened, wearing a frown. "But we can't count on a convenient storm in that specific area. Not even the gods would be that cooperative."

She just shrugged, turned, and winked at Telric. "An hour

ago as the candle burns you would have thought it impossible
that we'd be standing here without trying to kill each other.
But I looked at the sky earlier, and I can almost guarantee
there's going to be a big storm there.''

The king still frowned. ''It's days away from here. You
couldn't possibly . . .''

She squeezed his arm. ''Trust me.''

But he was not quite convinced. ''At last report, Kel
na'Akian had nearly five hundred men. That's twice the
force I've got with me. I'd planned to supplement my
strength with the garrison stationed here.'' He smacked a fist
against a palm in frustration. ''But they're gone—dead.''

She folded her arms and stepped back to look at him.
''Trust me,'' she repeated.

He paused, then consciously imitated her posture even to
the angle of her head. ''Trust you?''

''Trust me.''

Of course, she knew that he didn't trust her. She wouldn't
have trusted him, either, if their positions had been reversed.
Still, it didn't matter so long as they worked together to stop
her son.

She would send a storm to block the passes. Kel would
have to wait it out or ride a much longer course around the
hills. Either way, she and Telric, Riothamus, and all his army
would be between him and his tower.

Between him, she realized coldly, and Esgaria.

Chapter Fourteen

"They fear your son's magic," Riothamus said flatly.

The army waited nervously at the edge of the wood that surrounded the ruins of Kel's tower. Frost had listened to their gossip and silly speculation all along the way, but she had kept her silence. It was up to Riothamus to rule and encourage them, to lift their spirits. He was their king. She was only a stranger who rode at his side, and worse than a stranger to some. More than a few glanced her way with purest hatred in their eyes. Those were the men from Dashrani who had seen her fight with Yorul.

"I've told you," she said to the king. "Kel will be unprepared. Sorcery can't be done at a whim or a wish. It takes time and preparation. Kel has no reason to suspect a trap. He can be surprised."

"That doesn't mean he won't be dangerous," Telric reminded her. "I've seen him fight, and his men are the best money can buy."

"He may have small personal spells for his own protection, too," Frost added, trying to sound confident. "But nothing of the magnitude that destroyed Soushane."

Riothamus frowned and drew a short breath. "I trust you," he said lightly, almost tauntingly.

She smiled to herself. In the lion's den even a king's courage could fray. But Riothamus sat his steed proudly, looking resplendent in his finely crafted leather armor and the voluminous scarlet cloak.

She twisted in her saddle and gazed over the rest of the army. Every last man wore a cloak of red as she had ordered. There were fewer of them than she had hoped. She recalled that morning after Soushane's last rites when she had spied the patrol in her path. She had envisioned a huge army following, but fatigue had worked its will with her imagination. There had never been a large force—only two *krohns* of one hundred men each. More than enough, Riothamus had thought, to hunt down a band of outlaw rebels.

He hadn't realized how the band had grown, how swiftly the smell of money and the clink of gold coins could swell ranks. The promise of plunder and booty—or even battle itself—was enough to attract some breeds of men.

Well, no matter. Two *krohns* would be enough. She would make them enough.

"I need a high place," she told Telric.

"There," her comrade said, pointing to a high hill on the far side of the Lythe.

She raised an eyebrow. It was the highest point visible, but it was in Esgaria. She chose another, closer hill on the Keled side. "That might serve," she said, frowning. "I can't be sure from here." She turned to Riothamus, touching his arm. "Disperse your men as I told you, and remember: surprise is our greatest advantage. Keep them quiet."

He nodded. "What about you?" The Keled ruler looked down his nose. In his clothes, armored, and with an army at his back, he sometimes walked a borderline of belligerence with her. Or perhaps, she reminded herself, he was just tired from the long ride.

The gods knew she was. She patted Ashur's sleek neck and drew her hand away, startled by how thickly lathered the unicorn had become. It seemed even he was tired.

"Up there, I think," she answered Riothamus, indicating the peak of the hill she had chosen.

"Is it far enough?" he said with false gentility. "Are you sure you'll be safe?"

She winked at him, not bothering to hide her amusement or her scorn. "Safe enough to save your ass," she answered, "when my son comes to thrash it."

With Telric beside her, she rode across the field, past the ruins of Kel's tower, and into the woods beyond. The ground

had dried since the day when they were last here, but a
cloying dampness still hung in the air. The odor of rotting
verdure crept thickly up her nostrils.

They rode without speaking until they reached the foot of
their destination. Frost rose slowly in the stirrups, stretched,
and muttered a low curse. Telric watched her, expressionless.

"It won't do," she said, settling back into the saddle. "I
didn't think the trees were so thick." She ran a hand over the
stiff muscles in her neck. "I need an unobstructed view of the
entire field where the two forces will meet. This is no good at
all." She sighed and tugged the reins, wheeling Ashur around.

Telric caught her hand. "Then where else? What are you
up to, woman?"

"Tipping the scale," she said wearily, mysteriously. "And
I think there's only one place I can go."

They wound their way back among the trunks and knotty
bushes. Periodically, Frost glanced up through the leaves to
measure the sun's progress across the sky. She didn't know
precisely the time of her son's coming. She knew only that he
would come.

But doubt began to eat a hole in her heart, and she feared
her plan had been too hastily conceived. Riothamus's men
were all fine fighters and cavalrymen. They would fight well
on the open field. But what if the battle spread into the
woods? What if their fear of Kel's magic undid them entirely?
Had she made a mistake in her choice of battlegrounds? Was
she about to make a far worse error? So many questions
without answers: she tried to force them out of her head.

"I'll make my circle here," she announced when they had
regained the ruins. Telric stared at her, uncomprehending, but
he didn't question her intention.

She wished that he would question, though. Perhaps in
trying to answer him, her own thoughts would crystallize and
her doubts would vanish. He only waited, though, puzzled
but patient, and the only answer she could find to give him
was, "You'll understand soon enough."

Frost eased herself from the saddle and paced among the
shattered stones and broken rubble. Her lightning barrage had
done devastating work, but a scorched section of a wall yet
stood as high as she could reach. "Here," she said. "Come
and give me a hand."

She leaned her weight against a large chunk of blackened stone and attempted to move it. Telric was quickly there, his shoulder next to hers. "Where?" he grunted, straining. The stone rolled over a squared edge and fell heavily sideways. Frost bent and dug her fingers under the sharp edge. "Next to the wall," she answered, groaning as she tried to lift it again.

The sound of horses' hooves made her straighten. Riothamus and two of his soldiers came around the wall. He looked down at them impatiently. "What are you doing? I thought you went to hide in the woods."

She was growing tired of his attitude. "And you saw me ride out again. Get your two lackeys down here and call up more of your men." A hint of anger flared in his eyes, but she ignored it. "Hurry up. There are preparations I've got to make, or any surprise we see this day is going to be on us." She bent to the stone again.

"Your Majesty," he said.

She looked up. "What?"

"It's how I am addressed," he told her sternly.

She hadn't come so close to a true laugh for some days, and she bit her lip hard to choke back the sound. It wouldn't do, she realized, to embarrass a king, even Riothamus, before his soldiers. He had to keep their respect to command them. After all, she had asked him to cooperate. Could she do less?

She stifled her mirth with an effort. Instead, tight-lipped, she bowed her head to do him honor. In return, he granted her an imperious nod.

Their eyes met and locked. He knew how she truly felt, and she knew he knew. Yet his dignity was preserved before his men. He nodded again in secret acknowledgment of their new, tacit agreement. For now, he asked no more of her but the pretense of respect.

"By the wall," she instructed the two soldiers, who dropped from horseback and came to her aid. The four of them managed the stone handily and placed it where she directed by the standing remains of the tower. "Now another on top of it."

Quickly a series of uneven steps was erected to the wall's summit. By the time they had finished that task, ten more men had joined them, called forward by a gesture from their king. They dismounted and flung their cloaks over their saddles.

"We've got to work fast," she told them. "Clear the stones from around this wall. I need a circle, and not so much as a pebble within it except what we've erected here."

The Keleds fell to work at once. They labored without complaint in the hot sun until their hands were scraped and filthy and their sharp, neat uniforms were covered with dust. Another ten men joined them, and even Riothamus climbed down and lent his hands to the hard work. That surprised her; she wondered if he did it because he truly felt her urgency or to reinforce his image with his men.

The air grew thick with dust and the smell of sweat. Stones flew and bounced and cracked. Teams of men worried at the larger chunks of the once mighty structure, using them to fill gaping holes in the earth where the tower's basement levels had collapsed.

Once, Riothamus stopped and brushed his hands. He looked about to see what work remained and started to send for yet more of his warriors to come and help.

"We'll do with these," Frost said in quiet warning. "This is one-tenth of your force. Leave the rest fresh and rested for the battle."

He looked as if he would argue, then thought better of it. "You don't know when Kel will get here," he said. "It could be days. We may all have time to rest."

She shook her head. "It will be today. Only the hour is in question."

"By what witchcraft can you know that?"

She regarded him patiently, then wiped her chafed hands on her tunic and turned away. There was still work to do, stones to remove. There were her own special preparations to make. There was no time at all for his foolishness.

It took no magic to know when Kel would come. She knew her son, had seen the mad determinations that fired him. She had also studied his map over and over. She knew the distances and the time it took to travel them.

Days ago Kel had attempted a sorcerous assault on her storm. In her mind and heart she had felt the echoes of his efforts. Abruptly those resonances had ceased, though, and she knew he had failed to disperse the rains and the lightnings.

She was equally sure that, given his past behavior, he had turned his men and taken the longer route around the hills.

Her son was too impatient to wait out such a storm as she had raised. He was not given to waiting; he was driven to act. Such was her son's nature. Kel would push himself and his men relentlessly, resting little, forgoing food or sleep, and he would reach his tower today.

She knew it.

In fact, she counted on it. Kel would arrive with an exhausted fighting force, and he would ride unsuspecting into her surprise.

I loved you once, she thought of her son. *I'm sorry for what I must do.*

Then she kicked herself, bitterly aware of the turn her thoughts had taken. "Think of Kimon and Kirigi," she said aloud to herself. "Think of Soushane. Think of Lycho and Jemane and Pericant, Oric and Cleomen . . ."

Telric touched her shoulder. "What are you mumbling about?" He leaned down and peered closer at her. His fingertip lifted a drop of moisture from the corner of her eye. "Are you all right?" he said, his voice heavy with concern.

She blinked, then stared down at the broken rock she held in both hands. She drew a deep, weary breath, waited for a soldier to move out of her way, then heaved the stone onto a growing pile. "Fine, just fine," she answered unconvincingly, gently rubbing sore palms together.

He took her hands to examine them. "Let the others finish here," he said. "You'll have work aplenty when they're done."

"So will they," she countered. "Fighting's damn hard work, and killing's harder yet. There's no rest for anyone until this is over."

"There's rest for you right now," he insisted, taking a waterskin from another soldier. "Here, drink."

She accepted it gratefully and swallowed a large mouthful. It washed down the dust in her throat, but it also reminded her of the well at Dakariar—and Lycho.

That's right, she thought angrily. *Embrace that memory and all those other memories. Harden your heart. Use them to block out the fact that it's still your son you're preparing to betray.*

But it isn't betrayal, she argued with herself.

She took another long pull at the waterskin, stoppered it,

and handed it back to Telric. She caught his wrist as he took it from her. "Could you do this if he were your son?"

The Rholarothan's eyes narrowed sharply; for a moment she had the chilling feeling that he could see into her very heart. She remembered then that Telric had been Kel's prisoner. It wasn't fair to ask him such a question.

"Do you love Keled-Zaram?" he asked when he found his voice. "Did you love your husband and your younger son?" Telric brushed his fingers over her cheek. The touch was feather soft, yet it communicated much. "It isn't easy for you, is it?"

"It shouldn't be easy," she answered simply. "He's my firstborn."

His hand drifted down to her chin, tilted her head slightly upward. His finger played at the corner of her mouth. "You love him in spite of everything," he said, finishing her thought. His voice softened, and he spoke in a bare whisper. "But he'll destroy everything else you love if you don't stop him. He's killed his father and brother, and I know how you bleed inside for Soushane and Dakariar; it shows in your eyes when someone mentions those towns." He stepped closer and slipped an arm about her. "And how long will it be before he destroys you, too? If not your physical body, then the spirit within you?" He put his face next to hers and embraced her with a warm, protective strength. "I'll stop him myself before I let him do that."

She freed herself from his arms. He was gentle and comforting, but the war raging in her soul was not so easily ended. "I have a terrible foreboding," she said quietly, "as if there is so much more to this that we don't understand."

He tapped her lightly on the temple. "Sometimes, you have to stop thinking," he told her, "and just act."

But she shook her head, wrapped her arms about herself as if a cool wind had blown over her. "I can't do that," she said distantly. "I knew another child once who had killed father and brother." She looked up until their gazes met. "Also a mother."

They were interrupted before either could say more. Riothamus stepped between them, his bright garments and once gleaming armor covered with dirt and fine, gray stone powder. He pointed toward the woods. "Company," he announced.

Telric reached for his sword, but Frost stopped him. The riders all wore scarlet cloaks, and they emerged from the woods by the same path she had led from Kyr. She estimated their number at half a *krohn*. Straight across the field they rode toward the ruins.

Riothamus slapped his thigh. "Damn pup. I told him to stay home."

"That's the trouble with love," she quipped. She had already guessed who it was before the king's outburst. It was no great surprise when Sarius jerked his mount to a halt before them and removed his helm. The youth flashed a tight grin and bowed his head to his monarch.

Riothamus strode forward and seized the young governor's reins. "I told you to stay in Kyr." He couldn't hide the anger in his words, though he kept his voice low.

"No, you didn't." Sarius swung a leg over his horse's head and slid lightly to the ground. He didn't smile, but there was thinly veiled amusement in his reply. "You said I couldn't come with you." He looked over his king's shoulder at the working men and gestured for his own escort to dismount. "So I came on my own."

"Leaving Kyr undefended!" Riothamus snapped.

The fifty men were all that Riothamus had spared to man the garrison. At that, they were only a token force, insufficient for a city the size of Kyr.

Sarius was unconcerned. "The safety of the king is more important than the safety of any one city," the younger man countered with equal crispness. "Even my own." His voice dropped, and he continued as if he thought no one else could hear, "I came to fight beside you. Don't send me away. Don't shame me."

The two men regarded one another, and Frost felt the silent communication that passed between them like a spark. They were lovers, she reminded herself, and she wondered which would win this private struggle. It would be easy to side with Sarius this time. Fifty extra men would only make her task that much simpler.

So, she was relieved when Riothamus placed his arms around the youth and hugged him. It brought to mind how good it had felt when Telric had embraced her moments before. She had neglected to tell him so.

"Stay then, but keep close to my side." The king backed a step and clapped Sarius proudly on the shoulder. "If we fight, then it must be together." He put on a sudden grin. "That also means you get to help me lift that big stone over there, so take off your cloak and get to it."

Sarius paled. "Manual labor?"

Riothamus nodded sternly. "Right by my side." He beat his sleeves, making sure the dust spread to his lover. Then, for good measure, he brushed a finger over Sarius's cheek, making a dirty smear. With a laugh he turned and headed for the stone while a very puzzled young governor followed.

With fifty additional backs, the job was quickly finished. Frost told them all to stand away while she paced around the isolated section of wall. The cleared space was large enough for her purposes and free of rubble. She only hoped the damned wall didn't collapse when she climbed up on it.

"Give me that lance," she said to a soldier who stood closest to the horses. He obeyed instantly, sliding one of the long shafts from a carrier on one beast's saddle.

"Now," she said to Riothamus, "take all your men into the woods. Position them as we discussed and wait."

Sarius spoke up. "How long?"

The king answered before she could, "As long as we must."

"But those woods are full of mosquitoes and bugs!" Sarius protested glumly, but he added before anyone admonished him, "If you say wait, we wait."

"My hero." Riothamus grabbed the youth's neck and shook him playfully as a cat might its kitten.

"One last thing," she said as they began to mount their steeds. "If you think you see something strange happening when the fighting begins"—she fixed king and governor with a hard stare—"you must ignore it. Your part is to fight anything or anyone that doesn't wear a red cloak. Nothing else is important to you. Make sure your soldiers understand that."

Riothamus nodded. His next remark took her by surprise. "We'll try to take Kel na'Akian alive if we can."

She lowered her eyes and swallowed hard. She hadn't expected that from him, had not even allowed herself to think about it. It was certainly more generosity than Kel deserved from the king whose land he had ravaged.

"Can you forget so easily what my son has done?" she asked uncertainly.

Riothamus's face hardened. "I said I would *try* to take him alive, woman. I promise no more."

She stared, openmouthed, speechless.

"I've had time to think, Samidar," Riothamus continued, again startling her. She had forgotten that was the name he knew her by. It was the first time in the long ride he had used it. "I think Yorul must have acted rashly at Dashrani. Kel na'Akian was the enemy he was ordered to capture. There was no need to kill young Kirigi or to burn your tavern."

It was too late for such apologies, yet she was grateful. She closed her eyes and permitted one sweet, unblemished memory of that last morning with her adopted son. He had been naked; they had walked down the road and talked of so many things. "I'll never leave you, Mother," he'd said innocently.

But of course he had. He had been too young to know that life was a series of good-byes.

She put the memory away and opened her eyes. That had been another lifetime and another world. There was the present to deal with now, and the future to prepare for. "No matter what you have to do," she said grimly, regarding the king without flinching, "you stop Kel from crossing the Lythe River. No matter what it takes."

Riothamus looked as if he would say more, then thought better of it. He wheeled his horse and led his men into the woods. Frost watched as they fanned out in a semicircle and disappeared among the trees. There they would wait, a living barrier between the ruined tower and the river.

Telric stood by the wall, holding the reins of his mount with those of Ashur. He carried two red cloaks over one arm, and he held a waterskin.

She glanced at the sun. It was midday or a little after. When would Kel come?

"Don't think," the Rholarothan had told her. *Act when you must.* Maybe he was right. Maybe she could cling to that philosophy and make it through this day.

She spun around as if someone had called her name. Westward, there was Esgaria, where she was born. Only a narrow patch of woods and a river separated her from it. Was it her homeland that called to her? She listened, waiting to hear if the sound would come again. But the silence mocked her.

She remembered the sorceress Oroladian, and she remembered the gifts that Kel was bringing for her. Was it the wind she had heard blowing from Esgaria? Or was it Oroladian who called her name?

You'll never get them, Frost swore as if the sorceress could hear her thoughts. *Whatever these aspects are you've tricked my son into stealing, you'll never hold them in your hands. By all the dark gods, I swear it.*

Five paces from the wall section, Frost used the point of her lance to scrape a symbol in the hard-packed ground. "What's that?" Telric asked, coming near to see the glyph better.

"It would take too long to explain all its meanings," she answered. "And you still might not understand. Take your horse away from here. He mustn't disturb these."

He led his mount away and watched her work. She scratched a circle around the wall. At each of the cardinal points, she made the same symbol as the first. Then she scraped a second circle inside that, so that her markings were ringed and sealed.

Inside the second circle she carved new symbols at the eight major compass points. This time the glyph was more elaborate, and the hard earth made the work difficult. She cursed repeatedly as she erased portions of the patterns and made them again correctly. The lance point quickly dulled. She leaned harder on the haft and dug her scratchings as deeply as possible.

When the second ring with its eight markings was completed, she began a third.

"Sixteen of those things?" Telric exclaimed doubtfully. "There won't be room."

She didn't answer. There would be room, but just barely. It was the time she worried about. The final set of glyphs was yet more elaborate, and she didn't know when Kel would come. Would she have time?

"I thought you said a witch didn't need such things," the Rholarothan said. He moved as she worked, stepping carefully among the eldritch characters until he reached her side.

"I don't draw power from them," she explained. "There is no innate magic in this pattern. To Kel or any other sorcerer they would be useless."

Her comrade scratched his head. "Then why all this work?"

"Useless to a sorcerer, but not to a witch. The design will help me to focus my own raw power for a special purpose." The point of her lance suddenly snapped, nearly pitching her forward, but she caught her balance and continued with the jagged edge.

"You didn't need anything like this when you leveled the tower," Telric observed.

Frost straightened and leaned on her tool. She regarded him quietly for a moment. "It's far easier to pull lightning from the sky," she told him, "than to affect the mind of a man with magic." She gazed around at the ruins. "When I did this I was full of rage. Nothing makes magic stronger than rage and hatred, and destructive magic is always the easiest." She returned to her work. There were still three glyphs to finish. "Now, I still have that anger," she added without looking at him, "but there's also doubt and fear and trepidation."

There was little else to say after that, and she was grateful when he left her in peace and went to stand with his horse. She watched as he departed, assuring herself that he disturbed no marking, broke no part of the circle.

She completed the last glyph. There was only one remaining element to her pattern. After a pause to wipe the sweat from her brow, she moved outside the circles. From each of the cardinal points she drew spokes five paces in length radiating outward toward the edges of the field. Between those four lines she scratched four shorter ones, then eight more shorter than the second set.

When the final line was drawn she rubbed her back and let go a sigh. "It's done," she announced. She went to Telric and took the waterskin from his horse's saddle. Before she drank, she scanned the edge of the woods. There was no sign of Riothamus or his men, but she could sense the eyes upon her every movement. "Nothing to do now but wait," she said to her friend, and upended the skin.

Telric drank when she had had her fill. The liquid dribbled over his chin and into his tunic. He rubbed it over his throat and face, then glanced at the sun. "What do you want me to do?" he asked at last. "We're going to be right in the middle of this thing, you know."

Of course she knew. She also knew it wasn't fear that prompted his words, but Rholarothan impatience. "Have faith in me," she answered softly. "And let no man climb those crude stairs, because that's where I must stand." She pointed to the top of the wall.

Telric gazed at the summit, and his brow crinkled. He shook his head. "Don't be a fool. You'll be too exposed, and Kel has archers."

"I have to risk it," she said firmly. "If Riothamus does his part, Kel will be very busy."

But Telric argued, "A bow shot is a simple thing, woman, and your son outnumbers us two to one."

"He doesn't know that," she countered, "and if I do my part, he won't know it."

His dark eyes narrowed, and he glared at her. "What are you planning?"

She patted his head and smiled hopefully. "Wait and see. You're going to love it."

He could only shake his head and grumble, "What about your circles? They could be wrecked if the battle gets too close."

"Oh, it will get close. That's why I want you here. And Ashur will be with us, too. But by the time they get this close, my spell will either have succeeded or failed, and it won't matter what happens to the circles."

She knew he didn't like it, but at least he kept his worries to himself. He followed her back across the pattern, drew his sword, and laid it upon his lap as he took a seat on the lowest stepping-stone. Frost squeezed his shoulder, glad in her heart for his company. Then she climbed past him and up to the top of the wall. There, she also sat and stared toward the east, where Kel na'Akian would emerge from the woods. There would be no hiding for her or Telric.

What would he think when he saw his tower? She knew her son. He would be angry and vengeful. He would think of his grimoires and the arcane objects he had left behind accumulated over the years. She wondered where in all the rubble those evil things were buried. She hoped they stayed buried.

A motion below caught her eye. It was Telric's horse. Bored, it had begun to wander off, and she cursed herself for the oversight. She should have sent the creature with Riothamus. If it wandered into her pattern . . .

She didn't even finish the thought. Ashur suddenly chased after the horse and nipped its flanks until it sped toward the hidden Keleds. The unicorn herded Telric's steed to the first trees, then turned back toward the circles.

A red cloak appeared briefly to snatch the horse's reins and lead it out of sight.

Frost smiled, wondering what Riothamus had made of that. Not one of his men had reacted strangely to Ashur during their journey. Apparently, not one man among them had noticed his difference or perceived any small part of his uniqueness. How could so many be so blind?

She would never figure it out.

Chapter Fifteen

So darkness falls upon us all
And no one, no not one,
Shall walk away when day
Dies and the moon shines on battle lines.

See how we die, how our souls fly
On crimson wings to find a morning
Gone, forever gone.

How we dance and kick upon the lance!
With steely grace the cold, dark angels race
To tear our hearts apart,
And the last songs we hear are songs of terror,
  songs of fear.

"Only two *krohns*!" Telric argued from his position at the bottom of the stair. The waterskin was balanced on his knee. He had not moved for some time for fear of disturbing the pattern. "That man must be a fool."

"Not a fool," she answered patiently. "Just naive. He's been a sheltered king. In all his reign he has never ventured far beyond the gates of the capital at Sumari, except to hunt or take a country ride with his court. Riothamus has very little understanding of his own people. It's no real wonder that Kel

has been able to strike and elude him so often." She paused
for an instant, remembering. "Now Riothamus's father—
there was a hell-raiser."

Telric only scoffed. "His old man is dead. We're stuck
with what we've got."

"You worry too much. I said he was naive. But he's not
stupid, and he learns quickly." She yawned and stretched to
ease the stiff muscles in her back. "Bring me some of that
water before you guzzle it all."

He climbed high enough to hand her the skin. She took it,
unstoppered it, and tossed back a mouthful. It tasted good and
cooled her parched throat. If only she were not growing
hungry as well. She gave the skin back, and Telric returned to
his place.

The Rholarothan's grumbling had taken her mind from her
doubts and fears. The conversation had even lifted her spirits
somewhat. It didn't matter to her that he had planned to do
just that. He was probably smiling secretly to himself and
thinking how clever he was to have directed her concerns to
other matters.

She looked down upon his dark head, bared to the weltering
sun. Fine streaks of gray shimmered silvery when he turned a
certain way. *Old dog,* she thought, suddenly aware of the
growing fondness she felt for him, *what am I to do with you?*

"What are you doing here?" she asked impulsively, putting her chin on her palm and leaning forward. "Just who
are you, Telric?"

He twisted on the stone step where he sat and gazed at her.
His face remained impassive. A soft wind rustled his hair and
stirred the red cloak on his shoulder. She waited for him to
say something. She bit her lip; a strange constriction squeezed
her chest, and she felt for an instant as if she were folding in
on herself.

"Talk to me," she urged him. "Make me know you."

He turned away and stared into the distance, unmoving.
What ghosts had she disturbed to make him react so? Even
through the cloak the tension in his body showed. He drew a
long, slow breath; his head drooped between his shoulders.
Frost wanted suddenly to run down the steps and throw her
arms around him. The thought startled her, but it didn't lessen
the sorrow she felt for bringing such a mood upon him.

Yet she remained where she was, unable to take that step.

She stared at his broad back. Finally he rose, turned, and faced her.

"Frost," he said thickly, "Samidar, is it in you ever to love me? Is there any hope that you might ever call me husband? Or even lover? I would settle for that."

She gaped, caught off guard by the intensity of his speech. She, too, rose and descended the steps to stand just above him. Such pain in those upturned eyes! They stabbed into her heart.

She laid a hand on his cheek and caressed it. His questions rolled over and over in her head, thrilling and tormenting her, bringing joy and grief at the same time. And the answers rolled there, too, jumbled and broken and uncertain.

Her hand slid up into his raven locks. She had never dared to touch his hair before; it was silky smooth, as she had known it would be. She studied the lines that time had etched into his brow, stared into eyes that seemed unbearably familiar, deep as the Calendi Sea, eyes that haunted her dreams.

Her hand drifted down his shoulder, down his arm. Their fingers met and interlocked and squeezed fiercely. She thought she could answer him honestly if she searched her heart. The answer was there, yet it frightened and mystified her.

It was Telric's hand she held—but it was Kimon's face she looked upon.

She started to speak, but he reached out and pressed one finger to her lips. "You think I look like him, don't you?" he said.

She blinked. It was as if he had read her thoughts. "I loved my husband," she told him needlessly. Even as she said it, she discovered no pain or grief remained in her memories of Kimon. There was only a sweet, encompassing warmth. "Even in death I love him deeply. I can't forget him." She descended one more step, and they stood eye to eye. "I could sleep with you, if that was what you meant by lovers. But we both know it wasn't."

His face filled with sadness. "No, it wasn't." He looked away, then his gaze came back to her. The light of the sun reflected in his moist eyes.

"It's unnatural how much you look like him," she said in an awed half whisper.

She saw the truth, then, Robin, where it had always been,

unconcealable in those eyes. She let go of his hand and thrust her knuckles into her mouth.

"It's very natural," he admitted with barely controlled emotion. "Kimon was my brother."

She stumbled, caught herself, and sat down heavily on the step. Her mouth worked, but words eluded her.

"My half brother," he corrected, kneeling so they faced each other once more. He took her hands again and pressed them between his own. She closed her eyes, unable to meet that ghostly gaze.

"I've loved you just as I've said, and I've searched for you for years," he told her earnestly. "I didn't lie about that. I love you, woman, and I never would have told you this—I'd have kept it secret forever—but I hear how you speak of him." He swallowed, paused, and hung his head. "I see how you look at me, and I know it's him you're thinking of." He placed his hands on her knees. His voice took on a softer tone. "At those times I despair, because I fear I'll never have your heart."

She opened her eyes. Shivers ran up her spine as she regarded his face. It was so familiar, yet so different. "How . . . ?"

He tilted his head quizzically, then pursed his lips. "Father was very good to his bastards," Telric began sarcastically. "At least, the ones he knew about. Kimon's mother was a barmaid in Shazad. There were lots of barmaids, if you know what I mean." He waited to make sure she did. "Of course, they all fell out of favor with Father sooner or later. Sometimes, I think he only tolerated my mother—his legal wife— because her bloodline was older than his, and her fortune was a damn sight larger.

"The legitimate sons were never allowed to mix with the bastards, but Father kept a close watch on them all. Kimon quickly caught his eye. When his mother lost her job one winter, Lord Rholf gave him work to earn their support." He hesitated and looked thoughtful. "I think Kimon was nine, then. Rholf gave him a knife and taught him to skin and gut the catch from the day's hunting. That was his single chore all winter. Later, there were other jobs, and Rholf began to train him. He gave the boy his first bow, then his first sword.

"Let me tell you, I was as jealous as all my brothers. Father spent more time with his bastard than he did with us."

He paused again. Frost didn't say anything but waited for him to continue. Kimon had never talked much about his past; she had always assumed it was because of some deep, personal hurt, some memory he refused to touch upon. She herself had been acquainted with such pain, so she had never pried.

Telric took up his tale again. "Kimon began to disappear for days and weeks at a time. Sometimes, he was gone for months. His mother had died of some illness, and my brothers and I thought it was that melancholy that had turned him so sullen and caused his absences. But one night, he was summoned very late by my father." He stopped and smiled suddenly, an ironic and self-condemning smile. "By accident—no, it wasn't accident—my brothers and I were up late, too. We hid behind the arras in Rholf's room to hear what they discussed. That night, we learned he had become my father's personal—"

"Assassin," she interrupted, finishing his sentence. "I know that part."

Telric's lips drew into a thin line, and he patted her knee. "Of course you do." He rose and stretched, then, to ease the cramps in his legs. "If I have any skill with a sword today, it is because of Kimon. After that night, I redoubled my efforts at training in the hopes of recapturing my father's attentions." He smiled again. "In some ways, it worked. Kimon disappeared for longer and longer periods of time, and when he was home he and father always quarreled. Rholf began to spend more time with his true sons when Kimon was around—I think to put Kimon in his proper place, to remind him he was only a bastard." He kneeled before her again and tried to put on a grin. "He used us. It was no surprise to me when Kimon didn't come back from a mission. If only I'd known it was you Father had sent him after, I'd have followed. I loved you even then, Samidar."

She tried to see the young man he had been. "I saved your life in the Creel Mountains."

"And left me in the desert."

"We were enemies."

His smile was genuine. "It took me one night to realize we weren't." The smile broadened, chasing the sadness from his eyes. "Oh, the dreams that came to me that night!"

A silence rose between them, and their fingers intertwined once more. They regarded each other, and she saw in his face the years of hope he had nurtured. "Did you never marry?" she asked.

He shook his head.

"But there were women?"

He considered a moment, then began to tick them off on his fingers, counting soundlessly. She slapped his hands before he got far, then tangled a hand in his hair and tugged sharply.

"Faithless, disloyal . . ." She stopped. Though he joked and smiled, she knew the pain he carried. It was still easy to remember the touch of Kimon's arms around her when she was lonely or hurt, easy to recall waking curled around him when the sun streamed through their window. How could she ever have lived without that? How had Telric lived without it?

She reached out and touched his face again, asking herself another question. How could she not love him now? They had confronted so much together these past days, ridden and fought and suffered side by side.

It was just that way that love had come to Kimon and her. Danger and trial had knitted their hearts. Why shouldn't it happen again?

Because she couldn't look at him without seeing her husband. In his eyes she would forever see only Kimon.

"Oh, gods," she said softly, slowly, as a new realization stole upon her. Her hands folded into tight fists. "Kel is your nephew."

Telric only nodded.

Frost rose, numbed, and climbed back to the top of the wall. She looked out over the field and into the woods. Something inside her began to cry, but no tear misted her vision. Nor did she know whom it cried for, or why. For her? For Telric? She stood until her legs began to tremble, then she sat down and put her head in her hands.

A cool wind blew upon her neck. A cloud passed over the sun, casting a tenuous gray shadow. She craned her head upward and cursed herself with dull enthusiasm. It took no effort to still the song within her that had called the cloud, but it sobered her and reminded her to keep a tighter rein on her emotions and her witchcraft.

The cloud drifted away. The sun returned with its unrelenting heat. She shielded her eyes.

"It was only one little cloud," Telric called, using his

sleeve to wipe sweat from his face. "Couldn't you have left it awhile?"

A sheepish look curled the corners of her mouth upward. "How did you know?"

"Half the time I've spent with you I've been soaked to the skin by one storm or another." He raised his arms toward the sky and made a mocking attempt at magic gesticulation that mostly amounted to finger wiggling. "You think I'd blame nature now?"

"If there's any magic at all in your hands," she said, pointing to the east, "then you'd better direct it there."

The first line of Kel's force broke through the trees and stopped. Kel rode to the fore and jerked back on his reins. Neither he nor his men wore their skull masks; they hadn't expected battle on their own home ground. Her son raised his hand, motioned, and led the way across the field. Straight for the ruined tower he rode. His black cloak fluttered behind him, giving him the appearance of a great, winged bird in flight.

Frost could feel Kel's gaze upon her. His anger preceded him like a palpable wave.

Telric picked up his sword and smacked the blade against his palm in anticipation. *Well,* she thought, *it was magic of a sort, anyway.*

When Kel and his men were halfway to the ruins, Riothamus acted. The Keled army emerged from the woods in a large semicircle and swiftly closed around the outlaw force in a pincer movement. With their smaller numbers, it was a suicide maneuver.

Kel's army came to a halt, kicking clouds of dust into the air. The rebels wheeled their mounts, momentarily confused, uncertain. Weapons glittered in their fists as they drew steel. They stared toward the Keleds and toward their leader, waiting for his command.

Frost had to act quickly.

She seized the broken spear haft from where she had laid it atop the wall and raised it over her head. Already the song at the core of her soul was building; the power surged, stronger than ever, engulfing her. The eldritch music in her ears drowned all other sound.

The power erupted from her, up through her outstretched

arm and into the spear haft. The air crackled around her fist
and the hard, polished wood. The haft began to glow with an
azure radiance that only she could see. From either end twin
shafts of energy lanced downward and struck the innermost of
her circles. The symbols ignited with blue fire that spread to
the middle circle and the outer until all three rings and all
three rune sets blazed with arcane fury.

The flames reached the final parts of her pattern—the
spokes. Fire shot along the scratchings, but they did not stop
when the device was fully aflame. They continued outward
over the field until they licked the very leaves at the border of
the woods.

No soldier or horse gave any notice at all. No one beyond
the circle saw. The flames gave off no heat, no smoke. They
could not be felt by flesh. There was nothing for the mortal
eye to see. The fire was only a construct of her imagination, a
visualization of her power as it spread over the field. She
opened the deepest parts of herself, secret, forgotten places
long unexplored, and her magic flowed forth.

The field blazed with her energy, and the air sang with her
music!

"Gods and gods!" Telric cried. He stumbled from the
lowest stone, where he had stood watching, and twisted hard
to avoid stepping on one of the burning symbols. Within the
circles, he, too, could see the flames, and he cringed away.
"Woman, what are you doing? You'll burn them all!" He
clambered back upon his stone, staring outward, and again he
cried, "Gods!"

She smiled grimly, and the music began to diminish. "Only
an illusion, old friend," she told him. She lowered the spear
haft and leaned upon it. "No one will burn. Watch."

Riothamus's soldiers gave a tumultuous shout and charged,
closing inward on Kel's army. As they rushed deeper into the
blue fire, which only she and Telric could see, each red-
cloaked figure seemed to split and divide into three men. The
volume of their battle paean and the thunder of hooves seemed
loud enough to shake the earth itself. Sunlight gleamed on a
veritable ocean of steel. Like a mighty hammer, they smashed
into Kel's startled forces.

The clash and clang of weapons and the screams of the
slain were the only music now. Swords and axes rose and fell
with manic precision. Lances plunged, scored, withdrew in-

carnadined. Warriors toppled from saddles and were trampled; crushed and broken bodies bled into the uncaring earth.

To Frost's eye it was murder. Utterly confused, Kel's mercenaries fell like chaff before the Keled scythe. She looked down from her high place. Dust hung in a great, choking cloud over the battle, but it couldn't obscure the horror.

She bit her lip. There was a sickness in her stomach.

A handful of rebels broke from the fighting and ran full tilt for the woods. A band of red cloaks rode them down, hacked the bandits into bloody pieces, and turned to rejoin the conflict. She recognized Sarius at their head. There was none of the youthful enthusiasm in his face that had been there before. He wore a grim mask of hatred and determination.

She searched for her son amid the confusion. The field had become a chaotic swirl of men and horses. She couldn't find Kel, and there was a measure of relief in that. Perhaps he had fallen already. Or if he had not, maybe she would be spared the spectacle of his end.

"They strike at ghosts," Telric said gloomily. He ran one hand slowly up the flat of his blade as he gazed over the battle. "They can't tell the real Keleds from the false images."

He spoke truly. It was almost comic how the rebels swung and lunged at foes that weren't there. Imaginary swords couldn't kill, but imaginary enemies didn't die, either. Terror drove the mercenaries to a howling, disorganized frenzy. They distrusted their eyes; they began to chop at anything close that held a weapon—sometimes their own fellows.

"Do you pity them?"

The Rholarothan stood stiffly as if punishing himself with the sight before him. Then, "It doesn't seem fair or honorable."

An unreasoning anger suddenly boiled from her. She flung the spear haft, hitting him across his broad shoulders. He whirled, startled, eyes clouding with an anger of his own. Frost stalked down the steps, shaking her fist.

"Honor is a damn rare commodity!" she shouted furiously. "Too precious to waste on garbage. Was there honor in what Kel did to Soushane or those other towns? Do you think fairness ever entered his mind before he murdered all those people?" She raised her fists over her head, shivering with the strength of her emotions. How she wanted to knock that fatuous expression from his face. "Don't you dare speak to me of honor!"

"Those are men!" he shouted back. "This isn't battle—
it's butchery!"

What a fool he was! Whatever had made her think she
needed him? "It's just what they would have done to Riothamus
if I hadn't used my spell. Then where would the killing have
ended? How many more innocents like Kirigi and Kimon
would die before Kel was stopped?"

Telric took a step back, nearly falling off the stones again.
He looked at her, aghast. "Woman, he's your son! It was one
thing to *talk* about this battle. But this is real. He's your
son!"

As abruptly as it rose, the anger drained from her. She
straightened and wiped at the corner of her eye; it was sweat,
she told herself, and nothing more that made her blink. An
eerie calm settled upon her, but she couldn't bring herself to
watch the fighting.

"He's completely mad, Telric," she said at last. "He's my
son, but he's your nephew, also. You know what he is, and
you know why we must do this." His hand clenched spasmodically around his sword's hilt. She felt sadly sorry for
him, and she wondered if Telric had followed Kel from
Soushane to avenge her as he had claimed or for the chance to
know his brother's son. "It still hurts, though, I know," she
gently added.

Telric said nothing; he turned his back to her.

The battle was drifting closer. She spied Riothamus. The
king showed no lack of courage as he rode through the thick
of the combat. He rammed his steed into another man's
mount, sending horse and rebel tumbling, screaming. As the
mercenary scrambled to his feet, Riothamus leaned from his
saddle and drew the edge of his sword across the man's
unprotected throat. A vengeful shout of triumph warped his
features. He wheeled his horse about to hack at another foe.

The blue fire faded away; the last strains of music stilled
within her. She surveyed the field from her high vantage,
sickened by the carnage. Mercenary bodies littered the ground.
Few red cloaks seemed to have fallen. There was no need to
maintain her illusion any longer.

Suddenly her knees weakened, and she sagged prone upon
the wall. A barely audible moan escaped her lips.

Telric raced to her side and bent over her. He cradled her

head in his hand and brushed a strand of hair from her face. "What's wrong?" he shouted. "What happened?"

She moistened her lips to speak. "It'll pass," she managed with an effort. "I told you, it's much harder to touch a man's mind with magic, and there were so many men. . . ." She swallowed and struggled to sit up. "I didn't expect it to take such a toll." She gripped his shoulder and rose unsteadily to her feet. When she had ended her spell, all her strength had faded with it. She had expected to feel a weakness, but she hadn't anticipated it would hit so hard. She squeezed Telric's arm, using him to maintain her balance.

"Can you fight?" the Rholarothan questioned worriedly. "They're coming closer."

The tide of battle was definitely turning their way. In answer, she drew her sword. The sunlight rippled along its length. "Then let's go down to meet it," she suggested.

She let go of his arm and he led the way down the step stones. At the bottom he carefully avoided the glyphs as he set his foot on the ground. "Those are useless now," Frost told him. She rubbed the toe of her boot through the nearest one.

There was no order to the fighting. The red cloaks had begun as a disciplined unit, but the killing had eaten too far into their brains. Much of the combat was now on foot as horses had been lost or slain. Again, she searched for some sign of her son, praying to her gods that Kel was already dead.

Three rebels ran across the field to attack her, war cries ringing. Incredibly swift, Telric lunged in front of her, raising his sword high over his head to intercept the first descending blow. Then, in one smooth motion he raked his weapon over the mercenary's unarmored gut, cutting deep. Without pausing to draw breath, he met the second man. Rholarothan steel described a glittering arc and chopped through the rebel's sword hand. Telric's backswing drew a scarlet line under a chin.

The third rebel bore down upon her. Frost brought her sword up in both hands, and her gaze narrowed.

But before she could act, a black shadow rushed from the corner of her vision. There was a sickening *thud*, the ripping of flesh, a groan of utter surprise and despair. The rebel's eyes snapped wide with death fear.

With a shrug of his massive neck, Ashur lifted the man high into the air and tossed him away. The huge spike on the unicorn's brow glistened wetly. He trotted to her side, and she ran a hand gratefully through his thick, stygian mane. In the excitement she had nearly forgotten him. She sprang onto his back.

"There's nothing in this ruin to guard," she called to Telric. "Look after yourself!"

His hand caught a piece of her cloak, and he jerked hard. She tumbled backward over Ashur's rump and landed in the crook of her comrade's left arm. He waved his sword near her nose. "Don't be a fool," he hissed. Genuine rage showed on his features as he set her on her feet. "You're weak, and it's nearly over."

"It passes quickly," she snapped. "I'm all right."

Two more rebels charged them. Frost sidestepped, brought her weapon around to intersect the haft of a whistling battle-axe. Her foe grinned as she backed up a pace, and he followed her. The axe wove a dazzling butterfly pattern as he advanced. She waited a heartbeat, judged his timing, then brought her edge slicing over his bare bicep.

The axe pitched from fingers abruptly gone numb. The rebel stared at her in pain. He said nothing, but his expression begged for mercy.

With all her might, Frost lunged, pushing her blade through his chest until it protruded obscenely between his shoulders. With an equal effort she tugged it free.

The rebel dropped to his knees, clutching desperately at the spurting hole in his breast. Then, he fell forward. A red spittle oozed from his mouth into the dirt.

Mercy? she thought bitterly to herself. *If Kel has to die, then I have no mercy for his hirelings, either.*

Telric stood over his lifeless opponent, examining a gash in his sleeve. "Just a scratch," he announced, ripping the material away to show her. "I was careless."

She forced a mirthless grin. "Nearly over, I think you said."

But Telric had been right. The red cloaks fell on the few remaining mercenaries like starving wolves, riding them down, surrounding them, and hacking until the bodies hardly looked human. Seldom had she witnessed such savagery from trained soldiers.

Telric had spoken earlier of honor, and she had criticized him. The world was not generous to men with ideals. He had only to look and learn a lesson. When men fought men, honor was not involved.

The clamor of steel on steel faded. The battle shouts echoed away. There was no pounding of horses' hooves or hiss of arrows in the air. Only a dark and terrible moaning from the wounded or dying hung over the field. It, too, quickly diminished as Keled soldiers walked among the fallen, giving swift and final end to their enemies.

"The people of Keled-Zaram are avenged," Riothamus declared as he rode up to her. He dropped from his mount and stood holding the reins. "We have you to thank for it."

"Don't thank me," she muttered. "Help me find Kel. I lost sight of him when the battle was joined."

Riothamus gazed back over the carnage and rubbed his chin. "I'll help you," he replied quietly, almost apologetically. "But it may not be easy. Some of my men have done their work too well."

She knew what he meant. The body might not be recognizable. Her son could be lying dismembered, hewn apart by the overzealous Keleds. Or horses might have crushed him beneath their hooves, leaving only pulp and little else that resembled Kel.

Still, she had to know. She threw her arms around Ashur's neck and offered a silent prayer to her gods. Then she started across the field to walk among the dead.

Old memories rushed upon her of other times and other wars. The distinctive odor of blood crept into her nostrils. It mingled with the smell of men who had fouled themselves in their final moments. She stopped, her eye caught by something shiny on the ground. It was a jeweled medallion on a broken chain of fine gold. She bent, scooped it up, handed it to Riothamus, who, along with Telric, followed her. "To the victor," she said bitterly.

There was a sick feeling in her stomach. She had gotten out of this business long ago and thought never to return. Too much war had filled her younger days, and too many times she had wandered over fields like this one searching for her friends.

The faces were the worst. There were the hardened faces whose scars told of lifetimes in battle, old faces, and young faces of mere boys seeking a first taste of adventure. There was a shank of gray hair and a grizzled beard; there, a bare chin that never knew a razor. Blood stained them both.

But old or young, worldly wise or innocent as virgin children, every face bore the same expression. Fear-widened eyes, mouths frozen in twisted, soundless screams, skin already turned death pale.

Not one had expected to die. Not one had welcomed it. Death was a god that only claimed an enemy or a comrade. What man, soldier, farmer, or king had not convinced himself in his heart of hearts of his own immortality?

She winced at the upturned faces. Every one of them reflected the surprise and terror they had found on the point of a sword. She uttered another prayer to the god Orchos, who ruled the nine hells. *Let it be different with me,* she prayed. But she knew it would not.

Sarius came running up to join them, flushed and breathless with excitement. Blood splattered his finery, and blood dripped fresh from the sword he held. He rammed the blade's point into the earth and left it quivering while he flung his arms around his king. "We've beaten the bastards, every last one of them!" He pressed his lips to Riothamus's and hugged him again. "Now, we'll leave them to rot and their cursed bones to bleach, a warning to all would-be rebels."

"You'll bury them or build them a pyre," Frost said through clenched teeth. "Just as I did for the people of Soushane."

Sarius looked disdainfully down his long nose. "That's enough out of you, bitch. Your usefulness is ended. There's a cell back in Kyr waiting for you."

Telric's sword hissed from its sheath.

Riothamus put out a hand. "Hold, Rholarothan. Sarius still feels his blood racing and oversteps himself." He pushed the young governor back a pace. Sarius looked outraged and started to speak, but his king gave him a light backhanded smack on the mouth and raised a threatening finger. Sarius pouted but held his tongue.

"We'll make a pyre for the dead," Riothamus promised Frost. He gave the order to Sarius, who grudgingly carried it to the nearest red-cloaked officer. "There'll be no prison for you," he said when his lover returned. "I think you've paid a higher price this day than any of us."

"I haven't found my son yet." She turned away from him and resumed her search, kicking the hilt of a broken sword aside with her toe. *Broken weapons,* she thought morosely, *broken lives.*

"Dark angels without wings," she said aloud when Telric bent to pick up the hilt. He gazed at her, appearing to understand. He drew back and threw the bit of metal high and far. It sailed end over end, sparkling in the sunlight, then plummeted back to earth.

"I don't know how it happened," she overheard Riothamus say to Telric as she bent to examine a body. The face was ruined, but a tuft of dark hair sprouted on the chest. Kel was smooth-chested. "When the charge began," the king continued, "and the battle cry went up, it sounded like there were a thousand of us, and everywhere I looked there were red cloaks. Yet we were only two hundred and fifty!"

Telric looked appropriately grave but said nothing for a long moment. Then he rubbed at the scratch on his forearm. "This was your first taste of fighting, wasn't it?" He waited for Riothamus to nod. "In all the confusion, perhaps it only *seemed* to you that your men were more numerous. You won because your men surprised and disoriented the rebels." He paused and nodded toward Frost. "She's an excellent strategist."

She could not even smile at how easily her friend lied. A deep conviction began to gnaw at her, though. "He's not here," she announced with grim certainty. Still, she went from corpse to corpse.

Riothamus scoffed. "He must be here. Not one of them escaped."

"I tell you, he's not here!" She picked up a sword that laid abandoned on the ground; both edges were notched and dulled. She spun around, her gaze scouring the field again. In her frustration she brought the flat of the blade down sharply on her knee. It made a brittle *snap.* She discarded the separate pieces angrily. "He must have had some spell," she mumbled.

"You said he wouldn't have anything prepared," Riothamus reminded her. "You said his sorceries took time to ready. He must be here!" For the first time he stooped to examine a body with his own hands. He rolled it over, gave it a cursory glance, and moved to yet another. A growing knot of desperation stole into his voice. "He must be here!"

"A small personal spell, maybe," she continued as if she hadn't been interrupted. "Some charm that let him slip away."

At that instant, a horrible din rose from the far western edge of the field. Every man stopped in his tracks and turned, staring toward the source of the shrieking, seized by an uncontrollable shivering.

Frost felt the blood in her veins turn to ice. She knew that frightful sound. She whirled, shielding her eyes from the setting sun, and gazed upon all her worst fears.

Kel sat upon his big black stallion. The sun glinted redly on the short length of metal in his clenched fist. There could be no doubt that it was the dagger, Demonfang. Nothing else on earth made such a hellish cry.

Across his saddlebow, Kel held a bound and squirming red cloak. He cradled the Keled's head in the crook of one elbow as if he were holding a baby. The man twisted and writhed to no avail in the sorcerer's unyielding grip.

The dagger's shrieking strained to a wilder pitch. Even over such a distance it seemed to fill the air with its abominable hunger. Frost felt its power like a potent vibration that crawled on her flesh, that burrowed into her mind.

Still Kel waited, as if to be sure that everyone saw and knew who it was that mocked them. The red cloaks had drawn first blood in this battle; he would draw the last. He raised the dagger high above his head. The sun's glow touched the metal, and it shimmered like a short, scarlet flame.

Demonfang flashed downward, sinking to the hilt in the Keled's chest. The shrieking paused as hell yawned to receive another soul; then the dead man's mouth opened, and those same shriveling screams issued again.

Frost shut her eyes and counted her heartbeats until the dreadful chorus ended. When she opened them again she could barely see through a red film of hatred.

Kel pulled Demonfang free and sheathed it. Casually, he lifted one leg and dumped the murdered soldier in the dirt. With limitless gall he held up a saddlebag for them to see.

She could almost hear his laughter as he turned the stallion and rode into the narrow strip of forest toward the Lythe River and Esgaria. It required no witchcraft to tell her what was in that saddlebag. He had wanted her to know; he had meant to taunt her.

Kel had his Three Aspects at last. One from Soushane, one

from the well at Dakariar, and one from the Plain of Kings.
He had seized them and made them his despite all her efforts
to stop him.

Now, he would carry them to Esgaria and lay them at the
feet of the sorceress Oroladian.

But I'll still come for you. She sent the thought flying on a
burst of magic and drove it forcefully into her son's heart.
Even as he plunged into the Lythe's waters she felt him
stiffen at her touch. *I'll come for you both!*

She ran for Ashur, intent on following her son. But heedless of the bodies and the debris that littered the field, she
tripped and fell flat on her face. Dust filled her mouth, and
she stared into a dead man's eyes.

Chapter Sixteen

The wind had risen sharply as the sun drifted from the sky. The trees shook, and the leaves rustled dryly. The normally placid surface of the Lythe rippled with tiny, dancing white-caps. On the banks the grasses shivered.

A thick brown smoke churned among the branches, held down by the wind, unable to escape into the higher reaches of the air. It bore a nauseous tang that clung to everything it touched as it roiled up from the massive funeral pyre.

Frost brushed away the strands of hair that whipped at her face. The clear hoofprints on the soft earth led straight into the river, pointing the direction Kel had taken. She sucked her lower lip and stared across the Lythe into Esgaria.

A flock of cawing birds flew overhead. They wheeled slowly, gracefully, toward the sunset. She listened until their cries and honkings faded in the distance.

Did the gods send her a sign? Would they lead her to Kel if she followed them? Or had chance alone sent them flying into her homeland?

"An omen?" Telric said, displaying that uncomfortable talent he seemed to have for knowing her thoughts. He pointed the way the birds had flown.

She shrugged and looked back over her shoulder. The trees were too thick to see the field. She should at least say good-bye to Riothamus. Oddly, she felt as if some bond of friendship had been forged between them. But there was no time, and the king and his men were working hard at a sorry task, piling bodies on the pyre they had built on the very ruins of Kel's tower.

Sarius would think she had deserted or fled for fear of her life. Riothamus, though, would know where she had gone. He would understand.

She nudged Ashur's flanks with her heels. The unicorn started into the river. The water swirled about his legs, around her boots. The bottom fell away suddenly, and she submerged nearly to her chest. With a muscular lurch, Ashur began to swim.

An abrupt splash alerted her that Telric had decided to follow. He had said little since Kel's escape, and she had made no effort to breach his silence. There seemed little need for words.

The river chilled her. The strong midstream current threatened to sweep her from the saddle. She wrapped her legs around the unicorn and stubbornly gripped the saddlebow. These waters had almost claimed her life once; she wouldn't give them a second chance.

Ashur's hooves found purchase on the muddy floor. He scrambled up the side of the bank and tossed his soaking mane. She yelped and tried to shield her eyes from the cold spray.

"I'll get you for that," she swore in a low voice.

"For what?" Telric pulled up beside her. Without warning, his horse also shook itself, and she was showered a second time. Telric laughed as she wiped her chin. Droplets rolled down his face and into the beard that had begun to grow on his chin. "For that?" He laughed again.

She had to admit it was a good sound.

Then, an awful quiet filled her. The soul seemed to stir and tremble in her body. She gazed around at the trees, the deepening blue of the sky, the shadows that seemed to surround her.

She was home.

"I've found his tracks," Telric said roughly. The leather of his saddle creaked as he leaned over to study the markings on the ground. "I said I've got—"

"It doesn't matter," she answered softly. The wind died, and an odd hush settled over the forest. She was reluctant to disturb it.

But Telric had no such compunction. His voice was harsh

and jarring in the stillness. "What do you mean?" He pointed. "Look, he's gone this way."

She frowned. Didn't he feel it? Didn't he understand? This was Esgaria, and she had come home. She peered upward through the looming trees that seemed to lean over and whisper to her. The sunlight streaming through the leaves whispered and listened. The dark recesses whispered and listened.

"Not much light left," her comrade reminded her. A note of irritation had crept into his voice. He walked his horse a few steps down the narrow path. "We could lose him in the dark."

She turned her head from side to side and spoke in a muted murmur. "I've touched his heart with my magic." She closed her eyes and hugged herself, and her voice dropped even lower. "I can feel him. I know where he is. You needn't worry about losing him."

She opened her eyes again. The mood of the forest was overwhelming. She breathed deeply, and the odors of the leaves and the grass and the soil filled her.

Telric's brows knitted together; then he glanced away. The cloak he wore couldn't disguise the way he bunched his shoulders. His hands clenched around his reins until the knuckles whitened. "You don't need me for anything, do you?"

Suddenly, the forest was just another forest. The land could have been any country. The wind blew and the leaves rustled and the river made a bubbling roar, but the sound was the same as on the Keled side, the same as it was anywhere.

She rode close to Telric, leaned out, and put a hand on his thigh. "Don't talk like a fool," she said in a normal voice. If the forest could listen, she didn't care. "I have my witchcraft, but I also have a heart and all its failings. I'm scared, and I'm tired." She paused and waited until he looked up and met her gaze. "I feel so old, Telric. If you weren't here to see me through this, I don't think I could go on."

A wan smile parted his lips. He laid a hand on hers and squeezed it. "It's a nice lie," he said. "You're stronger, woman, than any man I've ever known. Magic has nothing to do with it. You had no power when we first met years ago in the Creel Mountains." He swallowed and wet his lips. "Nothing stops you, and you do what you have to do."

"So do you, Telric Lord Rholf." She pulled her hand

away and looked ahead into the dense foliage where the
tracks led. "Kel na'Akian is your brother's son. This is a
family matter."

He hesitated. "Family?"

A nod of her head closed the discussion. There was yet a
faint gray light from the setting sun. They could push deeper
into the woodland, then make camp for the night when it
was too dark to travel. She nudged Ashur onward and held up
an arm to knock the first low branch from her face.

Esgaria closed around them.

Frost leaned back, glad for the spongy piece of ground that
made her bed, and rested her head on her saddle. She stretched
and willed her weary muscles to relax. The small fire warmed
the soles of her bare feet, and she wiggled her toes deliciously.

Thousands of crickets and other insects filled the night with
their songs. An owl hooted, unseen in the impenetrable gloom
beyond the firelight. Overhead, the branches sawed back and
forth in an easy breeze. It was an age-old chorus, and she lay
perfectly still to fully enjoy it.

A twig snapped. Telric stepped into the circle of light,
returning from a short, private walk. He dropped down onto
the cloak he had spread beside her and folded his hands
behind his head. Only a very few stars were visible through
the thick overhang.

"You're too restless," she observed. "Try to sleep."

"You could catch up to him," he said. Clearly, his mind
was still on Kel. He raised up on his elbows and stared into
the fire. "I've seen Ashur run, remember? You could over-
take him easily."

She sighed, not wishing to surrender a rare moment of
peace. She folded her hands behind her head, hoping he
would take it as a hint. "The stallion was strong and swift,
and Kel knows his way. He has that advantage. All we can do
is follow."

He sat completely up. "You said you could tell where he
was!"

She shifted her feet a little closer to the fire, relishing the
toasty warmth. "I can, but that doesn't mean there's a neatly
paved road between us. I can't just ride over to him and say
hello. An unseen limb would knock me as flat on my back as
anybody."

Telric lay back again. He folded his arms over his chest, and his mouth drew into a tight line. Something weighed heavily on his mind, but he held it back.

"I've given it some thought," she said at last to ease his worrying. "And I've decided we've got a little time. We don't have to push so hard; we need rest ourselves."

He rolled over on his side to look at her. The fire gave an orange sheen to half of his face. One eye gleamed; the other was lost in shadow.

She decided to explain a few things to him. "Kel told me the objects he sought were the Three Aspects of a potent Chondite spell that would bring the dead back to life." She named the objects for him, ticking them off on her fingers. "The Eye of Skraal, the Lamp of Nugaril, the Book of Shakari—don't you see? This isn't any common spell, but true grand magic. High necromancy." She gazed upward, searching the sky through the thick branches. The moon was not visible to her, but she knew its present shape. "That kind of necromancy can only be done when the moon renews itself and the night is as black as hell's deepest pit. That's three nights away."

He frowned and shook his head. "None of that makes much sense to me."

She smiled. Impulsively, she rumpled his hair. "Of course not. You're a Rholarothan."

"I think I've been insulted," he said with a pout.

"Many times in your life, no doubt."

At last, he settled back and seemed to relax. He loosened his tunic to let the breeze play over his bare skin and interlaced his fingers on his belly. The gentle rush of his breathing became one more song added to the night's performance. But his eyes never closed.

For a long time she stared into the fire trying not to think about anything, and for a brief while she felt as if some part of her had merged with the land and the night. A sweet calm descended upon her, siphoning her fatigue, bringing a tranquil contentment. She knew it wouldn't last, but for now it was something very precious.

Her hand lightly brushed her companion's cheek. He rolled over again. She sat looking down at him until he, too, rose up.

"What about Kimon?" he asked slowly.

There was no hesitation in her answer. "I love Kimon. I'll love him forever and longer than that. But Kimon isn't here. He can't touch me, and I want to be touched."

He looked past her into the fire. "You're not in love with me, though. Not the way I am with you."

She took his face between her hands and made him see her. His features danced with firelight and shadow; his eyes glowed from dark depths.

"I do love you, Telric," she said earnestly. "At this moment, for this night, as much as I can, I do love you." She pressed her forehead to his. "Let that be enough."

He pulled her hands down, but he didn't let them go. "What about tomorrow?"

She shrugged. "Tomorrow is tomorrow."

Sadly, he shook his head and lay back down. He turned away and rested his head in the crook of an arm. "It's not enough," he told her honestly.

She sat there, silent, unmoving, watching his back. The crickets sang, and the breeze played in her hair, and the night waited with her. After a little while, he rose again and reached for her hand. "Maybe it's enough," he conceded, "for one night."

The fire had burned very low. Neither Frost nor Telric felt like getting up to hunt more wood, and they were warm enough next to each other. They lay quietly, listening to the sounds of the night. Then, in the gloomy forest depths among the twisted limbs and gnarled old trunks, something caught her attention.

"Look," she said, freeing herself from the arm Telric had thrown across her middle. She raised up on one elbow to see better. "Fireflies."

He peered over her shoulder, then put his head back down again. "Ummm, just a bunch of bugs."

She sat up and watched them for a long time, winking in the darkness, mesmeric and beautiful. Yet she remembered *Sha-Nakare* and moved a little closer to the fire.

By noon the next day they had reached the end of the forest. A small town and surrounding fields lay directly in their path. Frost pulled Ashur to a halt while there were still enough trees to hide them.

"You go on," she told Telric. "Get us some food and find out what place this is. I'll meet you on the far side."

He gave her a doubtful look. "Surely you don't think anyone here would remember you. It's been a long time."

She gazed at the nameless town. A part of her longed to ride beside him. Those were her people ahead. She shared a heritage with them. Yet she knew she could not enter, and a small pang stabbed her heart. "I'm still a woman wearing a sword," she reminded him. "They would shun me as something vile and despicable. Even if I kept my mouth shut so they wouldn't recognize my accent, even if they didn't guess that I was also Esgarian, I wouldn't be welcome. Women do not touch the weapons of a man—that is our strongest taboo."

Telric hawked and spat. "Stupid custom."

"Is it more stupid," she rejoined, "than the blood feuds that keep you Rholarothans at each other's throats?"

He appeared to think about that as he scratched his sweaty chest. Then he shrugged.

"I'll go wide around the fields." She pointed to the road that cut straight through the town. "You'll find me along the way when I'm out of sight of the citizenry."

He nodded, but then he pursed his lips and asked sheepishly, "Just how hungry are you?" He patted his clothing meaningfully. "I'm afraid you've caught me at a low moment—not a *minarin* in my pocket."

Her jaw dropped. She clapped a hand to her chest; the purse she wore on a thong was gone. Cursing, she remembered she had lost it at Dakariar during her confrontation with Kel.

She closed her eyes and let go a long sigh. Then she slipped the silver circlet from her brow and turned it lovingly in her hands, admiring the workmanship, savoring the memories it brought. The sun gleamed on the single moonstone set cleverly into the twisted band, and she imagined she could see in its polished surface the aged face of the woman who had given it as a gift on her first adventure. Frost had treasured the circlet all those years.

"Take this," she said, pressing it reluctantly into Telric's hands. "We both need a decent meal. My belly feels like an empty pit." Her fingers lingered briefly on the ornament as he accepted it from her. The metal was still warm with the heat of her body. "See that you bargain dearly with it though," she added. "Get a good price."

He frowned but thrust the piece inside his tunic. "You'r sure that Kel came through here?"

"Through and straight out," she answered shortly. "H didn't tarry, either. See that you don't."

She jerked on the unicorn's reins and rode away, followin the edge of the forest until she was beyond the range of th fields and the town was but a featureless smear in the dis tance. Then she cut westward, making a wide arc until sh rejoined the road.

A tree grew close to the roadside. She dismounted, unfast ened her weapon belt, and sat down with her back to th rough bark. Ashur stayed near and began to munch the thic grass.

The leafy branches shaded her from the sun, and sh opened the top of her tunic slightly to let the scant breeze coo her. She ran a hand along the grass, then dug her fingers int the rich earth.

Was it a tremor of fear or a thrill of excitement that ran u her spine? *Esgaria*. In every quiet moment that name spran into her thoughts. She had come home at last. The leaves, th wind, the sun all seemed to whisper *Esgaria*.

She opened her hand. The black, fertile soil sifted throug her fingers.

Yet her homeland had rejected her, made her an outcast denied her the right to be what she was. Esgaria, as much a she, with its laws and customs, had murdered her brother Esgaria was to blame for her parents' deaths.

The land that was so dear to her was also dangerous an alien. She realized with a deep, aching sadness that, althoug she had been born here, this was not her home. She loved thi land of dark forests, yawning valleys, and sharp cliffs. It wa a mysterious, spectacular land with a spirit all its own.

But she was a warrior and a woman—and for that Esgaria would not love her.

Love. She turned the word over and over in her mind. Sh longed for it where it was not offered, and she rejected i when it was.

What had driven her into Telric's arms? Loneliness? Fea of the future? So often she had seen men on the eve of a battle seek the solace of sweethearts, wives, or prostitutes

Perhaps some similar instinct had compelled her to reach out for Telric. In fact, it had been on the eve of her confrontation with Kel that she and Lycho had savored each other.

Lycho had given her so much, but Telric had given more. The force of his love had swept away her cares last night, and eventually she had found beside him the first restful sleep in months. But it had not ended, she knew. When the sun had come up she had seen into his eyes, noted the way he gazed at her as they rode. He had said little, nor had he tried to touch her again. But she had felt his longing.

In the night it had been sweet. In the light of day with time to think, she realized it had only been cruel. Still, she wondered if she would feel the same when darkness fell again. She had no doubt how Telric would feel.

Could she make a new life with another man? The thought startled her. She had given no consideration to anything beyond stopping Kel and settling with the sorceress he called Oroladian.

But after that?

Suddenly, she was thinking of Amalki and Teri, the friends who had saved her few belongings when her inn had burned. She found she missed her neighbors, and she wondered if Teri's baby had been born yet. Surely it had come by now. Boy or girl? She wished she had agreed to let them name it Kirigi.

She sighed and gazed down the road toward the town. No matter what, life went on. Kings and soldiers, witches and sorcerers struggled and schemed and killed each other. But the Amalkis and Teris and the babies seemed always to go on.

She leaned back against the tree and watched an ant crawl over the toe of her boot. Slowly, she relaxed. Home or not, it was a beautiful Esgarian day. Fleecy white clouds drifted idly in the blue heavens, and with nothing better to do, she indulged in her favorite childhood game, imposing shapes on the clouds with her imagination. There was a bear, and there an eagle. Another cloud wore the shape of a horse, and as she watched, the wind worked its own special magic and changed the horse into a unicorn.

Frost smiled, stretched on her back, and folded her arms under her head.

The rich smell of spiced meat woke her. She opened her

eyes and met Telric's grinning face as he waved a morsel under her nose.

She sat up, embarrassed. "I dozed. . . ."

Before she could say more he popped the bite of meat into her mouth. In his other hand he held an oiled wrapper with more meat. Beside him on the ground was a sack. It smelled of bread and cheese. "You were tired," he said, holding another tidbit to her lips. As soon as she swallowed the first he pushed it in. He seemed to take a peculiar pleasure in stuffing her mouth that way. She chewed as quickly as she could, and he took a piece for himself.

"By the way." He licked his fingers and reached inside his tunic. "You seemed kind of fond of this." He extracted the moonstone circlet. "So keep it. I've always liked the way it looked on you—like a third eye." He set it on her brow and grinned. Then he pushed another morsel into her mouth and folded the wrapper over the remainder. He stood and slung the sack over his shoulder, and she eyed him curiously, chewing. He went to his horse and put a foot in the stirrup.

"When you finish that," he said, mounting, "you'd better hit the saddle."

She stopped chewing, suddenly suspicious. The circlet on her head felt like a heavy weight. "How did you pay for all this?"

He glanced over his shoulder toward the town. "It was fun, actually," he answered, winking. "I haven't stolen anything since I was a boy." He patted the sword on his hip. "You should have seen the innkeeper's face. He packed all these goodies for us, and all he got for his trouble was a good close look at the edge of my sword." He shook his head and grinned again. "Got to credit him, though. He pointed out the nicks in the metal and how it needed a good honing, but forgive him, please, his throat wouldn't make a decent whetstone."

Frost clambered up, strapped on her weapon belt, and sprang onto Ashur's back. She stared down the road. "Any pursuit?" she said breathlessly.

He shrugged. "You don't look as tired suddenly."

She ignored his comment and took off at a gallop. Telric followed close at her heels, laughing in the wind. The sack of food bounced at his side. She cast a glance over her shoulder, but there was no sign yet of pursuers. Still, it didn't pay to take chances. The sooner they put some distance between the town and themselves, the sooner they could stop and eat again.

She prayed he'd had the good sense to steal a little wine as well. What was spiced meat without a good red wine?

They rode hard, slowing only when they entered yet another wood. The smell of water hung in the air. A short distance on, they stopped on the bank of a narrow, tranquil river.

"Break out the cheer," she ordered, pointing to the food sack. "I can't think of a more idyllic place for a picnic. Then, if no one leaps on us from the shadows, I'm going to take a bath." She smelled herself and made a face. How could Telric possibly have been attracted to her last night? She sniffed again. For that matter, how could she have been attracted to him? "You, too, but make sure your horse gets a drink first. The water won't be fit afterward."

She looked at him suddenly, feeling pleased with herself, unable to recall the last time a joke had passed her lips. It felt good, very good indeed.

The Rholarothan dismounted, came to her side, and held up his hands to help her down.

"Sir!" she exclaimed with wounded pride. "I'm quite capable of getting off and on this beast without you. I suspect you're looking for another opportunity to slip your brutish arms around me."

Telric put on an innocent expression, but he still held out his arms.

"Oh, all right." She swung a leg over her saddlebow and leaned toward him. "But mind your manners."

Instead of setting her on the ground, he caught her legs and cradled her in his arms. He brought his face close to hers, hesitated, then kissed her. When it ended there was a mischievous gleam in his eye.

"Telric," she said slowly, "put me down. I told you to mind your manners."

He took a couple of steps. The muscles in his chest and arms bulged. With a heave, he tossed her into the river.

She gave a shriek as the water closed over her head and she hit bottom. Sputtering, she leaped up and wiped her eyes. Telric had already spread his red cloak on the ground and started to pull a small feast from his sack.

"You overblown, pompous piece of dung!" She stopped, speechless as she watched him pull out a corked bottle and two delicate vessels of beaten gold. She waded from the waist-deep water, her gaze riveted on the red liquid as it poured from the container.

"Stay there," he ordered sternly. He set the vessels carefully on the ground, rose, and began to undress. "We stink." He dropped his tunic and pulled at a boot. "In Rholaroth we never dine with stinky people. It's bad for the digestion."

Frost removed her own garments and tossed them soaking onto the grassy shore. "Just make sure you bring the wine. I'll even consider forgiving you for a taste of that."

When he was naked he picked up the vessels and waded in to join her. The sunlight glinted resplendently on the gold as she accepted one of the wine cups and turned it in her hand. The liquid swirled within, rich and thick as blood. It had an outstanding bouquet. She shut her eyes and took the smallest sip, savoring it. As she had hoped—it was superb.

"Forgiven?" Telric asked over the rim of his cup.

She took another sip. "I'm still considering," she answered, and clinked her cup against his. He tried to embrace her, but she held him off. "You Rholarothans don't dine with stinky people, and I'm damned hungry. So wash." She knocked back the last of her portion and tossed the empty vessel back on the bank. It landed on the spread cloak precisely beside the bottle.

She moved out toward the middle of the river. It was deep enough to swim, and there was very little current. She took a few strokes and dived beneath the surface. The water was warm, glorious. Her tired muscles began to loosen immediately. When the need for air compelled her, she surfaced and swam back to Telric.

He stood near the shore, laving water over himself. His skin shone where the droplets clung to him. His muscles rippled as he worked. For a nobleman Telric was still in fine shape. He hadn't gone soft with easy living like so many rich men.

She moved closer. A fine tracery of scars lined his arms. A bigger scar told of an old wound on his thigh. A similar scar ran along the ribs on his right side.

Her feet found purchase on the muddy bottom, and she extended her arms the better to observe her own battle history. It was written in her flesh just as it was in Telric's. They both had seen too much of war in their lifetimes.

"How's the bicep?" she called, remembering the latest of his wounds.

Telric flexed his muscle for her and grinned. "I told you it was just a scratch. It's nearly healed."

She nodded and began to wash her body and her hair. A rude noise from her stomach reminded her just how hungry she was, so she hurried.

They climbed out together, and Frost gathered her clothes and draped them over some low branches in the hope they would dry before she had to wear them again. Still naked, Telric sat cross-legged on a corner of his cloak and carved slices of cheese with a small dagger he wore on his weapon belt.

The wine cups were already filled when she sat down beside him. There were two oil wrappers of spiced beef and pork. There was also a chunk of fresh bread still warm from the oven. She tasted the wine and reached for a share of the meat.

Only a bit of cheese remained when they were finished. Frost licked the lip of the bottle and upturned it, collecting the last droplet on her tongue. With a regretful sigh she tossed it over her shoulder into the bushes.

Her companion leaned close. "Samidar . . ."

She pulled away from him, rose in a swiftly graceful movement, and walked several paces away. There was a dull buzz between her eyes—the effect of the liquor—but she wasn't drunk enough for what Telric had planned. Half the day was before them yet, and there was a long way to go. "Get that look out of your eye, Lord Rholf," she snapped. But even as she spoke, her gaze wandered over his nude form. She forced herself to look away, recognizing the danger in their casual familiarity. She moved farther away and collected her garments from where she had hung them. They were still soaked, but she pulled on the tunic, suppressing a grimace at the clammy touch.

Telric sat watching for a moment, then reached for his own clothes. He dressed quickly and munched down the last piece of cheese while she struggled with a wet boot. "We probably should have saved some of this," he said, swallowing the final bite, licking his fingers. "But it was just too tasty."

She said nothing. They'd both eaten as if they'd been starved, without a thought for tomorrow. Too late to worry about it, though, and there was a pleasant, snug feeling in her belly. Her clothes, however, were not pleasant, and she resented Telric for the trick he'd done her.

"Help me with this damn boot," she called, balanced precariously on one foot while trying to shove the other into the damp leather. She glanced from the corner of her eye to see if he would fall for her plea.

Indeed, he fell. As he bent down to push on her heel, she placed both hands on his shoulders and shoved with all her strength. The splash he made as he hit the water was quite satisfying. The sight he made as he surfaced, muddy and sputtering, was even more so.

Frost folded her arms over her chest and smirked.

Telric staggered up the bank, wiping his face and new beard. Mud soiled his boots, his knees, and his backside. His garments clung limply to him. "There's a mean streak in you, woman," he averred solemnly.

She backed hastily away from him, took Ashur's reins, and mounted. "I prefer to think of it as my playful side." She flashed a grin that showed all her teeth. "See you on the other shore." She guided Ashur past him and into the river.

"Well, if I have to ride in wet clothes, at least I have the consolation of knowing that you do, too," he shouted as she went by.

So you think, she laughed to herself as she rode up the opposite bank. It was no greater a test of her magic now than it had been in Kel's tower to dry her garments. She did it surreptitiously so her friend wouldn't notice. He had pushed her in the river first; she had only avenged herself. He deserved wet misery—but she was having none of it.

She waited while Telric mounted, forded the river, and joined her. The expression he wore as he adjusted himself in the saddle was gratifying, but she hid a grin and instead shut her eyes briefly to listen for the tiny chord that echoed at her soul's core. It told her that Kel had passed this way.

It was enough to know they were on his trail, and she shut her heart against the faint music. She would not dwell on her son today. It was too fair an afternoon, and she felt too good.

A different music, she decided firmly. *I'll sing, instead.*

Her voice filled the wood. Songs she once had sung in her

kitchen poured forth. When those were exhausted she reached farther back into her memory. Battle songs, traveling songs, bawdy songs, ballads, laments, love songs followed one upon the other. She wished idly for an instrument to play upon, but no matter, it felt good just to open up and sing!

"You have all sorts of talents," Telric commented between melodies.

She answered scornfully with a mocking roll of her eyes. "You should see how I paint." She made another, uglier face.

He cocked an eyebrow. "Music *and* painting?"

She laughed at his surprise. "And sewing and cooking and languages. You forget that I was a nobleman's daughter and educated accordingly." She bit her lip. "Of course, I learned a lot of other things, too, from my mother—things you wouldn't want to know."

She regretted her words instantly. Memories surged up irresistibly, and a new mood settled upon her, dampening her spirit. All the old pain and hurt rushed upon her. Ghosts she had thought exorcised long ago threatened to rise again, and ancient griefs tugged at her heart.

She sang one last song, fighting to dispel the mood, but there was no joy in the music this time, and she stopped before the final verse was finished.

Riding close, Telric touched her hand. Her fingers intertwined tightly with his, and she clung to him as if he were an anchor.

Not for years had those memories bothered her. She'd put all the guilt to rest—or so she had thought. *Why now?* she pondered. Her past seemed suddenly to hang over her like a black cloud. Indeed, she glanced up through the branches to assure herself the sun still floated in the sky.

But the answer loomed all around. It was the land, Esgaria itself, that haunted her. It knew her crimes and called her to judgment. She might find brief shelter in Telric's arms or in a jovial picnic or even in a song. But the land was always there, waiting. The very spirit of Esgaria accused her, and for all her witchcraft she could not stop its voice.

She rode the rest of the day in silence, watchful of every tree in the forest, alert to every swaying leaf, to the rustling and whispering.

They traveled until the sun was gone from the sky. In the

murky twilight that remained, they made camp for the night. Telric gathered kindling for a fire while Frost found a few larger pieces of dead wood, fuel enough to see them through until morning. Neither spoke of food. They spread their cloaks next to the flames and lay down with their saddles for pillows. He snuggled up behind her, slipping an arm about her waist. In no time at all, his breathing slowed and sleep claimed him.

Frost sighed and tried to relax. Telric's nearness warmed her, but she was relieved when he sought nothing more than to lie beside her. On her side, she gazed into the fire. She could feel the Rholarothan's heartbeat, and she could hear her own like a counterrhythm. Slowly, the sounds lulled her to sleep.

But with sleep came dreams! Sweet dreams and troubling dreams. She rolled ecstatically in Kimon's arms. Or was it Telric? Then, armor materialized around her nude form. Kimon—or Telric—disappeared, replaced by Kel and his mercenaries. She swung her sword, cutting and killing until she stood knee-deep in bodies.

But every corpse wore her brother's face!

Those faces also faded, and she stared at the familiar visages of the men and women who had frequented her tavern. She danced and whirled for them, and they threw coins. But in midair the coins turned to fireflies that stung and burned her flesh. She ran stumbling, tripping on her skirts, until she came to a river, and she dived, but even as her feet left the bank she saw her reflection on the moonlit water.

Impossibly, the reflection reached up to embrace her. Yet it was not her image at all. The thing in the water wore her mother's face, and it laughed at her! Its arms closed about her and dragged her down into the murky depths. She struggled, gasping for air, inhaling the water, beating her fists against that mocking face while it laughed and laughed. . . .

Frost sat up, instantly alert, drenched in sweat. No matter the nightmare, she knew dream from reality. That hadn't been laughter. Only Ashur made a sound like that.

Telric came awake, too. "Huh? What is it?"

"Shut up!" she hissed. Her sword rasped from its sheath. The fire's glow rippled along the keen edge, casting an amber reflection among the leaves.

The unicorn screamed again, reared, and stamped his hooves

on the mossy earth. His eldritch eyes burned and crackled
with a wild intensity. He tossed his head, lashing the air with
his mane.

Telric's horse suddenly joined in, whinnying and chewing
at the rein that tethered it to a sapling.

Too late, Frost felt it, too.

"Get up!" she shouted. The air tingled with an unnatural
foulness. The forest reeked with evil and decay. Telric freed
his sword; his eyes searched the darkness as he leaped to his
feet.

Something swooped across the fire straight for her. Her
sword came up and cut a broad arc, encountering nothing.
But she had cleaved it—she knew she had!

A black amorphous shape wrapped around her, soft as a
spider's web, and a shriek tore from her throat. The touch
was icy; her flesh began to freeze and her limbs went numb.
She twisted, writhed, but her motions were too sluggish. The
creature clung to her like thick smoke.

Her sword was useless. She reached within herself, seeking
some spell to strike with, but to her horror the familiar music
was stilled. Not even her witchcraft could help her! She felt
her life being sucked away. The numbing cold reached inexorably for her heart.

Dimly, she looked for Telric. He stood helplessly by, the
sword hanging from his lax grip. His mouth moved in shouts
and curses she couldn't hear, and tears streamed on his face.
She saw his plight and cursed fearfully. The thing that was
draining her life had no substance. If he struck with his
sword, the edge would find only her flesh.

But she was not ready to die! She knew this thing and how
to defeat it. Desperately, she forced frozen lips to move,
tongue and teeth to shape words. There was so little time!

"Gray . . . gray spot!" she cried weakly, but the words
sounded wrong, slurred, incoherent. She tried again, begging
her gods to make her comrade understand. "In the black body
. . . gray spot!"

Telric stopped his mouthings and stared in confusion. Then,
suddenly his sword flashed upward, gripped in both his hands.
He shouted her name like a battle paean and stabbed downward with all his strength.

A psychic scream ripped from the creature. Telric stumbled
back as if struck, clutching his head, and collapsed. White

light exploded behind Frost's eyes as the cry cut through her mind like a saw-edge.

Then, the creature was gone.

Her knees buckled, and she fell dangerously near the fire, unable to move, gasping for breath to fill her frozen lungs. Her exhalations fanned the embers and shifted the flames. Yet there was no sensation of heat upon her face. An uncontrollable shivering racked her. Her head snapped back with its violence; her limbs flopped insanely, then rigidly locked.

Suddenly, Telric was beside her, lifting and cradling her, rocking and pressing her to his chest. "Samidar!" he groaned. "Samidar!" She tried to answer, but words would not form.

Gradually, the trembling ceased. Telric held her as the night crawled by, and she began to warm. He rubbed her limbs and swayed back and forth as near to the fire as he dared take her. In the comfort of his arms, with two red cloaks wrapped about her, she let go of her fear.

But there was the memory of that touch and the cloying, sucking cold—the cold of the grave. She searched the gloom and the shadows and hugged the sword that Telric had recovered for her.

Once he got up, spying his own sword at the edge of the camp where it had been flung by the creature's death throe. He carried it to her, incredulous.

The blade impaled a dirty, age-yellowed skull.

The eye sockets, full of reflected firelight, seemed to accuse her.

Chapter Seventeen

"A *shimere*," she repeated. Emboldened by the bright light of day, it was easier to explain the unnatural thing that had attacked her in the night. She held Ashur's reins lightly and let the unicorn choose his own pace as she answered Telric's questions. "Some people call it a *shimmer* and others a *sending*."

He nodded, but she knew he didn't understand.

"Remember, Kel is primarily a necromancer," she continued. "If he has the skull or any bone of a person who died a violent death, then he can conjure that spirit and send it forth to do murder. But somewhere within its form the spirit must carry that bone. It always appears as a gray or white spot." She swallowed. The *shimere*'s cold touch was still a vivid memory. It had held her helpless. "Nothing can defeat such a creature but a piece of steel thrust into that spot."

Despite the sun's growing warmth, she shivered. Against the *shimere* even her witchcraft had been useless. She owed her life to the man who rode beside her.

"It was a ghost?"

She smiled at the simplification.

Her companion didn't share her amusement. "Kel knows we're after him, then. He can strike at us anytime, just as he did last night."

"Not anytime," she corrected. "Necromancy is nightbound. He can't work that kind of magic during the day. In fact, all his strongest sorceries seem to require darkness. It's a major weakness in his talents."

"Like a vampire," he spat. "He sleeps by day!"

She frowned at his display of ignorance. "Don't spout foolishness. Kel is wide awake at this very moment." She hesitated and briefly shut her eyes. "He's reached his destination," she announced.

Telric arched an eyebrow. "You can sense that? What about Oroladian? We must be very close."

Yes, they were close. Sunset should bring them to Kel's hiding place if they rode all day. That troubled her; Kel would have time to prepare a welcome, and she had learned the hard way what his magics could do. She would have to be on her guard.

And if Oroladian was there as well? What if it was two sorcerers they faced? She reached within herself, listening and hearing only the disharmony that was her son. If Oroladian was near, Frost could not detect her.

She began to regret letting Telric come along. Clearly, the Rholarothan was out of his element. He knew nothing of sorcery or witchcraft, nothing of the powers he faced. It had been unfair of her and selfish to drag him into this.

Yet last night the victory had been his. Without him, the *shimere* would have claimed her life. Still, she was torn. It would be easy for Ashur to outrun Telric's horse. She could leave him behind. Of course, he would follow, but by the time he caught up, maybe she could finish this unpleasant business.

Yet Kel was his nephew as well as her son. He had come this far, fought beside her, stood by her through terrors he couldn't comprehend. She had no right to leave him. She had fought against magic before with nothing but her sword and her courage, and always she had won. Telric was no less a warrior than she. To deny him now would be an insult. If he knew nothing of sorcery, still he was a man. And men had made even the gods tremble.

"We must ride hard," she said at last, "to beat the sundown."

Telric looked thoughtful, then he frowned. He patted his mount along the withers. "This mare is stout-hearted, but worn. Ashur will make it easily." He patted the horse again. "I'm not sure of this one."

"Would you rather spend another night in the open?" she said ominously.

His eyes narrowed. "I guess Ashur can carry us double again." He stroked his beast a final time. "Sorry, horse."

Frost gave her own steed a pat, leaned low to whisper in the unicorn's ear. He snorted in response and tossed his mane. Then she touched heels to his flanks, and they were off.

Sundown found them deep in the heart of yet another wood. The rugged trail had slowed even Ashur. Telric's mare was lathered with a heavy froth and breathing heavily, but the spirited animal had made a valiant effort and kept the pace. Still, they would have to rest the poor beast soon or lose her.

"We're close," Frost said, smacking a fist against her thigh. "Damn close. Where in the nine hells can he be hiding?"

Telric peered up through the trees. The sky was an orange blaze as day ended. Narrow shafts of light stabbed weakly through the foliage, contrasting eerily with the deeper patches of gloom. He sniffed; the air was full of a rich, earthen odor.

"The strangest one yet," he said sullenly.

"What?" she called back over her shoulder.

"The forests," he answered quietly, subdued. "So many of them in your land, all incredibly beautiful, almost haunting, like none I've ever seen." He paused, staring around. "Yet there's a kind of subtle menace about them. I've seen no game but an occasional bird. And I feel like something or someone is constantly watching me."

"A tension," she added, "like you're being squeezed very slowly and can't quite draw a full breath."

He nodded.

Frost leaned low in the saddle and ducked under a fat limb that stretched across the way. She understood well enough what her companion felt. As a child she had played in forests like this one. As a young girl at her mother's side she had practiced the secret arts among the dark shadows and creeping old roots of such huge trees. Sometimes, to escape her carping brother—or just to find solitude—she had climbed into the high tops and hidden from the world.

Even then, she had known the sensations that Telric had described, the sense that something lurked among the massive, tangled roots, in the tallest, unclimbable branches, something alien and curious. She had courted it as a child, dared it, played with the fear that behind the next tree something was waiting to grab her.

She was older now, and the games of childhood were behind her. Still, as she peered into the darkening recesses there remained a subtle dread.

"Esgarians believe our gods live in these wilder, northern forests," she told him as they rode. "Perhaps it's true. Much of this land has never known the print of a human foot."

Telric barked a short curse, and she turned around to see him rip at a thin branch that had snagged his cloak. "Because no human foot could get through some of this brush," he commented gruffly.

The trail was treacherous with twisted root systems and creeper vines. It was impossible for Frost and her comrade to travel faster. Limbs bent low enough to sweep a careless rider from the saddle, and dusty cobwebs repeatedly brushed their faces. Sometimes the ancient path vanished altogether in the thick undergrowth. Fortunately, there was enough daylight for Telric to see where Kel's recent passage had broken tiny branches and crushed the impeding grasses. She also had her witchcraft, but that only told her where her son was—not the best route to take to reach him.

She ground her teeth in frustration.

"The light's fading," Telric pointed out needlessly. "Maybe we should make camp. If we stand a close guard all night . . ."

"No!" she hissed. Then she apologized. It was no use getting angry with him. She had led them into this tangle. "He's close, I tell you. I can feel it. We're practically on top of him." She searched both sides of the trail, peering deep into the gathering darkness. "What did you say the name of that town was? The one near the border where you stole our food?"

"Parkasyt," he answered dully.

She shook her head. The name didn't mean anything to her. Perhaps it had sprung up in the years of her absence. They had passed by no other towns, but that was not surprising. In the far south, along the tamer sea coasts, Esgaria was dotted with jeweled cities, rich in splendor and bustling with commerce. But in the northern half of the country there were only a few cities and a few more small towns; the coastline was too jagged for shipping ports, and the forests were too vast for agriculture. The region was guarded—that is, ruled—by a handful of powerful warlords with private armies. They were the bastion against the Rholarothan expansionists and the more peaceful Keleds.

Her father had been such a warlord.

"Do you smell something?" Telric asked, interrupting her thoughts. He touched his nose and sniffed again. "Salt air!"

She nodded. "The Calendi Sea! We must be near the coast."

All through the forest the crickets began to warm up for another night of chorusing. Telric called it noise, yet to Frost it was as much a part of life's pulse as her own heartbeat. A light winked very close to her face. Reflexively, she swiped at it. Then she opened her fist.

The evening's first firefly lay on her palm. She gave a shudder and tossed it away. *Fool,* she chided herself for her unthinking reaction, *not every firefly in the world is a product of Kel's enchantment.*

Something stung her across the face, and she gasped, jerking back on Ashur's reins. With a finger she hesitantly explored her tender cheek where a thin branch had carved a shallow scratch just below her eye. She hadn't even seen it in the gloom. She wiped at the cut with a saliva-moistened thumb and regarded Telric. He said nothing, just stared from side to side, watching the trees and the half-seen things that moved among them.

The forest, she realized. *It's getting to him. It's getting to me, too.*

They pushed on with little more than the fire of the unicorn's eyes to guide them. More and more, Frost reached inside herself, listening for the magical note that was Kel. It was a jangling in her soul, and it set her teeth on edge. It told her he was close. But where was he?

For that matter, she wondered, where were they? She realized how little she had ever seen of Esgaria and how little she knew about the country. Hers was a knowledge based on tales and stories and legends. She had never truly traveled in her own homeland.

"But we've traveled in a lot of other lands, haven't we?" she whispered into Ashur's ear, leaning forward. As if in answer, the unicorn tossed his head. She straightened hastily to avoid a faceful of mane and smacked him playfully. "I don't need a broken nose to match my cut, thank you."

Relenting then, she stroked his muscular neck, tangled a hand in his mane, leaned down again, and pressed her cheek to his smooth, glistening hide. "I've never actually said it, you funny beast, but I love you."

The Rholarothan spoke up behind her. "Break down and say it to me."

She didn't hesitate. "All right. I love you, too."

He scoffed. "Talk is cheap. Prove it."

She reached out in the darkness, caught the nearest convenient branch, and bent it forward. "Here comes your proof," she warned him.

It made a most satisfying *thwack!* as it struck him on the chest.

A bit of levity brightens even the blackest night, she told herself. But still she watched the forest, sensing things, listening.

The crickets were in full voice.

She rode with her hands before her. It was the only way to avoid another scratch. Something snagged her hair, and she yelped. It was easy to imagine one of Kel's demons, and her heart skipped a beat. Still, she knew it was no such thing. Ashur's eyes or her own witchcraft would have warned her. Nothing had grabbed her, nothing but the forest.

A wind swept abruptly through the trees, shaking the leaves, heavy with the salt tang of the Calendi. She drew a deep breath, marveling. The air was full of odors: the sea, the spongy earth, the dry and dusty foliage, rich bark.

Frost brushed back her hair, briefly toying with the circlet that Telric had returned to her. She treasured it even more for his special act of caring.

A new sound rose distantly to join the night's symphony. Barely perceived, it seemed to swell and fade, a wistful whisper, a rush, a lonesome and mournful sound.

"The sea," Frost said at last. "That's the surf you hear. We'll emerge on the cliffs soon."

Suddenly, the world opened before them. Frost bit her lip and slid from Ashur's back. Her legs were weak from long riding, and she nearly lost her balance, but she steadied herself and stared wide-eyed with wonder.

The Calendi Sea sparkled in the light of the countless stars. The last sliver of a dying moon hung over it. The black water churned; white-capped waves danced and rolled far out on its glimmering surface. Nocturnal sea birds wheeled in the sky, fleet shadows that appeared in the corners of her eyes but disappeared from a direct gaze.

She stared far, seeking the horizon. It was impossible to say where the diamond-capped water and the star-flecked heavens met. They merged instead and appeared to extend forever into oneness.

She walked to the edge of the cliff. The surf smashed and battered the jagged rocks below, throwing spray and foam high into the air. It failed to reach her lofty vantage, but she imagined its cool touch on her face.

Telric came to her side and slipped an arm about her waist. "It can't be the same world," he whispered as he looked out to the sea and back into the forest. "We stand on the threshold of two magical lands."

"And they both make me tremble," she confided.

For the moment, Kel was forgotten. Frost went to Ashur, put an arm about his neck, and hugged him close without taking her eyes from the sea. She stood there, mesmerized, swallowed up by her memories.

She had stood on cliffs such as these and gazed out at this same sea, this same sky. At her command the storm had come, full of thunder and lightning. The water had frothed, maddened by her witchly power. It had lashed the rocks with unnatural fury while the wind screamed.

She had clapped her hands and laughed as only a child could have, delighted with her magic. What a game it had been! So young, but at a whim she had tamed the sea when it raged and driven the calm sea wild.

That had been so long ago, almost another lifetime. *How we are changed and made different by the years*, she thought sadly.

"It never seems to change," Telric said to her.

It took her a moment to realize he had not read her mind. Her comrade had referred to the sea itself. He stayed on the cliff's edge, as much a prisoner to the Calendi's melancholy spell as she.

"Of course it changes," she countered. "It eats away at the rocks and the cliffs, altering its coastline, carving tiny inlets and bays. Sometimes it's tranquil; sometimes its fury is staggering. In the day the waters are blue as sapphire; at night, black as a murderer's heart—black as they are now."

She pressed her face to Ashur's neck again as the sea wind swept over her. "Everything changes," she affirmed. "Everything."

They both mounted. A narrow trail wound along the cliff and among the trees that grew to the very edge. They rode without speaking, listening to the sharp sound of their hooves on the stony path, to the contrasting rush of the sea foam below. No longer could they hear the singing of the crickets.

"Look there." Telric stopped his horse and pointed straight ahead.

The fortress reared in the distance, black and imposing. It rebelled against the night, blotting out stars with its tall, square towers and embattled walls and flat, massive buildings. At the rim of the highest cliff it squatted as if it dared the pounding surf to bring it down. It seemed to issue a quiet, grim challenge to the rest of the world.

Frost motioned for Telric to continue. She didn't need to tell him whom they would find in that dreadful estate. He nudged his mare and led the way, saying no more. The hand he kept at his sword's hilt was eloquence enough.

A strange, inexplicable sensation shivered through her as she gazed at the ancient edifice. Something nagged at the back of her mind, something important, but try as she might she could not grasp it. She listened for that small note of music inside herself that told her Kel was near. It rang, clear and strident, but it wasn't what bothered her.

The fortress itself seemed to reach out to her. Its walls echoed her name.

Unconsciously, she dropped the reins over her saddlebow and rode clutching a shank of the unicorn's mane. There was a measure of security in the familiar texture and in actually touching him.

In the shadow of the outer wall the trail made a sudden turn back into the forest. There was no choice but to follow it. The stars disappeared once again, shut out by the thick, leafy canopy. Though they could no longer see the Calendi, the sound of the relentless surf pursued them.

The trail ended before an immense set of gates. The doors were rusted iron, but even through the age and tarnish something glinted in the faint moonlight, a pattern of inlaid gold. Portions of the pattern had been gouged away, probably by lucky thieves. The forest had grown right up to the gates, unchecked. Creepers and ivy dripped from cracks and gaps in the old stone walls.

"Look," Telric said, pointing.

High atop the gate, almost obscured by a spread of branches, perched a giant stone raven. Its wings were outstretched, its head thrown back as if in cry.

A short, strangled sound gurgled in her throat. She slid from the unicorn's back, crept hesitantly to the gates, and laid her palms against the cool, pitted metal. Then she leaned her forehead against it and banged her fists in anguish.

She knew now why the fortress had seemed to call to her, why it resonated so fearfully in the most intimate places of her heart.

"This was my home!" she cried to Telric. "By the lost gods of Tartarus Lake! Oh, curse you, Kel, curse you for leading me back here!"

"This was your father's house?" her companion echoed in a subdued voice.

She nodded, straightening, brushing back the hair that had cascaded over her face. She took a deep, angry breath, striving to control herself. "Somehow, Kel has found his ancestral seat. This estate was my father's and his father's father's. That raven above the gate was the device of our family. According to legend this land was given to us by Tak himself, our god of the dark mysteries, who came to us in the bird form and promised that all our women would excel in his teachings."

"You mean witchcraft?"

"A true witch is extremely rare," she told him, "but certainly in sorcery and wizardry and all the dark arts."

He dismounted and came to her side. He leaned his weight against the heavy gates to no effect. "Now, it seems you have a male who also excels," he said with a grunt.

"No," she said. A grim note stole into her voice as she motioned him back. "*Excels* is the wrong word. Kel is very good. But he'll soon know that he's not good enough."

For more than twenty years she had lived stripped of her witchcraft. She didn't know why it had returned, and she didn't know how. She didn't even know when. For some weeks, at least, she had used her power unawares, causing the weather to reflect her moods or her fears, turning cards that told true fortunes, conjuring the steppe winds to fan the funeral pyre at Soushane. And before even that? She remembered the impossible storm on the day she had found Kimon's body. That had been nearly a year ago. Had that been her doing?

It didn't matter. Her power had returned, and nothing else was important. It swelled within her like a living, growing force. It was easy for her to wield, as easy as lifting an arm or bending a finger.

She used only the smallest part of it, gently brushing Telric aside. Magically, the gates swung inward. There should have been scraping and creaking, the groaning of ancient hinges, but there was no sound at all.

The effect on the Rholarothan was profound. He stared, agape, rubbing his shoulder where he had strained against the doors. His gaze shifted to her. There was no fear in his eyes; he was beyond that reaction. But his discomfort was plain.

She mounted Ashur and waited for him to climb into his own saddle.

"Is Kel within?" he said slowly.

"You know he is," she answered.

She led the way through the open gate, glancing up at the raven as she passed beneath it. It had been the symbol of a great house that once was respected throughout Esgaria. Now, it loomed over a ruin, seeming more than anything like a great, sated bird of carrion.

Inside the wall stretched a wide courtyard that made a full circle around the fortress. Weeds and brambles grew wild among the cobbled paving stones. A young tree flourished just inside the gate, part of some root system that had pushed under the bastion. Far to her left, Frost could make out the shadow of the barracks that once had housed a hundred men-at-arms. Past that, out of sight, would be another barracks, the armory, and the stables.

She remembered the sounds of practice combat, the *clack* of carriage wheels, the laughter of children that once had filled the yard. As clearly as if they were with her now, she heard her father's voice and her mother's, the voice of Burdrak, who had secretly and foolishly taught her the use of men's weapons.

And she recalled her brother, damn his worthless soul—his voice echoed here, too, bitter and jealous and hateful.

They were all dead, though, and the voices were nothing

more than the wind that sighed across the weedy ground and whispered over the broken stone. Dark crimes had been committed here years agone: murder, fratricide, suicide. The servants, even the soldiers, must have fled in confusion and terror, never to return, believing the land itself had been cursed.

Perhaps it is cursed, she thought blackly, *and I am the cause.*

"Where is Kel?" Telric asked uneasily.

She didn't answer. A broad stair rose up to the estate's main entrance. She halted at the foot of it and slid from Ashur's back. Her touch lingered on the unicorn's shoulder, then reluctantly she took the first step upward. Telric dismounted and hurried after her. His sword gleamed unsheathed in his fist as they approached the huge, carven doors.

More ravens had been chiseled into the antique wood. Some of them flew upon the smooth, worn surface. Some perched on delicate branches, variously displaying magnificent wings. Once painted in careful detail, the pigment had flaked away with the years. Frost examined the doors carefully before touching them, assuring herself that Kel had placed no magical wards upon them. Then, seizing one of the two iron handles, she pushed inward.

Dim torchlight greeted them. They stepped inside without making a sound and paused. Frost repressed another shiver. How many times had she climbed that curving stairway as a child and played in the rooms above? How many times had she played in this very entrance hall?

Yet it all seemed so alien and otherworldly to her.

"He's up to something," she whispered suddenly. "There's a vibration in the air; I can feel it."

Telric brought up the point of his sword. His knuckles had turned white around the hilt.

She padded quietly across the hall and paused before another set of doors. She touched it with her fingertips. The sensation was stronger. She opened them and started down a narrow corridor. There were rooms on either side, but she ignored them, increasing her pace.

At the end of the corridor a tapestry was hung. She brushed it aside. A slender staircase rose up, lit by a single torch in a sconce on the wall. She didn't need its light, though. Too many times she had walked this way to forget; she knew what lay at the top.

"This place is a maze!" Telric whispered, drawing no response. "Doors and more doors!" he hissed irritably when she stopped before another one.

She touched it lightly, assuring herself that she had found the source of the arcane vibration. Then, she listened for the tiny note in her soul that said she had also found Kel. She nodded to her companion. He drew a deep breath and nodded also.

An odd calm settled upon her as she eased open the door to her father's library. Kel's back was to her as she said softly, "Hello, son."

Kel whirled, startled, and his face went pale. He stood within a double circle pattern drawn on the bare wood floor with chalk. The symbols between the two circles were unknown to her, but they crackled with a vile energy. The air reeked of death and decay. On either side of him two tenebrous *things* floated, shifting and formless. On a small table before him rested a pair of skulls.

"No!" Kel screamed fearfully. "You can't be here yet. I'm not ready!"

Before Frost could act, Telric shouldered his way into the room, saw the *shimeres,* and froze. Then, realizing they had interrupted the conjuration before it was complete, he crossed the chamber and rubbed his bootheel across the outermost circle and through one of the glyphs, smearing them.

Kel screamed again.

The *shimeres* let go an ear-splitting wail, shot up to the ceiling, down to the floor. Desperately, they smashed into the walls and the high bookcases, overturning furniture, knocking over candles that illumined the room. Frost snatched one away from an arras before a fire could start and crouched in a corner.

The *shimeres* whirled in faster and faster circles. Their black substances began to melt and merge, spinning faster with each passing heartbeat until a small, tightly contained vortex raged at the center of the room.

Frost stared, her hair lashing wildly, her garments whipping about her. She shielded her candle with one hand, but the tempest fanned the flame to a blue, dancing blaze. Nearby, Telric was sprawled on the floor, clinging desperately to his

sword, struggling to unfasten the cloak that threatened to
choke him as the vortex sucked at the scarlet fabric. Kel was
flattened against the far wall, wide-eyed and hysterical. He
screamed curses, but his words were lost in the spiraling rush
of energy.

Books and scrolls flew about the room, chased by the two
skulls, the small table, anything that was loose. The air was
full of deadly missiles. Frost protected her head and crouched
even lower; she couldn't reach Telric's side.

Then it ended, and all the world seemed to hold a breath.
Books, bones, tables, all fell with a resounding series of
snaps, cracks, and thuds as the vortex lost its energy and
began to dissipate. When the tempest had subsided, only a
faint, dewy film of ectoplasmic material remained. That, too,
quickly evaporated.

Frost rose and set the candle, the only source of light, on a
shelf above her head and moved toward her son.

"Stay back!" he shouted angrily, but fear shone in his
eyes. "Stupid woman! I knew you were close, but not *so*
close. You and your lapdog"—he waved a hand at Telric as
the Rholarothan got to his feet—"you'll wreck everything!"

She took a step closer. "Kel . . ."

His hand shot into a pocket of his robe and drew out a ring.
Before she could stop him, he slipped it on his first finger.
His face was a mask of bitter hatred as he vanished.

Frost leaped forward, but her arms closed on emptiness.
"Telric," she shouted, "kick the door shut!" Without ques-
tioning he lashed out with his foot. The door shivered as it
slammed against the jamb, but Frost sensed it was too late.

"The ring," she explained as she jerked the door open and
raced down the stairs, "is a talisman. It hides him from
human eyes. That must be how he escaped from my inn when
Riothamus's soldiers came for him. He must have used it,
also, to get past the Keled army when we crushed his force at
the tower."

"What do we do, then?" her comrade called, running
behind her.

"I didn't need to see him to get us this far," she answered.
"I think I can find him now."

She hurried back the way they had come, through the
entrance hall, outside into the courtyard. Halfway across, she

stopped and caught Telric's arm. "He's just beyond the gate," she said warily. "I can feel him."

Ashur came to her side as she started across the yard again. The mare only glanced up at them, then went back to munching the weeds.

She moved cautiously. She could sense her son's presence, but not his precise location. He was out there somewhere, moving slowly.

They paused at the gate. The huge doors stood open, inviting. Frost eased her sword free, flattened against the cool iron, and inched her way around the corner. There was no sign of her son. She beckoned, and Telric and Ashur came around to join her.

"That way," she whispered, "but I don't . . ."

For a brief instant Kel appeared. His eyes burned into hers, and he wore a subtle grin. Then he turned and ducked behind the thick trunk of an old tree.

"There!" she cried, running along the outside of the fortress wall. But when she reached the tree, Kel was not there. He appeared again, though, farther down the wall. She gave chase, weaving among the trees, leaping thickets, brushing aside limbs that might have clawed her face. Ashur thundered along close on her heels. She didn't dare look back for fear of losing her son, but she knew Telric followed.

Kel ran lithe as a deer with his robes gathered in his arms. Suddenly, he stopped and turned to face her. Not even the darkness could mask the madness that shone in his gaze. He flung back his head and howled an insane laugh. "Do you know this ground, Mother? Do you remember it?"

She knew it was a mistake to listen to that silken, beguiling voice. She should cut him down without hesitation. But he was her son, and she stayed her hand. "No more games, Kel," she said sharply. "You've caused enough grief."

A malicious smile blossomed on his lips. He continued as if she hadn't spoken. "It's the cemetery, Samidar, my dear mother. We buried our soldiers here, the retainers and the servants." His smile widened. "And they've missed you. They want to welcome you home!"

He opened his hand. On his palm glinted fragments of teeth and bone. A surge of arcane force rippled through the air as he tossed them. Ashur screamed and reared; prominences of flame crackled from the unicorn's eyes. Frost felt the power like icy knives carving away her flesh. Where each ensorcelled fragment fell, the earth split open.

"Embrace them, Mother." Kel laughed. "Embrace your friends and loved ones!"

They shambled from the fissures. The red fire of hellish half-life gleamed in the corpses' vacant sockets. They groped for her, and their nails were long as dagger blades. Withered, rotten flesh and tattered burial garments dripped from ancient bones with every step the creatures took. The stench of them was overpowering.

Frost shrank back in revulsion. A foul taste filled her mouth, and she discovered to her shame that she had vomited on herself. She gaped, staring at a nightmare made real. They came for her, surrounding her, and more clambered from the earth as more fissures yawned, all with the same hungering look.

How many? she cried in silent terror. *How many are buried in this once hallowed ground?*

Beneath her feet the earth sank away. Reflexively, she leaped aside and bounced clumsily off the unicorn's flanks as Ashur, too, tried to get away. She fell on her face, swallowing dirt. Then she let go a shriek as something raked her ankle.

Without thinking, she rolled on her side and brought her sword over in a glittering arc, severing the grisly arm that reached out of the hole where, moments before, she had stood.

That was all it took to mobilize her. She scrambled up, spitting filth from her mouth, and smashed at the head that tried to rise from the same hole. Bone splintered with a hollow, snapping sound.

Her action was permission enough for Ashur. The unicorn plunged into the thick of them, slashing with horn and hooves, bellowing his strange war cry.

Far to her left she spied Telric. The Rholarothan's back was to the fortress wall. He swung his sword two-handed in wide, whistling strokes to keep the monsters at bay.

From the corner of her eye she saw a taloned hand reach. It caught her long hair, but before it could jerk her off-balance she cleaved off the arm. Her second blow sent a head flying from a pair of emaciated shoulders, and the creature collapsed.

Her heart gave a leap. "Strike at the head!" she shouted, praying that Telric could hear her.

She sprang at the nearest corpse. Its ribs showed bare on its right side, and the decayed scalp had slipped over the skull nearly into the creature's eyes. Still, it reached for her, finger bones clenching spasmodically, clacking its broken teeth in an obscene rhythm.

One clean stroke sent it to a second rest. *Was it grateful?* Frost wondered. *Or was even this perversion of life preferable to the everlasting hells?*

She wasted no more time on such troubling thoughts. Alive or dead, these horrors intended to kill her. Suddenly, her fear was gone. She moved through them, hacking with relentless fury, shattering skull bone, slicing limbs, decapitating. Two of them slammed into her from behind, bearing her down, but she twisted and flung them off with ridiculous ease. Even the freshest of them was little more than skin-covered bone. There was no weight to them and no power in their feeble blows. The things had only their claws, which more than once came dangerously close to her eyes or throat.

She caught a hasty glimpse of Kel as he stood beneath an ancient tree like some woodland god of myth, watching. The laughter with which he had so freely mocked her was silent now. His face was livid with anger and frustration.

Telric was not where she had last seen him. She couldn't spy him anywhere, but a series of shouts and curses and grunts, followed by the wretched snapping of bone, told her he must still be on his feet.

Ashur had taken the greatest toll. The corpses' nails were useless against the unicorn. He trampled the mindless creatures as they attacked him, and he pounded them back into the earth with his great hooves. He didn't always find the skull, though, and wherever the unicorn fought, pale cadavers twitched grotesquely on the ground.

Three of the nightmares shambled toward her. It was almost a duty, she had decided, to free them from Kel's insidious control and give them peace once more. Raising her sword, she ran at them, determined to do it swiftly.

Too late, she saw the yawning fissure and gave a choked cry. Her head struck the opposite side as she fell, and she landed at the bottom in a heap, stunned. She struggled to draw a breath, to get to her knees.

A grave, she thought, horrified. *I'm in a grave!*

Groping in the loose earth, she found her sword. As she pulled it from the dirt, she chanced to look over her shoulder and froze.

Three corpses jumped into the grave on top of her. Instinctively, she brought up her blade, impaling one of them through the eye socket. Its own descending weight tore the skull from the spinal column, but it also knocked the sword from her grasp again.

An evil face leered down at her; bony hands locked around her throat. The creature's touch chilled, and she tried to shrink away even as she fought to loosen its grip. But the confines were too narrow; she could get no leverage. Those red eyes burned into her; they drank the warmth and life from her body.

Desperately, she brought her arms up, trying to break the monster's hold. As she did, the third corpse began to tear and rip at her garments, trying to get to the flesh beneath them with its talons.

Again, she slammed her arms up, but the grip on her throat was arcanely strong. She could almost see the laughter in her murderer's gaze. Agony seared her throat; her lungs cried for breath.

She shoved her thumbs into the redly glowing sockets, hooking her fingers over the bony ridges. With all her fading might she strained. The muscles in her arms and shoulders bulged and trembled with her effort. Her vision clouded over with a crimson film, and a roaring filled her ears. An incessant pounding began to throb in her temples.

With a wrenching heave, she splintered the creature's skull with her bare hands. The broken fragments showered down upon her face. The remains of the corpse sagged atop her like some obscene and necrophiliac lover.

Fire shot up her calf. The third creature had torn through her trouser. Its nails gleamed darkly with her blood. It looked up at her with a slack-jawed grin, holding up the hand to show her its handiwork. Then, it lunged to sink those talons into her face.

With an effort, she flung the second corpse in its way, brought her feet up, and kicked it back against the graveside. Two ribs swung weirdly, broken by her blow. Quickly, she got her feet under her, but before she could rise, the shambler wrestled her back to the ground again.

But anger drove her now. As its fingers dug into her neck, she reached down, snapped one of the broken ribs free and twisted her body. Her gruesome foe tumbled sideways. As it struggled to sit up, Frost lunged. The jagged end of the rib flashed into the empty eye socket, striking the back of the skull. The length of bone reflected an eerie, scarlet luminescence as she leaned all her weight upon it.

There was a crunch. The red sheen faded at once. She let go of the rib and sagged back, wiping sweat from her face. The corpse grinned at her, pinned to the side of the grave. It flopped about, and the hands still reached for her, but the rib held firmly.

She recovered her sword and drew back. Bone and earth sprayed from the force of her blow, and the third corpse tumbled headless beside the other two.

She pulled herself out, looked around, and saw there was little more to do. Telric chopped down the two remaining shamblers as she crawled from the grave. Ashur sniffed at the corpses on the ground. If it twitched, he stamped on it until it didn't twitch anymore.

Kel was nowhere in sight.

Telric approached her, his weapon still unsheathed. He wore an expression of barely controlled rage. But there was more, too. He had the look of a man who had seen too much, who had walked to the edge of the cliff and barely resisted the fall.

"He's mine, Samidar," he said through clenched teeth. "He's my nephew, and he's mine!"

She shivered at the change in him. If his eyes had burned scarlet, she might have mistaken him for one of the shamblers. But for the dark growth that shadowed his features, his cheeks were colorless and hollow. His empty hand clenched and unclenched. He glowered at her.

"He's mine!" he repeated. It was almost a serpent's hiss.

She bit her lip. "Then we go back inside," she told him, finding within her soul the disharmony that would lead them to her son. She sheathed her blade, awed that it had done such killing work without a drop of blood to stain the edge. Ashur came to her side, and they went back to the fortress gate.

The mare was gone. There was no time to search for her.

They did not creep across the yard this time; there was too much anger in them for that. They strode up the steps, leaving Ashur at the bottom. Telric let out a growl and kicked open the doors. They stepped into the entrance hall.

"Have a care with my woodwork, you fool barbarian." It was a female voice, menacing in its calm. It filled the hall. "I doubt if such artistry is common in this world anymore."

Frost looked up and saw the woman who stood at the top of the broad, sweeping staircase. She peered down at them, clutching the balustrade, leaning on it. A torch burned in a sconce near the highest stair, but shadow obscured most of the woman's face.

Frost whipped out her sword. Though her witch-powers had returned, she still felt safer with a length of steel in her hand. "Oroladian!" She spat the name like a curse.

But the woman shouted back, "Gods, how you shame this house and your Esgarian heritage. Put your man's weapon out of my sight!"

"Who are you?" Telric's voice boomed in the hall. "Are you the sorceress Oroladian? Answer me, damn you!"

Frost moved to the foot of the staircase, her weapon still bared. She set her boot on the first step and stopped. A queer sensation gripped her, not unlike the one she'd experienced when she'd first looked upon the fortress from the cliffs by the Calendi. "Who are you?" The words rasped from her like a saw over dry wood.

"Don't you know me?"

That voice echoed in Frost's head, spanning years. It crawled up out of her blackest nightmares and choked her with a terror worse than anything she had felt in the cemetery.

The woman mocked her. "Of course you know me, Samidar." With spectral grace the woman started down the stair, passing from shadow into the light of the torch. Frost stared agape at her own face. No, it wasn't quite hers. The woman was younger by some years. Yet the resemblance told a chilling truth.

"Reimuth?" Frost could barely speak the name after so many years, after so much pain and bitter guilt. "You're dead!"

The woman grinned hatefully. "You should know, Samidar. You killed me."

Frost lowered the point of her sword and drew herself erect. She had tortured herself with that accusation for far too long, but she had finally come to terms with it. Kimon had helped her to see events as they had been, to accept what blame had been hers and to cast off what had not.

"You took your own life," she contradicted, and at last, she believed it. "I set the stage, but it was your hand that held the sword."

Telric touched her shoulder. "What are you talking about? Who is she? Where's Kel?"

Reimuth glowered at the Rholarothan and answered in a voice that dripped venom, "To get Kel you must come through me, Northerner."

Telric answered with equal menace, "If you say so, bitch, then that's the way we'll do it." But he turned back to Frost. "You're pale. Are you all right?"

She nodded, drawing a slow breath, sheathing her sword.

"What are you doing?" Telric insisted, catching her hand. "Is she Oroladian or not?"

Frost matched gazes with the woman on the stair, and again she nodded.

"Then why did you call her Reimuth?"

Frost felt the stirrings of her witchcraft. It beat and throbbed within her, crashed like the Calendi surf on the rocks of her soul. Its roaring was sheerest music as it filled her.

She knew at last why it had returned. "Reimuth is her true name," she explained to her friend.

Telric's expression was pure scorn. "You know her?"

"Do you know me, Samidar?" the woman mimicked. She started down the staircase again.

Frost held her ground but motioned her companion away. Without looking at him, she answered, "My mother."

Chapter Eighteen

I hear you when you sigh
Soft as raindrops pattering the leaves
Quiet as fading dew
I hear you
But you will not come near
I see you in the sunset
In a topaz moon
Reflected on a still pool
I see you
When I cannot hear
I feel you
Like a lingering song half-forgotten
But you will not come near me
Where I wander
And I cannot come to you

"Go outside, Telric."

He touched her sleeve, but this time she shoved his hand away. "Go outside. Stay close to Ashur and don't wander away from him."

Hurt was evident on his face. "What about Kel?"

"Get out!" Reimuth gestured threateningly, and the air tingled with the flux of her sorcerous power. But Frost stepped protectively in front of her friend and glared at her mother.

The two women locked gazes for a brief moment, then Reimuth relented. "Leave us, Northerner," she ordered with the barest civility. "My daughter and I are overdue for a family talk."

"I am family," Telric spat scornfully. "Kel is my nephew."

Reimuth gave him a cursory glance and frowned distastefully. She spoke again to her daughter. "Get rid of him—or I will."

Frost knew Telric's anger was straining toward the boiling mark, but before he could say another word she put a hand over his lips. "If you love me, Telric," she said softly, "then do as I ask and wait with Ashur." She turned and gave her mother a hard look as if to emphasize her next words. "Nothing more is going to happen this night. We're going to talk, that's all. This is between Reimuth and me."

"And Kel?"

"Forget Kel," Reimuth snapped from the stairway.

Frost ignored her as she steered Telric toward the door. "I'll find him, don't worry. He's still here. He knows I can find him wherever he runs."

Telric slammed his sword back into its sheath and made a gesture of his own to Reimuth. It wasn't magical, but it was quite rude, and the expression that flashed over Reimuth's face proved she knew its meaning. Frost caught his elbow and hurried him to the door. Before he stepped into the night, though, her touch softened and her hand drifted up to his cheek. He took her other hand, squeezed it gently, and kissed the palm. Then, he pulled the door closed and was gone.

She drew a deep breath and turned back to her mother.

Reimuth descended the stair. Long black hair flowed over her shoulders and down her back. Sea-green eyes flashed under dark lashes. She held herself imperiously, one hand resting lightly on the banister.

Frost repressed another shiver. She had never appreciated how similar they looked. Now, though, she was peering back through time, seeing herself as she must have been ten years younger. There was no gray in Reimuth's hair, no wrinkles at the corners of the eyes. Frost experienced a strange, unsettling jealousy.

"Take that thing off," Reimuth demanded, pointing to the sword her daughter wore. "It's an abomination. You'll not wear it in my house."

Frost moved toward her mother, tossing her head defiantly. "Go to hell," she answered stonily, curling her fingers around her weapon's hilt. Then she forced a smile. "Oh, I forgot. You've already been there—and back, apparently. Still, since you're fond of Esgarian law, then you know this property is mine through inheritance after the deaths of my parents and the only possible male heir, my brother. I doubt if Esgarian courts would recognize your resurrection." She shouldered past her mother and headed upstairs.

"Where do you think you're going?"

"To tour my property," she said flatly without a backward glance.

Reimuth followed her, and together they moved through the upper rooms of the fortress. The halls echoed with voices from the past, old conversations suddenly remembered with crystal clarity. Here she had fallen and bruised her arm while playing with a servant girl. There was the passage that once led outside to her favorite garden. Here was her brother's room.

She hesitated at the door to her own chamber, then pushed it open. She regretted it at once. Her bed was untouched from that night when she had slain her brother. The blankets were rumpled where she had thrown herself across the bed, crying with fear and guilt. The rich blue material of the spread, though, was gray with a layer of thick dust.

There was a trunk at the foot of her bed, and, driven by a terrible compulsion, she lifted the lid. She glanced at the piles of·folded dresses and gowns and lowered the lid again. So many memories! A table stood near a narrow, shuttered window; on it was a pretty stone and the musty remains of a feather. She didn't remember them. Perhaps she had found them in the forest and brought them home. So many years!

She turned and something behind the door caught her eye. She bent closer to see in the weak light that spilled from the hall torches. She straightened, holding a small pair of felt slippers. She made a quick swipe at the corners of her eyes, afraid her mother might see the tears that leaked out. She set the slippers on the trunk, gave the room another lingering gaze, and departed.

"You might at least show some remorse," Reimuth said.

Frost stopped in midstride. "It was you who taught me to be strong, Mother," she answered caustically, turning. For the first time she noted one difference between them. Reimuth was shorter by several inches. "Why did you come back?" Frost finally asked, the words hissing between her teeth. "How did you come back? I know you were dead."

A shallow smile parted Reimuth's thin lips, and the woman folded her arms over her breasts. "Do you doubt the power of my sorceries?"

Frost answered coldly, "I know your skill, and I know that death can be conquered. I've seen Chondite priests wrestle with the death god and win. But always resurrection followed quickly before the soul accustomed itself to a new existence, and assistance was required to guide the soul back to the body." Frost shook her head and folded her own arms, unconsciously imitating her mother's posture. "No, Reimuth, don't try to lie to me. Too much time has passed. It was Kel's doing, wasn't it?"

They wandered back down the stairs. Just off the entrance hall was another large chamber, where her father had held court and sat in judgment over the people in his charge. The walls were hung with rich, handwoven tapestries; a fine film of dust obscured the cleverly embroidered raven motifs, but Frost remembered how magnificently they had framed her father as he sat in all his finery dispensing justice.

"Yes, it was Kel's work," Reimuth admitted at last. "How he found his way here, I don't know. He said something about tracing your adventures. He's obsessed with you, you know." Reimuth drifted toward a large chair that perched on a low dais. She ran her hand lovingly along the back of it and down over the carven armrests.

Abruptly, Frost realized that her mother, too, was a victim of remembrance. Reimuth had married in this house, borne children under this roof. Her husband had sat daily in the very chair she ran her hands over. Frost felt a sudden, powerful urge to reach out and embrace her mother, to apologize for all that had happened between them, to ask forgiveness.

Yet she could not. She *would* not. There was blame for all to share, blame for her mother and father, for her teacher, Burdrak, and especially for her brother. Yes, and there was blame for her, too. But she refused to shoulder it all alone to please her mother. For years she had done that, until Kimon taught her better.

She longed with a potent yearning to feel her mother's arms around her, but she settled for her own, hugging herself.

"When he recalled my spirit," Reimuth continued, "he didn't know my name. I could not speak for some time; the shock of returning suddenly to this world was too great. But he had to call me something, so he named me Oroladian."

"Dear to hell and heaven," Frost interpreted, at last recognizing the name as a blending of Rhianothan and Esgarian dialects.

"I think he knew from the beginning who I was." She touched her face hesitantly. "We look so much alike; the conclusion must have been obvious to him." She stared at her daughter and shook her head slowly. "Then, my speech and my memory returned." She looked her daughter straight in the eye as she continued, "Then my powers, stronger than ever before. I'm not a witch like you. My magic must come from objects or special words or patterns. But my time in hell had taught me many things." A faraway look stole into Reimuth's eyes, and Frost wondered at the mysteries her mother must have seen. "Like the Chondite sorcerers, I tried to fight the death god. Orchos was strong, a fearful deity, but I kept my courage and struggled with all my dark might, and I won a partial victory.

"I could not return my spirit to its body, but neither was I trapped in the hell I had earned. I wandered all the nine hells. I saw such wonders, Samidar! And I learned much about the nature of power." She paused and continued in a more subdued voice, "I used my new power to see into Kel's heart and mind, and I saw that what he suspected was true, that he was your son and my grandson."

Frost stepped up onto the dais and faced her mother across the great chair. "Why couldn't you have been satisfied with that? Why did you send him to ransack Keled-Zaram searching for the Three Aspects? You abhorred war, Mother. Remember how zealously you guarded the peace of Esgaria?" She shook a clenched fist under her mother's nose. "Do you know how many people my son has murdered for you? He claimed the Aspects could restore life, but you already have life!"

Reimuth moved away from the chair and brushed her hand along a tapestry, stirring a cloud of dust. "As a necromancer Kel is very skilled," she said quietly, "but necromancy has its limitations.'' She looked at her daughter and her voice dropped a note. ''I am growing weak again and soon will die. Kel's magic gave me only one year of life, and it can give me no more. Time is running out.''

Frost fought against the emotions that churned within her. ''So you broke Esgarian law and taught him your sorcery, hoping he could find the means to extend your time.'' She couldn't keep the sneer from her voice.

''He already had power,'' Reimuth shot back defensively. ''I merely refined his abilities. During our studies we learned of the Three Aspects: the Lamp of Nugaril, the Eye of Skraal, and the Book of Shakari. Used in concert these objects had the power to give life to the dead. But the Chondites had hidden them. It took precious months to discover that all had been secreted in Keled-Zaram.'' A wan little smile danced over her mother's lips. ''As far as I know, it was coincidence that you had chosen to settle in the same land. Unless you believe the gods have conspired to bring us back together.''

Frost could barely control her anger. ''You sent Kel to find the Aspects, and you didn't care how he got them or what havoc he caused, so long as he won you more life!''

''I didn't send him!'' Reimuth answered, matching her fury. ''He disappeared one night. Eventually, my magic found him, and I learned he had gone after the Aspects. We communicated, but he refused to come home.''

''Why didn't you go after him? Didn't you see his madness? You might have tempered his actions!''

Reimuth's eyes flashed. ''Are you still as ignorant as you once were? Did I teach you nothing? My life-force is bound to this place. Travel to Keled-Zaram? I cannot go even beyond the fortress walls.''

Frost crossed the distance between them with swift strides, backing her mother up against the tapestry. ''Don't call me ignorant! I took enough of that from you while you purred over my simpering brother and pampered him.'' She caught her mother's thin gown in her fist and dragged her face close to her own. ''You encouraged Kel. You're as responsible for his crimes as he is. You used my son!''

Reimuth clamped a hand over her daughter's wrist and pulled her toward a door on the far side of the chamber. She took a torch from a wall sconce. ''Come with me,'' she demanded.

They plunged into an unlit passage with only the torch to show the way. Reimuth set a brisk pace, never releasing her grip on her daughter. At the end of the dark corridor she flung back yet another door. The interior glowed with warm amber light. "See what your jealousy has wrought, Samidar?" Reimuth snapped.

But it was Reimuth who caught her breath sharply. She stared with widened eyes and clapped a hand to her mouth.

Frost saw at once what had so horrified her mother. She squeezed her eyes shut and hated her son all the more.

Three skeletons gleamed in the torchlight. They had been carefully laid out in ceremonial respect on low slabs of stone. Blankets of purple covered two of them to the chests, and the hands had been folded in the traditional manner. Frost knew without asking whose remains she gazed upon.

But from each the skull had been removed. A gold coronet lay discarded on the floor. Reimuth slumped against the jamb, her face twisted with anger.

"The *shimeres*," Frost said bitterly. "My father, my brother, my teacher. Kel tried to use them to kill me. My own family." She picked up the coronet, unsure what to do with it. "You see how mad he is?"

Reimuth reacted as if she had been struck. She snatched her husband's coronet and whirled on her daughter. "Madness? You wail about the sendings and what Kel has done. But it's Kel's family—you and that bastard Rholarothan who dares to call him nephew—that hounds him and hunts him like he was a dog!"

Rage heated Frost's cheeks; her hands curled into tight fists. "You didn't see the towns and the bodies he left in his wake as he searched for your Aspects. He murdered his father and killed his own brother!"

"Really?" Reimuth snapped. She turned away long enough to place the coronet in the hands of the middle skeleton. "He takes after his mother, then, doesn't he?"

The torch fire flared and danced wildly as a sudden wind rose from nowhere and swept through the shrine. Frost started, recognizing the cause, and forcibly mastered her fury. She waited for the music within her to fade before she dared to speak again.

"Keled-Zaram has been my home, Mother. My husband is buried there, and Kirigi's ashes are mingled with its soil. I

have friends and good memories there." She fixed the other
woman with a hard gaze. "Kel bragged that he intends to
return and conquer Keled-Zaram. I won't let him."

Reimuth made herself equally plain. "I won't let you harm
him."

"He's my son," Frost said coldly. "Don't interfere."

"He's my grandchild," Reimuth countered. "He carries
the seed of our family, even if it is through such a tainted
vessel as yourself."

For long moments the only sound was the hissing of the
torch fire. The two regarded each other unflinchingly. It was
Frost who finally spoke. "How will the Aspects preserve
your life-force?"

Reimuth answered without hesitation, "During the new
moon I will stand in a golden circle and bathe in the light
from the Lamp of Nugaril as it reflects from the faceted Eye
of Skraal. All the while, Kel will read from the Book of
Shakari; the spell of power is hidden among the written
words."

Frost went to the door, then turned back to her mother.
"I'll wait until he finishes the ceremony," she said quietly,
"until you have the life you hunger for. But mark me,
Reimuth, when it's over I'm coming for my son. Not all the
powers of hell will keep me from him."

Reimuth tilted her head and raised a quizzical eyebrow.
"Are you challenging me, daughter? Would you repeat your
shameful past—fight and slay the only family you have?"

Frost was unmoved. "Don't get in my way, Reimuth.
Unless this time you think you can win your match with
Orchos." She left her mother then and made her way back to
the entrance hall. Once more she looked around the place
where she had so often played and heard childlike laughter
from the distant past. Full of regret, she opened the door and
went outside.

There was no sign of Telric. Ashur waited at the foot of the
long stair. She went to him and stroked him absentmindedly
while looking for her friend. She bit her lip, scouring the
darkness. *Damn it, I told him to stay close,* she cursed.
Leading the unicorn by his reins, she wandered around the
courtyard, but there were few places for her comrade to hide.

A fleet shadow moved near the gate. Frost dropped Ashur's
reins. Her sword hissed from the sheath, and she ran. At the

gate, she stopped again, recalling how Kel had cat-and-moused them to the cemetery. She started to reach inside herself for the note that would tell her where her son was, but before she found it, the shadow moved again.

It was Telric. The Rholarothan stared at her from the edge of the forest. "The mare's gone," he said as he came toward her. "I thought it might have wandered into the woods."

She resisted an urge to curse. The missing horse was a problem, but she'd had reasons for telling him to stay with Ashur. With the unicorn beside him there was a measure of safety from Kel or Reimuth. It annoyed her that he had not heeded her advice. Still, he was well enough and no harm had been done. She drew a slow breath and listened to the crash of the sea in the distance.

"Let's go," she said wearily as Ashur came around the gate.

"Go where?" He turned and watched the forest with a curious expression. "I can't find my horse."

"You won't find her in this dark," Frost assured him. "Maybe she'll turn up come morning. But I need sleep, and I won't get it as long as I can see this place. We'll go back down the trail and find a spot on the cliffs."

They walked back toward the sea. Every rustle of the leaves, every shifting branch, made her jump. Every shadow was another corpse come to claim her, every patch another hole to swallow her up. Not until they rejoined the cliff trail did she realize that she still carried her bared blade. She felt foolish but decided it wouldn't matter if she carried it a while longer.

When the walls of her father's fortress could no longer be seen above the trees, they stopped. There was no clearing and no place to make a safe fire, but Frost didn't care. She thrust her sword into the soft earth and slumped down against an old trunk. Telric sat down beside her; Ashur stood quietly by as if on guard.

The Calendi Sea stretched before them. Rolling wave after wave battered the rocks below, filling the night with a soul-soothing roar.

Yet sleep proved elusive. They talked, instead. She told him of the Three Aspects and the power they possessed. She explained how Kel intended to use them to preserve her mother's life. She couldn't bring herself to move against her son just yet. For some reason she didn't quite understand, she wanted her mother to have that chance to live.

"I have to let him use the Aspects," she insisted. "I swear I didn't kill my mother, Telric, but I set in motion the events that made her take her life. How can I deny her a second chance?"

"It's unnatural," he argued, hugging his knees. "What about those creatures that attacked us in the cemetery? Did they deserve another chance to live? When I saw them crawling up from their graves I thought I'd lost my mind. I froze." He leaned his head back on the rough bark and sighed. "I'm not sure now I haven't lost my mind. None of this can be real."

She placed a hand on his thigh. "This is real," she said softly. "Cling to this." She waited for him to answer, but he just stared up into the star-flecked heavens. Then his fingers intertwined with hers.

"It's so strange," she whispered, laying her head on his shoulder. "Reimuth is my mother. She even uses the same tone when she talks to me, as if I were still a child. Yet she's *younger* than me, and I feel this queer jealousy."

He squeezed her hand. Neither spoke for a while, then Telric squirmed uncomfortably. When he spoke, his voice was low and serious. "You haven't said much about Kel."

She looked away, feeling cold and uncertain. She wished he would stop talking and put his arms around her, hold her and warm her. Her bones ached, and her lids felt so heavy.

"Reimuth was only a child herself when she bore me," she heard herself say, but the words sounded remote, dreamlike.

Telric stood up suddenly and went to the cliff's edge. He clenched his fists behind his back, then spun around to face her. "What about Kel?" he said irritably. He threw himself down beside her again and took her by the shoulders. "Tell me, Samidar, what we've come all this way to do?"

She pushed him away. "I don't know anymore!" she shouted angrily. "I don't know. Nothing is clear to me. Nothing is simple anymore!" She pressed her head to her knees and hugged herself, rocking back and forth, afraid to look at her comrade, afraid to look inside herself for answers that might be too hard to bear.

"Maybe Kel deserves a second chance, too," she said at last. "He's insane and dangerous. I know what crimes he's done." She swallowed and found the strength to look up into Telric's stony face. "But maybe if I stay here, Mother and I can help him or find some way to control him. She loves him, too, despite what he's done. He'll listen to her."

Telric stared, full of bitterness and anger. Without another word he turned his back on her and strode away.

She called after him, "Telric, he's my son!"

He didn't go far. He leaned wearily against another tree, head down between his shoulders, and Frost heard what must have been a sigh. Still without speaking, he lay down and wrapped his cloak tightly about himself and cradled his head on an elbow.

She stared imploringly at his back. "Telric, everyone deserves a second chance!"

He didn't move, just lay there stiffly facing away, one more shadow on the ground.

He doesn't understand, she told herself as the stars faded one by one from the sky. Gradually, morning cast a new color over the sea, but still the Calendi roared its hollow, rushing note. She glanced again at Telric's broad back. Though the sun beat down through the leaves, she still felt chilled. *He doesn't know how hard it is for a mother. How can he?*

She could see his breathing, the ebb and swell of his body, as he slept. It made a kind of counterrhythm to the pounding surf. Overhead, sea birds began to dip and circle, calling their eerie, high-pitched cries. She watched them until the aching pressure behind her eyes grew too great.

What am I going to do? she worried, glancing yet again at her lover. The scarlet cloak hid his face from her. She didn't want to hurt him, though his silence had cut her to the bone.

She sagged back against her tree and closed her eyes, unaware of the moment when sleep finally stole upon her. With a sigh she tumbled onto her side.

Her last thought was of Telric.

She awoke suddenly from a bad dream. The last orange glow of the sun stained the Calendi as it sank below the rim of the world. She had slept the day away. She rose slowly, wondering why Telric hadn't roused her. She looked around, calling his name.

He wasn't under his tree. There was no sign of him anywhere.

A weird sensation crawled up her spine. Ashur was gone, too, but when she called his name the unicorn emerged from the forest chewing a mouthful of flowers. She went to him and ran a hand through the thick mane, along his muscled neck, taking a measure of comfort and security from his presence. Ashur licked her hand and tried to nuzzle her shoulder.

But the saw-toothed edge of some indescribable fear remained with her.

She moved to the spot where Telric had slept. The mossy grass showed the imprint of his body, but the ground was cold. He had been gone for some time, then. She leaned down, then lay down in the same place exactly as he had lain. She closed her eyes and waited.

The sensation became a raw jangling that made her flesh creep. She leaped up, rubbing herself and cursing bitterly. A red haze of anger clouded her vision.

Unmistakably, the taste of Kel's magic lingered in that spot. But what had her son done this time? Why had he made Telric his only target?

She swung up onto Ashur without taking the time to saddle him. She shot a glance at the horizon. The sun was down, its last rays fading.

It was the night of the new moon.

She kicked the unicorn's flanks and raced along the cliff trail, giving no thought to the treacherous turns and narrow edges, knocking aside limbs that slapped at her face. Her father's fortress loomed above the trees, threatening and full of menace as evening gathered around its parapets.

Frost knew why her witchcraft had returned. Her mother's suicide, like a blood sacrifice, had powered the spell that stole her magic. But when Kel brought Reimuth back to life, he inadvertently negated her final spell. The result was that Frost was a witch once more. She could feel the power singing within her, and the song was one of purest, white-hot fury.

She swore to Tak, the witch-god, and to Orchos, who ruled the realms of the dead. If Telric had been harmed, there would be all the hells to pay. Nothing would protect Kel or Reimuth. Kin or no kin, she would rip out their hearts!

At the fortress gates she jerked Ashur to a halt. The air was acrid with her son's magic. Sophisticated wards, visible to her witch's senses, sealed the massive iron doors against her. The pattern of her son's spell glowed, a faintly traceable outline of crimson radiance, constantly shifting and changing, deadly to touch.

The pathetic fool! Was he really so overconfident? Did he expect her to walk up and knock?

She lifted her gaze to the darkening skies, and her mouth fell open in a soundless song. Clouds formed, gathered, and thickened in response to her call, black and impending. Sheet lightning rippled through the heavens. A blast of thunder shook the trees. Frost molded the storm with her song, shaped and bent it to her will. A jagged blue bolt flashed. She shook her fist; thunder answered.

She called the wind. It came ripping through the forest, slashing leaves from their branches, swirling them in its powerful wake. Trees bowed before its force; limbs cracked and crashed to the ground.

Do you feel it, Reimuth? By giving you your life, Kel has given back my power. Even as a child I knew you feared my magic. It came so easily to me. You were a great sorceress, but you had to sweat over your stupid chants and potions and grimoires and talismans. Did you think I couldn't feel your jealousy? That's why you shunned me while you pampered my brother. You turned him against me, Mother. You killed him as surely as I did.

Frost raised both her hands; tiny lightnings coiled and crackled about them. *You were right to fear me, Reimuth. You could never do this!*

She slammed her hands together. The night split open with impossible thunder. A single alizarine bolt blazed downward from the clouds. All of Kel's careful, clever wards were as nothing. The gates exploded open on melted, smoking hinges.

Above the shattered gates the raven sculpture teetered and pitched backward. It hit the earth with a loud crack, and the bird's head rolled a few paces away from the body.

Frost didn't give a damn. For generations it had stood perched above the gates, the emblem of her family. If anything, broken it seemed a more fitting emblem. She looked away from it and fixed her gaze on the three figures in the courtyard.

She guided Ashur past the ruined totem. Telric took no notice of her. A dim aura of ensorcellment shimmered around him. In one hand he held the emerald Eye of Skraal. All his attention seemed focused upon it. In his other hand was the unlit Lamp of Nugaril.

Molten gold had been poured to make a circle, and Reimuth stood in its center. The runes and glyphs within the circle were also of gold. As Frost rode under the gate her mother spun about; her face mirrored desperation and anger. "Get out!" she raged, and she lifted her hands in an arcane gesture. "You can't interfere, not now!"

Her words were barely audible over the wind that screamed through the courtyard. It extinguished the torch in Kel's hand as he leaned forward to ignite Nugaril's Lamp. The dark hair whipped wildly about his head. The lightning reflected eerily in his eyes as he cast the useless torch aside and glared at his mother. His voice rose above the gale.

"Shut up, Grandmother," he shouted at Reimuth. "Stop waving your hands about like a fool." He moved away from the circle and smiled at Frost. "This bitch is mine alone."

Frost brought Ashur to a stop and glowered scornfully at her son. A simple nudge of her knees and the unicorn would pierce him through. It could be over that quickly.

But it would be too easy.

She pointed to Telric. The Rholarothan was oblivious to all that had transpired. It only made her angrier to see him so helpless. "Release him, Kel." Her voice was so low it grumbled in her throat, yet she knew he heard. "Or by the gods of Tartarus Lake, I'll boil the flesh from your bones."

Chapter Nineteen

Shall I sing, O gods,
And play upon the lyre
Songs unsung for you, alone
And if I sing, O gods,
Will you love me
If I falter
If I mumble
Words unheard by man before
May I continue, gods,
Until the last song is sung
Until my heart bursts
And the whirling stars become not stars
But fevered, fading illusions
And if I sing, O gods,
Will you dance?

Kel clenched his fists at his sides. "He's mine, Samidar," her son snapped defiantly. "While you tried to turn Grandmother against me, I lured him into the woods and set my mark upon him!" An ugly emotion warped his features. It was not her son, but a total stranger who railed at her. "You tried to take Reimuth away from me; instead, I took your lover from you."

His hand dipped into the loose front of his tunic. Frost didn't know what he had hidden there, and she didn't wait to find out. She'd have no more of his tricks. With the merest thought she shaped the wind and hurled it at him. It flung him backward through the air, and he fell with a choked grunt, flailing in the dirt. He struggled to rise, but the wind held him pinned.

"You've done enough evil, Kel," she said bitterly. "If you won't release him, I'll wrest him from you."

Another voice shouted over the gale. "What about me, daughter?" Reimuth called. "Are you strong enough to wrest him from me?"

Before Frost could react, her own wind turned against her. An invisible hand smashed her from Ashur's back. Its power rolled her relentlessly upon the ground, tumbling her as if she were a helpless plaything.

Then, Reimuth let go a shriek, and the gale lost direction. Breathless, prostrate, Frost looked up as Kel flung a fragment of the cobbled pavement at his grandmother. "I told you to stay out of this!" Kel shook his fist as Reimuth dodged the second missile.

Frost scrambled to her feet. She almost felt sorry for her mother. Reimuth was blind to Kel's insanity, seeing only a replacement for the son she'd lost and a hope for the future of her family. Even now, she had no true understanding of her grandson's madness. Her face mirrored only hurt and confusion at his rejection of her aid, and Frost had to wonder if Reimuth might not be as mad as her grandson.

But the time had passed for such concerns. She thought, instead, of Telric. He stood unmoving, unnoticing, like a dead man on his feet. She had a vision of the corpses they had fought in the cemetery, creatures of Kel's magic. Now, Telric was a prisoner of that same magic, and damn her soul before she would surrender him to it!

She gestured, and her witchcraft surged forth to do her will. All around Kel the cobblestones ripped themselves from the earth and battered him. He cried out in pain and surprise and threw his arms up to guard his face. There was a loud crack, audible over the rushing wind, and Kel screamed. He clutched his ribs and sagged to his knees.

Blood flowed from his nose and from cuts on his brow and mouth. One eye swelled nearly shut. Supporting himself on one hand, he shot her a look of pure hatred. But the pummeling continued. A rock struck him in the back, another in the cheek. Dozens of stones and fragments spun around him, a deadly vortex that slowly was stoning him to death.

A chill unlike anything she had ever felt raced up her spine, and sickness gnawed her gut. She was killing her son, the only child of Kimon's blood. She had given him life; now she was taking it back. She trembled, and tears sprang unbidden from her eyes and trailed thickly down her face. But she did not relent, and her power did its awful work.

Then, she heard the chant. It grew in volume and intensity. From the corner of her eye she saw Reimuth's outstretched arms. The swarming stones around Kel slowed and fell to the ground as Frost felt the sharp edge of her mother's magic interrupt her own.

"I won't let you have him!" Reimuth called angrily. "I told you! I *warned* you!"

This time, Kel did not oppose her aid. Unable to rise, his face caked with blood and dirt, he took advantage of the distraction his grandmother had provided and reached within his tunic. His hand came out in a tight fist. Scarlet fire danced between his knuckles. He pointed at Telric and shouted, "Kill her! Kill the loveless whore! Now!"

Too late, Frost remembered the amulet that Kel had used to control her at Dakariar. Carefully but swiftly, Telric placed the Eye of Skraal and the Lamp of Nugaril on the ground. Then, with a savage cry, he yanked his sword from the sheath and charged at her.

A moment of indecision nearly cost her her life. At the last instant she sidestepped, thrust out one foot, and tripped her friend. He rolled without losing his weapon and regained his feet. In a smooth motion, he turned to face her again.

She pulled her own sword free and looked around wildly, trying to gain time, trying to think. She glimpsed Reimuth watching from the circle. Was that an expression of fright her mother wore? Kel raised up on one elbow, his face alight with a hideous glee.

"I told you, Mother." He laughed, but his pleasure was broken by a fitful coughing, and he grabbed his ribs. In a voice strained with pain his words reached her. "He's mine; he does my bidding." He tried to laugh again, and again pain seized him. A trickle of crimson stained his lips. "To free your lover you'll have to kill me," he finally managed. "And to do that you'll have to kill him. Do you appreciate that, Mother? Do you hear me laughing?"

Telric circled her, looking for an opening in her defense. Suddenly he lunged, but instead of thrusting, his blade sliced in a high arc and whistled toward her head. Steel clanged and blue sparks flew. Twice more they engaged and Frost jumped back. Telric followed relentlessly. His eyes were vacant and staring, yet he moved with dazzling speed. Unexpectedly, the tip of his sword split her right sleeve open, and she knew the warm wetness of her own blood as it ran down her arm.

Telric gave her too little time to think. She feared to use her witchcraft against him. It wasn't really Telric attacking her; she didn't want to hurt him. Yet she couldn't continue to fight defensively. Sooner or later, he'd cut her badly and it would all be over. She used her sword to block his blows and searched for some quick way to stop him.

"Telric!" she shouted into his face when he closed again. She deflected his stroke, but the Rholarothan slammed into her, knocking her down. His sword bit into the earth where her head had struck as she rolled aside and found her feet. "It's Kel! Fight him!" She turned aside a nearly fatal thrust aimed for her midsection and spat in his eyes. Caught off guard, he stumbled back, wiping at his face. She kicked hard at his chest, hoping to knock the wind from him so she could turn her attention back to her son, but her friend was too fast. He caught her foot, jerked, and toppled her backward.

His blank gaze gave no answer as she screamed his name. The blade that descended to end her life was far more eloquent.

Then, a huge black shadow with eyes of bright flame saved her. Ashur crashed into Telric from the side, smashing him to the ground. The sword tumbled from his grip. He didn't even groan, just lay there, unmoving.

Frost thought her heart would stop. She thanked her gods that the unicorn hadn't charged with lowered horn or reared to attack with those deadly hooves. But the way he had hit the earth! The impact alone might have killed her love.

Telric's leg twitched, and she almost laughed with relief. But his hand groped on the cobbles for the sword he had dropped, and she knew it wasn't over. If he got up, it would only begin again.

Unless she finished Kel.

She scrambled up, sword in hand, and moved swiftly toward her son. There was panic on his face and fear. It brought her a strange satisfaction, and she tapped the flat of her blade on her palm as she bore down on him.

"You never loved me!" he screamed.

His words had no effect on her at all. He was mad, a rabid beast that she had to put out of its misery before it infected anyone else.

"You loved everybody but me!" His voice was a loud whine. "Never me!" He raised the fist that held the talisman. It burned with a scarlet coruscation as he bent its power upon her.

He tried to steal her mind as he had done once before. But that time, she hadn't been aware of her own power. With little more than an inward shrug she turned his spell aside. He exerted the talisman's magic, and she felt it nibble at the edge of her will. He was strong, but not strong enough. The glow around his hand became a red fire as he strained uselessly.

The razor-keen edge of her sword glimmered briefly in that occult light. Kel's hand flopped on the ground, the amulet impotently clutched in fingers that slowly uncurled. An inhuman shriek issued from her son's throat, and he stumbled back in agony, staring with disbelief at his gushing stump.

Instantly, another cry rose above Kel's screaming. She recognized the familiar sound and whirled in time to see Ashur rear and stamp in warning. His eyes blazed like furious, prominencing stars.

The sky erupted with a blast of thunder that rocked her on her feet. Jagged bolts of blue and orange raced across the clouded heavens, tearing the fabric of night, filling the air with a harsh smell of burning.

"Get away from him!" Reimuth raged. "Get away from my grandson!"

Her mother strode toward her with a terrible visage. Her eyes crackled with tiny inner lightnings, and her long hair whipped wildly about her face. The sorceress shook her fist; another blast shook the land.

Frost glimpsed the Book of Shakari at the center of the circle where Reimuth had stood. A rising wind not of her making fanned the pages, and she thought of the ritual she had interrupted. It was the night of the new moon, and her mother's last full night of life without the Aspects' magic.

Reimuth's voice soared over the tempest, full of power and anger. "I should have killed you on that dark night so many years ago. But I let my grief for your father and brother blind me. Now, you would slay your own son and doom me to a second death. You're a monster, Samidar, and it's time to put an end to your evil!"

Frost trembled with emotion as the indictments she had flung at Kel were hurled back by her mother with such bitterness. But Reimuth was wrong—as she had been wrong on that distant night.

"Don't make me fight you, Mother," she shouted, casting down her sword. "You don't understand. You never understood!"

Reimuth stopped. The storm still raged under her sorcerous control. The rippling lightning made a dramatic backdrop that illuminated the courtyard in unpredictable flashes. Her mother pointed an accusing finger. "Step away from my grandson," she repeated forcefully.

Frost hesitated, and an impossible wind smashed her backward. Her heel caught on a loose cobble and she pitched over, striking her head painfully. It was enough to anger her. With a small effort she turned the wind aside and rose to her feet, feeling the song in her soul swell to a frightening symphony.

"Shall I leave him to hurl stones at you again?" she called to her mother. "Or so he can defile your husband's remains again? Do you know what a *shimere* is, Reimuth? It's an enslaved soul that's been twisted and warped into something vile and deadly! That's what Kel tried to do to your husband and son. In fact, he may have done it. The gods know which one he sent for me in the forest that night!"

"Whatever he's done he's still my blood," Reimuth answered stubbornly. "He found me and gave me life again. He would have given me even longer life, but you've interfered!"

The cobbles sprang up around Frost as they had Kel. They tried to pound her, but she was faster. She waved a hand, and the stones turned aside. They thudded to the earth and stayed there.

"You're weak, Mother," she challenged scornfully. "And unimaginative. You imitate my spells. But you were always weak. When Kel told you to shut up, you did. He ordered you to remain in the circle, and you obeyed until you saw him defeated." Frost reached out with her witchcraft and began to subtly retake control of the storm above them. "You're pathetic," she continued, her voice full of contempt. "I loved Father, but he treated you exactly the same way. You were the greatest sorceress in Esgaria, but you were chattel to him, as all Esgarian women were chattel."

A searing bolt lanced down from the sky, but Frost sensed her mother's move and threw herself aside in time, rolling on her shoulder and regaining her feet. A small black crater marked the place where she had stood moments before, and fire swiftly consumed the bits of weed and brush that pushed up through the shattered paving.

"Liar!" her mother shouted. "Your father and I ruled together, and together we guarded the northern borders against Rholaroth." She waved toward Telric's limp form. "How shamed he would be to see the scum you've fallen in with!"

Frost held herself back, feeling the pattern of the storm, alert for another attack. "Guarded the border, you say? By all the hells, you made it your prison! Did you ever wonder what lay beyond the border, Mother? There's an entire world, but you were too weak and afraid to discover it. For all your sorcerous might, you hid behind these walls, cloaked yourself with the laws and traditions of this backward little nation." She spat in the dust. "You're not worthy of the magic you wield."

Reimuth screamed, enraged. She raised her fists, then brought them down in a sharp, commanding gesture.

But the lightning didn't respond. Frost extended herself, freeing the music within her, and seized control of the storm. "Yes, you're weak. That's why you took your own life those many years ago!" She turned from her mother and shouted to the storm. A barrage of lightning answered, and a section of the fortress exploded under the blistering force.

"No!" Reimuth stared horrified at the destruction. She shouted a string of words that Frost couldn't understand, and she stamped her foot.

The earth surged up like a giant wave and tumbled Frost helplessly. From the corner of her eye she spied Ashur. The unicorn bellowed and ran ahead of the wave, disappearing around the old barracks. The swell of earth struck the ramshackle building and smashed it into splinters.

Frost didn't know what spell her mother had spoken, but it

was a potent spell, causing almost as much damage as her lightning. She risked a hasty glance around to locate Kel and Telric. Both of them lay in supine heaps. She wondered if either lived.

"You call me weak?" Reimuth roared. "I've seen the horrors of the nine hells. You dare speak to me about the world?" Again she shouted something, and this time Frost recognized the language as an ancient Esgarian dialect unused for centuries.

The grass and weeds shot up at an impossible rate, coiling around Frost's limbs, twining over her body before she could get to her feet. The sharp grasses cut her as she struggled; the weeds constricted around her throat, choking her. The blood pounded in her ears, and her lungs burned.

"You are dead, daughter," Reimuth mocked. "Challenge me again in twenty years if you can find your way back to this life."

But Frost was far from defeated. She tore at the weeds around her throat, sucking for air. At the same time an arcane shimmering danced over her flesh, scorching the writhing verdure, turning it brittle and black until it crumbled at her merest shrug. Frost scrambled to her feet, furious.

Reimuth was prepared. She bent and scratched a sign in the dirt before her daughter could act. Then she spat in the center of her glyph and called out a word.

Beneath Frost's feet the earth turned to mud. She sank to her ankles, then the slime rose up around her in a massive, swelling mound. She barely had time to cup her hands over her mouth and nose before she was engulfed by the rising mire. Dampness seeped through her garments, cold and gelid, chilling her. Inexorably, it oozed through her fingers, threatening to fill her mouth.

Desperately, she swallowed the scant air trapped between her hands. The mud crept up into her nostrils.

She opened her mouth then, but the muck did not pour in. A high, keening note flowed from her throat, pushing back the viscous shell, creating a small pocket near her face. But there was no more air to breathe, and pain seared her chest as she sang. She emptied her lungs slowly, agonizingly, striving to maintain the single note.

The pocket grew and grew. Slowly, all the mud recoiled from her body, forming a new bubble. Straining, she pushed outward, opening her eyes, freeing the tears that welled in the corners. Her note began to quaver. She had almost no air left to sing. Yet she knew if she stopped, the mud would come rushing back to smother her.

As the bubble expanded, it achieved a murky translucence. Frost saw her mother limned in wild flashes of lightning. Reimuth chanted hysterically, her face dancing with light and shadow, arms outflung as she strove against her daughter's power and fought with all her sorceries to collapse the mud again.

Frost stretched out her own hands as if to hold the bubble back. The pitch of her song changed suddenly as she shifted her attack and poured her last breath into a piercing note.

Reimuth screamed in anger and surprise as her gown flew up about her face. The material snapped whiplike at her eyes, and thick folds stoppered her mouth. She ripped frantically at the rebellious fabric as it twisted about her with constricting force.

Distracted, Reimuth lost control of her spell. Deprived of the sorcerous energy that shaped it, the bubble of mud showered harmlessly down upon Frost. Sputtering, she wiped the slime from her face and eyes and gulped air into her tortured lungs.

When she could see again, she faced a naked parent. Shards of Reimuth's gown fluttered across the yard on the storm winds. Her mother began to chant again, but Frost strode implacably forward.

"I'm not dead, Reimuth," she called icily, feeling the music swell within her once more. "You learned much during your time in hell, but I've learned more from life. It's made me strong, Mother, strong as steel and stronger."

She gestured, and the firm ground beneath her mother's feet changed to a shallow pool of blood. Reimuth gasped and leaped to dry pavement. She stared horrified at the stains on her bare flesh, her chant forgotten.

"You made me an outcast in my home," Frost charged. With each step closer, her power grew. "You stole my witchcraft and drove me into the world with only a sword to carve my way."

Reimuth's fear shone suddenly in her eyes. She began a new chant and swiftly bent to draw another pattern in the dirt.

With a despairing cry she jerked her hand away as another
bloody pool formed where her finger touched the earth.

"I lived by that sword, Mother!" Frost shouted, giving full
vent to her anger. "I fought and I killed with it; I slept with it
and cared for it and cherished it, because to lose it meant my
death. Even when I thought I'd found peace at last, I couldn't
part with it, but kept it in a trunk near my bed."

She raised her fist and shook it. The sky answered with a
titanic blast of thunder. The wind roared over the wall and
rushed through the courtyard. A pelting rain began to fall
with stinging force, washing the mud from her face and
garments. Then the ground shivered as twin bolts of cobalt
fire struck the cobbled paving.

For the first time, Reimuth screamed in fear. She flung up
an arm to protect her eyes from the brilliant flash and explod-
ing debris. Her long hair stood almost on end as the air
crackled around her, and she staggered away from her daughter, blood squeezing from a score of small wounds.

"Even if your sorceries had been greater than my witchcraft, you couldn't have defeated me." Frost brought down
another bolt, forcing her mother to retreat farther. "You
haven't the sheer will to fight. You faced death once, and you
fear it."

She conjured a frightening display. Lightning rained down
upon her ancestral home, blowing gaping dark holes in the
walls. The westernmost tower exploded in a hail of shattered
stone. Reimuth screamed again and ran for the steps, but
Frost called the wind to lift her mother and hurl her back.
Head over heels, the tempest rolled the sorceress ever closer
to the entrance gates.

"You faced death once," Frost repeated, shouting over the
rising gale. "But I've faced it a thousand times on a thousand
glittering edges. I've lost my fear of the nine realms, and that
makes me stronger."

Two bolts clashed overhead like swords in combat, ringing
not with steel but with deep-throated thunder.

"Samidar, don't!" Reimuth implored. Her mother's nails
dug in the ground between the cobbles, seeking purchase as
the winds continued to assail her. "Please, stop!"

Frost thrilled with the arcane music that filled the deepest
reaches of her soul. The power was a maelstrom inside her.

Her anger churned it, and she laughed, drunk with its potency, glaring at the helpless naked thing before her.

"This was to be your night," she mocked her mother cruelly, "the night when you reclaimed your full life." She looked beyond the fortress gate, where Reimuth could not go. Kel's necromancy had bound her short life-force too closely to her home, and while his magic maintained her vitality, the gate and the wall defined her world. She drove her mother toward it. "Instead," she cried, "it's death that shall do the reclaiming!"

Reimuth raised a hand, pleading for mercy. She begged, but her voice was small and weak against the wind that pushed her toward her doom. In a last effort to save herself, her pale hands locked around the broken body of the raven sculpture that once had set upon the gate, but her strength faded quickly, surely. Bleeding, her fingers gave way, and she tumbled over the threshold.

She began to age at once. Her skin melted and sagged. Her porcelain beauty dissolved into cracks and deep wrinkles and thick folds. With astonishing speed her hair grayed. Her flesh lost its luster, turning a sickly pallor. Her breasts, so rich and full, withered in an instant.

The thing that once had been her mother collapsed on the ground. With a last effort, a rotting head lifted and rheumy eyes stared at her. A hand trembled in supplication, and a voice caked with the rust of years whispered to her.

It said her name, and no more, and died.

Samidar.

The music froze inside her. The wind failed, and the lightning ceased. The rain made only a soft patter on the cobbles, then stopped. The clouds rolled expectantly through the heavens.

Frost quivered with disbelief and terror at what she'd done. She had not intended this—to strike her mother down a second time! All her old guilts rushed in upon her again, the old nightmares, all the old fears. She bit her lip until a trickle of blood ran down her chin. Silently she cursed herself, and she cursed the power that throbbed impatiently within her.

Then, Reimuth's feeble limbs twitched. Her life, it seemed, was not yet completely gone.

With a sob, Frost ran to her mother's side, swept the frail body up in her arms, and carried it back through the fortress gate. She stopped and pressed Reimuth's head to her breast and waited. No breath came to those parched lips; nothing stirred in the brittle chest. Frost lay her face next to her mother's leathery, sunken cheek and rocked the woman as if she were a poor baby.

"Mother," she mumbled, spilling tears into Reimuth's vacant, staring eyes. "Mother!"

Something glinted on the ground ahead. Frost looked up and saw the circle of gold that Kel had poured upon the ground. Despite all the mayhem, it was miraculously intact. The Lamp of Nugaril lay just outside it, but there was no sign of the other Aspects.

She glanced up at the sky, swore, and bit her lip again. There was still time. Morning was yet a while off. But she would have to search for the Eye of Skraal and the Book of Shakari. She prayed to her gods it would not take too long.

Fired by her new resolve, she hurried to place her mother within the circle, pausing only long enough to smooth back the wisps of hair that had strayed across the empty face. With a thumb and forefinger, she closed Reimuth's eyes, noting with a stab of pain their deep green color so like her own.

The book proved easy to find. It lay spine up, open to the earth next to the bottom stair. Some of the pages had folded under, and a few others were smeared with mud. Somehow, perhaps through some magic of its own, it had escaped any damage by the rain.

The Eye of Skraal, however, was nowhere in sight. She began to wander over the grounds, searching for the jewel with a grim desperation.

"Is he dead?" a voice asked weakly.

She turned, startled. Telric leaned on his sword and regarded her with a dazed look. It shamed her to admit she had forgotten him. He repeated his question, and she looked around for her son. She spied his limp form in the darkness. "I don't know," she confessed. "I think so."

Telric started toward Kel. "I'll make sure."

She caught his arm. "No, I need your help. If we find the emerald, I can save my mother."

His brows shot up. "Save her? What in the hells for?"

She let go of him and stepped back, angry. "She died once because of me, damn you, and the memory haunted me for half my life. I won't let that happen again." She squeezed his arm again. "Help me, Telric. Don't you see? This is my chance for redemption!"

He pulled away from her and stared across the yard to where Reimuth lay. "She's dead already," he said. "You defeated her."

"But I can save her this time," Frost insisted. "I can use the Three Aspects myself. I have the lamp and the book. I need the jewel."

His face was full of doubt. "And when she wakes up, what then? She'll want revenge for Kel."

She shrugged. "I have to do this. I said terrible things to her when we fought, but in her own way, I know she loved me once." She gazed toward the circle and her mother's still form. Outside the gate those limbs had twitched, but she had no doubt now that Reimuth was dead. "And I loved her, too. After I fled from Esgaria, I used to get so lonely I'd cry for her." She looked up into the Rholarothan's eyes, begging him for understanding. "I've got to do this!"

Telric let go a heavy sigh. "Then let's find the god-cursed stone, get this over with, and get out of here. If I never set foot in Esgaria again, I'll die a happy man."

Leave Esgaria, she thought strangely, *leave home?* For all the grief and anguish that filled her, there was still room for the sadness such a consideration brought. Yet she realized in that moment that she would ride anywhere with Telric—away from Esgaria, away from the place where she was born— anywhere he wanted to go. Yesterday, this land had called to her, filling her with an awed wonder. Now, she longed only to be free from a ponderous shadow.

She resumed her search for the Eye of Skraal. "If I get close enough, I'll sense its emanations," she told her friend. "But it's dark; it might have rolled anywhere. You take that side of the courtyard."

He sheathed his sword and made his way toward the ruined gate in a half crouch, the better to see the ground. She worked her way gradually toward her son's body, searching with her eyes and her witch's senses. There was so much rubble, broken stone, cobbles. Quite possibly, she feared, the emerald was buried.

Down by the shattered barracks something moved. She froze in midstep, then straightened and watched the twin spots of flame that raced toward her. A small part of her brightened to see the unicorn, but she was too weary to rejoice—and too desperate for her mother.

A short distance from Kel's body, Ashur stopped. He snorted suddenly and pawed the earth; his eyes sparked. Then, to Frost's amazement, he charged and drove his ebon horn straight for her son's body.

Even as she screamed, Kel rolled aside. Still alive, then! But perhaps not for long. Ashur lunged again, and again Kel barely avoided that glittering point.

Frost ran, all thought of the gem vanished from her mind. Ashur reared over her son, and Kel's face went ashen with terror. He raised the stump of his right hand to ward off the unicorn's next thrust, too paralyzed with fear to do more as he stared at certain death.

Then she was between them. She shouted Ashur's name angrily as deadly hooves lashed out. The unicorn bellowed confusion as he tried to avoid her. He came down on top of her, brushing her shoulder with a foreleg, numbing her entire arm. She fell backward from the force of the blow, and the wind rushed out of her lungs as she landed on her son's knee. His outcry rang in her ears.

Then another cry drowned him out, a horrible and familiar shrieking that tore open the night with its sharp-edged fury. From the corner of her eye she saw Telric racing toward her as Ashur paced an uncertain circle. There was no help for her, she realized.

Demonfang gleamed above her, clutched in her son's one hand. He plunged it deep, ripping another scream from her to add to the dagger's demented chorus.

But an instant later, the dagger went silent. The blade grated between her ribs, yet Kel had missed her heart. She sucked in a short, painful breath, knocked his hand from the hilt, and rolled away from him. Gasping, she struggled to her feet and her sword hissed from its sheath. She raised it for the death stroke.

This was what she had come to do. Now, Kel would pay for the murder of his father and brother. Kimon and Kirigi could rest in peace. And how many others would also rest when he was dead? How many men and women, how many kingdoms, would be safe?

But her arm refused to fall. She added her right hand to the hilt, yet she couldn't bring the blade down. Her knuckles cracked as she wrestled with her weapon. Her muscles trembled. Her sword hovered over Kel, ready for a final blow that she couldn't bring herself to strike.

It was no charm, she knew, nothing of Kel's doing. He was at last helpless and without hope; it showed in his face as he cringed at her feet. It was no magic at all that stayed her hand. Only the knowledge that he was her son.

Slowly, then, Kel realized her weakness. He smiled, puckered his cheeks, and spit into his one good hand the missing Eye of Skraal.

A hot rage seared through her. He'd had the jewel all along and played dead, knowing that sooner or later its emanations would draw her close enough to give him the chance to use Demonfang. How he must hate her!

And how she hated him. Hated and loved—she saw it now like the two edges of the same sword.

Telric ran up behind Kel and paused. His steely eyes locked briefly with hers, and he saw her inability. His own sword made a swift, glittering arc as he swung, and he glared at his nephew with a cold determination, knowing evil when he looked upon it.

Frost unleashed a portion of her power to stop him. Death halted a hair's-breadth from Kel's neck.

"Release me, Samidar!" the Rholarothan shouted bitterly. "I've had too much of people controlling my actions. You know what he is. You know what has to be done!"

She heard his words dimly. Demonfang's power began to work its damnable magic. It had not found her heart, but it had tasted her blood, and that had satisfied it momentarily. Still, its hunger was unending, and she could feel it as it slowly devoured her life.

She reached inside herself, opened her soul, and matched her power against the dagger's. Demonfang recoiled, but she knew she could not hold it back for long.

The fear left Kel's face. A horrible, twisted mockery of a smile blossomed on his mouth, a leer that was both glee and accusation. "She can't kill me," he proclaimed for Telric's benefit. "She's my mother. She *loves* me." His lips writhed venomously around every word as he jeered and laughed at them. "Tell me how much you love me, Mother." He mimed a kiss, batted his lashes at her, and held out his bleeding stump.

The sword fell from her hands and stuck shivering in the earth. She said nothing, just sank to her knees. Then, his fear returned suddenly as she bent over him. He tried to crawl away, but she caught his tunic and pulled him to her. She tangled a hand in his hair, dragging his face close to hers. He tried feebly to push her back, but his strength had drained away with much of his blood.

"No," he croaked, and he grabbed for Demonfang where it was still between her ribs. She caught his arm and forced it gently down. "Don't. . . ."

"Don't fight me," she whispered urgently. "Don't resist." She took his face between her hands, ignoring the mewling sounds that issued from him. His eyes bored into hers, so full of fright, so green—like her own eyes and Reimuth's. He was indeed his mother's son.

She compelled him to meet her gaze. For a brief instant all his trembling ceased, but the fear never left him. "I love you, Kel," she told him, and she repeated it over and over.

Then she called her magic once more. It surged up, a wild music. She shaped it, melding the cacophonies and euphonies into dazzling lancets. She poured the full, eldritch fury into the only child of her body.

The air glowed around the two of them, mother and child, as they huddled on the ground in the darkness.

"I love you, son," she whispered.

Chapter Twenty

Frost released her son, sagged heavily to her right side, and caught herself on one elbow. She gasped with pain. A trickle of dark blood oozed from the corner of her mouth. With the fingers of her left hand she explored Demonfang's hilt where it rested just near her breast. The grip was wet and slick. So was her tunic. Warm liquid flowed down her ribs.

She felt the dagger's power rising again and heard its muted wailing in her head. Her lips parted to answer it. *Not yet,* she commanded. *Be silent.* She pressed her lips tightly together, denying the scream that the blade's curse urged on her.

Telric bent beside her. He grasped the protruding hilt, but before he could pull it free she caught his hand. "The sheath." She nodded toward Kel. "He's wearing it. Bring it here."

He looked uncertainly at his nephew. Kel hadn't moved since Frost had let him go. He sat with his legs wide, arms dangling limply at his sides. There was a vacant, childlike expression on his face.

As Telric unfastened the sheath belt from Kel's waist, he crinkled his nose. "He's wet himself," the Rholarothan said with disgust. "What did you do to him?"

She breathed hard. More blood trickled from her mouth, and she wiped it with the back of her hand. "I couldn't kill him, Telric." She grabbed his sleeve and tried to pull herself up, but he forced her gently back down. "I used my witch-craft to reach inside his mind, and I destroyed it. All his power, all his knowledge, everything he was or could ever be, it's gone.'' She drew a rasping breath and gazed at her son. ''He was a sweet baby when he was born. Now, he'll be a baby for the rest of his life.''

Telric swallowed. He grasped Demonfang's hilt. ''I've got to get this out,'' he said between gritted teeth. He hesitated, then jerked.

The blade scraped against a bone, and a blinding white pain did what Demonfang's power could not. Her head snapped back, and she screamed. Telric held the dagger up, staring fearfully as black blood ran over the tang and the hilt and dripped on his hand.

''Sheathe it,'' she gasped. ''Quickly, before it exerts its power.''

He did as she told him, slamming the dagger into the silver sheath. She snatched it from him, and before he could stop her, she managed to sit up and buckle it around her waist. Telric cursed, tore a scrap of cloth from his sleeve, reached inside her garment, and pressed it to her wound. She winced at the contact, but she also sighed.

She had beaten Demonfang. Its power had coursed through her, and she had turned it aside, saving her soul. But she could sense the damage the blade had done to her body. Blood poured through Telric's rough swab, and its bitter taste was thick in her throat. It was difficult to draw a full breath.

The Eye of Skraal twinkled in the dirt between Kel's legs. She pointed without speaking. Telric retrieved it and put it into her hand.

She said weakly, ''My mother—I've got to finish the spell.''

She tried to rise, but her friend wrapped his arms about her. ''You're hurt too badly.'' He kissed her softly on the brow. ''It's you we've got to worry about.''

''No,'' she insisted, pushing him away. ''I told you what I've got to do. Now, help me up.''

He gazed sadly at her, then lifted her in his strong arms. ''I can walk,'' she assured him, but he still carried her to the circle of gold.

''Tell me what to do,'' he said, lowering her. ''I'll do the work. You stay quiet.''

She propped herself on one hand. ''First, bring Kel into the circle, too.'' He hurried to obey and carried her son across the yard. He deposited his nephew on the opposite side of the design. A string of spittle ran down Kel's chin as he sat there staring at his thumbs. "Now bring me the book." She waited until it rested on the ground before her. "Now the lamp." He brought that, too, moving as swiftly as he could.

The song in her soul was weaker this time when she called it; the harmonies seemed disjointed and distant. But she extended her hand, and a tiny blue flame bloomed on her palm. "Stay close to me," she said to Telric, "no matter what you see."

She touched her flame to the Lamp of Nugaril.

A red light blazed forth, unnaturally bright. It gave no warmth at all. Instead the air turned strangely chill. Beyond the circle shadows sprang up around the courtyard and took on a weird life of their own. They danced and cavorted, drawn to the circle. They whirled and spun, stygian shapes without substance, soundless.

Nugaril was an evil god, Frost knew, and these were his spawn. The shadows radiated a vileness that made her shiver, and she thanked the gods of goodness that the circle's gold kept them at bay.

"Traveling with you, I should be used to such things," Telric muttered, kneeling beside her. It was clear from his tone that he was not and never expected to be.

A loud trumpeting from Ashur made her turn sharply, and she bit her lip at the agony in her side. She cursed herself. How could she have forgotten him? The shadow things flew at him, and the unicorn bellowed in torment, a sound that cut her to the soul, worse than Demonfang.

She staggered to her feet, breathless with the effort, and called his name. She feared, though. Ashur was a tangible creature, but also a creature of magic. Could he enter the protection of the circle? He came running, the shadows giving swift pursuit.

The unicorn's unearthly eyes blazed, trailing flame, as he leaped over the golden markings and crashed to a halt, hooves hurling a shower of dirt and stone pebbles on Reimuth's unmoving form. Frost threw one arm about his neck and hugged him. He nuzzled and licked her hand.

Pain flared in her ribs again, and new blood rose into her mouth. She gave the unicorn one more pat and sank down by the Book of Shakari. At her order, Telric took up the lamp and the emerald. "Hold them over my mother. Shine the light

on the gem like this.'' She showed him how to rotate the Eye
of Skraal between thumb and forefinger. The emerald reflected the light and cast it off in tiny spears of coruscating
radiance. "You mustn't stop once we begin. It may be a long
time.''

He hesitated, and he searched her eyes, full of concern.
"Are you all right?'' he said. Then he waved a hand at her
mother's body. "I don't want to bring her back just to lose
you.''

Frost nodded, forced a smile, and patted his cheek. "Let's
finish this, then I'm yours to do with as you will.'' She
winked, trying her best to be convincing.

Telric was not amused, but he scrambled to Reimuth's
side.

Frost closed her eyes as a wave of blackness swept over
her. A taste of her own blood came stronger than ever. A
momentary, unreasoning fear wormed itself into her thoughts,
but she fought against it.

The spell of the Three Aspects was its own potent magic. It
required none of her power. Instead, she called on her witchcraft to slow the flow of her blood, to block all sensation of
pain.

Telric lifted the emerald and the lamp. He began to turn the
stone, and a beautiful sparkling illumined Reimuth's withered
features.

Beyond the circle the shadow shapes danced, attracted to
Nugaril's flame, repelled by the circle of gold. She watched
them as she gathered her strength. *Life where none should be,*
she considered, *unearned and undeserved.*

She looked at her mother. In the last moment Reimuth
had called her name.

She picked up the Book of Shakari. Nugaril's Lamp provided enough light to read by. She turned to the first page.
The language was Old Chondite, a tongue that reeked of its
own peculiar magic.

The pages cracked and snapped with age as she turned
them. She read aloud, chanting the ancient poems and can-
trips as the priests of Chondos would have done.

The Aspects were the three god forces that governed the
cosmos: light, darkness, and neutrality. Shakari's wisdom
guided the lords of light. Nugaril was a minor but vindictive
god of darkness. The goddess Skraal was one of the neutral

powers that maintained the balance between good and evil.
Life, the book suggested, was not born of one or the other,
but was a union of all three influences.

Frost paused long enough to study the sky. The stars
twinkled serenely. No trace of morning yet tinted the heavens. *How much time,* she wondered, *how much time?*

She read on, understanding less and less as the pages went
by. It didn't matter. She knew the structure of the language
and the pronunciations. The words alone were words of power.

A sudden coughing seized her. Doubling over, she spat
crimson. Pain knifed through her side, and she clutched her
ribs in surprise. Not even her magic was enough to dull the
growing agony, it seemed. She ground her teeth and looked
up. Telric looked as if he would dart to her side, but he kept
his place bravely. He was pale with worry, illumined strangely
by the same shimmering that bathed Reimuth. She forced a
sheepish grin and read.

A shout from Telric interrupted her. She didn't stop but
glanced over the book's edge, chanting as loudly as she
could.

Reimuth's features blurred and reshaped into their former
youthful countenance. The flesh softened, the limbs grew
firm again. The long, brittle hair that splayed over the ground
thickened and turned dark.

Joy flooded through Frost when her mother's bosom heaved
with its first breath. She closed the Book of Shakari as she
completed the final page. The tome slid from her hand and
fell into the dirt.

Telric set aside the lamp and the emerald. He went to her
and wrapped his arms about her. His warmth suffused through
her, and his touch was comforting. "Your mother lives," he
said into her ear. "You've given her back her life."

She settled into his shoulder, letting him take all her weight.
She had not called upon her witchcraft, but her pain seemed
to fade away. "She lives, and maybe I am redeemed of that
foulest sin of my youth." Frost shut her eyes and trembled,
freed from a great burden.

"Why doesn't she move?" Telric asked.

Frost rubbed the back of his hand and locked her fingers in
his. "There's a vast gulf that separates life and death," she
explained, "and the crossing can be hard. Even a soul needs

rest. She'll awake soon enough." She tried to look over her shoulder for her son. "She'll have to take care of Kel."

All the strength went out of her then. She coughed, and blood dribbled on her chin. Weakly, she reached inside her tunic and pulled out the swab that covered her wound. It was soaked and useless.

Telric held her tighter, and she realized he was crying. She listened to the sound of his tears and for any faint note of power that still remained within her. At her soul's core there was unnerving silence.

She touched the hilt of the dagger at her side. "Demonfang has won after all," she whispered. She turned her gaze beyond the circle. The air was alive with the frantically dancing shadows. They seemed to mock her with their vitality. "Put out the lamp," she told Telric. "Let me rest by you without those damned creatures watching."

"Close your eyes, and they'll go away," he urged, pressing his cheek next to hers. "The lamp is out of reach. I don't want to leave you." His tears dripped onto her face. They rolled thickly, hotly, on her flesh. "Don't leave me, Samidar."

She turned her head from side to side. "Where's Ashur? Move me so I can see him."

He did as she requested. The gentle care he took was not enough to keep her from crying out and grabbing for her wound. But when the film cleared from her vision, the unicorn was there.

She reached up a shaking hand. Ashur lowered his head and licked her fingers as he had often done. His great spike bobbed near her face, and she ran her palm along its glistening length. His eyes burned like stars, flickering with slender prominences.

"Go, my good friend." Her words were barely audible. "Run to wherever you dwelled all those long years when I didn't think I needed you." Her lids drooped; she snapped them open. "I always needed you, though. You're a dream, my unicorn, and we all need dreams." Ashur bent his head lower yet, and she ran a hand through his rich mane. "Run," she repeated, "and everyone who has a dream will chase you."

Ashur only continued to lick and nuzzle her. She pulled her hand away and clutched Telric's sleeve. "Drive him off," she pleaded. "Make him run away. I want to see him run!"

But Telric shook his head. "The shadows are still out there."

"Then put out the lamp, and the shadows will die."

He refused to let go of her. "I need the lamp," he said slowly. "If you leave me, Samidar, I'll bring you back."

She cringed, but it wasn't pain that made the tears spring into her eyes. Gods, she didn't want to leave him. She could have been happy growing old by his side, spending days and nights in his arms. Suddenly, she longed to see his home in Rholaroth and to call it her home.

But it was not to be.

She brushed his lips lightly with the tips of her fingers. "Can you read classic Chondite?"

His expression was answer enough. He hugged her tighter than ever, and great sobs racked him.

"I can."

She felt Telric twist around, but she was too weak to follow. It was her mother's voice, though. Reimuth walked into her view, still naked, still beautiful, still younger than her daughter. In her hand she held the Eye of Skraal.

"You spared me, Samidar, and you spared your son."

Frost tried to shake her head. She rolled her eyes upward to her mother's face, but she couldn't focus her vision. "He's not the same. . . ." She gave up the effort. It was too much trouble to form the words. She sighed and stared across the circle. She couldn't see Kel.

"None of us are the same," Reimuth answered.

Telric spoke, full of sudden hope. "You're a sorceress. Can you save her?"

Reimuth kneeled and took her daughter's hand. "The wound is too grave." Her mother's lips pursed grimly. She picked up the Book of Shakari and blew the dirt from its binding. "But we have the Three Aspects."

Frost felt a surge of hope that quickly dimmed. It had to be close to morning; the night of the new moon was nearly at an end. She squeezed her mother's hand and drew her close. "Say my name again," she begged. "My true name." She watched Reimuth's mouth intently as the word formed. It sounded sweeter even than the witchly music that once had filled her soul.

Her gaze wandered to the sky. There was yet no hint of the

sunrise, but it had to be close. *If only there was time*, she thought sadly. *If only there was more time*.

Telric's breath was feather soft as he whispered in her ear. Yet it was not the Rholarothan's voice she heard. It was Kimon and Kirigi. The words came to her from across a yawning void. *Don't worry*, the voices said in chorus, *don't fear*.

She held on to those voices for a long time, drawing comfort from them. She had no fear. If she lived, then she had Telric to love. If not, then Kimon and Kirigi were waiting.

She glanced at the sky, and a wan smile flickered on her lips. She reached out for Ashur once more, to touch the unicorn that was only a dream. Her dream. His eyes seemed the only light in the darkness that pressed upon her.

The voices spoke again, but she didn't understand, and it didn't seem to matter. She felt her life fading. *Was it time?* she wondered. *Was there time?*

A last song rustled through the empty corners of her soul, and she closed her eyes. Sighing, she gave herself up to sleep, content to greet whatever world that waking brought.

Life
Undying,
Death-defying.